6/17

the IMPOSSIBLE VASTNESS of US

SAMANTHA YOUNG

the IMPOSSIBLE VASTNESS of US

HARLEQUIN® TEEN

ISBN-13: 978-0-373-21242-2

The Impossible Vastness of Us

This edition published by arrangement with Harlequin Books S.A.

For questions and comments about the quality of this book, please contact us at CustomerService@Harlequin.com.

Printed in U.S.A.

For my amazing agent, Lauren Abramo.

You were my very wise guide on this journey.
It is a tale that would have been quite different without you.

Thank you, my friend.

CHAPTER 1

"AND WHAT IS THIS?"

Jay and I broke apart from our kiss to find Hayley standing in the doorway. She stood looking young and attractive in her black-and-gold flight attendant uniform, glaring at us.

Her dark brown hair was pulled back in a severe bun that only accentuated her high cheekbones and big dark eyes. Hayley was really pretty and I'd been told I looked a lot like her. Except for the eyes. I had *his* eyes. People told me all the time how amazing my eyes were. I would have given anything for Hayley's eyes.

I knew without a doubt that my looks were one of the reasons Jay James couldn't quite give up on trying to get into my pants. Not that I was cynical or anything.

Jay was a year older than me, smart, but a total bad boy. Tattoos, check. Piercings, check. Motorcycle, check. Every girl in my school wanted a piece of him and for whatever reason he liked me.

We had been making out on my couch for about ten minutes. Jay had nice lips and I'd hoped that when he kissed me I'd feel something other than the wet touch of mouth and tongue against mouth and tongue.

The romance novels I'd found stashed in Hayley's closet said I was supposed to feel all hot and tingly.

Kissing was supposed to be exciting.

I didn't find it all that exciting. "Nice" was about as good as kissing had gotten for me. And as always my mind wandered due to the lack of excitement. This time it had wandered to Hayley. She was up to something. I knew it. As a flight attendant she was away a lot, but her trips were longer than usual. She was also acting weird and shifty, hiding her phone from me when it buzzed with a notification, and having whispered conversations in her bedroom. Something was up. I just hoped that something wasn't a guy.

It was like my wayward thoughts had conjured her.

"This is Jay," I said, crossing my arms over my chest in defiance at the stern look on her face.

I hated when she acted like she gave a crap.

"I don't care who he is." Hayley tried to fry his ass with her eyes. "You can leave."

Jay stared back at her with as much defiance as I did, making me like him more. He turned to me and pressed a slow, intimate kiss to the corner of my mouth. "See you at school, babe."

He laughed at the mischief in my eyes.

I waited until he'd brushed by Hayley without a word and I heard the front door close behind him. "Nice. Thanks."

Hayley's dark eyes narrowed into slits. "Don't talk to me like that. I'm tired, it's been a long day and now I come home and find my daughter being mauled by some walking hormone. Am I supposed to be happy that you're dating some guy who looks like he's seen the inside of prison more than once?"

"We're not dating. We're just fooling around."

"Oh, well, then, why am I so upset?" She threw her hands up in exasperation.

"Hayley."

She flinched, like she always flinched when I called her by her name (so she flinched a lot). "Don't 'Hayley' me. I have a right to be upset about this."

"Don't be. I'm not serious about him. And I'm not getting pregnant. Anyway, you're home early."

"They put me on a shorter flight." She dumped her purse on the couch as she moved farther into the room. "We'll discuss Jay later. I need to tell you something."

I tensed. "Yeah?"

She stared pensively at me for a few seconds before finally taking a seat by my side. "I've met someone."

Dread instantly filled me.

Scrutinizing me for a reaction and getting none, Hayley smiled reassuringly. "He's wonderful. His name is Theo and he has a daughter who's actually your age. He lives in Boston. We met on one of my flights out there."

My stomach churned. "How long?"

"Several months ago."

"I knew something was going on," I muttered.

"I'm sorry I kept it from you for so long… I just wanted to make sure it was real between us."

"And is it?"

"Very much so. We've fallen in love."

"That's some long-distance relationship."

"I stay with him when I fly out there. I see him as often as possible."

I snorted. "And you think he's faithful all the times you're not around?"

"Don't." She cut a hand through the air. "Those are your trust issues, India. Not mine."

My blood boiled with indignation. She was completely naive if she thought for one second this guy wasn't a loser. She had chosen badly before, after all. I had a right to the dread that was making me feel sick.

"I just wanted to give you a heads-up that it's serious."

"What does that even mean?"

"It means that if this is going where I think it's going, then that might mean a big life change for us."

Oh, hell.

I stared at her in horror.

Hayley sighed wearily at the expression I wasn't even trying to conceal. "I'm going to make a cup of tea. I'm tired so we'll talk about Jay another time." She turned but then stopped to stare sadly at me. "Thanks for being so happy for me, by the way."

That didn't even deserve a response.

There was a time Hayley couldn't give a damn about my happiness. I felt it only fair that I feel apathetic now about hers.

"So wait, what does that mean?" Anna stared at me with big round eyes. "Are you, like, moving to Boston?"

Thursday. Days after Hayley dropped her bombshell that included a possible "big life change for us." She'd left for Boston on Tuesday, and I'd barely heard from her. This lack of communication had finally made me tell Anna what was going on.

I leaned against my locker, glaring at the opposite wall. Unfortunately, said locker was situated right next to the guys' bathroom, which meant enduring Eau de Teenage Turd every day. "I have no idea."

"That's what she meant, though, right?"

"Probably."

"Why aren't you freaking out more?" She stood directly in front of me now, hands on her hips as she glared up at me. "I'm freaking out!" She flapped her arms around. "Freak out with me!"

"Why are you freaking out?" Siobhan said as she, Kiersten and Tess stopped by my locker. "Is it because Leanne Ingles looks like a walking thrift store today?" she called out loud enough for Leanne Ingles to hear as she passed us. I watched Leanne turn bright red and felt my blood heat.

"Don't be a bitch," I snapped at Siobhan.

"I'm just saying, terrible dress, ugly mess."

"You were being horrible." And it was hardly the first time. If it were up to Siobhan she'd rule the school with terror and meanness.

"Whatever." She sighed. "Why are you freaking out, Anna? And why are you doing it in front of India's locker? This whole area should be quarantined." She wrinkled her nose at the bathroom doors.

"Lunch," I stated firmly before pushing off my locker door. I strode away, knowing they'd follow.

I heard their footsteps and suddenly I had Anna on my right, Siobhan on my left and Kiersten and Tess right at my back.

"So?" Siobhan nudged me with her elbow. "What is Anna flipping out over?"

"India's mom might be moving them to Boston!"

The girls shot me stunned looks at Anna's outburst, but I ignored them as I also tried to ignore the swarm of butterflies in my stomach.

"Boston?" Siobhan gasped. "No. Ugh."

Siobhan was a California girl. As far as she was concerned there was sunny CA and then there was the rest of the world. I almost grinned at her disgust.

"You'll so lose your tan," Tess said sympathetically.

I glanced at her over my shoulder. "And that's my biggest concern?"

"No, her biggest concern is Jay," Kiersten insisted. "You can't leave Jay. He's totally in love with you."

I wanted to roll my eyes at the fairy tale Kiersten had obviously been weaving in her head these last few weeks. "No, he's not." I shook my head and looked forward. "And that's not my biggest concern, either."

"Her biggest concern is leaving me," Anna huffed.

Actually, the answer was none of the above. The truth was my biggest concern was the dude we would be moving to Boston for. But Anna was definitely up there, too. If there was anyone in my life that I truly cared about, it was her. I had lied to her about my past, I had kept my secrets and I didn't really tell her what was going on in my head most of the time, but I gave her more of me than I gave to anyone else. It didn't bother her, either. Our friendship was based on the fact that *she* trusted me. I'm a vault. Anna knew she could tell me anything without fear that I'd gossip about it. I had seen her through her parents' really freaking messed-up divorce and the fallout—she had sex for the first time when she was only fourteen and she was too young. It was a difficult time for her and I was there. Not judging her. Just being there.

It meant a lot to her.

She'd be sad if I left her.

I'd worry about her without me.

"I'm not going anywhere," I told her, wishing I felt as confident as I sounded.

"Hey, India." A group of juniors waved as they headed into the caf.

I threw them a smile and followed them in.

"Remember we have our first dance committee meeting this afternoon," I reminded the girls. "We have to start planning Winter Formal."

"I don't even see the point in organizing the vote for Winter Snow Queen this year. We all know you're going to win." Kiersten's voice held more than a hint of envy.

I shrugged, but I couldn't argue. There was more than a passing possibility that my classmates would vote to make me queen.

If there was one thing I'd mastered more than any of my classes, it was the art of being well-liked. I wasn't rich, I wasn't snooty, I didn't judge people and I had the ability to hide how different I felt from everybody else. I made an effort and I tried to be friends with people from all cliques. I was on the school newspaper. I was on the debate team. I was on the girls' soccer team. I was the theater manager.

I was really, really busy.

And that was just the way I liked it. *Needed* it actually. Being popular wasn't about the attention. It was about the control it gave me. It was much harder to be hurt, and much harder to lose the game, when I held all the right cards. I was the most popular girl in junior year, and if Hayley didn't ruin everything by moving us to the east coast, I'd be ruling the school next year.

After standing in line for food that resembled something a cat might throw up we settled down at our usual table.

"Is someone going to fill me in on the whole Boston thing?" Siobhan asked, a gleam in her eyes.

Siobhan was captain of the girls' soccer team, pretty, smart and rich. As far as she was concerned I was sitting in her seat. I bet she was secretly thrilled I might be taking off for Boston.

"Hayley met someone there. It might be serious."

"That sucks. Sorry," Tess said.

"Hey, it's Hayley. They'll probably break up in a week."

"Seriously, if you move to Boston I'm moving with you." Anna's expression was glum as she stared at her sandwich.

"Eat." I nudged her elbow.

"You and food." She sighed but picked up the sandwich.

I bit into my own and stared around the cafeteria, drinking it all in. I really hoped this time next year I'd still be sitting right where I was now.

In life's driver's seat.

As if Hayley heard my inner longing, my phone buzzed in my pocket, and when I pulled it out there was a text from her.

I need you home after school. We need to talk. xx

The sandwich turned to dirt in my mouth but I kept eating. I chewed slowly as my chest started to feel a little tight.

"India, you okay?"

I swallowed hard and shoved my phone toward Anna. "I think I'm moving to Boston."

She paled and looked down at the text. "Shit."

I stared out at the Fair Oaks High School parking lot, more aware of the fast thump of my heart in my chest than I had been during soccer practice. Practice had run a little late and I knew Hayley was probably getting antsy.

I felt nauseous but it was time to face the music so I took out my phone and called her.

"Where are you?" she said instead of "Hello."

"Soccer practice ran late and Siobhan had a dentist appointment so she couldn't give me a ride home."

"Damn, I forgot you had practice. I'm on my way."

Lowering myself to the curb, I flicked through my phone, checking social media and answering notifications. Anna had sent me a Snapchat. It was a picture of an ice pop with the Boston Red Sox logo Photoshopped onto it. Over the picture she had scrawled a message.

Tell Hayley to suck it! YOU'RE NOT MOVING TO BOSTON! Xoxo

I smiled grimly and waited.

When Hayley arrived I got into the car without a word and we drove home to the apartment in silence. Once inside, Hayley finally spoke.

"I thought we could do takeout tonight."

We couldn't afford to do take-out nights all the time. Take-out nights were reserved for birthdays and the last night of school summer vacation. Sometimes even Thanksgiving.

Something was up. "Aren't you supposed to be on a flight somewhere right about now?"

She shrugged, avoiding my gaze as she wandered into the kitchen.

I followed her, watching as she pulled take-out menus out of our kitchen drawer.

"What do you want? Chinese, Indian, Thai, Lebanese?"

"I want to get this 'talk' over with."

Hayley regarded me, taking in my tension and the hard look in my eyes. Finally she sighed. "This is good news, India. Truly it is."

"Just say it."

"Theo proposed. I said yes. And we don't want to wait. We're getting married this December."

My mouth dropped open. "I haven't even met him!"

She pinched the bridge of her nose at my shout. "And that would be a concern if you were younger. But you're starting junior year. You're sixteen. Before we know it, you'll be going off to college." She stepped toward me and grabbed my hand. I let her squeeze it. "And, sweetheart, you can go to any college you want now."

"How?"

"Theo is...well, he's wealthy. And he's already made it perfectly clear that he wants the very best for me, and that means the very best for you."

"Are you trying to buy my acceptance of this whole ridiculous thing? You are aware that this isn't normal, right?"

Hayley dropped my hand. "Don't be melodramatic. I just want you to know that, yes, of course it will be difficult to leave behind school and your friends here and move to Massachusetts, but the upside is that we'll never have another financial worry in our lives. Ever."

Jesus, how wealthy was this guy?

As if she read the question on my face, Hayley smiled dreamily. "He's an incredibly well-respected attorney from a wealthy family. Boston's elite."

"And he's marrying you?"

"Nice," she snapped. "Very nice."

"I didn't mean it like that." I shrugged. "I just... I thought those people stuck to their own."

"Usually. But Theo doesn't care about that stuff. He just wants to marry the woman he loves." She waved away my negativity with a shake of her hair over her shoulders. "He married a well-to-do woman, and they had a daughter, Eloise, before she died of cancer a few years ago. He hasn't been serious about another woman since, until me."

"Oh my God." I shook my head in disgust. "You think you're living in a fairy tale."

"Don't talk to me like that."

"You're hauling me across the country to move in with some guy I've never met!" I heard the hysteria creep into my voice, but couldn't seem to stop it. "Let's remember the last guy you chose that I had to live with. Or have you already forgotten?"

Understanding dawned on Hayley's face. It was shocking that I even had to say it out loud. A good mother would have known exactly why I was taking this so hard. "Oh, sweetheart." She moved toward me but stopped when I flinched back. "Theo is not like him. Not anything like him. I'm not a stupid kid anymore. I wouldn't make that mistake again."

I stared at the floor, trying to will my heart rate to slow. I could barely hear anything over the whooshing of blood in my ears.

I started at Hayley's touch and looked up. She'd decided to ignore my body language and cross the room to take hold of my arms. She ducked her face to stare into my eyes.

"No one," she whispered fiercely, "no one will hurt you. I promise."

Liar.

LIAR.

LIAR!

The scream rang out inside of me but somehow I swallowed it.

This was happening.

She was taking my control away.

I slumped beneath her touch, dropped my eyes from the

promises in hers and nodded. She kissed my forehead and squeezed my arms.

"Why do we have to move? If he has so much money, why can't he move here?"

"Because it's not like he's a lawyer who can move to another firm. He *owns* the firm. Plus, Eloise goes to a very good school in Boston. It just makes more sense for us to move there."

"We're two weeks into the semester already. What about my classes?"

"Classes at your new school don't start until next week. By the time you start there it will be the end of September, which means you'll only have a missed a few weeks of classes instead of a month.

"Sweetie, this is going to be the best thing that's ever happened to either of us. And didn't you hear the part about Theo being a lawyer? I know you want to work in the district attorney's office one day. Theo can open doors for you there."

I was stunned she'd even considered that for me. I wanted to put criminals behind bars where they belonged, and so I didn't want to just study to be a lawyer, I wanted more. I wanted to work my way into the district attorney's office one day, and in my secret heart of hearts...I wanted to *be* the DA. I didn't realize Hayley had actually listened to me about my career aspirations.

But still... I wanted to do it on my own. I didn't want to depend on anyone to get me there, especially not Hayley's new sugar daddy.

Fries. Pop-Tarts. Cap'n Crunch. A Hershey's bar. Burger. With cheese. I really like cheese. And mustard and ketchup on top. SpaghettiOs with little hot dogs cut up into it. Like Mommy used to make.

Stop thinking of food.

I can't even cry. It would hurt too much to cry. Take too much effort.

Too cold. The shower in our tiny bathroom in the trailer wasn't the best place to sleep. I had water. But the water was starting to hurt my tummy.

How long had it been? I needed food.

I tried to get out but he'd done something to stop the door opening on the other side and I could see he'd boarded up the tiny window above the sink.

Sleepiness kept coming for me.

I was so tired of thinking about food.

Just be sleepy.

I heard the stomping of feet outside the door.

A cracking sound.

I felt a sudden tingle of warmth over my face.

"Open your eyes, Trash."

I opened my eyes.

He glared at me from the narrow doorway. "Punishment is over. I'm sick of using Carla's bathroom."

My mouth felt dusty. Dry. Gritty. Like our road outside in the hot summer.

"Well?" He grabbed my arm and hauled me up. It hurt more than usual. "Get the fuck out."

He let me go and I fell against the door frame, then slumped to the ground.

My legs didn't work right, *I thought, panicked.*

Suddenly pain flared up my side and I turned.

He drew his foot back from contact with my hip. "I said get the fuck out."

Somehow I managed to crawl.

The bathroom door slammed shut behind me. I lay on the floor of our kitchen, staring up at the cupboards.

Finally I whimpered.

There was food. But I was too tired to reach for it.

I WAS TOLD WHEN I GET OLDER ALL MY FEARS WOULD SHRINK!

I shot awake at the blaring sound of Twenty One Pilots coming from my phone. My alarm. Fumbling for the phone, I turned off the alarm and sat back.

My body was coated in sweat.

I hadn't had a nightmare like that in a long time but it didn't take Freud to figure out why the bad dreams were back.

After all, in a couple of weeks I was moving all the way across the country to live with a man I'd never even met.

Groaning, I dragged myself out of bed, wondering why I had been blessed with the most selfish, irresponsible mother on the planet.

"I can't believe India is really moving."

At the mention of my name I halted before turning the corner in the hall. I was on my way to a dance committee meeting after school.

"I can. It's the first thing since she got here that's ever made sense," Siobhan said.

I narrowed my eyes. She was such a bitch.

"How do you mean?" Tess said.

"Oh, please, Tess. You and I both know that India doesn't bring much to the table. Look where she lives compared to me. She's way trash. I'm way live. I have the big party house and the pool. And my house is by the beach. She lives in some poky little apartment that only Anna has seen the inside of. It's a crime that she's as popular as she is."

I barely heard anything after "She's way trash."

Panic had seized my chest at those words.

No.

This was supposed to be my safe place.

No one could talk about me like that here.

As long as I was still here, this was my kingdom. I whirled around the corner. Tess was already striding down the hall toward the classroom the dance committee used for meetings.

Siobhan had been staring after her but jerked a little at the sight of me.

I eyed her carefully as I passed. "Well. Are you coming or not?"

"*I* am, but why are you?" she grumbled as she fell into step beside me. "It's not like you'll even be here for the formal."

"*Then*, no. But I'm still here now," I reminded her.

And I got more joy than I should have when everyone in the room greeted me enthusiastically and barely acknowledged Siobhan, and still more when a lot of my suggestions were taken despite the fact that I'd be long gone by the time of the actual dance.

I was in control.

Siobhan and her words couldn't touch me in that room.

"You look tired," Anna told me quietly once the meeting was over.

I couldn't exactly tell her that was because, for the fifth time this past week, I'd had one of the old nightmares. It had woken me up at three that morning and I couldn't get back to sleep.

"Just exhausted. Packing and stuff, you know."

"I know. Don't remind me." Anna wrapped her arm around my waist and pulled me into her. "Did Hayley tell you any more about this guy?"

"A little. And I Googled him."

Her eyes grew round with curiosity. "What did you find?"

Nothing incriminating. But still something terrifying. "Hayley said he was wealthy. She meant *wealthy*. This guy is high society. She's moving me into high society. *Me*." I felt the growing panic in my chest, knowing that climbing the social ladder in Boston was going to be near impossible. Being bottom of the social hierarchy was a nightmare. People didn't notice you down there, and when you were almost invisible there was no one to care if anything bad happened to you. No one to swoop in and stop you from being hurt.

It was a different kind of social ladder altogether in Theodore Robert Fairweather, Esq.'s world. "How am I ever going to fit in there?"

"Not everyone at your school will be wealthy."

Unfortunately, Anna was wrong. "Most of them will. I'm going to private school."

She looked as horrified as I felt. "No joke?"

"No joke."

"Like with a little plaid skirt and stuff?"

"I checked out the school's website and there doesn't seem to be an actual uniform, but it's on a whole other level academically." Which was good for my application to college, but would mean having to work that little bit harder, and working that little bit harder meant cutting into my plans for social climbing. "The tuition fee is insane. Apparently *Theodore* got me in without an interview thanks to his name alone."

Anna wrinkled her nose. "Wow. I can't believe you're moving in with Mr. Moneybags and you haven't even met him. Your mom is such a flake. This is like a TV show."

I gave a bark of bitter laughter. "My whole life is like a TV show."

CHAPTER 2

THE HOUSE IN WESTON, Massachusetts, was a mansion. An actual mansion.

I stood on the driveway outside, my neck craning back, and took in the massive redbrick building. It had gray slate tiles on the roof and bright white wood-framed windows. It also went on and on and on.

"Do you like it?"

I swallowed hard and glanced over at Hayley's fiancé and my soon-to-be StepVader—I mean, stepfather. Theodore Fair-weather was in his midforties, tall, athletically built and, I guess, good-looking for an old guy. To top it off he owned a home that could fit our California apartment inside it twenty, thirty times over.

"It's big," I said.

Theo laughed, his eyes crinkling at the corners. They did that a lot. I supposed that meant he laughed a lot. That didn't mean he was a kind man, though. Those laughing blue eyes could still be hiding cruelty. People were, after all, masters at deception. "It is big," he agreed.

"You know *I* love it." Hayley laid her head on his shoulder. "I can't believe we're finally here."

"I can't, either." He kissed her forehead. "It feels like forever I've been waiting for you to show up."

Theo had picked us up at the airport. We didn't have a lot of stuff with us because Hayley told me not to pack too many clothes. She said we'd need to go shopping for clothes that would help us fit in better.

Right.

I could tell she was excited at the prospect of spending Theo's cash. I, on the other hand, didn't want to owe this guy anything. Unfortunately, I was already into him for thousands in tuition fees at some stuck-up school in Boston.

"Let's get inside." Theo strode in through the double front doors. We stepped into a marble entrance hall with two large inner double doors that led into the main hall. A grand staircase swept down toward us in a curve. I stared around wide-eyed at the expensive furnishings.

Growing up I tried my best not to feel like trash. I knew people thought we were trash. But I worked hard to remember that no matter what they said, *I* wasn't.

But standing in cheap clothes in that big, expensive house, I suddenly felt this overwhelming fear that I would never find my power here, my control. I felt awkward. Unsophisticated. Uncultured.

I felt like trash.

And if possible I hated Hayley and Theo even more for bringing me here and making me feel that way about myself.

"I'll show you around and then to your room, India."

The rest of the house made me sick to my stomach with its

beauty. I lost count of how many stunningly decorated and lushly furnished reception rooms Theo led us through. The kitchen was twice the size of our apartment. Finally he led us to the back of the house into a more casual TV room. Three of the walls were made up of floor-to-ceiling glass and a twin set of French doors that led out onto a large patio area. I could see a barbecue, large outdoor dining set, lounge chairs and beyond that in the near distance was a massive swimming pool and a pool house that was a miniversion of the main house.

Sitting around the pool, laughing and talking, were a group of kids about my age.

Theo frowned at the sight but as soon as he became aware of my scrutiny he grinned. The sudden change only reinforced my decision to be wary of his character. "Eloise's out there with some friends. Why don't we take you out there and then Eloise can show you to your room later."

I couldn't think of anything worse.

Immediately the sick feeling in my gut became a swarm of butterflies.

My feet might as well have been weighted down with anchors as Theo and Hayley forced me outside into the late-September sun.

"Eloise," Theo called, and a pretty redhead stood up from a lounger. She was wearing a beautiful yellow silk dress that looked great against her pale rose skin and probably cost a fortune.

She stepped forward and beamed at her father. I felt a twinge of something I refused to call jealousy as father and daughter embraced—a tight hug that was so full of feeling they would have to be really freaking great actors for it to be faked—and then smiled into one another's faces.

Theo murmured something that I couldn't quite hear and

Eloise looked chastened. "I'm sorry, Daddy." Eloise looked squarely at Hayley. "I apologize for not coming out to welcome you properly."

"That's okay, sweetheart." Hayley waved her apology off while I tried not to scowl at them both. *Sweetheart?* Really? Just how close were Hayley and her new soon-to-be daughter?

"Eloise, this is India. India, Eloise," Theo said.

Light hazel eyes connected with mine and I tensed. The warmth in them had disappeared.

"Welcome." She gave me a tight smile.

I gave her a terse nod, which only made her smile tighter.

"I'm going to help Hayley get settled in. Why don't you introduce India to your friends and then show her to her room. Okay?"

"Sure thing, Daddy," she chirped.

Hayley squeezed my hand and gave me a bolstering look as though she cared whether or not she was leaving me to my doom. I turned away from her to stare warily at Eloise.

She stared back, not saying a word until we heard the click of French doors behind us.

Eloise crossed her arms over her chest. "You're here."

Yes, definitely not the warmest welcome in the world. "So it would seem."

She frowned at my clothes. "You'll need to go shopping."

I didn't give her or her friend who giggled from a lounge chair beyond us a reaction to her insinuation that my clothes were too cheap for her world.

Pulling on my armor, I did the only thing I could and pretended like I wasn't intimidated. "Who're your friends?" I said, walking toward them.

The giggler was a petite girl with flawless golden skin and rich dark brown hair. She was perched on a lounge chair.

Sitting on the edge of the pool with their pant legs rolled up were a sun-bronzed blond-haired boy and a stunning blonde girl with perfect porcelain skin and features—they looked like an Abercrombie & Fitch ad. In the pool on a blow-up lounge was a guy with black hair and a curious smirk. Finally my eyes swung to the boy leaning against the pool house wall. He was tall with naturally tan skin, dark hair and dark eyes, one of those boys that were too good-looking to be real, and he was staring at me with cold indifference.

I stared right back with my best *I'm so bored I could die* expression before turning my attention to the giggler.

To my surprise she gave me a little smile. "I'm Charlotte."

"More importantly, I'm Gabe," the boy in the pool called out. He paddled toward our end of the pool and held a hand out while he grinned up at me. He wore his close-cropped black hair in waves and water glistened on his warm brown skin. Freckles a shade darker sprinkled his cheeks and the bridge of his nose, giving his handsome face a hint of adorable. His smiling dark eyes roamed my face.

I bent down and tentatively shook his wet hand. "India."

"Awesome name." He reclined back in his lounge chair, drinking me in. His perusal was much different from Eloise's and I relaxed a little. Maybe I still had a little power. After all, I didn't magically stop being pretty in Massachusetts.

"I'm Joshua." The boy with his feet in the pool held out his hand.

The girl next to him hit him in the gut with her elbow and glared at him.

"Ow." He scowled. "What?"

She shook her head in disgust. "Idiot."

I ignored her and took his hand. "Nice to meet you."

"You, too."

It was his turn to nudge the girl. She sighed heavily and looked up at me, giving me the same kind of once-over Eloise had. “Bryce,” she muttered.

I glanced over my shoulder at the boy by the pool house. At my scrutiny he straightened up and walked toward me. He stopped at a lounge chair and sat down on it with a casual elegance you could only be born with. “Finn Rochester,” he said curtly, his voice deep, rich, around those two sharp words.

He was the only one to introduce himself using his last name and I immediately knew I was supposed to register its importance.

I decided then and there I liked him the least—this beautiful, pretentious boy.

“My boyfriend.” Eloise strode toward him and put her hand on his shoulder.

The gesture seemed forced and I had to wonder how *Rochester* felt about Eloise’s less than subtle claim of ownership.

“And just so you know, Joshua is my boyfriend,” Bryce piped up.

Laughter in my voice at their desperation to claim their boys, I said, “Good to know. I’ll be sure to shelve my inner man-eater around them.”

Gabe chuckled. “No need to shelve it around me.”

“You two—” I flicked my hand between him and Charlotte “—aren’t…?”

“Oh God, no,” Charlotte said.

“Hey!” Gabe splashed some water at her and she squealed like a five-year-old.

“So, California?” Joshua said.

I nodded. “Arroyo Grande.”

“Ugh, the west coast,” Bryce sneered.

I immediately thought of Siobhan and her aversion to all

things *not* west coast. Had I stumbled upon her mirror twin in Massachusetts?

"Maybe 'ugh' but I would kill for nice weather all year round." Charlotte sighed in longing.

"You'd bore of it," Bryce said. "Four seasons are better than two."

I didn't bother telling her that California *had* four seasons; they just didn't contrast with one another as much as they did here. I was guessing that information wouldn't make a bit of difference to change her mind about the west coast.

"So…how strange are you finding all this?" Joshua said. "Theo and your mom getting together… It's pretty sudden, right?"

I felt Eloise's eyes on me and understood that she was interested despite herself so I directed my answer to her. "I think our parents are dicks."

The guys burst out into laughter. Well, Joshua and Gabe did. Finn eyed me like I was some weird science experiment.

Eloise narrowed her eyes. "My father is not a dick and I don't appreciate that kind of language."

I crossed my arms over my chest. "Your father is richer than Jay Z and yet no one thinks it's a good idea for him to fly out to Cali so I can get to know the guy I'm supposed to call stepfather. Instead I've got to leave my life behind and move in with some strange man I've never met. That doesn't sound at all dickish on the part of our parents?"

"My father wanted to fly west to meet you," Eloise told me with calm disinterest. "Your mother is the one who didn't want him to."

I winced and felt an ache slash across my chest. Of course Theo wanted to meet me, and my mother talked him out of it. She probably thought I'd ruin everything for her by telling him the truth or, you know…just by being me.

Pretending I didn't care, I shrugged. "So do you guys all go to the same school?"

"We—" Eloise circled her finger to include the group "—*are* Tobias Rochester High School. Finn's great-grandfather was the founder."

Suddenly things were becoming clearer.

I looked at Finn but he was staring stonily at the ground.

So these were the cool kids. My "in." How did I even begin winning them over when Eloise's chilly demeanor wasn't exactly inviting?

My eyes slid past Eloise to Finn, who was looking at me again. Or should I say *through* me again.

Unnerved, I glanced back at Eloise.

She waved halfheartedly to the house. "I could show you to your room, but you probably want some alone time to adjust."

Hopes falling, I recognized her polite comment for what it was. She was definitely *not* welcoming me into her group.

"Right." I pasted on a smile I hoped was civil. "Later, guys."

"Definitely," Gabe returned.

I gave a nod to Charlotte as I passed but she dropped her eyes.

I did my best to walk calmly inside and out of view.

Once I had privacy I collapsed against the nearest wall and struggled to draw in breath. I felt shaky, my face was tingling and my breath was trapped in my throat.

I felt like I was dying.

Recognizing the impending panic attack, I struggled to get control over it.

Eloise had made it clear she didn't really want to be friends, and I didn't know if it was because she hated my mother—if it was about not wanting a replacement or not wanting her father's attention divided—but I did know I was being left out in the cold.

School on Monday was going to be just delightful.

Trembling, I slumped to the ground and pressed the heels of my palms to my eyes. I was used to feeling alone in a room full of people who liked me, but I wasn't used to actually being alone.

I was surprised by how much that terrified me.

I almost hyperventilated again trying to find my new bedroom. I got lost in the myriad hallways, stairways and rooms in the mansion.

When I finally found my room I was stunned.

Spacious didn't even cover it.

In the middle of a grand room that had French doors that opened onto a beautiful Juliet balcony was a massive four-poster bed with champagne drapes. The wall the bed was situated against had been wallpapered in gold damask. I had white French-style furniture—bedside tables, a dressing table and mirror with a matching stool. A desk with a Mac sitting on top of it, school supplies piled next to it, a flat-screen TV hooked on the wall opposite my bed with a little shelf holding a DVD player. On the wall by the door was an iDock so I could play my music and hear it through the small speakers that had been fitted high up in every corner of the room. To finish there was a generous dressing room/walk-in and a private bathroom with a rainfall shower and huge claw-footed tub.

It was a suite for a princess.

I loved it. And I hated that I loved it.

It was the kind of room I'd dreamed of escaping to when I lived with my dad. The kind of room I'd never imagined I'd ever get to sleep in.

So I loved it.

I just wished it had come to me in a different way.

"So what do you think?"

Hayley stood in the doorway, smiling gently at me. She was alone.

Eloise's words from earlier came back to me and I turned around to fully face Hayley. "I think you're either ashamed of me or ashamed of yourself."

She stepped into the room and closed the door behind her. "What are you talking about?"

"I'm talking about the fact that Theo wanted to come to California to meet me, get to know me, before hauling me across the country into this strange place with strange people. You didn't want him to meet me…not until it was too late."

A guilty-looking Hayley shook her head. "That's not true."

"Eloise told me that Theo wanted to meet me, but you said no."

She stared at her feet and said nothing.

It never failed to surprise me that she could still hurt me. Angry, I pushed. "So…what was it? Ashamed of me or ashamed of you?"

"I…" She shrugged and looked up at me, seeming helpless. "I didn't want to take the chance that you'd tell him the truth. I haven't told him and I know how angry you still are with me, and I… I didn't want to lose him."

I laughed bitterly at her confession. "Isn't that always the way with you, Hayley? Always doing what's best for you. Not giving me time to get to know this guy, for him to get to know me… No, that doesn't work for you, right? So who cares if you rip my world apart again and toss me in with these sharks? As long as *you're* okay."

She rushed toward me suddenly, gripping my biceps hard as she pleaded with me. "This is the best thing that will ever happen to us. I know you don't believe me but Theo is a good man and he can take care of us. No one can hurt us here."

"No one but each other."

Her grip fell away. "Are you going to tell him?"

I looked around at my room, knowing that a guest room would never have been tricked out like this—with the laptop and speakers and school supplies. Whatever Theo's true character, he'd gone to great lengths to make me feel welcome in his home. "You know, I almost feel sorry for the guy." I turned back to her. "Marrying a woman he doesn't really know."

As I stared into Hayley's tortured eyes I crumbled. The truth was this could be my perfect revenge, taking him away from her by giving him cold hard facts. But I didn't have that kind of spitefulness in me. "I won't tell him."

Hayley sagged with relief. "It's the right decision, sweetheart. I promise. I am trying to make this up to you. I've been trying for six years. What else can I do?"

"Stop trying."

I flinched as she raised her hand and brushed her thumb across my cheek. Her eyes were wet as she whispered, "Never."

I held strong and silent until she left me alone in my room. That's when I finally let my tears fall.

"This is exciting," Theo said. "Our first dinner as a family."

Hayley beamed at him while Eloise and I looked anywhere but at each other as we sat across from one another at the eight-seater dining table.

After being forced from my new bedroom by Theo and Hayley I discovered Theo employed a driver, a cook, three maids and a groundskeeper. Apparently I'd missed the tennis court and badminton court situated beyond the swimming pool.

They had "staff."

Staff.

Seriously?

I felt like Cedric Errol in *Little Lord Fauntleroy.*

As we were served dinner by said staff, I ignored Hayley and Theo as they twittered lovingly with one another until Theo said, "Eloise, why don't you join Hayley and India tomorrow? They're shopping for a new wardrobe and could use you as a guide."

Eloise smiled at her father. "I would, Daddy, but I have a chemistry lab paper to write with Charlotte tomorrow. The paper is due Monday."

"Oh, well, your education comes first." He looked disappointed but didn't push her on it.

I slumped with relief that she wouldn't be joining us.

"Charles Street has some very nice boutiques," Eloise said warmly to Hayley. "And of course there's Newbury Street. You'll find everything you need there."

"Thank you." Hayley turned to Theo. "I've never been shopping in Boston."

"Gil will drive you but Back Bay and Beacon Hill aren't an easy place to get lost. That's where your new school is, India. Beacon Hill," Theo said. "Gil will drive you and Eloise there in the morning and pick you up after school. If you and Eloise end up with different schedules we'll work something out. Your mother tells me you're a great soccer player.

Tobias Rochester, unfortunately, doesn't have a girls' soccer team but we do have a lacrosse team."

"I've never played."

"Perhaps you'll be good at it."

"Does the school have a paper?"

His eyes brightened at my sudden interest in conversation. I think he was pleased that my interest lay in academics. Of course, he didn't understand that my true motivation wasn't really about academia, although I did want to get into a good college.

"It *does* have a school newspaper. An award-winning school newspaper."

"India was coeditor of her school paper," Hayley said proudly.

I was surprised she knew that.

Theo was pleased. "Well, we will definitely need to see about getting you on the *Tobias Rochester Chronicle*."

"Thank you," I forced out.

"You're welcome. Now what else are you interested in?"

"I was on the debate team and I was the theater manager."

"Well—" Tobias grinned at his daughter "—Eloise has been the lead in the school play for the last three years. Usually they give the leading role to juniors and seniors but Eloise is so talented that she has won every part since she was fourteen. You could surely find India a job behind the scenes."

"Daddy, our theater isn't some public school theater. Our theater manager is not a student—he's an experienced, paid adult."

He shrugged. "I know that. But India could be an assistant."

"Yes, I could be an assistant," I added, imitating Eloise's big doe eyes.

She looked almost pained. "I think we have all the behind the scenes staff we need."

"Pish posh," Theo said. "It's the start of the school year."

Pish posh, I mouthed at Hayley. Seriously? Did all Boston upper crust families talk like they thought they were still British?

To my surprise Hayley hid her smile in her napkin at my teasing.

"Yes, pish posh," I said to Eloise. "You're the talent. I'm sure you can pull a few strings."

Hayley choked into her napkin, not hiding her chuckle at all well.

Theo didn't even seem to notice. He was too busy eyeing me with new appreciation. "A go-getter. I admire that. I think you're going to fit in very well here, India."

"I think so, too." I forced myself to smile back at him.

"When your mother told me you planned to go to law school, that you have aspirations to work in the DA's office, I was impressed," Theo added, seeming sincere. "And I'm even more so now that we've become acquainted. I cannot tell you how wonderful it is to have a budding lawyer in the family."

I couldn't tell you if a word out of his mouth was true, but I could tell that her father's approval of me put a wary look in Eloise's eyes I just didn't understand.

CHAPTER 3

I HAD TO admit I was charmed by Charles Street.

Gil, our driver, was a pleasant, tall bald man who looked to be in his early forties, with broad shoulders and thick biceps. I think he was more bodyguard than driver.

He somehow found a spot to park on the street that was paved in red brick, lined with trees and had quaint gas lamps, antiques stores, restaurants and boutiques. The smell of flowers filled the air and it felt like we weren't in a city at all.

So far Hayley had bought two dresses that were hundreds of dollars each.

I had bought a cute notepad.

"You have to start looking," Hayley said as we strolled toward where Gil was standing at attention by the car.

"What am I supposed to be looking for?" I said. "I have no idea how the kids at this school dress."

"I never thought of that. Damn. I should have asked Eloise. Sorry."

"I don't think she would have helped."

"What do you mean?"

"Behind the 'Daddies' and chirpy smiles is a girl who is not happy to have me here."

I waited for Hayley to tell me I was being silly. She surprised me again by eyeing me carefully and replying, "Has she been rude to you?"

"No, but she wasn't that welcoming, either."

"Give her time." She nudged me with her shoulder with a coaxing smile.

"Whatever."

"You better tell me if Eloise crosses the line into rude. Her father has spoiled her a little."

"I can handle myself," I said, too stubborn to accept her help.

"Finn!"

I jerked at Hayley's random yell.

And then I followed her gaze and realized she wasn't being random.

My stomach flip-flopped.

Finn Rochester had just come out of the boutique I'd bought my notepad from earlier. He glanced over at us, his eyes narrowing on me.

Before I could stop her Hayley hurried over to him.

"Hayley." Finn nodded politely.

I hadn't realized Hayley had met Eloise's boyfriend but then I'd forgotten she had actually spent months around these people before dropping me in the middle of it. Not only had they apparently met, but they knew each other well enough to be on a cozy first-name basis. My resentment simmered to the surface.

"Finn, how are you?" She smiled at him like he was the

most interesting boy in the world. I knew Hayley well enough to know that she was impressed by his family name and his natural air of cultured superiority.

"Well. And you?"

"We're shopping." She raised the bags in her hands to elaborate.

He took in the one tiny little bag in my hand. "You don't shop?"

He seemed so bored by his own question I wondered why he'd bothered to ask.

Before I could say anything, Hayley said, "Well, India has a dilemma. Perhaps you could help."

"I'd be happy to."

I snorted. Loudly. Because he sounded like he'd rather do anything else in the world than help me.

His eyes cut back to me but I refused to be intimidated by him and his masculine beauty. I stared back until he turned his attention to Hayley.

I did a little inner fist pump of triumph over winning our staring contest.

Hayley seemed to eye our interaction with interest. She smirked a little as she said, "What do the girls at your school wear? India needs a wardrobe for the semester."

Without looking at me he shrugged. "Stick with designer. There are numerous stores on Newbury Street. Introduce yourself to the staff, explain she's attending Tobias Rochester and they'll be able to help you."

"Wonderful, thank you." Hayley beamed, not at all annoyed that Finn had referred to me as "she" rather than by name.

What? Was he afraid to say my name in case my trailer trashiness rubbed off on him?

Dipshit.

"You're welcome." He gave us a nod. "Enjoy the rest of your day."

As we watched his tall form stride away, I decided he was perfect for Eloise. He had the broad shoulders and narrow waist of a swimmer, long legs, a face worthy of the Greek gods and expensive clothes that fit him to perfection.

He was beautiful and wealthy just like his girlfriend.

And he was just as welcoming.

"I like him," Hayley said quietly. "There's something mysterious about him."

"He's a snob."

She frowned at me. "No. I don't think so. I think he's just sad."

"Sad?" I made a face. "How so?"

"I don't know. Maybe he needs a friend." She nudged me pointedly.

I gave a huff of laughter. "Oh, yeah, I can see that happening."

"What?" Hayley seemed confused as we started walking toward the car again. "I think you two might get along if you just make an effort. You know he's the kind of boy I would have loved to see you with if Eloise hadn't gotten there first. A boy like that needs someone to shake him up a little. You're so good at shaking people up."

I grunted and rolled my eyes at her teasing. "You, Hayley, I'm good at shaking you up. I'm pretty chill with everyone else."

And anyway… Hell would freeze over before Finn Rochester would ever look at a girl like me.

And it would seriously, seriously take a miracle to make a boy that cold appealing to me in any way. It didn't matter how pretty his face was.

★ ★ ★

Large wrought-iron gates swung open into a courtyard from the sidewalk and hugging that courtyard was Tobias Rochester High School. Housed in an imposing Federal-style building that was set back from the street, it looked like the king of the pretty row houses in the fancy neighborhood in Beacon Hill.

I stared up at the building, trying to ignore the pounding of my heart.

Unfortunately, my morning had gone speedily downhill. When I woke up it was to sunlight spilling into my beautiful, peaceful new room. I was surprised by how well-rested I felt. Seriously, now I understood why people often described beds like a cloud.

I'd then taken an awesome shower in my huge new bathroom and I'd put on one of the many outfits Hayley had forced me to buy the day before. I was wearing Armani skinny jeans and an oversize Alexander McQueen T-shirt. Hayley (or Theo actually) had even bought me jewelry, and I was wearing a new watch and bracelet, as well as a pair of small diamond studs in my ears. A pair of Tory Burch flats finished the casual but expensive look and, as much as I hated to admit it because I felt like the walking privileged, I looked pretty good.

And that's where all the "good" stopped.

Theo wasn't at breakfast because he went into the office really early. Hayley was still in bed and Eloise was sitting at the breakfast table being waited on hand and foot.

I decided to help myself in the kitchen, hoping to make conversation with the cook, Gretchen, only to discover Gretchen really didn't want me in her kitchen. I think it was the glaring and the shooing hand gestures that gave her feelings away.

I ended up out in the dining room with my new soon-to-be stepsister. The silence between us was so thick it was stifling as we ate.

Gil came to inform us that it was time to leave for school and I grabbed up my new school satchel (I never, ever thought I'd use the word *satchel*), and hurried after Eloise.

The tense silence continued between us during the thirty-minute drive to school. When we pulled up to the school, Gil opened the door for Eloise and she shot out of the car as if I had the plague.

Gil gave me a sympathetic smile as I got out and told me to have a good first day.

So far Gil was pretty much the only person in the whole Massachusetts experience that I might actually like.

I got a few curious looks from kids as I walked through the gates and into my new school life. Theo had sent Hayley a class program list a few weeks back and I'd filled it out. Within twenty-four hours I'd been given a schedule and he'd sent on textbooks so I could be somewhat up-to-date on what we would be discussing in class. Plus the school had an intraweb and the teachers were cool enough to list each upcoming class discussion and the reading that was expected for it.

As organized as I already was, I still had to register my arrival. Following signs for the school office, I took in the modern interior that was incongruous with the building's exterior. The school office was chic—all shiny glass, white, glossy painted wood and expensive computers.

"May I help you?" A middle-aged woman with short blond hair smiled at me as I stepped inside the office.

I gave her a small smile, hoping I didn't appear as nervous as I felt. "My name is India Maxwell. I'm new."

"Oh, Miss Maxwell, of course." She came around her desk

to offer me her hand. As I shook it she introduced herself. "My name is Ms. Llewellyn. I'm the head of administration at Tobias Rochester."

"Nice to meet you."

"You, too. We've been expecting you." She turned to her desk and shuffled through some papers before producing a large envelope. "This is for you. Inside you'll find important information about the school, including leaflets on a list of extracurricular activities we have here at Tobias Rochester."

"Thank you," I murmured, feeling overwhelmed already.

"Headmaster Vanderbilt would like to introduce himself."

Headmaster Vanderbilt turned out to be a guy probably only five years or so older than Theo. I expected someone stuffy, pretentious and more than a little condescending, but Headmaster Vanderbilt—a tall, reed-thin man who wore a tiny pair of rimless glasses perched on his big Roman nose—was warm and welcoming.

His welcome, in fact, would be the warmest I'd receive that day.

My first class was Microeconomics and to my horror Eloise, Finn and their whole crew took the class. I hadn't been expecting to see them all together in one class and while the teacher introduced me I had to quickly put my mask of indifference on.

Eloise didn't acknowledge my presence as I took a seat on the other side of the classroom. My eyes drifted to Finn but he was staring at the teacher, almost too studiously, like he was trying to avoid my gaze. I shook that suspicion off, knowing Finn thought he was superior to me—I probably wasn't even on his radar.

Not that I cared if I was on his radar or not.

My Microeconomics teacher was pretty cool and I got

through the class not feeling totally out of my depth. I considered that a positive for the day.

Fiction Writing was next and Charlotte was in my class. When I walked in, her eyes lit up and I thought I detected the beginnings of a smile before a thought passed over her expression. Her shoulders slumped, and she looked like she wanted to blend into the background.

I decided to ignore her weirdness and waved at her as the teacher approached to introduce herself. The teacher saw my exchange with Charlotte and insisted I sit with her.

"Hey," I said as I took the seat beside her.

Charlotte gave me a half smile, half grimace. "Hi."

"Don't worry, I won't cheat off you."

Her answer was a tremulous smile.

Encouraged, I nodded at her violet dress. "That color looks awesome on you."

Appearing almost taken aback, Charlotte glanced down at the dress and ran her fingertips over it. "Really? Bryce said it washed me out. She said I look trash in it."

Of course she did. I got more than a few mean girl vibes off that girl. "Well, she's wrong. It's really cute."

"Thanks." Charlotte gave me a shy smile before wariness replaced it and she turned determinedly to face the front.

Her body language told me not to push talking to her, but I felt hope.

Smiling inwardly, I faced forward, too, and listened to the teacher as she started class.

Two classes passed and I already had more homework than I'd ever had back at Fair Oaks High. I wasn't freaking out about it just yet, considering I had no friends and no extracurricular activities to distract me from all the schoolwork, but once I did I'd have to find a way to juggle it all.

As I was walking toward my next class I noticed the glances and full-on stares from my new schoolmates. Their looks varied from curious to sneering and I felt a tingle of wariness across the back of my neck. Turning a corner on my search for my Modern European History class, I came face-to-face with my stepsister-to-be and her girls. They sashayed down the hall like an ad for a TV show about beautiful popular high school kids, long hair fluttering out behind them like silk, long trim legs on display in their designer dresses and elongated by their Jimmy Choo sandals.

Eloise saw me, looked right through me and kept on walking without a word.

My skin felt hot with embarrassment at her obvious cut.

I watched her disappear around the corner with her best friends before looking around the hallway. That's when I realized I hadn't been imagining the sneers of my classmates.

A sick feeling settled in my gut as I wondered what the hell was going on.

Determined to pretend I didn't care, I threw my shoulders back and continued on my search for my class. To my relief I discovered the classroom without having to ask anyone for directions. The last thing I wanted to do right then was interact with anyone. I strode inside, cursing Hayley all over again for bringing me to Massachusetts, unaware of anyone else but the tall faculty member standing by the whiteboard.

He caught sight of me in his peripheral vision and turned. He was my youngest teacher so far, probably in his late twenties, and he was cute in a nerdy, intellectual kind of way.

"Hi." He smiled.

"I'm India Maxwell. I'm new."

"Oh, India, yes. I knew that." He held out his hand for

me to shake. "I'm Mr. Franklin, but most of these guys drop the 'Mr.'"

I smiled back, liking his down-to-earth vibe immediately. "It's nice to meet you."

"You, too." He looked out at the class and I followed his gaze.

I felt a horrible jump in my heartbeat at the sight of Finn Rochester sitting in the middle of the room and things pretty much got worse from there.

"Finn," Franklin said, "you've got an empty seat beside you, right?"

No. NO. NO!

I did not want to sit beside that stuck-up ass. Only seconds into the class and already I knew it was going to suck worse than anything that had happened in my day so far.

Finn glanced at the table and chair beside him and then looked over at me. His expression was carefully blank. "Yes, it's empty."

Franklin gestured toward it. "Take a seat, get comfy and we'll get started."

I murmured my thank-you and slowly made my way to the chair I'd just been allocated. Finn stared straight ahead at Franklin, much like he had done in our Microeconomics class. As I sat I glanced at his profile.

There was a weird flutter in my stomach that I put down to nerves. After all, it *was* messed up that someone as influential as Finn had decided I wasn't good enough. It would make the school social climbing that much freaking harder. More than that, I realized…it hurt. I didn't want it to hurt. But it hurt nonetheless. It reminded me too much of a time spent with a man who thought I was worthless.

Shaking that black hole of memories away, I found myself studying Finn.

The flutter in my stomach intensified.

It was a damn shame that someone so good-looking was such an incredible dipshit.

I noted his broad shoulders tense. Slowly, he turned his head to lock eyes with me. His look was dark and fathomless; mine was challenging.

Something weird happened to me as our silent interaction drew out. Franklin's voice became just a murmur in the background and my blood turned hot. The whole world faded out—everything but Finn's eyes and the squirming heat under my skin.

I began to worry that the longer he stared into my eyes, the more he'd see, because the longer I stared into his, the more I saw to my surprise that Hayley was right—there was a sadness in Finn's eyes. And what surprised me even more was how curious I was to know what put it there. I hadn't expected it. What could ever have made someone as lucky as Finn sad?

Finally his eyes narrowed and I could have sworn his expression turned wary a split second before he wiped it blank and turned his head away.

Feeling strangely unsettled, I decided to take a page out of Finn's book and pretend like he didn't exist.

When class ended Finn shot out of there before I could dare to say a word to him. I was okay with that. In fact, I waited for everyone to filter out before approaching Franklin.

"India, great job today. I'm delighted you did all the reading before joining us. Tobias Rochester is a competitive school. Sometimes it's hard for new students coming from a less competitive environment to keep up with us."

I thought that was an extremely diplomatic way to put it and knew my smile said so.

I pulled out one of the leaflets Ms. Llewellyn had put in

my packet. "I see that you are the faculty member that oversees the school newspaper."

"Yes. Usually it would be an English teacher but I minored in journalism so…" He shrugged modestly, as if to say, *Here I am.*

"Great. Well, I was coeditor of my paper back in Arroyo Grande. I was hoping that there might be a place for me on *this* paper."

"Oh. Well, you know, we've got most of the team together already because we're a few weeks into the school year…however, we are looking for a book reviewer. I know a critic isn't a journalist but is that something you might be interested in?"

"Yes." I nodded eagerly. "I love books. And really, I just want to be part of the team on the paper. It's a start, right?"

"Definitely. We do have a couple of other students interested. However, I always choose those who have potential to bring more to the paper over time. So why don't you email me some of the work you've done on your previous paper if you can?"

"I can do that."

He chuckled at my eagerness. "Great. My email is on the intraweb. Send it to me ASAP."

"I will. Thanks, Mr. Franklin."

"You're welcome, India."

There was a little skip in my step as I left his class. I was hopeful that things were looking up.

That thought was quickly dashed when I wandered into the cafeteria for lunch period.

Tobias Rochester was a much smaller school than my last, which made the cafeteria drama much more pronounced. And today's drama? Me. New Girl.

No one had made any friendly overtures yet and I was still

receiving weird looks. Everyone was gaping at me: disgust in some cases and curiosity in others.

The disgust was worrying.

As I strode to the lunch line to be served, I searched for and eventually found Eloise sitting at a table smack-bang in the middle of the room. Of course she'd want to be in the center of it all.

Bryce and Charlotte sat on either side of her, and Finn, Gabe and Joshua sat opposite them. The girls saw me and immediately looked away. Bryce said something and whatever it was made the boys glance over their shoulders in my direction. Finn and Joshua quickly looked away but Gabe grinned over at me and started to get up.

Bryce snapped something at him. He threw a fry at her with a chuckle and she turned a dark shade so red I thought her head was about to explode with all the blood rushing into it.

As Gabe made his way toward me I braced myself, not sure what kind of greeting to expect from him.

"You made it," he said, wearing an expression of amusement.

I didn't detect any meanness in him. "Yup."

"Well, you look great."

"Should you be over here complimenting me?"

"Are you talking about Bryce?" He chuckled. "She should know by now that I'm not one of her cliquey bitches. I talk to whoever I want. And Elle hasn't said you're off-limits and we all know Elle's the one really in charge."

Huh, that was interesting. I would have thought for certain Eloise would have called for me to be ostracized by her friends.

As if he saw the thought in my eyes, Gabe shook his head. "Elle's a good girl."

Hmm, I wasn't sure I believed that.

"So you're being nice to me?"

He laughed at my suspicious tone. "Believe it or not, yes."

"Okay." I shrugged, still not one hundred percent sure of his motives. Although to be fair he was cool to me when we first met, too. "So if you're really trying to be nice… maybe you could tell me why everyone is looking at me so strangely?"

"Ah." He suddenly looked sheepish. Guilty even. "Yes, about that." He stepped toward me, lowering his voice. "Look, when your mom and her dad started dating Eloise didn't exactly like Hayley. She thought it was strange that as time went on Hayley never once brought you with her or let her dad go visit you. She said she was afraid you might be in rehab or something." He rubbed the back of his neck, looking embarrassed. "I might have told someone else that you were in rehab and, before I knew it, it was all over the school. But it was weeks ago," he said defensively. "I thought they would have forgotten it by now."

My eyes bugged out, my anger simmering beneath the surface. "Everyone thinks I was in *rehab*?"

"Yeah. I am really sorry."

I gave a huff of disbelief, trying to gauge his sincerity. He did seem genuinely embarrassed by the rumor he'd spread. "Are you going to tell people it's a lie?"

"Eloise overheard a few seniors talking about it this morning and she told them it wasn't true."

Hmm. Probably didn't want the rumor to hurt her reputation. "Then why are people still looking at me funny?"

"It'll take time for it to die down. Sitting with us would help," Gabe offered.

Was he nuts? I gave him a look that clearly questioned as much and he laughed.

"I'm asking you to."

"I'm not welcome."

"Okay, if you say so. You know where I am if you change your mind." He winked suggestively and backed off.

I shook my head at his flirtation, feeling a teensy bit better knowing there was a student at this school that didn't hate me, even if he accidentally spread a stupid rumor about me. As I was reaching for my tray of food, I heard Gabe call my name loudly.

I turned and stepped out of line to find him halfway between me and Eloise's table. Everyone was looking at us.

"You look remarkably good for a recovering drug addict."

I should have been mortified, but instead I felt a renewed resolve within me to not let these people think they could embarrass me or force me to duck my head and hide from their curiosity and judgment. I grinned at Gabe's mockery of the student body for believing his stupid lie and called, "Thanks, dipshit."

His laughter rang out around the room, and I found myself chuckling. I looked beyond him to Eloise and found her watching me uneasily. Gabe was oblivious as he walked back to the table. I moved to find an empty table, and my mood plummeted harshly when I realized I was going to have to sit alone.

I hadn't eaten lunch alone since I lived with my dad.

Doing what I'd gotten so good at since I'd arrived in Massachusetts, I pretended I wasn't bothered by my loner status. Instead I pulled out the book I was currently reading and got lost in the words while I ate my pasta salad.

Only a few minutes later my face started to tingle and I felt the little hairs on the back of my neck rise. Not moving my book from covering my face, I discreetly looked up over the top of it, searching for the cause of the tingles.

My eyes locked with Finn Rochester's.

Those little flutters awoke in my stomach again and I flushed hot.

Finn wrenched his gaze away, frowning down at his plate. No one at his table seemed to notice he'd been looking over at me.

I focused back on the pages of my book, but the words just became blurry blobs.

The truth was Finn unsettled me. I honestly didn't know why.

I just knew I didn't like it.

Forcing myself to concentrate on the book, I eventually got back into the story and for a while I forgot I was in hostile territory.

I wish I could say that the day improved from there but it was pretty much the same as the beginning. Classes were fine, if a lot more challenging than my old school, teachers were overall welcoming and none of my fellow students bothered to introduce themselves to me.

I walked out of school at the end of the day the way I'd walked in.

Alone.

Gil was waiting with the car and when he saw me he got out to open the door for me. "Good afternoon, miss. I hope you had a good first day."

I thanked him as I slid into the car.

Once I was settled inside Gil got back in the driver's seat and started to pull away.

"What about Eloise?"

"Miss Eloise informed me that she will be getting a ride home from Finn later this afternoon."

I nodded and turned to stare out the window. I'd found myself forgetting throughout the day that Finn and Eloise were a couple. They didn't act like Bryce and Joshua, who could barely keep their hands off one another. I knew not all couples liked PDA, but there was usually something to let you know that a couple were into one another. They acted like friends, for sure, but I hadn't seen them kiss or hold hands or cuddle.

But I guess one day wasn't really long enough to form an opinion about them as a couple.

As the streets of Boston passed us by I let my thoughts drift away from Eloise and Finn. Instead I thought of all the homework I had to do, all the work I had ahead of me to get involved in my new school and how miserable it was that I hadn't made one single friend. I'd decided Gabe didn't count. I knew when a boy had sex on his mind and Gabe was definitely flirting with me.

"Tomorrow is a new day."

I was startled from my forlorn musing by the sound of Gil's voice.

He was smiling sympathetically at me in the rearview mirror. "The first day is always the worst."

Grateful for his insight and kindness, I gave him a small smile. "It can only get better, right?"

"Definitely." And it sounded like a promise.

I hoped it was a promise. A solid one. Because I'd worked too hard to get out of my previous miserable existence for my mother's new romance to take that all away from me.

Upon arriving home, I had to remind myself to let Gil

get the door for me. When I stepped out I thanked him and hoped he knew I meant it sincerely. So far he was the only person from the house, other than Theo, who had been warm to me. I appreciated it.

Thinking of the staff, I decided to brave the kitchen despite Gretchen's grouchiness that morning because I really wanted a soda. Entering the vast space, I found it full of hustle and bustle as Gretchen and one of Theo's maids prepared for dinner.

I gave them an unsure smile and headed toward the huge refrigerator.

"May I help?" Gretchen called over.

"I'm just getting a soda."

"I'll get it for you, miss," she said gruffly, stepping away from the vegetables she was cutting.

"It's fine. I can get my own soda," I assured her with more than a hint of amusement in my voice.

Gretchen frowned but nodded.

"Do you know if Hayley is home?"

The maid was the one that answered me. "Ms. Maxwell is out. Wedding plans. She said she would return in time for dinner."

Wedding plans. Of course. "Thanks," I muttered, and strolled out of the kitchen with my can of soda. I headed straight for my room.

Hayley had broken it to me last night that she'd quit her job. I'd tried not to get really angry at her for giving up her own means of independence, because I knew her well enough to know that this wasn't a decision she was going back on.

As I'd gotten older and started to question why Hayley made the choices that she made, I started to form the theory that my inept mother had always wanted to be a princess. She didn't want reality. She wanted fantasy.

Theodore Fairweather was finally giving her that.

She could live a life of leisure as the wife of a wealthy, influential blue blood.

Never, I decided, never would I put my entire financial and emotional well-being in the hands of someone else. Never!

Nope. I was going to metaphorically kick ass at my new school and forge a new path to total independence. On that thought I got on my laptop, found some editions of my old school paper and sent them to Franklin to look over.

I studied a little, impatiently waiting for time to pass. Anna was going to FaceTime me but since there was a three-hour time difference between us, I had to wait for her to get out of school. When my laptop started ringing like a phone, I thought I hadn't heard such a nice sound in a long time.

"Oh my God, come home!" Anna yelled.

"Believe me, I would if I could. How was the first day of school without me?"

Anna rolled her eyes. "Um...what do you think? Siobhan is totally acting like Winter Snow Queen already."

"Yeah, like we didn't know that was going to happen. As long as she's not being mean?"

"So far not a lot of meanness, just a lot of 'fall at my feet and kiss my toes.'"

"Literally?"

"Thankfully, no. I don't care how many pedicures that girl can afford, I am not getting near her feet."

I laughed and then immediately sobered. "I miss you guys."

"We miss you, too. You know who else misses you?"

"Who?"

"Jay."

"Jay? He said that?" Somehow I couldn't picture the too-cool Jay actually uttering those words to Anna. I realized by

Anna's giddy tone that I should probably feel excited that Jay missed me. But I just…didn't.

"No, but he asked if we'd heard from you. Of course Siobhan tried to use his attention to flirt with him but he was really only interested in talking about you." She sighed heavily. "Oh, to be India Maxwell, breaking the hearts of bad boys everywhere."

I snorted. "Yeah, because my life is so charmed right now."

She clapped her hands together and stuck her face closer to the screen. "Tell me how *your* day went."

And so I proceeded to fill my best friend in on the grim start to my new life in Boston.

"India Maxwell does not sit alone at lunch!" Anna was gratifyingly indignant on my behalf. "I'm sorry you had such a shitty day. But trust me, they will realize how epic you are soon enough." Her sympathy and reassurances were soothing, and after we signed off, I did actually feel a little better for connecting with her.

I wandered around my room, trailing my fingers over all my new things and wondering if material possessions ever made anyone truly happy, and was stopped in my tracks at the French doors. Outside I watched as a light blue convertible pulled up in front of the house.

Sitting in the driver's seat was Charlotte and getting out of the car was Eloise. Eloise blew her friend a kiss and sashayed into the house, disappearing from sight.

A smiling Charlotte pulled away from the house.

Hmm. I thought Gil had said Eloise was with Finn.

"There you are."

I spun around to find Hayley standing in my doorway. "When did you get home?"

"About thirty minutes ago." She wore this goofy grin on her face as she sank down onto my bed. "How was school?"

"Fine, I guess."

"You guess? Was it really that bad?"

"I don't want to talk about it."

She looked hurt by my curtness so I changed the subject. "How goes the wedding plans?"

And just like that she lit up again as she told me all about the wedding planner she'd met with, the venue they'd by some miracle managed to book on such late notice, the flowers they were considering, the colors…

Unfortunately, I had to listen to it all over again at dinner later that evening.

When she'd finally run out of steam, Theo smiled indulgently at her and then turned to me. "So now that we know your mother had a wonderful day, how was yours, India?"

Like the previous nights, we sat around the informal dining table, the four of us, pretending that we were all comfortable in one other's company.

"It was good," I lied.

"Did you show India around, Eloise? Introduce her to everyone?"

"Of course, Daddy." It was Eloise's turn to lie.

I noted the way her fingers tightened around her fork so hard her knuckles went white.

It gave me pleasure knowing she was waiting for me to out her for not doing her daughterly duties.

I let the moment pass and watched her hand relax.

"Are you liking your classes?" Theo said.

"So far." I looked over at Eloise. I wanted her to know that maybe I didn't need her, after all. "And Mr. Franklin, my Modern European History teacher, is the head faculty member on the paper. He asked me to send some old articles to him. Kind of like an interview for a spot on the paper."

Hayley and Theo looked delighted. Hayley actually wore a look of pride as she said, "Well, that's wonderful."

"First the paper and then the theater," Theo said, his attention now on his daughter. "Eloise, did you ask about a job for India behind the scenes?"

"No, Daddy. Not yet."

He frowned. "India has already missed out on the first few weeks of school. Time is of the essence. I'd like you to try harder tomorrow."

She blushed at his admonishment. "Yes, Daddy."

The rest of the dinner conversation was carried by Hayley and Theo and it mostly covered the wedding and Hayley asking for my soon-to-be stepdad's opinion on flowers and themes and crap I'm sure he really wasn't that interested in.

I was happy to be excused from the table once I'd finished my dessert but I refused to completely give in to my new life. I found myself grabbing up my plate before Theo's staff could, ignoring him as he called out to me that "Janelle will do that!"

Instead I took my dirty plate and glass into the kitchen and then promptly stopped short at the sight before me. Gretchen was scraping a huge chunk of leftover meat loaf into the trash. An oven dish half-filled with potato dauphinoise was sitting on the counter, ready to be thrown out, too.

My skin tingled unpleasantly as I felt an immediate cold sweat prickle my face, my palms and under my arms. My heart was hammering way too hard in my chest. "What are you doing?" I said shakily, taking a step toward her.

Gretchen looked up in surprise. "Clearing up."

"Stop." I hurried over and looked down into the trash can.

My chest tightened at the sight of the food inside it. "You just threw away half a meat loaf!"

"Miss, leave your plate and glass. I'll clean it up," Gretchen said tetchily as she reached for the potatoes.

"No!" I grabbed ahold of the other end of the dish and her eyes grew round with surprise. "You can't just throw perfectly good food out!"

"Miss, please let go of the potatoes."

"No!"

"Miss, please." Her face grew pale.

"What is going on in here?" I heard Theo's authoritative voice behind us.

My grip on the dish tightened.

"Sir, I'm just trying to clear up the waste and Miss Maxwell got very upset."

"India." A hand curled around my wrist and I followed it up to Hayley's concerned face.

"It's not waste," I whispered. "It's perfectly fine leftovers."

I saw the pain in Hayley's eyes at my words and she reached up to brush my cheek with her fingertips. "Sweetie," she whispered back.

"We can't just throw it out."

"I know." She nodded and looked over my shoulder. "Darling, India's right. We should be keeping the leftovers or giving them to a local shelter. It's a lot of food to throw away."

I felt the warmth of Theo's presence as he stepped up beside us and peered into the trash can. "Do you throw out this much food every day?"

Gretchen swallowed hard. "Not every day, sir. Sometimes."

"Well, it does seem like a lot. India and Hayley are right. You and the staff will share the leftovers between you from now on, is that understood?"

"Yes, sir." Gretchen slumped with relief, I imagine because Theo hadn't given her any more crap about it.

As for me, my heartbeat began to slow but I still wasn't completely reassured. "You will use the leftovers, right?"

I could tell she thought I was nuts but still she answered soothingly, "Yes, miss. I have a teenage son who eats me out of house and home. The leftovers will be welcome."

The tension drained out of me. "Good." I sucked in a huge breath of air. "Thanks."

She gently tugged on the oven dish and I let it go, stepping back.

"I must say, India, I find your attitude quite refreshing." Theo gave me an affectionate smile.

My return smile was tremulous.

He thought I was being socially and economically conscious. He had no idea about my issues with food.

Hayley knew, though.

She rubbed my arm and turned me away from Gretchen. "You've had a long day, sweetie. Why don't you make it an early night?"

I nodded, and turned around to find Eloise standing near the door to the kitchen, watching me.

Crap.

The last thing I needed was her witnessing my weirdness.

CHAPTER 4

HE WAS EATING DOUGHNUTS. They were fresh and I could smell them. Carla had brought them.

My stomach clenched painfully.

"I can't keep eating 'em if she's gonna look at me like a feral cat," Carla complained. "Just fucking give her some food, Ed."

"Little bitch isn't getting a thing until I say so. She knows what she did." He glared at me.

I didn't know what I did.

I just knew it didn't take much.

"Well, she's freaking me out." Carla shoved the box of doughnuts away.

"Fine." He stood up abruptly and grabbed up the box of baked goods. Eyes on me the whole time, he strode across the trailer to the trash can, stood on the pedal that opened the lid and one by one he dropped the doughnuts inside.

I hated him.

I tightened my arms around my knees and shoved my face against my skin to block him out.

"I gotta go to work."

"She ain't going to school?"

"Nah. They'd feed her."

"She could just eat while you're gone."

"I emptied every inch of the place." He laughed, a wheezy sound I hated just as much as I hated him.

"You're sick," she said.

If she thought so, why didn't she do something?

I felt a stinging burn against my head, the crack of his hand echoing in my ears. I winced and looked up at him.

He sneered down at me. "Don't move a muscle or I'll know."

I nodded, so relieved when they were gone.

I waited a while before I dragged my tired body over to the trash can. I pulled the doughnuts out, wiping cigarette ash and some spicy sauce off a few of them before I shoveled them into my mouth. And I cried the whole time.

By the end of second period the next day, I knew *bulimic* had been added to my roster of fictional problems after a girl I didn't know leaned across her desk as I finished an energy bar before Calculus 2 started.

"Bryce Jefferson told me all about you so I need advanced warning if you're going to puke that up, because I don't handle vomit very well." She wrinkled her nose at me.

I blinked at her, confused for a few seconds, before it dawned on me that Eloise had told Bryce about my kitchen escapade the night before, and Bryce had clearly told everyone else. It was bad enough the whole thing had given me nightmares I didn't want—I didn't need this crap.

"I'm not bulimic. But it's good to know you are so concerned about a possibly life-threatening disorder affecting a classmate. You should win an award or something for most compassionate student. No, wait. I mean the most self-centered dipshit award."

Her mouth fell open in outrage and she shifted her entire desk away from mine with a screech across the hardwood floors.

That probably wasn't the best way for me to go about making new friends.

As it turned out I shouldn't have worried too much about alienating one of my classmates. By Day Four at Tobias Rochester, Eloise's friends had done that for me. I had not made one friend and the only classmate that spoke to me at all was Gabe, and that was to flirt with me briefly in the cafeteria. It didn't make me feel too special, however, because it became clear as he mingled with other students that Gabe flirted with a lot of girls.

I'd also exhausted all avenues regarding extracurricular activities. It turned out every team was full—the debate team, yearbook, events committee… I'd even asked about the math and science teams but apparently only geniuses were allowed and I was rejected because of my mere above-average brain. As for athletics, they had no soccer team so I was already at a disadvantage. I couldn't play basketball or lacrosse, I couldn't fence or dance (at least not at the level Tobias Rochester dance team could), I couldn't sail, row or play rugby or squash. The only thing I was good at was running but the cross-country team was full, which left me with just plain old running. Not exactly a team sport but I signed up, anyway.

Tobias Rochester was a small and competitive school. If you didn't get your foot in the door of a team the first day of the school year it was doubtful you ever would.

The only other extracurricular options left to me were the *Tobias Rochester Chronicle* and whatever Eloise could rustle me up in the theater. I still hadn't heard from Franklin and every time I walked into Modern European History I braced myself for disappointment.

On Friday I did just that as I strode into his class.

"India," Franklin said as soon as I stepped into the room, "see me after class, please."

I sucked in a breath and nodded, not wanting to get my hopes up. Part of me wished he would just tell me before class started so I knew one way or the other if my school career was destined for the toilet.

Settled at my seat, I kept my head down, not looking up when the seat next to me scraped back. My breathing came a little faster and I hated that Finn made me apprehensive. I refused to acknowledge his presence just as he'd ignored my existence for the last four days. We'd passed one another in the hall and, like Eloise, he'd looked anywhere but at me. He never spoke to me in the three classes we shared and he'd also ignored me last night when Eloise had her crew over to hang out by the pool and eat pizza. Thankfully Theo and Hayley hadn't been home so I wasn't forced to go out and sit with them all.

I did think it was weird that last night was the first time I'd seen Finn at the house since my first day there. Plus, he'd never been there alone. It bugged me that I was so curious about his and Eloise's relationship. Why should I care?

I cut Finn a look out of the corner of my eye. He was wearing a dark blue Henley with black jeans. All week I'd seen him in shirts that were rolled up at the sleeves and suit pants. Today his top was more fitted, highlighting his broad shoulders and slim waist. I'd discovered Finn was the only junior on the school's very distinguished rowing crew, and to top that he was the stroke, the most important position in the boat. The stroke was the rower closest to the stern and set the stroke rate and rhythm for the rest of his crew to follow. In a way he was kind of like their leader, their captain.

Turning my focus on Franklin, I listened as he went over what we'd been discussing all week. Toward the end of class he sat on his desk and grinned at us in a way that made me wary. That was a grin that wanted something from us.

"So," he said, "I'm going to split you into pairs and each team is going to give the class a verbal and visual presentation in two weeks."

The tops of my ears got hot at Franklin's announcement. This could either be a very good thing for me, or a very bad thing. If Franklin teamed me up with someone I didn't know, then there was a chance I could straighten out a few of those rumors and actually make a friend. But if Franklin teamed me up with—

"Finn and India, you'll be partners. Your topic is the Lisbon earthquake of 1755 and its social and political effects on the rest of the world."

I was screwed.

I tensed as Franklin smiled at us, completely unaware of the major disaster he was creating.

I didn't hear a word he said after that.

Bracing myself, I turned to Finn.

The muscle in his jaw ticked.

So he was pissed.

Well, that just pissed me off.

"Looks like you're going to have to make eye contact with me," I said.

He turned his head slightly to look at me. "Looks like it."

"You know I'm not really a drug addict, right? Your good buddy Gabe made that crap up."

His lips quirked at the corner.

My God…was that an actual semismile?

"I know," he said.

"So that should make working with me a little more reassuring."

I got no reply.

"You do also know that there is actual talking involved in a verbal presentation?"

"Was it the word *verbal* that gave it away?" he said.

I smirked. "I'm just pointing out that you're going to have to work on this whole brooding monosyllabic thing you've got going on if we're going to get a good grade."

"Noted."

"I guess you're going to start working on it tomorrow, then."

He sighed and sat back in his chair to look at me fully. "Do you have a smart reply to everything?"

"Not to Toaster Strudel."

If I wasn't mistaken that little quirk at the corner of his lips came back.

Did Finn actually have a sense of humor?

Before I could say anything more the bell rang, ending class. Finn immediately gathered his stuff.

"Before you go, we should arrange a time to meet up for this presentation."

"After school Monday? I don't have rowing then."

"Sure. Where?"

"Front gate." And with that clipped response he strode away.

Once the class had filtered out to head for lunch, I made my way over to Franklin. My heart rate was a little fast.

Do not get your hopes up. Do not get your hopes up, I chanted over and over in my head.

"India, thanks for staying behind," Franklin said when I approached.

"Of course."

"I'm sorry I've taken all week to get back to you. I was hoping to let you know what the situation was sooner but one of our students on the *Chronicle* surprised us by quitting. Too many after-school activities apparently."

That meant there were two spots open on the paper, which gave me a better chance.

Do not get your hopes up.

Franklin smiled widely at me. "India, I have to admit that I'm really impressed by what you accomplished at your school paper. The stories you oversaw were current, important and on point. I particularly loved the article you wrote on your interview with the mayor. You asked some hard questions about city council budget cuts. *Relevant* questions."

I flushed with pride at his compliment. "Thank you."

"The other candidates were good but they weren't good enough. I doubt any of them are truly interested in the *Chronicle* as much as they're interested in adding as many extracurriculars to their schedule as they can to impress the Ivies."

I raised an eyebrow at the comment and he laughed.

"I never said that."

"I never heard it."

"No matter my theories, the truth is at the end of the day you're the best candidate. That's why I'd like to offer you a place on the paper."

Finally I was getting somewhere. "Thank you."

"You're welcome. I see you doing well with the *Chronicle*. I think if you work hard enough this year the goal of making editor in your senior year wouldn't be a fanciful one."

Just what I had in mind. I grinned. "That would be wonderful. I'll be the best book reviewer the *Chronicle* has ever seen."

Franklin chuckled. "I'm sure you will. You'll hopefully also be our final reader…our Ethics Maven. If you like?"

I was stunned by the offer. The Ethics Maven may not be a reporter but it was the person that gave reporters and editors the third degree on their stories, made sure they'd done their research properly, that their sources were legit and basically that they'd covered all their bases before the story went to print. It was a much better position than I'd hoped for because it meant I was involved in the process of mostly everything that went into the paper.

"Yes." I gave a huff of pleased laughter. "Yes, of course. That's great."

"You can cope with both? Of course, I'll be the final reader for your book reviews to keep things fair."

"Fine, great."

Franklin nodded and started to walk me toward the door. "Fantastic. Then welcome to the *Tobias Rochester Chronicle*. We'll see you Monday after school in the newspaper office."

"Great," I agreed, and strode out of there feeling much happier than I had in a while.

It wasn't until I hit the cafeteria and caught sight of Eloise's table that I remembered I was supposed to meet Finn after school on Monday.

Crap.

I failed to find Finn to rearrange a time to meet to start on our presentation, but I'd probably see him over the weekend at the house or first thing at school on Monday.

For the first time ever I returned to Theo and Eloise's house feeling not entirely grim about my new situation. For once Hayley was home when Gil delivered Eloise and me to the house but she was with her wedding planner. They were surrounded by magazines, pieces of material and a couple of large folders overflowing with what I could only assume was mind-numbing wedding "stuff." Not wanting to get dragged into it I called out a quick hello and ran up the staircase. From what I could hear Eloise didn't make her escape quick enough and had been drawn into the wedding zone.

Smirking at her misfortune I got settled in my room and did my homework for a few hours before Hayley stopped by to tell me dinner would be ready in thirty minutes.

I waited for her to leave and then decided I was done with homework for the night. Taking the back staircase so I could grab a soda from the kitchen before dinner, I was passing the second floor when I heard Theo's raised voice coming from his office.

The sound made me tense and without even thinking about it I tiptoed closer to his office door. It was open a crack and when I peeked inside I saw Eloise sitting in a chair opposite her father's desk. Theo sat behind what was possibly an antique desk, glowering at his daughter.

"Do you want to know how I know you're lying?" he snapped.

I flinched back so I wouldn't be caught, but holding my breath, I stayed to eavesdrop. I thought eavesdropping kind of sucked, but I'd been dumped into this strange house with a guy I didn't know at all, and I'd do anything to uncover who he really was.

Eloise hadn't replied to his angry question.

I heard Theo sigh. "I asked Headmaster Vanderbilt to keep an eye on things at school and report back to me on India's progress. Would you like to know what he told me?"

More silence from his daughter.

"He told me he overheard a student aid in the office gossiping with a friend about how you are not only *not* making India feel welcome but that there are some suspicions you are responsible for a heinous rumor spread about India on her first day at school. Something about her recent stay at a drug rehabilitation center and being a bulimic as well as a recovering drug addict?"

"Daddy, I didn't spread those rumors. That was Gabe and Bryce. I told people they weren't true. I did, I promise." She actually sounded like she meant it.

I heard Theo sigh again. "I believe you. But that doesn't change the fact that you have shirked your duties this week. I specifically asked you to look out for India. Instead you've left her out in the cold. Is there something I'm not aware of? Are you unhappy with my relationship with Hayley and taking it out on India?"

"No, Daddy. I'm happy you're happy. I like Hayley a lot."

She sounded sincere about Hayley and I felt a pang of unease at the thought of the two of them growing close.

"So why aren't you being welcoming to India?"

"I didn't mean to be unwelcoming. I just… I don't know how to be around her. We're very different. It just felt easier to go on as I did before…before she got here."

I was shocked by the whole conversation. It would seem Theo did care about how well I fit into my new life. I still didn't know if that was because it reflected well on him or if he really cared about my feelings.

"Eloise, you've lived a very privileged life." His voice had softened now. "India has not. You're right. Our world is very different than the world she's used to, and I can only imagine how overwhelming it is for her. You have to try to put yourself in her shoes. Compassion, Eloise. Compassion and kindness. You *will* show both to India. You *will* help her navigate the academic and social world of Tobias Rochester and you *will* teach her everything she needs to know in order to thrive here. Next week I expect to hear something very different from your headmaster. Is this understood?"

"Yes, Daddy."

I stepped away quietly, hurrying down the hall and downstairs out of sight. The conversation I'd overheard made me feel unsettled and I wasn't quite sure why. What I was sure of was that nothing would change come Monday morning. Sure, if Theo had threatened to cut off Eloise's allowance, then maybe she would listen to him, but he hadn't so I suspected I'd still be enjoying my lonerhood come Monday.

Not too long later I found myself at the dining table with the configuration that called itself my new family. Theo had immediately asked Hayley about her day so we got to listen to her go on about wedding plans *again* for another night. When she stopped to draw breath, Theo quickly asked me about my day at school.

I thought about the happy way it had ended. "I got two positions on the *Chronicle*." I shot a look at Eloise but she had her head down, her fork moving some chicken around and around her plate, not seeming to hear a word I said. I turned back to Theo and Hayley. "I'm their new book reviewer and their Ethics Maven."

Hayley grinned. "Sweetheart, that's wonderful news! Oh, we should have gotten your favorite dessert to celebrate."

"Ethics Maven?" Theo's grin was almost as big as Hayley's. "Really? India…that is fantastic. I'm very proud you made that happen in your first week. On your own, too," he added meaningfully.

It sort of bugged me that he got how important that was. I didn't particularly want to like anything about him.

"What's your favorite dessert?" Theo asked me.

"Pecan pie and vanilla ice cream," Hayley replied for me.

"Well, Eloise and I love pecan pie and vanilla ice cream, too. We'll send out for it. One second." He disappeared from the table before I could say anything and when he came back a minute later he smiled. "The local bakery is closed but Rosa is running out to the store to see if she can get a frozen one. Not quite the same but it should do."

Hayley looked at him like he'd just said he'd solved world hunger. She leaned over the table to kiss his cheek. Her eyes flicked to me as she sat back in her seat. "What do you say, India?"

I just stopped myself from frowning. I hated it when anyone prompted me to act a certain way. Since it was a pretty decent thing he'd done, though, I managed to say thank you without adding a growl of annoyance.

"Ethics Maven on the *Chronicle*." Theo squinted thoughtfully. "This year Ethics Maven, next year editor."

"That's the plan."

"Good." He looked over at his daughter. "Isn't Finn the *Chronicle*'s photographer?"

I was surprised when a subdued Eloise nodded.

Finn was on the paper?

I would be working with Finn at the paper and we'd be working on a presentation together? Maybe that was a little bit too much Finn for my liking.

Wait…

If Finn was on the paper, then he had lied to me about meeting up after school Monday. He must have known he had a school paper meeting so that meant he'd planned on standing me up.

RUDE!

Quietly seething, not even the warmed-up pecan pie that arrived on my plate a while later was enough to dispel the cloudy thunderstorm above my head. I retreated to my room after dinner, angry at Finn and feeling generally gloomy about the quality of people in my new world.

I sat on my big princess bed watching the sun dip below the trees at the back of Theo's grounds, my room welcoming in the shadows.

And when those shadows were swallowed up in the dark of the night I crawled under the covers to sleep and to escape the fact that not even the spots I got on the newspaper could change the fact that I was right where I was yesterday.

All alone.

CHAPTER 5

THE NEXT MORNING I opened the French doors and felt the chill breeze on my skin. Although the sun was out, it seemed the unseasonably hot weather was coming to an end. It was a beautiful morning, though, and I decided to enjoy a little of my new life and have my breakfast outside.

I sat down in a lounge chair on the back patio and let the muted sun warm my face as my teeth tore into a huge chunk of the fresh croissant I'd gotten from the kitchen. *Mmm, flaky goodness.*

And that was the second best part of my day.

Like I suspected, Eloise had no intention of being friends with me. She took off with Charlotte and Bryce for the day. I had a swim in the gigantic pool despite the cool air and then spent the rest of the day studying. The best part of my day was when Anna FaceTimed me. We talked for a couple of hours before she had to get ready for a party at Kiersten's. I did my best not to look glum when we said goodbye because I knew

Anna would spend the rest of the night worrying about me if she detected I was sad.

When I came out of my room it was to discover that Eloise was off to a party. Theo thought I was with her so he and Hayley had gone out for dinner and Gretchen had taken off for the night. I was a little intimidated by the cook so I didn't want to go into her kitchen and start moving things around. When the head housekeeper, Rosa, realized my predicament she gave me this look of sympathy that was akin to a knife in the chest. Rosa offered to make me something to eat, but her sympathy and the fact that I had been left out of my "family's" plans just pissed me off.

Rosa scrutinized me. "Can you drive, Miss India?"

Although Hayley couldn't afford to get me a car, I'd gotten my driver's license that summer. "Yeah."

"Miss Eloise's car is in the garage. I'm sure she wouldn't mind you borrowing it, if you'd like to eat out this evening."

Eloise had a car...that was something I did not know. I'd never seen her use it. I smiled at the thought of the freedom it would bring me. Really, I just wanted to get out of this godforsaken house. "That sounds perfect."

I ran upstairs to get my purse and shoes and when I came back down Rosa was waiting on me. She handed me the keys to the garage house. "It's the red Jaguar. Miss Eloise doesn't like driving so it will be nice for the car to see some use."

The large separate garage house was on the west of the property. Pressing a button on the keys I watched as one of the large doors automatically opened, revealing a number of cars. I wandered around the garage, checking out each one. There was a black Range Rover Sport, a white Mercedes SLK that Theo had gifted to Hayley a few days ago, a black Porsche 911 Carrera and a Jaguar F-type convertible.

The Jaguar was gorgeous. I ran my eyes over it, a little taken aback by how much I was drawn to a freaking car. I wondered if I had drool dribbling down my chin as I admired the deep metallic red.

Why did Eloise not drive this thing?

I walked over to the wall of hooks near the side door entrance and found the keys to the Jaguar. With excitement in my belly at the thought of driving the hot car, I slowly, carefully, got into the Jaguar. It still smelled of new leather.

I wrapped my fingers around the leather steering wheel and grinned.

Okay, so maybe there *were* perks to Theo's world.

When I pulled out of the garage, I decided there was no maybe about it. The Jaguar was smooth and swift, and fit around my body like it had been built just for me. I'd lowered the roof to allow the cool night air to whisper over me as I drove, that whisper turning into a rougher caress as I picked up speed.

I didn't know where I was going but in a car like this I didn't even care. I headed east on the Boston Post Road until I saw signs for a diner called Maggie's. I ended up about fifteen minutes outside Weston in a place called Waltham.

The diner had a retro look about it. Even the waitresses wore pink retro aprons over a cute white button-down shirt and a short black pencil skirt. Both girls had long hair pulled up into a high ponytail, tied with a pink ribbon, and they wore white bobby socks and white sneakers.

"Take a seat, honey," a girl who didn't look that much older than me called out.

I nodded and found a two-seater table in the corner out of the way. The smell of fried food made my stomach grumble.

After the waitress took my order, I slid the book I'd stuck in my purse out and I started to read.

And that's how I whiled away my Saturday night.

It wasn't depressing at all. Nope. Not. At. All.

I had to admit, though, I was pretty sad to put the Jag back in the garage. I couldn't believe Eloise didn't drive it more.

"India." Theo practically ambushed me when I stepped inside the main house, striding into the entrance with Hayley at his back.

"Theo," I said warily, wondering what had put the concern in his eyes.

"Your mother and I got home an hour ago only to discover you weren't at the party. Rosa told us she gave you Eloise's keys so you could get something to eat."

"Yeah." I shrugged, not wanting them to think that I thought it was a big deal. "I found a diner in Waltham. I ate and read there for a while."

Both Theo and Hayley looked upset and not a little guilty. "We assumed Eloise had taken you to Bryce's party. If we'd known she hadn't, of course we would have arranged for you to have dinner with us."

I clenched my jaw, my blood hot with humiliation. "I'm fine, okay? I told Eloise I didn't want to go to the party." Don't ask me why I covered for her. I didn't know the answer to that.

"Sweetheart, it's not fine." Hayley looked almost near tears. "I want us to be a family, not for you to feel alone."

"It was one dinner, Hayley. Not exactly scarred here."

She narrowed her eyes at my sarcasm, the tears having dissolved at my tone. "I'm trying to apologize."

"Apology accepted. May I go to my room now?"

Annoyingly, Hayley looked to Theo for the answer to this.

He didn't look happy, but he nodded, and I quickly skirted past them and up the stairs.

Of course I'd lied to Hayley. It wasn't fine. In fact, I could feel my resentment simmering on a higher heat day after day.

A shadow fell over me as I lazed on a lounge chair by the pool the next morning. I'm sure Theo and Hayley thought my absence from breakfast was some teenage tantrum about what happened last night, but honestly, I just wasn't in the mood to face them. I'd nabbed a bowl of cereal in the kitchen while Gretchen was out of sight.

I sighed, thinking the shadow belonged to Hayley, and looked up and to my side.

I tensed.

Eloise stood over me, studying me, a million questions in her eyes. Once she had my attention she sat down on the chair next to mine.

This time she was the one who gave a heavy, almost defeated-sounding sigh. "You told Daddy you didn't want to go to the party instead of telling him I didn't invite you."

Since it wasn't really a question, I didn't answer.

Her expression was guarded. "Why?"

I shrugged.

A few seconds of silence passed between us but it felt more like minutes.

"I didn't spread those rumors at school," she suddenly said.

Surprised that she felt the need to proclaim her innocence to me, I kept my own expression guarded, wondering what she was up to. "I know."

Eloise raised one slim, perfect eyebrow. "You do?"

"Gabe told me he spread the rehab rumor. And I heard Bryce was responsible for that b.s. about my being bulimic."

Biting her lip, Eloise nodded. "The bulimia rumor was partly my fault. I told her about the way you acted over our leftovers. But she came up with the bulimia thing on her own."

"I bet she did," I murmured.

Eloise studied her peach-painted toenails for a while. "I haven't meant to be a bitch to you." She looked up warily. "I just… I don't think we have a lot in common."

As much as I wanted in with the "in" crowd, I couldn't deny she had a point. "I guess we don't."

She nodded, seeming to relax knowing that I agreed with her. "Daddy's really mad at me right now. He doesn't get mad at me a lot. He asked me to look out for you at school and found out that I didn't."

"I don't need you to look out for me."

"Yes, but I imagine it's not really fun sitting alone during lunch."

I didn't reply because it wasn't.

"I love my father," Eloise said abruptly. "He's one of my best friends. I don't like disappointing him."

I'd kind of worked that out for myself, and in my secret heart of hearts I was jealous as hell.

"Okay…"

"Tomorrow at school things will change. You'll sit with us at lunch, walk with us in the hall." She looked off in the distance, her shoulders hunched to her ears. "We can't force friendship, but we can certainly be civil to one another."

She was so proper, so constrained. It occurred to me that her demeanor was a defensive strategy. It hid her emotions. It hid her vulnerabilities. It was a different kind of defense from my own, but a defense nonetheless, and I found that it was a small piece of common ground between us.

So I replied, "That works for me. Thanks."

Eloise looked back at me, apparently surprised by my response as her face softened with questions and curiosity. But the look was fleeting and just like that the warmth was zapped from her hazel eyes, the cold distance crystallizing in them once more.

"Well—" she stood up "—I'm off to Finn's. I'll see you later."

"Bye." I watched her leave, more confused than ever. Like her father, I couldn't figure Eloise out. As much as I'd been convinced she and Theo would be the villains in this chapter of my life, now I wasn't one hundred percent sure that was true.

No matter my confusion, the apprehension I'd been carrying around with me for the past week was draining from me.

Tomorrow at school I was to make my first appearance with the "in" crowd. I had a lot to overcome, what with the rehab and bulimia rumors, but those would be so much easier to get past while walking at the side of the most popular juniors at Tobias Rochester High.

I smiled, my shoulders melting into the lounge chair. I was on my way to making my way back up to the top again.

CHAPTER 6

WHATEVER I WAS expecting the next morning, the usual awkward, tense silence between Eloise and me wasn't it. Yet awkward, tense silence was what I got.

I'm not going to lie—I had a moment of panic as we slid into the town car, thinking yesterday's encounter had been a dream and I was back to being persona non grata with her.

Thankfully, as Gil pulled out of the drive, Eloise spoke.

"When we arrive at school you'll walk in with me."

I looked at her. She wasn't looking at me. She was staring forlornly out the window.

Maybe if she'd been pissed off about the fact that she had to give me the time of day, I would have enjoyed the situation more. As it was, the wary look on her face not only confused me but it almost made me want to cut her some slack and tell her to forget about helping me. If it were any other rich princess I'd say Eloise was bothered by the fact that she had to associate with a lowly peasant such as myself, but somehow I knew that wasn't what was bothering her.

It was something deeper.

Something more troubling.

And that confused the hell out of me.

It also made me a little uneasy.

"Okay," I said softly.

My tone made her look at me and just like that the forlorn expression she'd been wearing was wiped away. The cold distance was back.

"You'll be okay." Her words were kind, but her tone was empty.

"Yeah." I nodded and looked out the other window. "I always am."

We were silent the rest of the way to school and I knew for sure then that Eloise may be welcoming me into her group for the sake of appearances, but I was still an outsider to her.

Gil gave me a bolstering smile when he saw that Eloise was waiting for me to get out of the car. I wished him a good day and followed my new "friend" through the school gates. Walking at her side, I immediately drew stares from our fellow students. Confusion seemed to be the most popular expression among them.

I knew by the unsurprised looks on Bryce's and Charlotte's faces that Eloise had already forewarned them about me. Bryce gave me this cool little chin nod of acknowledgment, while Charlotte full-out beamed at me.

"Hey, India."

Her warm welcome soothed me a little. "Hey." I smiled back, doing my best not to feel like a total fish out of water as we stood by Eloise's locker.

"Do you need to go to your locker?" Eloise asked, but she was putting books in hers so I didn't know who she was talking to.

"She means you." Bryce sighed as if I was an idiot.

I ignored her. "Yeah, I do."

Eloise slammed her locker door shut. "Well, let's go, then."

Wow. She really meant it when she said we would hang out in the halls. I led the way, Eloise at my side, while Bryce and Charlotte chatted behind us. They were gossiping about some girl called Katherine who had "so obviously been coming on to Finn" at Bryce's party that Saturday night.

I glanced at Eloise for a reaction to this. I saw a flash of something that looked an awful lot like jealousy cross her eyes before she turned to stone.

"She is so delusional. As if Finn would ever go for her," Bryce said.

"She's a senior. And she's very pretty," Eloise suddenly murmured.

Was that insecurity I heard?

"Uh, not as pretty as you," Charlotte defended her friend heatedly.

"And let's not forget the fact that you're a Fairweather, Elle." Bryce rubbed Eloise's shoulder reassuringly. "Katherine's only a Kelter. Rochesters don't date nobodies like that."

I just barely contained my snort at the outrageous comment. These people were crazy choosing who was cool enough to date based on their family's last name. Not only had I moved across the country, I'd moved into a freaking Jane Austen novel.

Eloise didn't seem to hear her friends. "As I was saying, she's a senior and she's pretty, but Finn and I are solid. No one is breaking us up." It was the first time I'd heard any kind of passion from her. And it was about Finn. Clearly he was more important to her than I'd thought.

Her tone made Charlotte quickly change the subject to

the calculus homework she was struggling with. Eloise offered to tutor her as we reached my locker, and as I sorted books into it and got out my Microeconomics stuff, I realized I hadn't once been invited into the conversation and my response wasn't really expected.

I sighed inwardly.

I could cope with that.

For now.

The bell rang and the four of us walked to our Microeconomics class. I started toward my seat on the other side of the room when Charlotte's voice stopped me.

"Where are you going?"

"My seat." I gestured to it.

Bryce sighed. "I don't think so." She rolled her eyes and motioned me to the seat next to Charlotte's. If I remembered correctly it also happened to be the seat in front of Finn. "Sit."

"Isn't that someone else's seat?"

"It was. Now it's yours," Bryce insisted. "Sit."

I looked at Eloise, who was settling in. She nodded. "Sit."

Okay, then.

I'd just put my ass in the seat when Finn wandered in with Gabe and Joshua. My eyes clashed with Finn's first and this time he held my stare. The fact that he did made me breathless for some weird, stupid reason. My cheeks felt hot as he approached, but he broke the moment by looking away. Without acknowledging me he passed us, squeezing his girlfriend's shoulder. "Hey," he said to her as he took the seat beside her.

Eloise gave him a small smile. "Hey. You okay?"

"Yeah."

"You're here." Gabe sat on my desk, taking my focus off the couple. He was grinning down at me. "I knew this day would come."

I smirked at him. "Apparently my charm is too great to resist."

Bryce snorted derisively as Gabe laughed.

"Yo, India," Joshua said behind him as he took the seat next to Bryce.

I nodded a hello and looked back at Gabe. "Are you planning on staying there?"

"Well, we could remove the desk between us." He waggled his eyebrows at me suggestively.

It was my turn to snort. "Unless you're Channing Tatum I really don't want a lap dance."

Charlotte giggled.

"Pfft," Gabe huffed. "Magic Mike ain't got nothin' on me."

"What kind of accent was that?" Joshua turned around to tease his friend.

"Street," Gabe said as if it was obvious.

"What street?"

"Shut up. Dude, you're salting my game."

I burst out laughing. "Okay, get off my desk."

"Yes, Gabe, get off her desk," our Microeconomics teacher, Mr. Adams, said as he strolled into the classroom.

Gabe pouted comically and then just as swiftly he grinned, winked at me and jumped up to take the seat beside Finn.

Now that Gabe wasn't in my face I took a quick look around our classroom and, sure enough, most everyone was staring at me.

I shrugged it off and faced forward, but inside I had happy little butterflies.

They all thought I was "in." I could have kissed Gabe.

Relaxing, I was readying myself to put thoughts of my popularity on hold and concentrate on class when I felt this tingling on the back of my neck.

As Mr. Adams talked on, the tingling got worse until my whole neck was hot.

Was Finn looking at me?

The thought made me catch my breath again.

For some reason I really needed to know if he was looking at me.

Trying to be as subtle as possible I pretended to knock my pencil off my table. When I reached down for it, I looked behind me and my eyes immediately collided with Finn's. He looked away quickly and I shot back up, gazing at the whiteboard.

That didn't mean anything… I'd dropped my pencil, drawing his attention.

But then…no one else was staring at me. Not even Gabe.

Unnerved, I spent the rest of the class more aware of the tingling skin at the back of my neck than whatever it was our teacher was trying to teach us.

I was warming more to Charlotte. I knew that she was pretty much a follower, but I also didn't think she was a bad person. In fact, I thought she could be pretty sweet. In Fiction Writing we were paired up for a writing exercise and she chatted animatedly to me the whole time. I discovered her maternal and paternal grandparents were from Puerto Rico and moved to New York when Charlotte's parents were kids. Her parents grew up together in New York, and then moved to Boston for her dad's job—he taught Latin American Studies at Boston University. However, her parents divorced three years ago and Charlotte lived with her mom, who was a successful interior designer, and spent every other weekend with her dad. I got the impression she missed her dad a lot.

When class ended and we broke apart at the door to head

in opposite directions for our next class she drew stares as she called out, "See you at lunch, India!"

I grinned and waved back at her, my smile only deepening when a few students smiled tentatively at me as I walked by them.

Progress!

My smile died, however, as soon as I walked into Modern European History, and it had nothing to do with the class or Franklin and everything to do with Finn.

I just didn't know what kind of response to expect from him at any given time, and more frightening still, I didn't know what kind of response to expect from *myself* any time I was in his vicinity.

He was already sitting at his desk when I came in. I ripped my eyes away from him, hating that I was so aware of him, and smiled hello at Franklin.

When I took my seat next to Finn I didn't know whether I should say hello or not so I didn't say anything.

He reciprocated.

Great.

And just like our last class together that morning, I spent most of it hyperaware of him, and kind of desperate to get away. So that's what I did, and it wasn't until I was sitting in my next class that I realized I hadn't rearranged a time for us to meet up and work on our presentation.

However, I didn't sweat it because, of course, I'd be seeing him at lunchtime. Although given his propensity for not using words around me, I wasn't sure how lunch with Finn would go.

By lunchtime, I had racked up quite a number of smiles from my fellow students. That meant I had a little spring in my step as I walked into the cafeteria, and that spring only got springier when Charlotte immediately spotted me and waved me over to the center table. I pointed at the lunch line and she nodded in understanding.

I looked for Eloise as I walked to the line. When our eyes met she gave me a little nod of acknowledgment and I nodded back. It wasn't Charlotte's warm enthusiasm but it was definitely an improvement.

"Hi, India."

I blinked in surprise at the two kids who passed me with their food trays piled high. "Hey." I returned their smiles, having no clue who they were and not caring.

The moment felt a little like my old life back in Arroyo Grande.

I tried not to grin openly in triumph, something that was a lot harder to do when the girl in front of me in the line turned to say hi to me.

Once I had my food I wandered over to the center table and took the seat next to Charlotte. I greeted everyone as I sat and was gratified to get hellos in return, although in different levels of warmth.

"Is it just me, Miss Maxwell, or are the good people of Tobias Rochester being a little friendlier to you?" Gabe teased.

"You are not at all mistaken," I replied. "Despite the fact that you told them I'm a drug addict, they've been surprisingly cordial this morning."

He threw his head back and laughed, Joshua's and Charlotte's chuckles joining his amusement. More surprising: Bryce laughed and Eloise and Finn managed a smirk.

I dug into my sandwich, and they started up several conversations among themselves, once more not really inviting me into them. In a way it was a chance to observe who they really were around one another.

"I bought that red Dolce we saw on Saturday," Bryce said, looking a little too pleased with herself.

Charlotte's mouth fell open in dismay. "You know I was thinking about buying it for the wedding."

Bryce gave her this pitying look. "Sweetie, it made you look fat. I did you a favor buying it."

"Stop trying to make her feel bad," Eloise snapped, her hazel eyes flashing with anger.

Eloise's defense of her friend surprised me and I found myself watching her interaction with Bryce, curious, despite myself, about the "real" Eloise.

"I didn't call her fat. I said it made her look fat."

"It did not. And buying that dress was mean."

"Elle, it's okay," Charlotte said, resting a hand on Eloise's arm.

Eloise covered her hand with her own in a comforting gesture. "It's not okay." She whipped her head back around to Bryce. "You're supposed to be her friend."

"I am her friend. Just because I don't coddle her, doesn't make me not her friend. The dress did not look good on her. Being honest is my way of being a friend."

"Your way of being a friend could use a little more diplomacy these days."

"Why are you getting in my face about this?" Bryce sighed and turned to Charlotte. "Sweetie, it was not my intention to be mean to you. Will you forgive me?"

Charlotte looked like she wanted to do anything but that, yet she nodded before staring at her plate.

Eloise slid her arm around Charlotte's shoulders and gave her a tight squeeze. Charlotte smiled up at her in gratitude and affection.

Through all of this the guys continued to talk about music,

either completely oblivious or smart enough to stay out of the girls' conversation when it turned bitchy.

As for me, I felt like I'd learned a lot in just that short confrontation.

After lunch we all went our separate ways. That is...all of us but Finn and me who ended up walking in the same direction. We walked in silence for a few seconds, the tension between us unbearably thick.

When the back of his hand accidentally brushed against mine we both jumped—me from the little shocks that rippled up my arm.

"Uh." I cleared my throat as we stared suspiciously at one another. "I can't meet after school because I'm on the *Chronicle* now. Meetings are Monday after school."

He nodded slowly. "Okay."

That was it? He wasn't going to say, "Hey, me, too!" It wasn't like I wasn't going to find out after school that we were both on the paper.

"So we'll need to reschedule..." I prompted.

"Yeah, sure." He shrugged and then waved at a classroom door. "This is me."

And without a goodbye he was gone and we still had no plans.

"Great," I murmured, my dark mood only somewhat lifted when a student I didn't know smiled and said hello to me.

"India, you made it," Franklin greeted me as I stepped into the media room after school.

"I did." I nodded, looking around. There was a large table in the middle of the room, and individual desks with iMacs on them all around the edges.

There were just over a handful of students all sitting at

the desks, completely focused on whatever they were doing. None of them were Finn.

Huh.

Franklin came to stand next to me, surveying the room right along with me. “Everyone, middle table,” he called.

A few minutes later the kids were at the table looking up at us.

“This is India Maxwell, our new book reviewer and Ethics Maven. India, this is most of your new team at the *Chronicle*.” Franklin walked around the table and stopped behind an überconservative girl with rich dark brown skin and intelligent hazel eyes. She was wearing an argyle sweater vest over a long-sleeved white shirt, and there was a short string of pearls around her neck. Not an inch of her dark braided hair was out of place, pulled tightly back into a thick ponytail. “This is your editor, Alana Allbright. She’s a senior.”

“Hello.” She nodded politely and sharply, almost like she was eager to get the introductions over with so she could get down to work.

“And this—” he stopped behind the redheaded guy beside her “—is Paul Worthington. He’s our copy editor. He’s in your class.”

Paul looked bored behind his rimless glasses as Franklin moved on to the girls a few seats down.

“This is Honor Ruffalo and Katherine Kelter, both seniors. They’re our news and entertainment reporters.”

The two brunettes smiled politely at me. One wore her hair cut short to her chin, and wore a similarly conservative outfit as Alana. The other had lighter brown hair that was styled in perfect loose curls around her shoulders. She had the kind of pretty face that would get her noticed even if she wasn’t dressed like a supermodel.

I realized that one of these girls was the girl Bryce had been bitching about flirting with Finn at her party. If I had to guess it was Miss Flawless.

Franklin walked around the other side of the table to stand between two boys, drawing my thoughts back into the room. One of the boys was good-looking and dark-haired and the other a glum blond. "Jasper Oliphant—" Franklin nodded to the dark-haired boy "—senior. He's our sports writer." Jasper grinned at me cockily and I practically smelled the arrogance wafting off him. "Lucas Young, a junior." Franklin gestured to Glum Boy. "Our online guy. He does all our web content."

I nodded at the table. "Nice to meet you."

"Our graphics girl isn't here today. Nadiya Dewan, she's a senior. She puts the paper together. We meet on Thursday after school before the paper goes to print. You'll meet her then. The media room is open every night after school so you guys can work in here. Friday after school we meet to discuss the next issue." He smiled apologetically at me. "I didn't ask you to last Friday's because I had to explain to the team about losing our former Ethics Maven and gaining you."

"No problem."

"So, guys—" Franklin clapped his hands together "—do you want to get India up to speed on this week's issue?"

"Honor is covering a social issue brought to our attention via Twitter." Alana took charge immediately. "Funding for a community center in Mattapan has recently been pulled because it was felt by certain members of the charity funding committee that it was wasted money. They believe the community center will inevitably be destroyed and taken over by the unsavory elements of Mattapan. The whole point of the community center was to get young people off the streets and into activities—to give them something to focus on that would keep them out of trouble. Honor's piece will cover whether or not the attitude of the charity is perpetuating the social problem."

I nodded, impressed by the choice of coverage. "Sounds really interesting."

Alana preened. "Thank you. I'm known for my discerning eye when it comes to spotting a good story. Now Katherine is covering the dance committee's progress on the Fall Masquerade, our annual senior dance. We also have Winter Formal but that's for both juniors and seniors in December."

"Right." I eyed Katherine. She *was* the stunning brunette. I wondered for a second if Finn was flirting back with her or if he was a loyal kind of guy. For some reason, I couldn't picture Finn flirting with another girl in front of Eloise. I thought maybe he was too classy for that. Maybe. I didn't know.

Stop thinking about Finn!

"I'm—" Jasper jumped in before Alana could continue "—covering our rowing crew. They have their second race this semester. They only do three this year, the rest take place next spring. This race is against Plymouth, our biggest competition, so it should be cool to see us kick their ass." He winked at me, causing Alana to groan loudly.

She shot him a dirty look and then turned to me. "India, you'll be reviewing last week's number one on the *New York Times* list. I do hope you're a fast reader."

"Yup," I assured her, wondering what book she was referring to. I didn't exactly pay attention to the *New York Times* list. I didn't know anyone who did. Correction: before meeting the people at Tobias Rochester—the place where status and rank was all anyone seemed to talk about—I didn't know anyone who did. "So, I won't be reviewing just literary stuff, then?"

"Oh, no." She shook her head. "I feel it's important we comment on popular fiction in whatever guise it may come. Over the year I'm hoping the book review section will successfully highlight whether or not popular fiction is killing the general population's brain cells or feeding our intellectual souls."

Wow. My editor was in no way intense. "Okeydoke, then."

I shot a look at Franklin and saw he was trying to hide a smile. He literally wiped it away by scrubbing his hand over his mouth. "Okay, then." He strode toward me. "Now that you've met the team, I have one more member to introduce you to. You guys get back to work while I introduce India to our talented photographer." He gestured for me to follow him out the door. "He works in a traditional darkroom setup down the hall. The school insists our amateur photographers learn to master the art of film development before moving on to digital, and the *Chronicle*'s photographer seems to prefer film."

I got the impression Franklin was looking forward to surprising me with Finn so I didn't have the heart to tell him I already knew who the photographer was.

As soon as Franklin and I were out of earshot I grinned at him. "You didn't tell me about my editor."

He chuckled. "If I had, would you have turned down the job?"

"No, of course not. She's a little intense, but I actually like where she's going with the paper."

"Good. I'm glad you can see past her...*intensity*, as you say." He led me into an empty art room and right to the back of the room where he stopped at a closed door.

He knocked three times.

"Come in," I heard Finn call.

I sucked in a breath at the sudden flutter of butterflies in my stomach.

Dammit.

"I think you already know Finn." Franklin grinned at me as he ushered me inside the darkroom.

My eyes adjusted to the red-hued room, and I saw Finn standing by a small sink. He was staring at us over his shoulder.

"Finn, India is our new Ethics Maven and book reviewer. Finn is our photographer."

"I see that," I murmured, wrenching my attention from Finn to the photographs clipped with the little pegs on strings of thin rope that hung from one length of the small room to the other.

"I better go check on the team," Franklin said. "You check out Finn's photos, India, and then come find us when you're finished here."

I opened my mouth to protest at his leaving me but he was gone in seconds. The door shutting sounded extraloud in a room that was now thick with silence.

Feeling the heat of Finn's eyes on me I wondered if I should just leave or try to be mature and talk to him. I decided on staying, mostly because I was more than a little curious about his photographs.

I shot him a look out of the corner of my eye. He'd turned around and was now leaning against the sink, one ankle crossed over the other, his arms crossed over his chest, and he was watching me as if he were almost daring me to leave.

I couldn't get a handle on this boy. One minute he was arrogant and intimidating, the next avoiding all eye contact, and then back to Mr. Intimidating.

Well, I refused to be daunted by him.

Taking a small step closer to the rope, I began to study the photographs. As I did, I grew still with surprise and something else…

Wonder.

Every one of them was a photograph of people and every single one captured something vulnerable about their subject matter. There was a picture of a young family on the beach. The little boy looked happy, oblivious to the fact that his parents were holding themselves apart from one another, the mother watching her little boy with sadness in her face she couldn't hide, while the father was distant from them, looking out at the ocean.

I sucked in my breath, feeling Finn at my side.

"I took some of these in Florida. My grandparents live there. I've only just gotten around to developing them."

Shocked he was offering up information, I could only nod.

"I don't know who they are." He gestured toward the photo I'd been studying.

"Something's happened. They're fighting, I'd guess," I said softly.

"Yeah. At least, that's what it looks like."

Feeling brave I looked at him, realized how close we were standing and immediately felt like a heavy weight was pressing on my chest. He wore a hint of cologne. It was kind of woodsy, a little spicy. Nice. And I bet Eloise gifted it to him. Ignoring those thoughts, I said, "Why did you take their picture?"

He slowly looked from the picture to me, and I could have sworn he was struggling with some internal debate over whether or not to tell me. In the end he just shrugged and stepped away.

Disappointment flooded me and I felt a little prick of hurt

that he hadn't shared. Shocked by this, I quickly moved along the photos. I stopped suddenly at a beautiful shot of Eloise. She was lying on a pool lounge wearing a bikini that showed off her slim, elegant figure, and she was smiling up into the lens. Her smile was incredibly sad, and yet at the same time it was intimate, suggesting more than a passing closeness and familiarity between them.

She was showing him something of herself. She trusted him with it.

Not sure why I felt so off-kilter, I hurried away from the picture and stopped immediately at a photograph of a little girl.

She was sitting near a vandalized swing set and she was digging at the soil around her with… I gasped. "Is that a switchblade?"

"Yeah," Finn said, his voice tight. "I went to Mattapan to take some photos of the building they were planning to turn into a community center."

"The story Honor's covering?"

"Right." He nodded and our eyes met again. The pressure returned to my chest. "Franklin wasn't keen on Honor going out there alone so I went with her to take some shots. While we were there Honor wanted to ask some of the local moms questions about the abandoned project. That's when I caught sight of the little girl with the blade. Her mom saw her at the same time I did." He pointed to the picture. "I managed to take the shot just before her mom ran into it."

"It's a powerful photo," I said, impressed.

He nodded, but I don't think he meant it in arrogance. "I didn't go there expecting to capture a moment that would sum up the problem so perfectly, but it happened."

"You spotted it, though. I probably wouldn't have."

"I'm maybe more observant than you, then." He smirked a little and turned away, and I couldn't help the answering tug of my lips.

"You're a great photographer, Finn."

He leaned against the counter by the sink, seeming surprised by the compliment. "Thank you."

"You're welcome."

Silence stretched as we could do nothing but stare at each other, and my skin started to feel tight and hot, as if I was seconds from bursting out of it.

"Uh." I stepped back, suddenly needing more space between us. "So we should probably arrange a time to meet up for the presentation. That's if you're not planning to stand me up."

He frowned. "What are you talking about?"

"You said to meet you after school today even though you work at the *Chronicle*."

"I don't always come to the meetings. I only decided to come work here because you said we couldn't meet," he explained, and if I wasn't mistaken he sounded a little annoyed.

"Oh." I refused to feel guilty for thinking badly of him. Refused. "Okay. Well, we need to meet up sometime soon."

"Yeah," he agreed, looking at his feet now.

"I'd suggest Theo's but it might be distracting for you with Eloise there."

Finn looked up at me. "Theo's?"

Confused by the question I raised an eyebrow.

"You said 'Theo's.' You didn't say 'my place.'"

"Because it isn't." It was my turn to cross my arms over my chest.

Sensing I wasn't going to elaborate on my feelings about

the house I was living in and the people I was living with, Finn eventually nodded. "Okay. My place, then. Tomorrow."

Glad we'd finally organized a time but not so glad it meant spending more alone time with Finn, I just nodded and stepped back toward the door. "Okay. I'll meet you out front after school."

"Do you need a ride home tonight?"

I looked back at him, surprised by the offer, but not surprised to find him staring at his feet rather than at me. "Eloise's director has upped her rehearsals so she's still here, too. Gil's picking us both up in an hour." I would've thought he'd be fully aware of Eloise's schedule.

"Right." He straightened and turned his back on me.

There was something about it that was vulnerable. Something about him that was vulnerable. I was probably insane to even think that about him—this beautiful, rich boy—but he was getting to me.

Nobody got to me.

Crap.

"But thanks," I found myself saying quietly.

He glanced over his shoulder. "You're welcome," he replied just as quietly.

Crap, crap.

My fingers slipped around the door handle as I tried to get out of there at superspeed.

Unable to bear the silence any longer, I was going to be polite and ask Eloise how her rehearsals had gone when she surprised me by beating me to it.

"How was today for you?" she said quietly.

Gil had picked us up ten minutes ago and we were on our

way home to have dinner with Hayley and possibly Theo, if he wasn't still at his office in the city.

"Better, thanks."

"Good." Eloise nodded and she actually did look relieved. "I feel it went well, too."

"Did your rehearsals go okay?"

"Yes, thank you. I got you a position. Sound assistant."

"Really? Thanks." I couldn't actually believe she'd pulled through for me. Now I had two extracurriculars. Yay!

"You're welcome. How was your newspaper meeting?"

"Good. I'm excited about it. I have to review last week's number one *New York Times* bestseller. I don't suppose you know what that is?"

"I don't. Sorry. I'm sure you'll be able to Google it."

So the conversation was strained but it was polite and it was actual dialogue between us. And after a day spent in her circle I found myself more curious about my housemate. "You and Charlotte seem close."

Eloise turned to me with narrowed eyes, looking almost suspicious. "Yes. So?"

"You've known each other long?"

"Since the first grade." Suddenly she smirked. "Bryce shoved her in the sand pit during recess, and Finn and I got Bryce back by sticking worms in her lunchbox. Charlotte has been grateful ever since."

I laughed at the idea of a mischievous Finn and Eloise. "Bryce is kind of mean to Charlotte, huh?"

Eloise shrugged. "She's too direct with her sometimes. Charlotte is very sensitive."

I wanted to roll my eyes. Why was Eloise defending Bryce?

"Bryce comes off as a little mean-spirited but that's not who she really is. She can be really sweet and despite what you saw today she loves Charlotte. Bryce is very loyal."

If you say so.

That seemed to be enough conversation for Eloise because she stared out of the window the whole drive home, not inviting any more questions.

CHAPTER 7

"ARE YOU GETTING IN?"

I blinked out of my trance and stared at Finn. He had the passenger's side door of his car open for me. It was gorgeous. I didn't know what kind of car it was, but I knew it screamed money. I nodded and slipped past him, murmuring a thank-you as I sank down low into the black leather seat.

It took me a moment to realize that he'd opened the door for me. I couldn't remember a boy ever doing that.

I jerked again at the sound of the driver's door shutting as Finn settled into his seat.

We'd walked in awkward silence to the parking spot not even thirty seconds from the school gates and I'd immediately frozen at the sight of the jet-black convertible.

"Nice car," I murmured as he pulled out into traffic. "What is it?"

He shot me a quick look before focusing back on the road. "It's an Aston Martin DB9 Volante."

Whoa. Even I, who knew very little about cars, knew that an Aston Martin was hugely expensive.

"Your parents bought you an Aston Martin for your first car?" I said, not disguising my disbelief that they trusted a kid with a car like this.

He sighed. "You're not in Arroyo Grande anymore, India."

I looked at him sharply. That was the first time he'd ever said my name. I shrugged off the deep feeling of pressure on my chest that I seemed to get a lot around him. "I know that."

"Do you?" he murmured.

I didn't know what he meant by the question or his tone. "Kids at this school get hundred-thousand-dollar cars from their parents."

Something in his smirk made my eyes grow round with disbelief. "More than a hundred thousand dollars?" I touched the black dash with its thin red piping, unable to imagine ever spending that kind of money on a car. It was on the tip of my tongue to ask exactly how much a car like this cost.

He shot me a quick look and apparently guessed my thoughts. "Don't ask. It's considered crass to talk about money."

I snapped back in my seat, feeling like a chastised little girl. My cheeks were hot and I stared straight ahead, hoping he wouldn't sense my hurt. I disliked him more than ever right then.

"I didn't..." His voice was soft. "I didn't mean it like that. I meant it as a heads-up for later. You know...when you're at society events. People around here...they think it's beneath them to talk openly about money."

"Right," I muttered.

The atmosphere between us changed from charged to wary. I peeked at him from out of the corner of my eye. He looked tense.

I shifted uneasily, hating that he hated being in my presence so much. I could have killed Franklin for putting us in this position.

And I wasn't sure that Eloise didn't want to kill Franklin, either.

Lunch today at school had kind of gone and ruined whatever small progress I'd made with Eloise the day before. Well, *I'd* kind of gone and ruined it by asking a back-to-not-talking-to-me-Finn if we were still okay to meet after school.

The group had instantly wanted to know why, and I'd felt Eloise's narrowed eyes on me the entire time as I explained Franklin had partnered Finn and me up for the history presentation. She didn't say anything about it; in fact, she didn't say anything to me at all after that, and Bryce cut me a warning look that had made me regret mentioning it in front of everyone.

These girls were so freaking territorial! I'd never understand it. *Never.*

It suddenly occurred to me that we weren't driving out of Boston the way Gil took us. At all. "Where are we going?"

"My place."

I rolled my eyes at his dry tone. "I know that, but I was under the impression your place was in Weston."

"Dover."

"Is that near Weston?"

"About thirty minutes or so away."

"Eloise said you guys have known each other since you were kids?"

"We have. Both of our families lived in Beacon Hill when we were little. Our parents were good friends."

I waited for him to tell me more but he just stared straight ahead in silence. Usually, I would have allowed him his silence but not this time. I was too curious to know more about him and Eloise. "So why did you move out of Boston?"

He shot me an annoyed look but sighed before answering. "Elle's mom died of cancer when she was thirteen. Theo wanted a fresh start so he bought the house in Weston."

I felt more than a flicker of compassion for Eloise, knowing what it was like to miss my mom and have to move someplace unknown. "And you?"

His grip tightened on the steering wheel again. "My mom died of cancer when I was a kid. My father moved us to Dover but I hardly spend time there. I spent most of my time at Elle's before they moved, but Josh and Gabe still live in Beacon Hill so I hang out there a lot."

I sucked in a breath at this information I had not known.

My chest ached for him.

For them both.

And that's when I suddenly got them—Finn and Eloise. I got them. They shared something no one else could understand.

"I'm sorry, Finn, I didn't know."

"It's fine," he said, his voice gruff.

I blew out air between my lips, trying to shift the heaviness in my chest. "What are the odds," I murmured, so sad for them.

Finn didn't reply and I did him a favor by not pestering him with any more questions, the answers to which were none of my business.

For most of the journey to his place, I watched the world go by me in a daze, but when we passed a pretty sign that said Welcome to Dover, Massachusetts, I sat up straight, alert. We drove through a very small, well-landscaped town.

"It's nice here. Do you like it?"

Finn shrugged. "Like I said, I don't spend a lot of time here so I don't know much about it. If I'm here I'm at the house."

I was confused. How could someone not know the town that they lived in? But as we turned off what seemed to be part of the town's center, I began to understand.

Finn drove down a tree-lined road, taking us away from the center of town. We passed a few driveways and I caught glimpses of large homes among the treetops.

About five minutes later we turned down another road, passing a sign that said Snow's Hill Lane, and Finn began to slow.

The Aston Martin turned sharply onto a sloping drive and I wasn't surprised by the building in front of me.

A mammoth mansion with pale-blue wall shingles dwarfed us.

Without a word, Finn got out of the car, taking long-legged strides around the hood and to my side. I looked up at him as he opened my door for me, wondering at the flutters low in my belly as I got out of the car.

Nervous? I was nervous? No. I refused to be. I wasn't going to let Finn's place intimidate me any more than Theo's did.

Confident words, India.

"Ready?" he said, sounding grim.

I furrowed my brows at his tone. "Are you planning on murdering me when I get in there?"

His lips twitched but he just shook his head and started walking toward the white double doors.

A maid opened the doors and I had to school my expression at what I saw beyond.

Finn's place was grander than Theo's. I was staring at an imperial staircase. An actual imperial staircase. My neck craned back as I gazed up at the massive vaulted ceiling, and then brought my eyes back down to the marble flooring underneath my feet.

"Hello, Hannah," Finn said congenially to the maid who had let us in.

She smiled brightly at him. "Good afternoon, sir."

His polite smile dropped as he asked quietly, "Is my father home?"

"No, sir. I believe we're to expect him at his usual time."

"Good." Finn nodded and tension seemed to leave him.

I frowned at his relief to hear his father wasn't home. What was that about?

He gestured toward the hallway. "This way."

I followed him as he led me through the opulent home, taking me past a formal dining room, what I assumed was the kitchen from the sounds coming from behind the doors and a few closed doors. I caught sight of a swimming pool out back when we passed the open doors to a library.

Finally Finn led us into a room at the back of the house. It seemed like a much more relaxed place than the rest of the house with huge, comfortable-looking sofas and a television. Near the doorway was a large table and chairs. It wasn't just any table, though. It was one of those dining tables that converted into a pool table.

Finn pulled out a chair at said table. "I'll just go grab my stuff. Do you want a drink, snacks?"

I studied him for a moment. He was much more relaxed since we'd discovered his father wasn't home. He frowned at my perusal. "What?"

"Nothing." I pulled my bag up, pretending I couldn't give a crap about working this boy out. "Soda, please—whatever you have."

He left and I got up to look out of the pretty rectangular

windows with their narrow white frames. The pool glimmered in the sunlight out back. It was twice as big as Theo's pool and so was the pool house beyond it.

I shook my head and turned around to survey the room I was in.

Finn was right. This wasn't Arroyo Grande. I thought I was used to Theo's place by now, but the truth was I wasn't. I still got up every morning feeling like a guest—feeling like it was temporary.

Because it probably was.

I shrugged off the feeling, the concern, wondering what would happen to Hayley when it all fell apart, and hurried back over to the table. I didn't need those thoughts on my face and in my eyes when Finn returned.

I couldn't, however, keep the shock off my face when Finn walked in carrying a tray with cans of soda and snacks on it. He laid it on the table in front of me and then slipped the laptop bag he'd been carrying off his shoulder.

"You went into the kitchen?" I gaped at him.

"I know how to grab a snack, India."

I winced at his curt tone. "I didn't mean it like that. I meant your cook lets you into the kitchen?"

His eyes lit with understanding and, if I wasn't mistaken, a little amusement. "Gretchen," he murmured knowingly.

"So it's not just me? She's mean, right?"

Finn actually chuckled. Chuckled! "Our cook, Etienne, is definitely more laid-back than Gretchen."

"What a diplomatic way to put it," I muttered, turning back to the tray.

As I reached for a soda, my hand stopped midway at the snack Finn had put on a plate.

Toaster Strudel.

Surprised, I looked at him.

His expression totally deadpan, he said, "I have it on good authority that you're partial to Toaster Strudel."

A feeling, warm and lush and giddy, moved through me and I found myself throwing my head back in laughter. My giggles started to slow and when they did our eyes met. My breath almost completely escaped me because Finn was full-on grinning.

I'd never seen him smile before and it completely transformed him. His smile was boyish and a little lopsided, and completely and utterly appealing.

That warm giddiness settled in a pool of flutters in my belly and my laughter faded.

In that past minute I'd learned three things about Finn Rochester.

He definitely had a sense of humor.

He really did listen to me when I talked.

His smile could light up the world.

I'd also learned new things about me, but I didn't even want to think about those things and what they meant for how I felt about Finn.

Smile gone now, Finn got out his laptop while I flipped to my notes from history class.

The strangest thing happened over the next hour: we actually worked well together. We were weirdly in sync from the outset. Finn had asked if I would mind if he played some music because it helped him concentrate. I didn't mind because I needed to listen to music while I worked, too, and when the Torrents started playing, a band I happened to love, I gave him a smile to let him know I liked his music choice.

The band played quietly in the background as we worked through what each stage of the presentation would consist of.

We were coming to the end of our plan and now that I'd had a couple of glimpses of Finn as a real person I was curious to know more. I took a sip of my soda and watched him as he finalized our summary on his laptop.

It wasn't a hardship to watch him.

Not. At. All.

Sensing my stare, he stopped typing. "What?"

"So…a photographer, huh? Is that what you want to do with your life?"

And just like that the newfound ease between us disappeared. His expression went blank. "It's a hobby."

The fact that he'd completely closed down on me suggested otherwise. Before I could stop myself, I said, "It's definitely more than a hobby."

"No, it's not. I'm a Rochester. I'll end up working with my father."

Did I detect a hint of bitterness in his tone? I leaned closer. "What does your father do?"

"He's the CEO of a corporate holdings company."

"Sounds fancy." And for some reason not exactly what I pictured Finn doing with his life.

He smirked, relaxing a bit at my lighthearted tone. "It is." His eyes narrowed on my face. "And what is it you want to do?"

I guessed it was only fair I share. "I want to be a criminal prosecutor in the DA's office."

Finn's eyebrows rose. "That's pretty specific."

"I know what I want."

"And you're free to take it."

"You sound almost envious."

Finn pushed back from the table, closing his laptop. "You

know my father is friends with a professor at Harvard. I think he might be able to get us access to primary sources for this."

It bugged me when he shut down. I knew it was more than a little hypocritical of me, but I couldn't help how I felt. I was disappointed he refused to let me get to know him.

That was probably a warning sign.

I allowed his subject change. "That would be great." I began packing my notes away.

"I'm free Saturday afternoon. We could work here again," he said.

It wasn't like I had plans. "Sure."

"Okay." Finn stood up and I followed suit, shaking off my strange reluctance to leave. "I'll drive you home."

CHAPTER 8

ALTHOUGH I WAS grateful to Eloise for hooking me up with another extracurricular, I had to admit I had absolutely no idea how to be a sound assistant. Apparently, that didn't matter when you were Eloise Fairweather's stepsister-to-be. That and the promise that I was a fast learner had me through the door, following Eloise into rehearsal the next afternoon after school.

I knew from the very professional posters pinned up around the school that the upcoming performance was of *Our Town*. I also knew from Eloise's discussion with her father at the dinner table the previous evening that she was exceptionally happy about that considering she'd campaigned to the director—our English Lit teacher, Mr. Draper—against the original plans to perform *Almost, Maine*. The problem with *Almost, Maine*, she'd said, was that it gave her less time to shine on-stage considering it was one play broken into nine plays performed by a large cast.

Playing Emily Webb/Gibbs in *Our Town* obviously made Eloise happy and I had wondered why she wasn't pursuing a career in acting until a discussion she had at the dinner table with Theo. Eloise did not want to be a lawyer but Theo was like any cliché successful parent and wanted guaranteed success for his daughter. Acting couldn't give her that so she was pursuing something else she was passionate about—medicine. Eloise had grand plans to be an oncologist and would be applying to premed at Harvard.

It was one more thing we had in common—our future career choices were consequences of our history with our parents.

"You're just going to learn as much as you can watching today," Nadiya said once Eloise left us after our introductions. It turned out Nadiya, who was the graphics girl for the *Chronicle*, was the sound director.

"Great." I nodded, realizing this might not be a job that kept me that busy. But the important thing was how it looked on a transcript.

I stood next to Nadiya, her pretty face framed by a striking green hijab that set off her large dark eyes. She had the longest eyelashes I'd ever seen.

I tried to take in what she was doing as the actors got ready to rehearse. We'd done *Our Town* our sophomore year back at Arroyo Grande so I knew the play pretty well. Today it appeared they were rehearsing Act III.

The boy playing the Stage Manager was pretty good but I was waiting impatiently for Eloise to appear. This was the scene of Emily's funeral when she appears at the graveyard to sit with the other members of the dead, including her mother-in-law.

I stilled at the sight of Eloise and leaned forward to hear

better as she sat down beside Mrs. Gibbs to chat with her about her husband, George, and their farm. When she suddenly stopped and said the line "Live people don't understand," I was held rapt by the loneliness in her voice as she went on to discuss how distant she felt from the living.

I couldn't take my eyes off her through the entire act. While others flubbed their lines or read them over the top or flatly, Eloise didn't miss a cue and her realness was captivating. When the boy playing her husband, George, threw himself on his wife's grave as she looked on, and she turned to her mother-in-law and said, "They don't understand, do they?" little fleshy goose bumps rose up all over my arms.

The Stage Manager appeared, his monologue ending the play, and I was jerked out of the world I'd just been taken to by Mr. Draper clapping his hands together and yelling, "From the top! Some of you have a lot of work to do. Eloise, you were wonderful!"

And she was, I realized, a little dazed.

"She's good, right?" Nadiya smirked at me.

I nodded, still disbelieving Eloise was that freaking talented. "Yeah."

"As for you, sound assistant… You weren't paying attention to anything I did, were you?"

"No." I winced. "Sorry."

"It's okay. It was your first Eloise performance. You're forgiven."

I gave a little huff of laughter and tried my best to follow what she was doing, but I was still reeling a little.

Eloise seemed kind of young to be such a strong actress and I could only guess she was doing a method acting thing where she used her own experience to help her perform a role authentically.

I knew she'd been through something terrible, but seeing her vulnerable, it sank in for the first time how much Eloise was still hurting from losing her mother.

I wrapped my arms around myself, staring blankly at Nadiya's sound gear. I was suddenly uncomfortable with the knowledge that I'd been kind of self-involved.

Since arriving in Massachusetts, all I'd cared about was how the move affected me—how I was hurt by it. It never occurred to me someone here could be hurting, too, let alone Eloise.

Gil collected us after rehearsals and Eloise and I quietly got into the car. As soon as she had approached me at the school gates, I felt like I was looking at an entirely new person from the one I'd walked into school with that morning.

The fact was that I didn't know Eloise at all well so I'd played a guessing game of her character in my head. There were still things about her that I couldn't work out—like her relationship with Finn, although his rare moment of honesty about both their mothers gave me insight—but for the most part I'd thought I'd gotten the gist of her. Privileged, entitled, aloof, arrogant, principled, fair, determined, driven, kind to her friends, spoiled, blessed, charmed and a total daddy's girl.

Now I wasn't so sure.

I was thinking I needed to knock off "blessed" and "charmed," for a start, and add "sad" and possibly "lonely," along with "extremely talented."

Knowing there was sadness there, a vulnerability, actually made me curious about her. A little like I was curious about Finn, I guessed.

Drawn to sadness.

Huh.

I wasn't sure what that said about me.

"You're really talented," I said into the quiet of the car.

Eloise jerked out of the daydream she'd been in and raised an eyebrow at me. "Excuse me?"

"I said you're really talented."

Her eyes dropped, shielding her expression. "Thank you."

"You should be applying to Tisch, not medical school."

She shot me an unhappy smile. "If Daddy had his way it would be neither. It would be prelaw."

I frowned. "But he so obviously supports you."

Eloise wrinkled her nose and looked away, out the window. "Hmm."

What did "hmm" mean? Did Theo not really support his daughter? Were their conversations at dinner all for show? What was I missing?

"At least he'll have a lawyer in the family now," Eloise muttered against the window.

Unease shifted through me at her comment.

Perhaps I'd been right all along? Perhaps Eloise's behavior when we first met was born from some kind of resentment of me. She didn't think I was going to steal her father's support and affection, did she?

This was me! Did she not realize I didn't trust the guy? Or anyone for that matter.

"Finn and I have been dating since we were fourteen," Eloise said.

I blinked, confused by the abrupt statement. "O-kay."

She looked at me, still distant, still expressionless. "Two years. We're solid."

Um…was I being warned off the boyfriend?

I swallowed hard, feeling truly uncomfortable. "We're just writing a presentation together."

"I know." She shrugged and looked away again. "I was just making conversation."

I barely contained my snort. My ass she was just making conversation.

I did not need to be warned away from Finn. I wasn't doing anything! So why did my cheeks feel hot with guilt?

Dammit!

As soon as we pulled up to the house, I got out of the car before Gil could open the door and I tried my best not to slam it behind me. Eloise waited for Gil to let her out, so I stormed ahead into the house, pissed as hell at her warning and my reaction to it.

"You're home!" Hayley bounced into the hallway like an excited little girl. She smiled over my shoulder. "Hey, honey."

"Hayley," Eloise murmured behind me. "I have some homework I need to do before dinner, if you'll excuse me."

"Sure thing, sweetheart," Hayley called after her. When Eloise was out of sight she turned to me with that huge pretty smile of hers. "So you two seem to be getting along."

"Or at least we're pretending to." I patted her shoulder as I passed her.

She ignored my sarcasm, stopping me in my tracks with her next sentence. "I need you to come to the bridal shop with Eloise and me this Saturday. We have an appointment to find all of our dresses."

I spun slowly on my right heel, horror-struck. "Please do not tell me we're your bridesmaids."

Her hands flew to her hips. "Well, of course you are. Take that horrified look off your face—it's not funny."

"I'm not being funny. I'm truly horrified."

Hayley rolled her eyes on a sigh. "You'll be there. No arguments."

"I can't. I'm studying with Finn on Saturday."

"Finn?" She took a step toward me, frowning. "Eloise's Finn?"

"No, Nemo's Finn."

She glared at me.

"Yes." I threw up my hands. "What other Finn do we know but Eloise's Finn?"

"Does Eloise know about this study session?"

Not liking the accusatory tone in her voice, I snapped, "Yes."

Hayley closed in on me, her voice dropping to an almost whisper. "The last thing this burgeoning family needs is boy drama."

"Have you ever known me to be involved in boy drama?"

"What about Jay?"

"He wasn't boy drama. He was a make-out session you walked in on. Finn and I are study partners for a history presentation. That's it. Besides...didn't you get the memo? He's a Rochester. Rochesters don't date nobody Maxwells."

Hayley smiled at me like she knew something I didn't, and tucked a strand of my hair behind my ear. "Sweetheart, you are so very far from a nobody I worry about you all the time. Maxwell, Fairweather, Rochester...you're smart, you're intimidatingly self-assured and you're beautiful. In other words, a guy like Finn could probably not give a crap what your name is considering you're teenage boy catnip." She dipped her head closer. "So I'm asking...not this boy. Okay?"

I looked at my feet, hearing her opinion of me ringing in my ears. I couldn't believe that's how she saw me. Self-assured? Me?

I guess I'd really gotten good at pretending.

"Definitely not this boy," I reassured her, lifting my eyes to meet hers so she could read my sincerity.

She nodded, seeming relieved. "Saturday morning you will be at this appointment. You can meet Finn later."

I blew out air between my lips, already dreading it. "Fine." I turned to head upstairs and stopped when a thought struck me. I called back to her. "But no pink. Or peach! Or yellow... or pastels of any kind!"

I heard her laughter trailing behind her as she disappeared down the hall.

"That wasn't reassuring." I grimaced as I stomped upstairs.

October's weird warm weather was definitely over, and it had up and disappeared with an abruptness similar to my life in California. Wearing a short jacket and long-ass scarf I'd followed Eloise, Bryce, Joshua and Charlotte behind the rowing center at Lake Quinsigamond to the dock to watch Finn and his crew beat Plymouth.

Afterward Gil dropped us off at a coffeehouse and the entire time we sat at the table together Finn acted like I didn't exist. He'd been acting like I didn't exist the whole day. Except for the moment he got annoyed at me because Jasper was flirting with me instead of watching the race for the school paper. Annoyed at me! Like I wanted that creep to flirt with me. The rest of the day could be counted as having gone well, though, with everyone else seeming to be used to me now.

When Saturday morning came around, I definitely counted the crew race as the highlight of my week.

Mirrors covered the walls on either side of the circular room I found myself sitting in. It was a bright room, lights reflecting off the glass; a sweet perfume hung in the air and oversize vases filled with dusty pink hydrangeas sat on either side of the entrance to the dressing room.

The stylish and immaculately turned-out sales assistant handed me a glass of champagne, and Hayley said, "Oh. Okay. Just one. To celebrate."

I was sitting a foot apart from Eloise on a silver velvet chaise longue and we'd managed nothing but polite conversation since we'd arrived on Newbury Street that morning.

"I think this might be the one, ladies," the sales assistant, Kelly, said as she appeared out of the dressing room.

Hayley slowly glided out behind her, and I felt Eloise still beside me.

The gown was formfitting, hugging Hayley's figure until her calves, where it flared out into a slight fishtail and train. Its ivory satin was overlaid with lace that had a shimmer through it. It was sleeveless with wide scalloped lace straps and a demure neckline. But when she turned to step up onto the platform to look at the dress in the mirror, I saw the bodice was backless, the lace rejoining in a row of pearl buttons from the small of her back down over her bottom.

It was classic but hot, too.

She looked amazing.

I watched as Hayley's eyes lit up as she took in her reflection, turning this way and that to see the dress at every angle.

For once she was speechless.

Looking up at her, seeing how happy she was, I felt this weird mix of resentment and hope. I was still mad at Hayley for uprooting my life, for bringing me into a family that was as guarded as I was, making it impossible to truly know them or understand their motives. I resented her for putting her happiness before mine. But I found myself, day by day, beginning to wonder what life would be like if this thing with her and Theo was real and permanent. I wanted to believe that Hayley could grow up, stand still with someone and perhaps eventually, one day in the very distant future, earn my trust.

I had a safe place for myself back in Arroyo Grande where I didn't need Hayley to provide me with that safety or stability. Yet, now that my life was all over the place, I found I *did* need that from her. And to get that from her I needed her to be happy.

And that made me resent her all over again. Resentment, hope, resentment.

Vicious circle.

"It's perfect, Hayley," Eloise said, her expression soft and her tone the warmest I'd ever heard it.

She sensed me looking at her and raised an eyebrow.

I shrugged at the unasked question.

She sighed, seeming to understand what I wasn't saying. "I want my father to be happy," she whispered. "Hayley makes him happy. She'll make him even happier in that dress. That's all that matters."

For not the first time I found myself envious of Eloise. She loved her father so much.

What must it be like to want your parents' happiness instead of resenting them for it?

What kind of person had my parents turned me into?

I looked up at Hayley, my chest aching.

Her eyes met mine in the mirror and there was something like desperation in hers. Desperation for what, though? For my love? My acceptance? My trust? Did she genuinely want that from me? Was it not just that she felt guilty and ashamed?

I didn't know. But I did know I didn't want to be the kind of person who didn't want happiness for the people in my life.

"What do you think, India?" Hayley asked, her dark eyes pleading.

And for the first time since we'd been reunited five years ago, I gave her what she wanted. "I think Eloise is right. It's absolutely perfect. You look beautiful."

Her whole face lit up. "You really think so?"

I felt a sudden sting in my eyes, this overwhelming need to cry taking hold of me. "Yeah." I nodded quickly and looked away.

The sales assistant stepped forward to talk to Hayley about the dress, and I excused myself to use the bathroom, hearing the words "Carolina Herrera" and something about ten thousand dollars. I disappeared into the ladies' restroom and hurried over to the sinks, my chest tight, my skin hot. Splashing cold water up onto my face, I was struck by my expression. It was that of a trapped animal.

My fingers bit into the cold ceramic of the sink.

"You can't trust her," I reminded myself.

But I'm tired of being alone.

"I know," I whispered.

I was. I'd never felt more alone. I could handle it in Arroyo Grande because I had Anna and school but here I didn't have any of that. The only familiar thing I had was Hayley, who wanted me to trust her.

Maybe I should. It's exhausting not trusting anyone while I'm all alone. The dress. The wedding. Eloise. Theo. Maybe we really could be a family.

But what if I gave in and she hurt me, *they* hurt me?

Suddenly, without wanting to, I saw my father's face in my mind.

I pushed away from the sink, my resolve returning.

I just needed to handle being alone for a little while longer.

CHAPTER 9

THE CAB PULLED up to the Rochester mansion and I felt that unwanted flurry of butterflies in my stomach again. I'd paid the driver the small fortune it cost me to get out to Dover, money I would have blanched at paying not too long ago, and got out of the cab just as the mansion's door opened.

Finn stood in the doorway to his home, his hands in his pockets. His dark eyes burned right through me.

Sucking in a huge breath, I shifted my backpack on my shoulder and made my way toward him. The last couple of days at school had been interesting, to say the least. While Eloise's friends warmed up to me—even Bryce, who seemed to enjoy a little sarcastic banter with me—Eloise and Finn remained quiet and distant with me. Finn more so than Elle. In fact, I would go so far as to say he was almost cold.

At the Thursday meeting of the *Chronicle* he'd appeared to give us his photographs for the next morning's issue and then he was gone without a word. At Friday's meeting he'd sat around the table with us as we discussed the next issue and he only looked at me once. I drew his attention when I brought up my problem as a book reviewer to Alana.

"I'm sorry..." She'd raised an eyebrow at me. "A problem? Already?"

I ignored the gibe and the very subtle warning in her eyes that suggested as a newbie I should keep my trap shut. The problem was I may be a newbie but I was the Ethics Maven so my trap would be remaining firmly open. But my problem wasn't regarding anyone else's articles.

"You said I have to review the number one on the *New York Times* bestseller list every week. What do I do when a book stays at number one for more than one week?"

Our editor had stared at me while everyone tried not to look openly amused at the fact that their efficient leader had not thought something through.

Alana had shifted uncomfortably in her seat. "I may have overlooked that particular possibility. Well, if that occurs you can pick a book from the top five."

"Thank you. Also, what if the number one bestseller isn't appropriate. Say, an erotica novel?"

In answer I received a pointed scowl. "Again, choose a book from within the top five or twenty, if you have to, that *is* appropriate." *Now shut up*, her eyes seemed to say.

"Don't worry about it." Jasper, who had insisted on sitting next to me, leaned in, putting his arm around my chair back. "She's like that with everyone."

His lips touched my ear, and I jerked back from him, immediately searching out Finn.

He was watching me with Jasper, this time his expression blank. Like he could give a damn some guy was being a jackhole to me.

It was fair to say that I was not looking forward to our study session together.

As I approached, Finn stepped to the side to let me into his home.

"Hi," I said, not able to meet his eyes.

"Hey. You got a cab?"

I finally looked up at him as I moved into the grand hallway. "Yeah."

"I thought Gil was bringing you. I would have picked you up if I'd known."

"It's fine." I shrugged, not sure what to do with his supposed chivalry after the last few days of nothing from him.

"I'll give you a ride home when we're finished."

"You don't have to."

"I don't. But I will." His tone brooked no argument.

"Finn, you have a guest?"

I whirled around and came face-to-face with an older version of Finn. A tall, broad-shouldered man stood in the hall between the twin staircase, staring at me sternly. Finn had his facial features but where his eyes were deep and dark, this man's were steel gray and very cold.

I shivered, getting an instant vibe off the guy that I didn't like. Not. At. All.

"Sir, this is my classmate and Eloise's soon-to-be stepsister, India Maxwell. India, this is my father." Finn closed in on me, his hand touching my lower back as he stood so near our sides brushed against one another.

I hid my surprise, peeking up at Finn from beneath my lashes. I could feel how rigid his whole body was, and I got the distinct impression that his sudden touchy-feeliness was born out of protectiveness.

I looked up at his father, wary.

He marched over to me, his features like granite as he held out his hand. "Nice to meet you, Miss Maxwell."

I took his hand out of politeness.

"I hope you're settling in nicely."

"Yes, thank you."

"And what are you doing here today?"

I knew he didn't actually care what I was doing at his home. All he cared about was that he didn't like it. His polite manners couldn't hide his distaste. "Finn and I have a history presentation to work on."

"And we need to get on with it. Excuse us." Finn put pressure on my back, nudging me forward. I took his lead, moving around his father.

"Where are you working on it?" his father called after us.

Finn stopped. "The TV room. We won't disturb you there."

"Leave the door open," his father ordered.

I stiffened at the implication that we might get up to no good with it shut. My blood turned hot. I bet he didn't imply that kind of behavior around blue-blooded girls.

Rochester was a judgmental asshole.

"Yes, sir," Finn replied, the words tight with annoyance.

We walked toward the TV room we'd worked in on Tuesday and Finn didn't offer up an explanation for his father or *his* behavior around his father. He was brittle around Mr. Rochester and as soon as we got out of his presence Finn's whole body relaxed.

As for me, my stomach was churning. There was something in the atmosphere, something I couldn't quite put my finger on…but it made me *more* than uneasy.

"Drinks, snacks?" Finn said as we strode into the room.

"Sure," I mumbled, my mind whirring as I tried to work out what the hell it was I was feeling.

"I'll be right back."

Not too long later Finn returned with soda and Toaster Strudel and placed them on the table. My eyes flicked to the door. He hadn't left it open.

When I turned to him I saw he'd been watching me and he gave me this sad, defiant little smirk.

It made me smile back and to my surprise his whole face softened for a split second.

"Your father…" I said as he took the seat beside me. "He's…"

"A dick," Finn supplied. "My father's a dick."

I gave a huff of surprised laughter and Finn looked at me, smiling. I grinned back. "Yeah, he kind of is."

He chuckled and pulled his laptop out onto the table. "What about your father?"

Little bitch isn't getting a thing until I say so.

Open your eyes, Trash.

I pushed my father's voice out of my head and slipped my notes out of my backpack.

"Sorry," Finn said at my silence. "I didn't mean to pry."

"It's okay." I gave him a reassuring smile.

We were silent for a moment, and then I found myself offering, "My dad was a dick, too."

Our eyes locked, and for a tiny split second I didn't feel so alone anymore.

Finn looked away first, clearing his throat. "We should get started."

Yes, we should, I thought, determinedly focusing on my notebook.

Like before, we got on easily as a team, time flying by as we worked out the first half of the presentation. After an hour, Finn sat back in his chair and rolled his neck.

"Break?" I said.

He nodded. "Just five minutes of not looking at the screen would be good."

"Sure."

Silence fell between us.

"So..." Finn said as the silence became awkward. "I want to apologize."

"For what?"

"For being...a little off with you."

I studied his profile, waiting for him to look at me.

Finally he did.

His apologetic expression was sincere, and he also looked a little lost. I didn't understand why, but I also didn't like that, for whatever reason, he might feel lost. So I found myself saying, "You're forgiven."

Tension seemed to leave him. "I know you weren't flirting with Jasper at my race, either. Or ever."

"No, I definitely wasn't."

He looked around the room, shifting in his seat. He cleared his throat again. "So...did you leave a boyfriend back in California?"

His question made my pulse speed up. "Jay... Jay wasn't really my boyfriend."

"But you dated?" His eyes snapped back to my face.

"We hung out." I gave him a rueful smile. "I don't really date. I'm not big on commitment. I mean, you and Eloise... two years... That's a little scary."

Finn's eyebrows rose. "Did Jay know you didn't date?"

I snorted. "Yes."

"And he was okay with that?"

"Yeah."

He shook his head, his eyes roaming over my face in a way that only increased my pulse rate. "I don't believe that."

I wanted to ask him what he meant but all of a sudden he closed down, like he'd said too much or something.

"We should get back to work." He pushed his chair back in contradiction to his words. "I'm just going to get more soda."

The door slammed shut behind him before I could say anything, and it occurred to me as I sat there that I really needed to pee. If Finn came back with more soda my problem was only going to get worse.

There had to be a bathroom nearby in a house this size.

As quietly as possible, not wanting to seem like a snoop, I left the room and began my search.

When I heard Finn in a room up ahead I grew still.

And then I heard his father's raised voice and my good manners urged me to turn back. And I was about to when I heard Finn say, "For the third time, we're just working on a school project."

I stiffened, my breath catching as I realized they were talking about me, and I crept even closer, peeking through the crack in the door. It looked like they were in an office. Finn's dad's office. I watched Mr. Rochester stride around his desk to stand face-to-face with his son. How did I keep ending up in these situations? I was turning into a creepy serial eavesdropper!

Finn held himself rigid but didn't back away, even as his father got obnoxiously in his face. There was something hostile in Mr. Rochester's body language that I did not like one bit and any thoughts of turning away were stifled.

"I do not want her to return to this house again, do you understand me?"

Finn scowled at him. "She's my friend."

Surprise shot through me at that. Finn thought of me as his friend?

My belly fluttered in delight.

His father sneered. "*Friend.* Oh, yes, I'm sure your feelings for a girl like that are purely platonic. I saw the way you touched her earlier." He took another step forward, his nose almost touching his son's. "A little protective, are we? Use her if you must, but be discreet so Eloise doesn't find out. When you're finished, you make sure there are no complications. My son does not date trash."

I flinched in hurt before bristling with indignation.

Finn's face flushed. "India isn't trash. Don't talk about her like that."

There was a blur of movement and I blinked, heart slamming in my chest, as Finn's father grabbed him by his collar, his face red with fury.

Finn shoved off his father's hands and broke free, pushing the older man back. He shrugged down his shirt, glaring hatred at him. "Let's not forget I'm not a little boy anymore. I hit back now."

Rochester's nostrils flared with impotent rage and he raised a shaky hand at his son. "Watch your step, young man. Your future is in my hands. Your inheritance is in my hands. College, everything! You want that future, you listen to me. Eloise is a *Fairweather.* You will not jeopardize your relationship with her for a girl from a questionable background."

I tiptoed back, the blood rushing in my ears as I escaped quietly down the hallway. I found a bathroom in the opposite direction and rushed to lock myself inside.

I couldn't seem to catch my breath.

"Let's not forget I'm not a little boy anymore. I hit back now."

I squeezed my eyes closed, the pressure on my chest increasing.

Now I knew. I *knew* what the uneasiness I was feeling earlier was from. It was familiarity. Finn's brittle behavior around his dad, the coldness in his father's eyes, their interactions with one another...it reminded me of me and my own dad. It reminded me of how tense I'd been around my father because every second in his presence was a second he might attack.

Finn's father abused him.

He was always ready, always on the defensive, because he lived in a war zone, and I knew what that felt like. Whether it was his fist in my face or starving me for days, I was once a prisoner of war in my father's house.

So yeah, I knew better than I'd like how Finn must feel.

I covered my mouth, feeling a wave of nausea roll over me.

I didn't want that for him.

Sliding to the floor, I felt the strength go right out of me. Suddenly, I felt helpless. Hopeless even.

This bond, this sudden, desperate bond I felt with Finn—hell, I'd gladly be the loneliest person in the world if it meant we didn't share this kind of a connection.

"Where were you?" Finn asked sharply as I stepped back into the TV room five minutes later.

"Bathroom," I said, closing the door behind me.

We stared at one another, and I knew I wasn't hiding my newfound knowledge in my eyes.

Finn paled. "What...where..."

"I overheard you and your father."

The muscle in his jaw ticked as he turned away. "I don't know what you're talking about."

"Finn, we should talk about it." I hurried toward him. "Look, I get it—"

"You don't get a thing." He whirled on me, eyes blazing. "My life is none of your business."

"Finn—"

"You say a word of this to anyone—"

"I wouldn't!" I exclaimed, infuriated he'd even think that of me. "Please—"

"This." He ran his hand through his hair, beyond aggravated. "We're done for today. We'll finish it at school. I'll call you a cab."

I let him walk out of the room, my compassion for him overwhelming. I knew what he was feeling. I hated people knowing that my father beat me. I couldn't help wonder if they thought perhaps I'd brought it on myself, because what father could ever hurt their own kid?

Even though I was this mess of emotions, suddenly desperate to confide in Finn, to have someone to talk to who actually got what I'd gone through, I stifled that selfishness. Finn didn't need that right now.

So I kept quiet, packing up my stuff, and without waiting for him to come back to me I let myself out and stood on the curb waiting for my cab to arrive.

Distance from Finn allowed me to see reason.

For a minute there, seeing the panic in his eyes at my having discovered the truth of his family life, I'd contemplated telling him about me. About what my father did to me.

I'd never told anyone about it. Not even Anna.

Pacing my bedroom floor, my heart racing in my chest, I thanked God that I hadn't blurted it out, ripping myself open and laying myself bare and vulnerable to Finn, a boy I really knew very little about.

A boy—no matter how much I might feel drawn to him because of what we now had in common—I had no right bonding with.

He was Eloise's to bond with.

I didn't bond with anyone.

Groaning, I leaned against one of my bedposts and wondered how Finn would act with me at school on Monday.

Yet somehow I couldn't bring myself to care if he iced me out and destroyed my social status.

I should care!

But all I cared about was the fact that I got to escape my father and Finn hadn't. He was stuck there.

Stop!

No more caring about Finn Rochester. On Monday I would walk into school with Eloise and if Finn wanted to ignore me, then I'd let him, because I'd be too busy building the path to popularity.

I had a plan and for both Finn's and my own sake I would pretend like I had no clue about his relationship with his father.

That's what Finn would want.

I'd give him that.

CHAPTER 10

I WISH MOM were here.

I knew I shouldn't say it.

But it slipped out.

I'd gotten my period. I didn't know what to do. I didn't have money to buy what I needed. I had to ask him for money. He'd asked what for. I'd been too embarrassed to tell him.

I thought how much easier it would be if she'd never left us.

And it slipped out.

He screamed at me.

I could still hear his voice screaming in my ears as the pain started to recede and the darkness came for me.

Blissful darkness.

"STOP!" I thought I heard Carla scream.

But that was the last thing I heard as the black overwhelmed me.

My eyes flew open, adjusting to the darkness and revealing my bedroom. My heart started to calm as I remembered where I was and how old I was.

I was no longer twelve years old and lying on the floor of my father's trailer as he beat me to near death.

That was the last thing I ever said to him—*"I wish Mom were here."*

My chest hurt so bad with the memories, and I let the tears loose in hopes that it would relieve the ache. *I wish Mom were here.* Those fateful words led me to her, but when I got her I didn't know what to do with her except not trust her.

I squeezed my eyes closed, not wanting to think about our complicated relationship. I just wanted to sleep and wake up on Sunday and do nothing.

Not think of him or her or Finn.

It took me hours to fall back to sleep.

And all I did was think of them.

There didn't seem to be any negative change to Eloise's usual demeanor at all that morning. I had to assume that Finn hadn't said anything to her or decided to oust me from the group for my knowledge.

As for me, I was completely determined to act indifferent around Finn and just get on with life as I knew it at Tobias Rochester.

I fully believed that I could ignore what I knew.

And then I saw him.

He sat, head bent, at his desk in our Microeconomics class, and at the sight of him I felt this rush of emotion wash over me. I think it was affection.

Confused, uncomfortable, I followed Eloise and the girls in and sat down without saying hello to the guys.

"You're quiet this morning."

I studied my desk. It was the first time I'd noticed there

wasn't a scratch on it. Back at my old school the desks were covered with unoriginal epigrams such as "I was here." But not at Tobias Rochester. Oh, no. Kids weren't allowed to act like "vandals."

I felt something bounce off the back of my head and turned sharply around in the direction of the originating trajectory of the offending missile.

Gabe was grinning at me. "I said, you're quiet this morning."

"So you decided to hit me with—" I glanced down at the floor "—an eraser."

"Well, you didn't respond when I spoke to you. Physical assault seemed like the appropriate next step."

I rolled my eyes and turned back around, pretending not to care that Finn was staring determinedly at his desk, ignoring the interaction.

"That's it? That's all I'm getting? An eye roll." When I didn't respond Gabe gave this dramatic intake of breath. "Did your California boyfriend visit you this weekend? Is that why I'm suddenly persona non grata?"

I glanced over my shoulder. "Yes, that's exactly right. He found out about our secret love and threatened to maim you. I'm trying to save your life by ignoring you, so do me a favor and go along with it." I sighed and looked back up front, relieved to see our teacher walk into the room.

"You know your sassiness drives me crazy, Maxwell," Gabe murmured flirtatiously.

"*You* are driving me crazy." Eloise twisted around in her seat to huff at him. "Learn to read between the lines. She's not in the mood. Leave her alone."

Grateful, I shot her a look, hoping she could read my expression. If she did she didn't acknowledge it, just turned back around to focus on our teacher.

When class ended Finn leaned down to kiss Eloise on the cheek before leaving, something he didn't usually do. She seemed surprised by it, but when he marched out of the room without speaking to anyone I saw her expression change to concern. I looked away before she could make eye contact with me and work out I was the reason for Finn's frostiness with everyone but her.

Things were even chillier in Modern European History. With none of our group there as buffers the atmosphere between us was horrible. I'd experienced unfriendliness when I first arrived at Tobias Rochester, but back then I hadn't cared on an emotional level. I'd cared on a social and academic level.

Now I cared emotionally.

I didn't want to.

But I hated that Finn was giving me the cold shoulder.

In fact, I'd go so far to say that it killed.

Franklin had decided we were working on our oral presentations since we had to present those at the end of the week. Finn's whole body had locked up tight when I moved my desk closer to his so we could work together. He wouldn't make eye contact with me. His words were toneless. He flinched when our hands brushed.

I felt rejected.

My chest ached the whole time I sat next to him.

As he avoided looking at me, I felt like screaming at him to see me, the urge bubbling up under my skin, making my toes curl in my shoes in agitation. I saw him. I think he was the first person I'd ever truly seen and I couldn't help it—I wanted him to see me, too.

I wanted to be his friend.

That desire made me feel small. Like a little girl all over again.

Stop!

You don't need him.

But it was hard to remember that when I'd finally found someone who could truly understand me, and who *I* could truly understand. And I'll admit it now, even before I knew about the horrible thing we shared, I'd felt drawn to Finn in a way I'd never felt drawn to another person.

I gazed sadly at his face.

Didn't he feel drawn to me in return?

How was it possible for me to feel so strongly and not have him feel it back?

The bell rang suddenly and I flinched as Finn's chair screeched away from his desk. I could do nothing but watch in stunned silence as he packed up his things at superspeed and bolted out of the classroom before I could even move a pinkie finger.

I stared down at my desk, fighting a sudden and very weird urge to cry.

"India, are you okay?"

My head jerked up at Franklin's voice. He stood over me, brows pulled together in concern.

"I'm fine," I said, and got up slowly.

Franklin didn't look convinced. "Is everything all right between you and Finn? Are you going to be able to do this presentation together?"

He saw too much.

I gave him a twisted smile. "We'll get the presentation done, Mr. Franklin."

"Okay." He nodded slowly and stepped back.

That's when I realized the entire class had gone.

How long had I been staring blankly at my desk after Finn walked out?

"You know if you ever need to talk I'm here."

"Thanks. Really. But I'm fine."

But I wasn't fine.

I dreaded lunch period.

"Where's Finn?" Charlotte said as she and I took our seats at the center table in the cafeteria.

Eloise's expression was blank and I was beginning to wonder if she used her blank face to hide behind when she was particularly upset or concerned about something. "He went with the seniors on his row crew to Lulu's."

Lulu's was a coffee shop near the school where the seniors liked to have lunch.

"He's acting strange," Charlotte said. "Did something happen?"

"Not that I'm aware of."

Gabe grunted. "Something happened. He's got extra broody eyebrows today."

Joshua shot him an annoyed look. "You know how much pressure his father puts him under. He's probably just had a bad weekend."

You can say that again.

It was my understanding from the knowing looks exchanged that if Finn's friends didn't know about his father's physical abuse (and I had more than an inkling that they didn't), then they knew of his father's "intensity."

Eloise noted my interest in the conversation before saying primly, "Let's talk about something else. Charlotte, how was your date with Lawrence?"

I ignored them as Charlotte described her tedious date with

the son of a diplomat. A date that she'd been more than excited about last Friday. Gabe had teased her mercilessly about Lawrence and how boring the guy was, and was enjoying his "I told you so" moment way too much.

But I didn't care about Charlotte's disappointment right then, or Gabe's smug jokes about being right.

I cared about Finn avoiding me. Too much.

"Excuse me," I muttered, not capable of sitting among them feeling the way that I did. I stood up with my tray of food.

"Where are you going?" Gabe frowned, all his usual joviality gone.

"I've got a lot going on. I should probably use this time in the media lab. I'll see you guys later." I walked away before any of them—Gabe—could try to talk me out of it.

Instead of going to the media lab, I found myself in the empty darkroom.

I don't know why I went to the one place that was all Finn but I stood in the middle of the room, hugging myself, feeling sorry for myself and also berating myself.

What had happened to my determination to concentrate on my social rise?

Every day at that lunch table was an opportunity to build on my status at this school and I'd just walked away from it today because of a boy.

But not just any boy, I finally admitted.

A boy I wanted as my friend.

I *needed* a friend.

Everyone needed someone, right? Why was it so hard for me to admit that? I blinked back the sting of tears and kicked out at the cupboards in front of me in frustration. I was turning into an emotional head case.

I spun around…

And found myself face-to-face with one of Finn's photographs.

My breath caught.

It was a photo of me.

When had he taken that?

It was a close-up shot, but from what I could tell I was standing outside the front gates of the school.

He'd caught me in profile while the wind blew my hair lightly away from my face and I looked...sad.

Why had he taken this?

I sighed and looked away, unable to see the emotion he'd captured, emotion I thought I did a pretty good job of hiding. Not there. Finn had caught me while I was vulnerable.

Why did he care enough?

Was I just another subject to him or did he take my picture for a reason?

Before I found out about his dad, had Finn wanted to be my friend, too?

"Dammit!" I snapped, grabbing up my book bag.

If I was spending this much time agonizing over the guy I needed to do something about it. End of story.

I'd make Finn stop ignoring me.

I'd make him see that for now, while we were both powerless and trapped, we could eke out a measure of control together.

Attempting to get Finn to stop ignoring me was a lot harder than I'd anticipated. Over the next few days the boy came up with every excuse on the planet to avoid me. The only time he couldn't avoid me was in our history class because we were working on the presentation together.

Of course, we couldn't talk there.

By Thursday, I'd lost all of my patience. We did the oral presentation, and it went pretty well considering how stiff and cold Finn had been with me. I could see our classmates giving us odd looks and still had enough of my ambition in me to worry that his behavior would affect people's attitudes toward me.

Thursday after school was a busy night for the *Chronicle*. I'd worked my butt off that week so I'd done both my jobs and had really nothing left to do but help Alana oversee the issue as Nadiya put it together on the computer.

Before walking into the media lab I'd seen Finn head into the darkroom. I'd itched to go after him but knew I needed to be seen at the *Chronicle*.

Once it looked like everything was in hand, I approached Alana.

"You don't need me right now, do you?"

She threw me a distracted look. "Nope."

"I just need to do something. I'll be quick."

"Fine."

I tried not to look like I was hurrying but my feet seemed to have a mind of their own as they took me out of the media lab.

The truth was I couldn't remember the last time I'd felt this nervous. My stomach was fluttering, my palms were sweating and I could not get my heart rate under control no matter how much I tried to with calming breathing exercises.

There was nothing stopping me from turning back around and returning to the *Chronicle*.

Nothing but this pull toward Finn that I could no longer deny.

I wished I didn't feel it.

But I did.

I hated the idea of him hurting alone.

And I hated being alone.

Giving the halls a quick check to make sure there was no one else around I slipped inside the darkroom, taking a moment to adjust to the light.

Finn stood in the middle of the room, a few feet from me. He stared at me, and I could feel his displeasure fill the small space.

He dropped the photo he was developing to fully turn to me. "What are you doing?" he said, ice in his voice.

I sucked in a huge breath.

Here goes nothing.

"We need to talk about what I saw."

"You didn't see anything."

"Finn—"

"I don't have anything to say to you. What part of me avoiding you all week did you not get? You need to keep your nose out of my business."

"If you—"

"Get out," he said as he strode toward the sink, giving me his back.

"No." I stubbornly took a step forward. "I'm not leaving until you hear what I have to say."

"Why?" He looked at me over his shoulder, dragging his gaze down my body in this insolent, horrible way. "You think *you* can help *me*?"

Although I knew he was just lashing out in defensiveness it still hurt, and I could only stare at him a moment as I tried to remind myself why I wanted to do this.

He gave a huff of bitter laughter. "Stay out of my life, India." He turned to stare at the wall.

And then it happened.

For Finn Rochester I ripped myself wide open.

"When I was eight Hayley left me and my dad. Just left. No explanation."

Finn went rigid, and I took that to mean he was listening.

I took another step toward him, my mouth dry, my hands shaking right along with my knees. I would never have guessed how hard and scary it would be to tell someone my story. "My dad got really sad, and then really mad, and then really drunk. He lost his job. We lost our house. And he moved us into a trailer park on the edge of town. I went from a popular kid to a kid everyone called trailer trash.

"But I could have lived with that. That would have been easy…because that was nothing compared to my drunk dad. Nothing compared to the fact that he grew to blame me, to hate me, for Hayley's leaving us. And I mean *hate*, Finn. The deep, dark kind of hate." Tears filled my eyes as I remembered the vicious look my dad got on his face when he stared at me too long.

My words seemed to penetrate, and Finn turned slowly around. His eyes tore through me. He wore a haunted look I knew only too well.

"The beatings weren't great, but fists and feet, bruises and blood, I might have been able to deal with just that alone. But the hating me part was the rough part. And the locking me in the bathroom for days, the starving me as punishment for some transgression or other—that was the part that could have…" *broken me eventually.* I swiped at my tears, angry at how vulnerable the memories still made me feel.

"I'd become almost invisible at school. No one seemed to notice me disappearing. Well…there was this one teacher when I was ten. She noticed a couple of bruises. But Dad sobered up long enough to charm her into thinking he was a good dad, that I was just that kid who was always playing where I shouldn't." And too afraid to speak up, I didn't contradict him. I'd always wondered who else knew or suspected that my dad abused me and didn't do a damn thing to save me. The thought hurt too much, however, and whenever it crept up I threw it aside as quickly as I could.

"It wasn't until I was twelve when things started to get really bad and then finally it stopped. I said something that made him lose it. I don't know what happened. I woke up in the hospital and the nurse told me that my dad's girlfriend, Carla, had called an ambulance because she thought I was dying. He almost killed me. And on top of the injuries I was malnourished." I gave Finn and his horrified expression a sad little smile. "All very maudlin. The authorities tracked down Hayley, and over time she got custody of me. She moved me to California with her, and I've been with her ever since."

"Why?" he whispered, his voice hoarse. "Why are you telling me this?"

I shrugged helplessly, feeling raw. "I've worked hard at not needing anybody. Not Hayley. Not anyone. But…it's getting really shitty." I laughed bitterly. "I don't trust easily. In fact, not at all, really, and that's kind of exhausting. I don't know what's going on between you and your dad but I know enough to suspect he's been violent with you. I hate that for you. But I saw how you stood up to him and I felt… I don't know." I shrugged again. "Maybe it's twisted, but I felt like finally there was this person that might get me. Someone maybe I could trust. And he could trust me, too."

Silence fell thick and fast upon my last word and I swear I thought my heart was going to break a rib, it was thudding so hard.

And then he moved, taking slow, long strides toward me, and my breath got caught in my throat.

He stopped close to me, his expression warring between stunned and something else—something that made my heart sink. "I... I'm sorry that all that happened to you, India. I am. Believe me. But I can't..." He looked away, the muscle in his jaw flexing. "I can't be that person for you and you can't be that person for me. I don't want to talk about this. Ever. I'm sorry."

I'd been wrong before.

Finn's earlier rejection was like a bee sting compared to this.

I'd put myself out there for the first time ever and...

Nausea rushed over me.

Trembling from head to foot, I didn't wait for him to say anything else; I just turned and shot out of there, ignoring the concern in his voice as he called out my name.

CHAPTER 11

"HEY."

I looked up from my ereader and the angsty, heart-wrenching romance I was reading. The hero and heroine's problems were a nice escape from my own.

And Hayley was intruding upon that escape.

She smiled tentatively and stepped farther into my bedroom. "I just thought I'd check on you. You were quiet at dinner. Everything okay?"

There was a part of me that was stunned she'd noticed. Hayley was kind of wrapped up in her engagement party and wedding planning. "I'm fine."

"Oh, it sounds like it."

I stared sullenly at her. "Even if I'm not fine, when have I ever come to you?"

Hurt flickered over her features. "You used to come to me."

"Yeah, before I was eight and you abandoned me."

She sucked in a breath at the attack and I quashed the flicker of guilt. “Right.” Hayley stumbled back a little. “I’ll leave you alone, then.”

My fingers bit into my ereader as she slipped out of my room.

I wondered if she was going to cry.

For some stupid reason my own eyes started to sting at the thought.

With blurry vision I looked back down at my ebook and forced reality out.

If I were honest, what I really wanted to do was wallow in self-pity for...well, forever. However, despite the awful day I’d had, I managed to get some sleep that night and things looked...not different, but I could focus again on what was important.

I was a little reassured by the fact that although I’d made myself vulnerable to Finn, he wasn’t going to share my sob story with anyone else. So there was that.

And then there were my social plans.

Was I really going to throw them out of the window because a boy had hurt my feelings? A boy who wasn’t even a romantic interest? I wasn’t like those girls I’d always kind of felt sorry for—you know, the ones that couldn’t make a decision based purely on what they wanted, but on what they thought the boy they liked wanted.

Plus, I was the master at masking my true feelings.

I could do that around Finn.

I could pretend I wasn’t hurt. Like his rejection meant nothing to me.

“You seem better this morning. Your appetite is back,” Hayley noted as we sat at breakfast with Eloise. As per usual Theo had already left for the office. After our first few weeks of settling in, Theo had gone back to what I gathered was his normal routine of working long hours. He was never there for breakfast and he was only home for dinner a couple of days out of the week—mostly the weekend. I wondered how Hayley felt about how much he worked. I wondered if she cared or if it was an easy compromise in order to obtain the life she'd always wanted.

I glanced at Eloise to see if she was paying attention. She was staring at her breakfast as she ate, but I could tell by the tilt of her head that she was listening.

"There was nothing wrong with me last night," I said.

Hayley smiled weakly at my impatient tone. "Okay."

"I'm done," I said to Eloise. "Are you done?"

She looked over at me. "In a minute."

"While I remember, I need you girls to write out your guest list for the engagement party. Invitations had already gone out when I realized I didn't give you both a chance to invite some friends."

Eloise nodded. "I'll get the list to you by the end of today."

Hayley smiled gratefully and then looked at me.

I grimaced. "Her list is my list. Or did you forget my friends live three thousand miles away?"

Her dark eyes dimmed at my caustic response.

Not wanting to see the hurt there, I swept out of the house and slid into the car Gil had waiting for us. He seemed to sense my mood and sat in silence with me while we waited for Eloise.

A few minutes later Gil got out of the car to open the door for her and she climbed in beside me. We were quiet as we waited for Gil to return to the driver's seat. As he pulled the car out of the driveway, Eloise said, "You were a little harsh to Hayley, don't you think?"

I flushed inwardly with guilt.

Outwardly I shrugged. "I don't know what you're talking about."

Eloise seemed amused.

"What?"

She stared at me a moment and then shrugged before looking away. "Sometimes I forget you weren't born here. You're a natural."

"I've had my game face perfected since long before arriving in Massachusetts."

"I noticed." She shot me a look and we shared an unhappy smile.

Not for the first time I wondered if there was more to her sadness than her mother's death. And if so…what?

"You like Hayley, don't you?" I found myself asking.

Eloise seemed surprised by the question. "Does it matter?"

"Kind of. We're supposed to be becoming a family."

"Okay. Yes, I like Hayley. She doesn't seem all that complicated. She takes people as they are. I've never heard her pass judgment on anyone or bitch about them. That's refreshing."

I laughed. "Refreshing. Right."

We were silent for a moment.

"India, she's your mom. Just be grateful she's here, okay?"

Guilt and anger mixed together and clogged in a giant lump in my throat so I couldn't respond. I was pissed at Hayley and I didn't want to stop being pissed at Hayley. I had a right to be pissed at her. That didn't mean there wasn't a part of me that felt bad, that didn't feel like I was taking the fact that I had Hayley for granted when I lived with a girl who'd lost her mom in such a way that there was no hope of getting her back.

School that day was interesting to say the least. If I could have willed it to, I would have made my heart rate stay steady the moment I saw Finn. Unfortunately, the heart has a mind of its own, and as soon as we saw one another in the hall, mine started banging and thumping in my chest like a panicked nerd who'd been stuffed into her locker by the most popular kid in school.

Finn's eyes seared into me, soulful, almost tortured.

Then as Eloise drew us nearer, he seemed to remember himself and all that I'd seen in his expression disappeared like smoke in the wind.

"Hi," Eloise said, touching his chest briefly as we stopped in the hall.

"Hey." He tucked her hair behind her ear and gave her a small, intimate smile she returned. His eyes flickered to me and he mumbled a "Hey" before turning his attention back to her. "Are we seeing each other tomorrow?"

Eloise nodded. "It's Paul's birthday party tomorrow, remember."

I did. Paul, our copy editor, had invited me last week. His mother was Diana DuPont Worthington, heir to DuPont Diamonds, one of the most long-standing giants in the mining and selling of diamonds.

In other words, Paul's family was a big freaking deal and anyone who was *anyone* would be attending his party.

"Right," Finn said. "Is everyone going?"

Was it just me or did that *everyone* actually mean "India"?

I felt my hurt turn to anger and that was a good thing. I was better at handling anger than hurt. "I'm going to catch you guys later," I said in a voice that sounded so normal I was proud of myself. "I have to get to class."

Eloise bid me goodbye but I got nothing from Finn. For whatever reason, despite my confession, he'd decided not only were we not friends, we weren't even acquaintances. He was still going to treat me as if I didn't exist and that pretty much made him a shitty person. I'd told him things that I hadn't told another soul. I was more vulnerable to him than anyone else, except Hayley.

And he was acting like the world's biggest dipshit.

That helped me get through the day because I didn't want a dipshit for a confidant.

If I'd been blown away by Theo's home and Finn's house, I was overwhelmed by Paul Worthington's family's sprawling mansion. It was exorbitant in its grandeur. I couldn't imagine living in a place like it.

We'd taken Eloise's car, and she was more than happy to let me drive, which was a nice bonus. The Worthingtons lived in Weston so it was only a five-minute trip to his home, but I got the impression Eloise felt it was important that we turn up in a Jaguar rather than a cab—or heaven forbid walk there.

I followed Eloise through the party, wearing a short stretch-knit blue dress by Balmain. It had long sleeves, a round neck and a jacquard pattern in darker blue lace down the bodice and sleeves. I wore it with Michael Kors open-toed black suede booties. I'd never worn a more expensive outfit in my life. But looking around at everyone else I knew it was the right choice. Everyone was dressed to party wearing designer.

Eloise led us into the billiard room (yes, billiard room!) where our crew had congregated. I braced myself, about to follow Eloise as she moved toward her boyfriend, when a strong arm hooked around my waist and stopped me in my tracks. I was jerked back into a hard body, one that I pushed against as I twisted around to see who had captured me.

Jasper.

Great.

I pushed against him again and he eased his hold but didn't

let me go. "You look hot, India." He grinned. "Appropriate, considering your namesake."

I rolled my eyes and tugged out of his grasp. He scowled in disappointment.

"Hey, where you going?" he said, grabbing my wrist when I turned to leave.

Touchy-feely asshole. I scowled and pulled my hand away from him. "You know, if you want to talk to me, try doing it without touching me."

His eyes turned frosty so quickly I shivered, and he leaned in to purr viciously, "Awfully stuck up for a poor bitch."

I reeled back. "Showing your true colors there, Jasper."

And just like that the ice was gone and he was grinning at me beseechingly. "Come on, I don't want to be enemies. I want to be friends. Very *good* friends."

"You know what? You should just stick to being good friends with your right hand."

His friends who had been eavesdropping burst out laughing and Jasper's face darkened with anger.

I whirled away from him before the creep could get any creepier and I smacked right into Gabe's strong chest. He lightly grabbed my arms to steady me. "You okay?" His eyes narrowed behind me and he looked uncharacteristically pissed off.

"I'm fine," I assured him. "Nothing I can't handle."

He searched my eyes and whatever he saw made him smile. "Okay, warrior girl." He grabbed my hand and started leading me over to Finn and Eloise. "*Be friends with your right hand.* You crack me up, Maxwell."

I chuckled, feeling relieved to be with a friend and away from Jasper. I hadn't gotten the best vibe off the senior before tonight, but now I sensed something aggressive in him.

I didn't know if it was alcohol, or if it was my turn to be paranoid, but I did know I wanted to shake off my feeling of unease.

That wasn't the easiest thing in the world to do when I found myself standing next to Finn. I did my best to keep enough distance between us so we wouldn't touch. As my eyes swept over everyone they locked with one of the seniors on Finn's crew. He was the second tallest guy on the crew next to Finn, but more built, with big wide shoulders. His light red hair was cut close to his head and he had piercing blue eyes. Good-looking with sharp, angular features that were a contradiction to the smattering of freckles across his cheeks and nose, the guy was this very nice mix of cute and hot.

And he was smiling at me.

I smiled back.

He moved forward, close to the middle of the group, and held out a large hand. "Patrick Donaghue."

"India Maxwell." I shook his hand.

"You haven't met?" Eloise said, brow furrowed. "Apologies. India, Patrick's father is the other senior partner in Daddy's law firm—Donaghue & Fairweather."

"Oh. Well, it's nice to meet you."

"You, too." He smiled. "I saw you at the race but you disappeared before Finn could introduce us. I've seen you around school, too. I kept meaning to come over and introduce myself. I'm sorry it took me so long."

I grinned at his obvious flirtation, glad for the distraction from the brooding boy beside me.

"Okay." Gabe puffed up his chest comically and stepped between us. He gestured to Patrick as he turned to me. "You're not going to fall for this guy's so-called Irish charm, right?"

Patrick laughed as I made a face that suggested I was considering it.

Gabe clutched his chest dramatically. "Baby, you're killing me here!"

"And you're killing me here." Finn nudged him out of the way. "I'm bored." He took Eloise's hand and led her away, Bryce and Joshua following in their wake.

Taking it in stride, Gabe shrugged. "Drinks?" he asked me and Charlotte.

I was so busy "ignoring" Finn's departure that it took me a moment to understand his question. "Uh, sure. Soda. I'm driving."

Charlotte glanced between us. "Um…beer."

Gabe frowned at her. "A beer?"

"Yes," she said primly.

"Okay. Be back in a second."

He moved out of the way and I was almost a little disappointed to see Patrick and his teammate that I hadn't been introduced to had been diverted by Katherine Kelter and a pretty blonde I recognized from Eloise's play.

Sighing, I turned away to look around the room, attempting to pretend I wasn't wondering where Finn had taken Eloise.

"I'm sorry about Finn," Charlotte said, her expression sympathetic.

Confused and alarmed, I was a little sharper in my response than I meant to be. "What do you mean?"

She winced. "Well, it's obvious that he's not thawing toward you. But I don't think it's personal if that helps."

"It's not?"

"No, I think…well… I think he's keeping his distance deliberately to reassure Eloise."

My heart was pounding. Did quiet, sheep-like Charlotte see more than I'd given her credit for? "I don't understand."

"You're beautiful."

"Thanks?"

Charlotte laughed. "Most girls would be threatened by you. I know Bryce is." She smiled as if she found the notion of my upsetting Bryce amusing. "Finn's just really loyal to Elle, and I think he's just reassuring her that no matter how pretty you are he still thinks she's the most beautiful girl at school."

"But she is," I said, wondering why I felt so glum about that.

"I don't know. Guys seem to really like you." She gestured behind her and I found Patrick staring over at me while Katherine chattered away to him.

"And Gabe is half in love with you." Charlotte laughed again, but it sounded somehow hollow.

"Gabe? No, he's just teasing. You know he flirts with every girl he meets." I searched her face, wondering at the melancholy I saw in her eyes. Realization hit me. "Oh my God, Charlotte, do you like Gabe?"

"Shh." She glanced around her frantically to make sure no one had heard me. "Of course not."

Liar! "Oh, you so do."

"India," she whined at my teasing.

I laughed. "Look, I won't tell anyone. But you should know that I do not like Gabe. Not like that. He's just a friend. Always will be. And he's only flirting with me for fun. If it were serious he'd have asked me out by now."

"True," she mused. "His parents probably wouldn't let him date you."

My face prickled hotly. "Oh?"

"A lot of the families here are from old money. They tend

to want their sons to date a girl from a powerful and wealthy family. Both Gabe's parents are from wealthy families. His grandfather is the guy who co-created the first computer software program or something and now Gabe's dad is a CEO for a security company. As for his mom, she's like the daughter of El Salvador's biggest chocolate producer, and now she runs her own elite matchmaking business. They're not like Finn or Eloise's family. They can't claim to be blue bloods. But they sure can claim wealth and power and they have no intention of going backward. You haven't got the right status, and parents around here want their kids to date other kids from a similar background. Until Theo and Hayley have been married for a while, they won't see you in that light, if ever."

I masked my hurt with indifference. "I'm not interested in dating, anyway. But you should ask Gabe out."

"I couldn't." She shook her head. "He doesn't see me that way."

"Then make him. You're gorgeous. He'd be an idiot not to see that. Maybe he thinks there's no way you'd be interested. If I remember correctly, you did shudder with horror when I suggested you two were a couple."

She bit her lip. "I didn't want him to know I have a crush on him. I've liked him since the beginning of sophomore year. I was dating Matt Schneider over that summer and then he was a total ass to me when we got back to school. He publicly dumped me and then got really mean. He made me cry, it was so embarrassing. Gabe was really there for me, though. He talked to me for a long time and basically said that if I stood up for myself nothing bad was going to happen. He promised me. And I believed him. He said I just had to be brave."

She smiled dreamily and pressed a finger to her cheek. "And then he kissed me right here and hugged me. He told me I was too good for Matt." Charlotte suddenly looked glum. "I stood up to Matt because of Gabe. In that moment he helped me find the courage to be brave. I've liked him ever since but he flirts with almost every girl but me. Bryce made this crack once about how I'd have to be the last girl on earth before Gabe would ever see me as anything but a 'little sister' type and that stuck with me, you know. So now I pretend that the thought of dating Gabe disgusts me. A defense mechanism."

"Mixed signals. Not good. And Bryce could not be more wrong."

"How do I fix it then? Do you think I should?"

"Yes. Gabe would be ridiculous not to want to date you. Start slowly. Be a little flirty with him. I've seen you flirt. You can do it."

"Yeah? He won't laugh?"

"Never. I promise."

Charlotte heaved a sigh and then smiled at me. "I know Finn is being a jerk and Bryce is Bryce…but you should know I'm glad you're here. I like having you as a friend. It looks like Eloise's coming around, too."

Although I knew Charlotte would stop talking to me in a heartbeat if Eloise asked her to, I also knew that despite her weaknesses, she was a sweet girl.

A few minutes later Gabe returned with our drinks.

"A beer," he said, handing it to Charlotte. "Although I don't think you'll like it."

Her eyes flew to mine and I gave her a pointed "go for it" look. She cleared her throat. "I like beer."

"You do?" He took a swig of his own.

"Yeah."

And two beers later Charlotte apparently found some Dutch courage. Gabe and I were in the middle of discussing a movie we'd all seen that week when Charlotte suddenly stepped into his personal space, silencing us.

She gave him a flirtatious smile. "You know, Gabe, there's a lot about me you don't know."

His eyes grew round at her husky tone and I could tell he was trying to work out if she was messing with him. "Like what?"

She smirked mischievously and shrugged. "*Stuff.* I bet there's *stuff* I don't know about you."

Gabe stared at her as if he didn't know quite what to make of her. "Uh…"

Charlotte tapped his chest playfully. "A little flustered there?"

"Uh…"

"It's just me, silly." She rolled her eyes and then gripped his bicep as she sidestepped him. "Ooh, have you been working out?"

"Uh…"

"Very nice." She made this humming noise in the back of her throat and then let go of him. "I'm getting another beer."

"My biceps?" He turned to me, shocked, as Charlotte walked away. "What?"

I shrugged, grinning.

"Was she…?" His expression darkened. "Did she just…? Okay. She's had too many beers."

Laughing, I watched as he pushed through the partygoers, shouting Charlotte's name.

As for me, I couldn't wait to see how that played out over the coming weeks.

Having gotten used to being ignored by Finn, I was surprised on Monday in Modern European History when he leaned in to speak to me.

I turned to stare at him, my heart rate picking up at his nearness. I felt like a freaking metal detector around him.

Beep, beep, beep, BEEP, BEEP, BEEP, BEEPBEEPBEEP-BEEP!

Finn was brooding as usual. "You need to watch yourself."

"Excuse me?"

"With Jasper," he said impatiently. "Apparently you said something to piss him off at Paul's party. You don't piss Oliphant off, and you definitely don't do it in front of all his friends. *You* especially don't."

"What does me 'especially' mean?"

"You know what it means. To him you're a nobody, but a nobody he wants to use, and he's an arrogant, entitled asshole so he thinks he has the right to. Whatever you said..." He shook his head in annoyance. "Are you trying to cause trouble for yourself?"

I looked down at my desk, feeling like a scolded child. "He was being a dick."

"I don't like the way he's looking at you," he muttered. "Just...watch your back."

I peeked up at him and saw he was staring straight ahead again, disinterest on his face.

I gave a huff of bitter laughter. "I know how to watch my back, Finn. I'm the only one that ever has."

He jerked like I'd hit him and his mask of disinterest slipped. Guilt replaced it. I felt that look right down to my soul.

"Okay, let's talk the French and the British problem!" Franklin called out cheerily as he entered the room, and just like that the moment was broken.

CHAPTER 12

FINN WAS STILL avoiding me—and frustrating me because when he thought I wasn't aware he stared at me. I didn't know why, but I wished he'd stop watching me because it made it harder for me to forget the fact that he knew so much about me.

Thursday was much of the same but I had a lot to take my mind off it. I was still being kind of a bitch to Hayley and on top of all my schoolwork I had my work for the *Chronicle*. Eloise's director was sick so rehearsal had been canceled after school. I'd told her to just go home with Gil and I'd get a cab because I intended to stay behind after the *Chronicle* went to print to work on school stuff.

Really, it was just an excuse to stay out of the house as long as possible so I didn't have to interact with Hayley about the upcoming engagement party.

Finn stopped by the *Chronicle* for about two seconds to drop off his photos before leaving for crew practice, and Jasper thankfully treated me as if I didn't exist.

Once everyone had left for the night I headed to Franklin's classroom. He had to close up the media room because of all the expensive equipment in it, but he offered me his room and I took him up on it. He left me to get on with it, heading home, grumbling under his breath about papers he had to grade.

Half an hour later, I'd gotten through my Microeconomics homework and looked up at the clock to check the time. Something caught my attention in the doorway.

I startled at the sight of Jasper leaning against Franklin's doorjamb.

Unease crept down my spine. "How long have you been standing there?"

"Awhile." He shrugged off the door and sauntered casually inside.

My pulse sped up in warning like it knew something I didn't. "What do you want?"

Jasper snorted, casualness disappearing from his expression to be replaced by anger. "What do I want? An apology for trying to embarrass me in front of my friends last Saturday."

If I hadn't been so concerned, I might have laughed. "I made a smart-ass comment that everyone but you has forgotten about."

He raked his gaze over me as he took another few steps in my direction and instinct had me rising from my seat. "Maybe so. But I'm thinking you and I need to talk."

I began to stuff my things into my bag as my pulse started to race for real. "If you've come here to intimidate me, it won't work," I lied.

"Let me rephrase, then," he snapped. "I'm going to teach you a valuable lesson about how things fucking work here, India."

"No, you're going to turn around and walk out this door," a familiar voice warned.

Jasper jerked around at the menacing tone and relief moved through me at the sight of Finn striding into the room. He deliberately brushed past Jasper, nudging him hard with his shoulder so he stumbled into a desk. Finn kept walking until he was by my side.

"You okay?" he asked, eyes raking over me in concern.

I nodded, silent.

"What was the plan?" Finn bristled as he glowered at Jasper. "Get her alone and then what?"

Jasper sneered at us. "Are you insinuating what I think you're insinuating? Please," he scoffed, "I've never needed to force myself on a girl in my life. Do you really think I'd need to force myself on a piece of trash like her?"

Finn lunged for him and I was just fast enough to grab his arm and haul him backward. "He's not worth it. I don't care what he thinks of me."

Jasper laughed. "But Finn Rochester cares. I wonder how interested Eloise would be to find out her loyal lapdog wants to get in her freeloading 'sister's' pants."

"You piece of—"

"Finn, don't." I tightened my hand around his wrist to keep him still. "He's slime who doesn't know what he's talking about. He's also never going to come near me again. Right?"

"You're already a bad memory."

"We're serious." Finn stepped up to him, towering over him. "I'll ruin you if I even so much as see you looking at her."

"Jesus! Fine." Jasper held up his hands as he backed off.

There was a tense moment when I thought Finn was going to change his mind and go after Jasper again. Finally Jasper made a move toward the door and I breathed a sigh of relief when Finn let him.

But he just couldn't leave quietly. "Remember who you are, Rochester. Don't go making enemies with the wrong people over a nice piece of ass."

I saw Finn tense, but he didn't make a move toward Jasper and the scum left us alone in awful silence. Finn turned back to me. As I gazed up into his face I knew I'd never been more thankful to see someone in my life. "How did you…?"

Finn ran a shaky hand through his hair. "Patrick got me after practice today to say he'd overheard Jasper making a bet with some friends that he'd nail you by the end of the night."

My stomach twisted at the thought. "Do you think he would have…?"

"I don't know." His face turned red with anger again. "As far as I'm aware he never has before but I couldn't take the chance."

"I'm glad." I drew in a shaky breath and realized I was trembling.

"I wouldn't let anyone hurt you," Finn said quietly, so quietly I wasn't even sure I heard right.

We stared at one another awhile and as I fell into his dark eyes something began to build in me, swirling hot and thick in my chest. It scared me because it was a feeling I could never act on. I looked away, tears stinging my eyes. "Thank you."

I felt his warm hand on my shoulder. "India…"

Despite myself, my eyes were drawn back to his.

He opened his mouth as if to say something and then he stopped as if thinking better of it. Instead he said, "I'm going to get you some water. You sit down for a second. I'll be right back."

My immediate reaction was to grab his hand and beg him

not to leave me, afraid to be alone, but I quashed that instinct and nodded. I took Finn's advice and sat down, not believing that one stupid smart-ass comment could cause such a horrible drama.

Finn came back with two cups of water from a nearby water machine.

"Here." He placed the water on my desk and took his seat beside me.

We sipped in silence for a little while.

And then I had to ask, "So…you were worried about me?"

Finn heaved a massive sigh. "Yes."

"But you said you didn't want to be friends."

"I said I *couldn't*."

"There's a difference?"

"Yes." He searched my face. I didn't know what he was looking for. "I wanted nothing more than to be there for you when you told me all that stuff about your dad. And even though I said I couldn't be the person you were asking me to be, I went home that night and for the first time in a really long time I didn't feel so alone."

Emotion welled up in my throat, constricting it and anything I might have said.

"You've never told anyone what you told me, have you?"

I shook my head, pushing past the constriction. "Not even my best friend back in Cali."

He looked pained. "India, if I could change the way I reacted I would."

"This, today, went a long way to making up for that."

"No, it didn't. What you gave me…trusting me like that." He sat back in his chair and rubbed his hands over his face. When he moved them, he was looking at me in that soulful, tortured way of his that made me want to wrap my arms around him. "I… I've known Eloise since we were kids."

I froze, the blood rushing in my ears, as I suddenly wondered if he was about to admit what I refused to contemplate.

"I care about her a whole lot," he continued, "but our situation isn't like other kids our age. My dad…well, of course you're right about him. He's always been that way. Very controlling, with a major anger management problem." His voice lowered, thick with pain as he confided, "He used to hit my mom. When I witnessed him hitting her, she told me it was a secret that I couldn't tell anyone. She was a doctor. A pediatrician. A smart woman. Now I find myself wondering how someone like her could have stayed in that…taken it from him." He shrugged but I could tell it tortured him still. "When she was diagnosed with cancer my father was nice for a while. And then she died and he got worse than he was before, except now *I* was the one he controlled and used as a punching bag. Unfortunately for him I grew up bigger and stronger than him. The physical stuff stopped, but unfortunately for me the control issues did not.

"I was fourteen and my father caught me making out with our cook's daughter." He gave me this rueful, boyish smile that I felt deep in my gut. "He punched me in the ear so hard it was ringing for days. That I could handle, but the constant being on my back about dating the 'right kind' of girl started to really stress me out. So… I began dating Eloise to appease him."

Now I felt something else hit me in the gut, and it was a something I did not like. "Finn."

He leaned toward me. "India, I'm not using her. I mean, I am, but it's not like that. Eloise is getting what she wants out of this relationship, as well."

"Like what?"

"I can't tell you."

"You *are* using her."

"I'm not." His chair screeched as he pulled it closer so our knees touched. His dark eyes moved over my face and I sucked in my breath at the open appreciation I saw there. "I'm not using her...but we are in a relationship together. I guess it just never occurred to me that I might actually meet someone in high school. Someone I..."

That feeling in my chest, that thick, hot feeling, threatened to overwhelm me at all the things he wasn't saying. "Finn, Eloise is going to be my family."

He looked so forlorn it took everything within me not to reach for him.

"What is it you're hiding?"

"I can't tell you. Please, just trust me."

Hurt and frustration swept through me in equal measure but I tamped it down. It wasn't my place to demand his secrets.

My frustration was suddenly mirrored in his eyes as he looked up at me. "I wish things were different."

But they weren't different. They were the same, history repeating itself. I cared about someone and they didn't care enough about me back to be honest about what was really going on.

I didn't know if I was angry at Finn or just angry that nothing ever seemed to be easy for me. Everything was always a fight.

It felt like I lived in a constant clusterfuck.

I gave a huff of laughter. "Story of my life." I shook my head, grabbed up my bag and, unable to look at him, said, "Thank you for your help tonight."

"You're not leaving without me."

His protectiveness confused and pissed me off even more. "I'm not? Funny, it looks like that's exactly what I'm doing."

His familiar scowl was back in place at my sarcasm. "You're also not going home alone after what happened here. I'll give you a ride."

"Finn." I slumped, suddenly feeling exhausted. "I don't think that's a good idea."

Sadness flittered through his eyes before he managed a carefully blank expression. "I think I can handle driving you home."

Still a trembling mess after everything that had happened, I gave in and followed Finn out to his car.

The tension that we'd shared before was nothing compared to how it was now. Now that Finn had in a roundabout way admitted he liked me and I'd realized that what I was feeling for him was attraction, the tension could not be mistaken for anything else but sexual.

I'd never felt anything like it before—it was the most frustrating, scary and exhilarating feeling in the world.

When we eventually pulled up outside the house, the guilt washed over me. I shouldn't be feeling this way about Eloise's boyfriend and he certainly shouldn't be feeling this way about me.

I felt like we were to blame for the whole thing but I didn't know why.

I hadn't asked the universe to make Finn *like* me.

And I had definitely not intended to like him in return.

"India," he said just as I moved to get out of his car. "I've never really cared what anybody thought of me before...but I really don't want you to think I'm a bad person."

I stared into his beautiful eyes. "I can't imagine ever thinking you're a bad person. I meant it earlier...thank you for coming for me tonight. I'll never forget it."

"This feels weirdly like a goodbye," he said with a bitter twist to his gorgeous lips.

"Maybe it is. I guess we're both just a complication the other doesn't need."

Slowly, so slowly my heart had time to increase in hard, steady thumps, Finn slid his hand over the center console between us and stroked his thumb along the side of my hand. I felt that simple touch in every nerve, my body reacting to it in a way it never had to the touches and deep kisses that had come before it.

I stared at our hands for a moment, wondering how different my life could be if Finn wasn't Eloise's boyfriend, if we'd just met as strangers at school, felt the inexplicable bond between us and were free to do something about it.

Suddenly very aware of how long I'd been sitting outside the house in his car, I fumbled for the door handle. "See you around, Finn."

He didn't say anything in return.

Hurrying into the house, I couldn't look back, and I was more than grateful that I didn't bump into anyone as I rushed upstairs to my room, where I locked the door, fumbled for my phone and called Anna. Not only did I want a distraction, but I badly needed to hear a friendly voice.

CHAPTER 13

THE SCHOOL SEEMED to tower over us more than usual.

"Are you coming?" Eloise's eyebrows drew together.

My stomach felt sick with guilt every time I looked at her.

I nodded, full of trepidation. Last night I'd done my best not to dwell on Finn. I had even skipped dinner so I didn't have to face Eloise, using my long conversation with Anna as an excuse.

Anna did a good job of distracting me but talking to her only made me long for Arroyo Grande and my uncomplicated life there.

Now it was Friday morning, and I had to face Finn. I had to face Finn and our feelings and learn how to pummel those feelings into the ground in order to continue on with my life at Tobias Rochester.

It would have been helpful if the freaking school were named after someone else's great-grandfather.

"You're acting strange," Eloise said as we walked toward her locker, where Bryce and Charlotte were waiting.

"Not sleeping much."

"Mmm."

I looked at her sharply. "What does 'mmm' mean?"

God, she doesn't know, does she? How could she know?

"Nothing." She shook her head. "You and Hayley are creating quite the atmosphere in the house, that's all."

"I'm allowed to argue with Hayley."

"You never call her 'Mom' or 'my mother.'" She slanted a look at me. "It's…interesting."

Glib, I said, "Don't tell me you're actually getting curious about me, Eloise?"

She smirked. "I said it was interesting, not fascinating. There's a difference." Her head jerked to the side. "Finn!"

I tensed, following her gaze.

Finn was coming out of a classroom near Eloise's locker. He blinked, seeming surprised to see us there for some reason. His eyes flicked to me before quickly flitting back to Eloise.

"Hey," he said, waiting for us to draw up next to him.

"What are you doing here?"

"Handing in a late paper."

She frowned. "You've never had to hand in a late paper."

He studiously refused to look at me. "Uh, yeah. I have a lot going on."

Eloise's concern was so genuine that I felt like even more of a bitch for contemplating the things that I wanted with Finn.

"I have to run." He pecked her cheek and rushed off with just a nod to Charlotte and Bryce when he passed them.

Bryce wandered over to us, turning from watching Finn's retreating back to Eloise. "Well, he's acting strange."

Her words mirrored what Eloise had said to me earlier. They made my sister-to-be's head snap back to look at me. I did not mistake the suspicion I saw in her hazel eyes.

I kept my expression bland and shrugged, like I had no idea what was going on.

I must have done a good enough job at not looking guilty because the suspicion died, and she turned primly back to Bryce. “He has a lot on his mind.”

You have no idea.

Finn didn’t sit with us at lunch again. He went to Lulu’s.

And the entire time Eloise kept looking at her phone.

He was doing such a crappy job of pretending nothing had happened between us (and technically nothing had happened between us!) that I wanted to kill him.

Here I was, doing my best to pretend that everything was la-di-da, and he couldn’t even show his face at lunch.

It’s not like he had to do anything! We barely spoke at lunch before any of this happened so no one would notice us not talking.

It was fair to say by the time I got home that afternoon I was frustrated, worried and lamenting the fact that apparently I *wasn’t* so different from girls my age. A boy could make my world stop.

He was just the wrong boy.

“There you are!” Hayley said as I wandered through the informal sitting room to get to the kitchen.

I was no longer so afraid of Gretchen that I couldn’t go into the kitchen for a soda.

I grunted at Hayley and continued past her.

“Hey!” she snapped.

Irritation bubbled up inside me and I spun around to raise my eyebrows at her as if to say, *Well, get on with it.*

“I am sick of this.” She shook her head and stood up from

the pile of folders and papers scattered over the coffee table. *How long* does *it take to plan a wedding?*

"Sick of what?" I crossed my arms, feigning boredom. "Playing princess?"

"You. The way you talk to me. We were fine a couple of weeks ago. What happened between then and now? What are you taking out on me?"

My life. I'm taking my life out on you.

Curbing my inner melodrama, I shrugged. "I don't know what you're talking about."

"Yes, you do. *I* don't know what you're talking about. But maybe if you told me what was bothering you, I could fix it."

"You know what I want. I want you to do what you've been good at my whole life...and stay out of it." I strode out of the room, banging through the kitchen doors.

Gretchen shot me a dirty look for my loud entrance but for now this was my home and I was too pissed to be intimidated by the cook. I grabbed a soda and hauled ass to my room.

Unfortunately, I couldn't hide out there because Eloise would know something was up, so I went down to dinner that night.

Theo was home and he and Hayley were already seated at the table when I got there.

Eloise, however, was nowhere to be seen.

"Where's Eloise?" I said, standing in the doorway.

Theo shot a look at the chair she usually sat in and said, "With Finn. I said she could skip dinner with us this evening to spend time with him. Apparently, schoolwork has kept them apart for the last few weeks. I saw no harm in it."

"Oh." My stomach dropped at the thought of Eloise and Finn together. Talking. Touching...aahhh! I was not allowed to feel jealous! I shoved those feelings down and then

I stomped on them a few times before hocking a loogie on top of them. "So, does that mean I can be excused?"

Hayley stiffened, her lips pursing at the request.

Theo raised an eyebrow. "Do you have plans?"

"I'm not hungry."

"You should eat."

"I don't want to eat."

"Well, I haven't seen you all week so I'd really prefer if you sat down to dinner."

"I'm tired," I insisted.

"India—"

"Just let her go," Hayley bit out.

Theo stared at Hayley in concern before turning to me in disapproval. "You may be excused," he muttered.

India: Why can't you hear a pterodactyl going to the bathroom?

Anna: Why?

India: Because the *p* is silent.

Anna: Oh, man, I just snorted diet soda out of my nose. That hurt.

"India, may I come in?"

I looked up from grinning at my phone, my smile dropping at the sight of Theo standing in my doorway with a plate of food in his hand. "Um… I meant it when I said I'm not hungry." And I *had* meant it. I hadn't eaten a thing since yesterday. There was no room for anything else in my belly but butterflies.

Theo put the plate down on my dresser. "Okay. I'll just leave it here if you change your mind."

I waited for him to leave but after a few seconds of just staring awkwardly at one another, I said, "Was there anything else?"

He pointed to my desk chair in question.

I shifted, uncomfortable with the idea of having a "chat" but I nodded out of politeness and put my phone down beside me on the bed.

Theo heaved a massive sigh. "I'm not happy with how things are between you and your mother."

That's not any of your business!

It was like he read my mind or something. "I know you think it's not my business, but the truth is, it is my business now. When your mother and I get married, I will be your stepfather."

"I'm aware."

"India—" he leaned his elbows on his knees, concern and what might have been sincerity in his eyes "—I am not a stupid man. Do you think I don't know something happened to you? Your relationship with Hayley is…well, even before this argument between you flared up this week things were strained. And from the little I've gleaned from Hayley about your father I can hazard a solid guess that he was not a good man."

"What did she tell you?" I said sharply.

Theo's expression softened. "Not much. But I can put together the puzzle pieces. I think he hurt you and I cannot tell you how incredibly sorry that makes me. But I need you to know that you are safe here. I would never let anything happen to my family. You can always come to me whenever you need to."

I looked at my duvet, not able to see his kindness when I didn't know if I could trust it.

"I'm patient. I can wait for your trust."

There he went again being weirdly perceptive.

"As for you and Hayley… I should know better than to get between two fighting women…"

I looked up to see his wry smile.

"Hayley thinks you're upset because you're missing your friends in California."

She wasn't completely off base.

"So, what if I sent you there for a weekend? Whenever you want. You can choose."

My spirits immediately lifted. "Seriously?"

He grinned. "Yes."

Gratitude, real gratitude, swept through me and for once resentment didn't stop me from accepting. "Thank you."

"You're welcome." He stood up and gave me a soft smile. "I just want everyone to be happy."

And I just wanted to believe that was true.

Maybe one day I would.

Later that night, before bed, I was returning from the kitchen with a bottled water, and as I walked down the hall toward my room I almost jumped out of my skin when Eloise appeared around the corner. The house had been so quiet I could almost imagine I was the only one in it.

Eloise had startled at the sight of me.

"You okay?"

"I'm fine," she said. "I was heading downstairs for hot cocoa."

"You're up late."

"Working on a paper." She shrugged. "Daddy said you might be going back to the west coast to visit friends."

"Yeah. I don't know when. Things are hectic now. But hopefully soon."

She cocked her head to the side pensively. "You want to go back to Arroyo Grande, don't you? Permanently?"

I thought about lying. But I chose the truth instead. "Yes."

My stepsister-to-be didn't seem horrified by my confession that I'd rather stay in California with friends than here with my supposed family. Instead she looked thoughtful as she started walking toward me. She stopped a few inches from me. "I'm sorry this is hard for you."

I tried not to show my shock at her unexpected kindness. Instead I said, "I'm sorry this is hard for you, too."

And for a moment, just a tiny moment, we truly understood at least one thing about one another.

"Good night," she said before strolling past me toward the stairs.

"All right, I hate to ask," Bryce said in a beleaguered tone at lunch, "but who is the hottie in this photo?" She pointed to a picture on her phone.

I leaned past Charlotte to see. It was a photo of me and Jay, our arms wrapped around each other, as we laughed on the beach at a party last summer. It was on my Instagram. "Snooping, dear Bryce?" I teased.

"And hottie?" Joshua frowned at her.

She waved away his concern. "I thought he might be famous, that's all."

"He's not famous. That's Jay." I flicked a glance at Finn and saw he was glowering at Bryce's phone.

Finn's eyes flicked to me at that comment, and I looked away quickly.

"Did you date him?" Bryce almost looked impressed.

"I guess. We were never serious."

"It certainly looked as though you had fun together," Bryce said, waving another picture of me. One of Jay and me dancing. And kissing.

"Would you stop creeping?" I scowled at Bryce.

"Let's see." Gabe reached over the table and snatched the phone.

He made a face at the photo as he sat back down and to my mortification Finn leaned over to check out the picture. His face went completely blank.

Gabe handed Bryce her phone back. "You two looked awfully cozy, India."

"You're not her keeper, Gabe," Charlotte snapped, two little splotches of red coloring her cheeks.

He looked surprised by her attack. "I know that."

"Well, leave her alone. She's allowed to date. You're not her boyfriend!" At that she stood up, leaving her food, and flounced away with more indignation than the situation warranted. Although I had to wonder if her frustration was actually masking jealousy.

"Um…what was that?" Gabe asked.

"She's probably PMSing." Bryce waved away the incident.

"Bryce!" Eloise hissed.

"What? She's seriously melodramatic and all teenage angst during her time of the month. It's irritating."

Eloise looked at her like she was scum water, and I was guessing my expression wasn't far off the same. "Where are your manners?" she huffed, and stood up, rushing to catch up with Charlotte.

Bryce rolled her eyes. "Such drama today."

"Why are you being a bitch?" Joshua snapped before he took off.

"What?" Bryce threw up her hands. "So I'm bored. Look at these photos." She waved her phone at me. "You had more fun at a terrible, dirty party in, ugh, California than I've had in ages."

"So you decide to piss off half your friends?" Gabe sighed. "I'm out." He got up and took off in the direction of the others.

Apparently irritating the unshakable Gabe seemed to snap Bryce out of her mean girl stupor and she hurried from the table to catch up with him.

That left me with Finn.

I frowned at all the food that had been left behind, feeling anxiety build as I tried to figure out what to do with it.

"Charlotte's mother started dating Bryce's father," Finn suddenly said. "That's what's really going on."

"Oh." I knew from talking to Eloise that Bryce's parents were divorced, too. "That's a problem?" I glanced at Bryce's nearly full plate of tuna pasta salad. Maybe I could get a box or something from the lunch workers and get it to Bryce later.

"Charlotte's mother is the first woman Bryce's father has dated since the divorce. Eloise says Bryce isn't dealing with it too well and has been taking it out on Charlotte."

"That's tough." I winced in sympathy and then flinched at the table. Eloise's sandwich was half-eaten. That didn't bother me as much as Bryce's and Charlotte's entire trays of food... *they may have to go in the trash*. My knee started to bounce at the thought.

"Why are you staring at all the food?" Finn said.

I glanced over at him, feeling a little mortified I'd been obvious.

Oh, what the hell. I'd told him pretty much everything else.

"My dad... I went hungry a lot. I have a thing about wasted food." I shrugged like it was no big deal.

Concern warmed Finn's eyes. "Oh." He looked at Bryce's and Charlotte's trays. "Okay. One second."

Bemused, I watched as he got up, lifted a tray in each hand and sauntered toward the back of the cafeteria where a few guys on the boys' rugby team were eating. He said something to them and the boys grinned and gestured to the trays. Finn set them down and the guys descended on the food like wolves.

Something sweet and beautiful swept over me as Finn walked back over. He slipped back into his seat. "Better?"

Stop making me feel this way, Finn.

"Yes. Thank you," I said, grateful. "For that and for not thinking I'm a giant weirdo."

"I think you're extraordinary."

Words have this power over us. I knew that.

My father's words had the power to cripple me. For so long they made me think less of myself.

At school in California, kids were complimentary most of the time, and whether it was sincere or fake I used those words to build my self-esteem back up. They became a defense against negativity.

Words were what I was looking for from Hayley. Magical words that didn't exist.

And Finn's words—given sincerely and by someone like him—for a moment washed all the bad ones away.

It was obvious from the way he flushed and looked anywhere but at me that the words had just slipped out. Which kind of made them more special. "So...uh, you had a lot of fun back in California, huh?"

Now I was uncomfortable with the new subject. "Yeah. I miss my friends there."

"So that guy?"

I glanced around us to make sure no one was listening. "Finn..."

"I'm just asking a question." Was he mad at me?

That wasn't fair.

"Jay and I weren't serious. We don't even talk anymore. Not that we shouldn't, if we wanted to," I reminded him gently.

He glanced away.

We sat there, not moving even though one of us should have gotten up and left.

"I hate this," he said.

I didn't have to ask what "this" was.

He abruptly pushed back from the table.

I watched him stride out of the cafeteria, wondering why everything had to be so impossible.

Somehow we all got through the next week. The heated antagonism between Bryce and Charlotte cooled a little, although there was definitely still awkwardness between them. I didn't know Charlotte had it in her to be openly pissed at her friends, and I was kind of impressed that she'd be so confrontational and opinionated, when all along I'd thought she was more of the sheep type.

On a positive note Gabe was certainly paying a lot of attention to her, giving her a shoulder to cry on. I wondered how it was that no one else could see those two could be perfect for each other if Gabe would only open up those pretty eyes of his.

As for Finn and me...well, I didn't let myself think about that.

"Nope," I said, shoving him right out of my thoughts as I

stood in front of the mirror in my dressing room. For a second I'd contemplated what he'd think of me in this dress. "Butt out, demon," I joked to myself.

Time as a junior seemed to be moving at warp speed. Before I knew it, it was November already and I still hadn't made it out to California to see my old friends.

Now the evening of Hayley and Theo's engagement party had arrived.

It was our debut into society as a family and Hayley's nervous energy was a little catching. She was always so giddy and chirpy about the wedding and Theo that I almost forgot that she was as new to this place as I was. I knew she desperately wanted to be accepted as Theo's fiancée, and it would help if her daughter acted like a loving, mature teenager for the evening.

I could do mature and if not exactly loving, then at least better than distant.

All my new friends would, of course, be at the party, along with some other people from school Eloise had invited.

"India?"

I turned slowly around as Hayley appeared in the doorway to my dressing room.

As always, she looked amazing in her figure-hugging emerald green dress. Her beauty hurt me because if we were a regular mom and daughter that beauty would be just one more thing that would make me proud to walk at her side.

She smiled at me as she took in my dress. "You look beautiful, sweetheart."

"Thanks," I said. "You, too."

Her smile widened.

Things had definitely been a little better between us lately. After the whole revelation about Finn and his dad, I realized how much I took out on Hayley—even the stuff that wasn't her fault—and I guessed it wasn't fair to make her my emotional punching bag any more than it had been fair of my dad to do that to me.

"Black isn't a statement about how you feel about this wedding, though, right?" Hayley teased.

I was wearing a black lace cocktail dress with long sleeves, a high neckline and a pretty short hemline. "Not at all." I grinned and then I wrinkled my nose in thought as I brushed my hands down the front of the dress. "It's not too short for you?"

She contemplated the hemline and then shook her head. "No, you look perfect. You look like a young woman and that makes me feel old, but you look perfect."

"You don't *look* old and you know it."

Hayley laughed and placed her hands on her hips and struck a pose. "I try my best."

I smiled and followed her out of the room and into the hall. Theo was coming toward us, looking dapper in his tux. Hayley immediately gravitated toward him.

"So are we doing this thing?" I said.

"Yes. Eloise's holding the fort downstairs." Theo gestured for me to take the stairs first. "You both look lovely, by the way."

I muttered my thanks, listening to Hayley compliment Theo. He whispered something in her ear that made her giggle like a little girl and I just stopped myself from rolling my eyes as we descended the stairs to where the party was already in full swing.

Eloise stood in the large entrance greeting guests as they arrived at the door. Hayley had hired staff for the party—staff to take and check people's jackets, catering and waitstaff.

There had been people in and out of the house all day decorating and setting up. There were simple fairy lights twisted around the banister of the staircase, and sprinkled in the vines and glittering reeds that had been placed in large silver vases throughout the front of the house. Out back along the pool lit candles were everywhere, creating a romantic outdoor space that no one would use because it was too cold to stand out there in formal wear. Music from the classical trio she'd hired played from the middle of the house in the sitting room.

Waitstaff passed through the guests carrying trays of hors d'oeuvres and glasses of champagne.

I was about to make my way over to Eloise when I noted the tall figure beside her and halted.

Finn.

Crap.

Hayley almost stumbled into me. "Are you all right?" She frowned.

"Sure. Just wondering where Gabe and the others are." I peered into the informal sitting room but I couldn't see anyone I recognized.

"I'll send over Eloise and Finn." She patted my arm and moved away with Theo at her side to take over greeting the guests.

Well, damn.

Feeling stuck, I waited as Finn and Eloise moved over to me. I felt Finn's gaze but tried to ignore it. Eloise looked beautiful in a red silk dress. She was standing close to Finn, staring around the room with an almost dazed expression.

"You okay?" I said.

"Champagne," she muttered in answer, and grabbed a glass off the tray of a passing waiter, drinking it in one huge gulp so, I assumed, our parents wouldn't catch her.

"Not okay, then?"

"She's probably just realized that you're definitely going to be her stepsister." Bryce's wry voice reached us before she did. She sidled up to Eloise, slipping her hand around her friend's waist. "I'm here for you, darling."

I rolled my eyes at her mocking but Eloise barely seemed to register it.

Joshua strode around to stand beside Finn. "Where's Gabe and Charlotte?"

"Not here yet," Finn said.

"I think he said he was going to bring her."

"Yeah?" I asked, wondering if perhaps Gabe was finally seeing the light.

"Yes, dear Gabe has been awfully sweet to Charlotte while her tramp of a mother seduces my father." Bryce sneered.

Joshua shook his head in what was definitely near disgust. "I need a drink."

"A lot of that going around," Finn murmured.

Our eyes met and we shared a bemused smile before I remembered where we were and looked away.

It could have turned into an enjoyable night.

Patrick Donaghue was there, being all attentive and cute.

But everywhere I went there was Eloise alternating between champagne and the giant glasses of water Charlotte kept force-feeding her.

Mostly, however, there was Finn.

Staring at me with those soulful eyes, making me feel guilty. Making me feel like if I didn't touch him or comfort him, my legs would give out, and breathing wouldn't come so easy.

Breathing *wasn't* coming so easy.

Finally, I gave up on trying to salvage the night. I made my excuses to Patrick because…

I needed to escape my feelings.

Mostly everyone had gone into the house for Theo's speech so I found the keys I wanted, dashed out, checked around to see no one was watching and I let myself into the dark pool house. The blinds were drawn so it took a moment for my eyes to adjust to the shadowed room. The only light that spilled in came from the candles around the pool, and peeked in under the blinds that didn't quite reach the floor. I moved into the room, easing down onto the sofa.

Finally I felt like I could breathe again. Who knew it would be so exhausting pretending you didn't have feelings for someone?

My head jerked up at the slight squeak of the pool house door opening and closing, Finn's face illuminated in the light from outside before shadows crept over it once he was inside.

With me.

Alone.

"What are you doing in here?" I was back to that whole having difficulty breathing thing again.

"We need to talk." His voice seemed to fill the entire room and I winced, afraid someone might hear him.

"Did anyone see you follow me in here?" I whispered, shooting up off the couch to have a peek through the blinds.

"Everyone is still inside. It's too cold out. Would you please look at me?"

At his harsh tone, I did. I could see from the quick rise and fall of his chest that he was struggling to breathe normally, too.

"What did you want to say?"

His eyes roamed my face, something like desperation flickering across his features. And suddenly that desperation turned to determination. "This," he said, and in a blink of my eyes he'd closed the distance between us.

His lips came down on mine as he gripped my arms tight.

I inhaled in surprise, his warmth and the smell of his cologne overwhelming me.

Finn is kissing me!

At the touch of his tongue against mine, my skin turned hot and tingly, and those butterflies in my belly erupted to a riotous flutter. Finn's groan vibrated down my throat, and I found myself crushed harder against him as our kiss deepened.

Suddenly I got why everyone made such a big deal about kissing. With the right person it was…*wow.*

Somewhere beyond the fog he had created in my mind, I remembered Eloise. It was enough to dampen the butterflies and reluctantly I pushed against his chest and wrenched my mouth from his.

Finn just as reluctantly loosened his hold, his dark eyes scorching me. "Don't," he whispered.

"Eloise," I reminded him, gently extricating myself from his grip.

"Let's just forget everyone else. Eloise. Patrick."

"We can't just forget. This would hurt people." I gestured between us.

"Right now all I care about is you."

"That's a fantasy, Finn."

"Don't say that. You feel it, too, right?"

"I do. But I also don't want to hurt anyone."

"We won't." He tried to reach for me again, and I could hear something like panic in his voice. "Don't you want to feel happy, even just for a moment? I'm sick of being miserable."

Unease started to creep over me, and I stepped away toward the door. "Sometimes I'm sick of that, too." I liked him. I wanted him. Maybe even needed him. More than I'd ever wanted or needed any boy. But despite the fact that he was the first guy to give me that romance-novel kiss I'd been waiting on, his selfishness made me wary. "And maybe we could be happy for a moment, but it would cause other people sadness. I won't hurt people to be with you. And I have to wonder what kind of person you really are if you can't see beyond this to how much it would kill Eloise." I shook my head, disappointed in him, in me and in the whole situation. Feeling stronger in my resolve, I bit out, "Just forget me. I mean it. You're not who I thought you were."

"She's gay!" Finn cried hoarsely as I turned my back on him.

And suddenly I felt like the idiot who was standing up on an open-top bus and didn't see the heavy metal sign up ahead until it was too late and slamming right into my head.

I spun slowly around to find Finn was staring at me in horror.

"Eloise is gay?" I whispered.

"Oh fuck." He rubbed his hands over his face, muttering, "Oh fuck, oh fuck, oh fuck."

"Finn." I hurried over to him. "It's okay, calm down."

"It's not okay!" he snapped, his eyes shimmering with tears. "I can't believe…oh fuck."

"Finn." I stood there, feeling useless and helpless as he paced in front of me, gathering speed in his panic. "Stop. Please. Stop. I won't tell anyone."

I saw nothing but self-recrimination in his eyes. "You're right. I'm a selfish asshole." He bowed his head and closed his eyes, pain etched on every feature.

Silence fell over us as I came to terms with what Finn had just told me.

Eloise was gay.

And so scared for anyone to find out...she and Finn were using one another?

"Is that what you meant?" I said. "Before? You said she was getting what she wanted out of your relationship, too."

He nodded and slumped down onto the sofa.

I carefully sat down next to him, not wanting to spook him with sudden movements.

"We really have been friends for a long time," he said. "Our mothers dying the way they did only made us closer. But like brother and sister closer."

"Does she know about your dad?"

"She knows he's a dick but I hid the violence from her. I was..."

"Ashamed," I said.

He looked up, our eyes locking, and he nodded solemnly. "Ashamed."

I blinked back the spring of tears in my eyes. "So how did you...?"

"Things had been weird with her for a while before her fifteenth birthday and the night of, Elle got drunk for the first time. Wasted. I got her out of a situation with a guy in our class and hid her out in my room while I tried to get her sober.

"She just suddenly started to cry. It wasn't... She told me she was gay. You have to understand her dad is a major donor to the Republican party—he's conservative and traditional," Finn explained. "He campaigned back in 2004 against same-sex marriages and wasn't happy that Massachusetts was the first state to issue a marriage license for same-sex couples. I mean, he's not going to react well to Elle's secret—that's a given. And he's Elle's entire world. She's terrified of losing him. Of losing another parent. And she's just plain terrified of being considered different. You've seen how much people here care about image. This is a conservative community. But it's more than that. I mean, most people are more accepting now. They'd probably get over it. I tried to tell her that but there's something more… something about her mom, I think, and whatever it is has Elle scared of how her dad will react. She's afraid she'll lose everything and everyone."

Well, look at that, I thought. Our circumstances may be different but in a way our motives were the same—we both needed the safety of being popular, being accepted. I had yet another thing in common with Eloise.

"Theo…" I let the words fall away. There was a lot there to suggest Theo would be unhappy to learn Eloise was gay, but I had seen them interact. I could see how much love was there. I had to wonder if he would turn his back on his daughter. I couldn't see him doing that. But then you just never knew about people. I wondered *exactly* what had happened with her mom, too. Instead I said, "So you struck a deal?"

Finn nodded. "We pretend to be boyfriend and girlfriend until college and that way my dad stays off my back, and no one suspects the truth about Eloise."

"Wow."

I didn't know what else to say.

I think I was shell-shocked.

"She knows how I feel about you. At least…she knows I like you." He wore a look of apology. "I would never have dreamed that I would betray her… I just… I feel like I'm going crazy. All the lies, all the hiding." He seemed to plead with me. "Most of the time I feel like I can't breathe inside my own life. Like I'm just existing. Not with you, though.

I feel like I'm breathing fresh, clean air whenever I'm with you. I feel alive."

Holy... Wow.

Finn turned his hand, sliding his fingers through mine, and then he brought my hand to his lips and kissed it ever so softly.

"I promise that I won't ever tell anyone. I would never do that to you or Eloise."

"Thank you," he said hoarsely.

Warmth moved through me that he believed me without even having to question it.

"So, what—"

The pool house door opened and the light from outside spilled over Eloise's face as she stepped inside and closed the door.

She crossed her arms over her chest as she stared at us. "What are you two doing in here?"

It was the worst time ever for me to lose my natural cool, my ability to pretend, something I had perfected over the years. But lose it I did. I jerked away from Finn so fast I slipped off the couch and narrowly avoided crashing onto the floor when he reached out and caught me. Perched on the couch beside him I knew my behavior screamed, *We just got caught doing something we shouldn't.* "Shit," I muttered, brushing my hair back with a shaking hand as I looked at Eloise for her reaction.

She wobbled in her heels a little, not any more sober than she had been when I'd last seen her. She narrowed her eyes. "Finn?"

Apparently Finn had also lost his ability to fake it. "Elle, I'm..." Guilt shone out of his eyes and, drunk or not, able to see in the dimness of the room or not, Eloise clearly sensed his guilt.

She stumbled back from us, pure fear in her eyes. She shook her head. "Finn?"

Finn stood up, letting go of my hand. "Elle, I'm sorry. It slipped out."

"Oh God, you didn't?"

"Eloise." I stood up now, too. "I won't tell anyone."

However, my words didn't seem to penetrate.

"Oh God." She raised a shaky hand to her forehead and slumped against the wall. Her back hit the light switch and light flooded the room, making me wince.

Eloise didn't even notice. She was struggling to breathe and her face had gone unnaturally pale.

"Elle." Finn rushed toward her but she warded him off with her palm outward.

"I'm going to be sick," she gasped out before she dashed toward the bathroom.

Finn went to follow but I cut him off, chasing after her.

I just managed to pull her hair out of the way as she slumped over the toilet and began throwing up everything she'd eaten and drunk at the party. Even when there was nothing left she kept making these whimpering, retching sounds that soon turned to full-out sobbing.

Tears burned my eyes. I hated that I was the cause of her pain and fear. "Shh." I crawled closer, rubbing her back. "Eloise," I whispered, my voice shaking, "this doesn't change anything for me. You have nothing to be ashamed of. But I get you're scared, okay. I get it. I won't tell anyone. I promise."

She jerked back to glare up at me. Her face glistened with sweat and she had mascara smudges all around her eyes. "And I'm just supposed to trust you?"

"Yes."

"Well, I don't." Sliding away from the toilet, she pressed

her back against the bathtub and with a quivering hand she pushed her hair off her face.

Finn stood in the doorway, hovering uncertainly.

The atmosphere was so thick and horrible it reminded me almost of grief. When Anna's parents had split up a therapist had told her mother that what Anna was going through was a form of grieving. I'd sat with Anna every day after school and she wouldn't say anything. But the atmosphere said it all. It was heavy and scary, made up of that singular feeling of having lost the innocence of believing in a magical forever, the loss of permanency…of safety.

That's how it felt in that tiny bathroom, and it was mostly all coming from Eloise.

"We're going to be family," I finally murmured.

Her eyes flashed defensive fire. "And?"

"And I would never hurt my family."

She looked away, her expression clearly saying she didn't believe me.

"I mean it," I said, and my jaw clenched against all the emotions threatening to rise up out of me. "I know what it's like to have someone who is supposed to be family betray me. And I would never, *ever* betray my family."

Whatever Eloise heard in my voice made her look straight into my eyes. It was only seconds as she peered into my soul, but it felt like forever. Finally I watched, relieved, as a measure of tension left her. "Promise?" Her lips trembled around the word.

"I promise."

"Okay." Her trembling turned to tears and she swiped quickly at them, as if to hide them from me.

"India, can I talk to Eloise alone?"

I nodded at Finn and he held out his hand to help me to

my feet. Grateful for the help, because there was really no way to get up elegantly in my dress and heels, I took his hand and let him pull me up.

When I looked down at Eloise she was staring at us, a million and one questions in her eyes. I'd leave Finn to answer those. For now, I wanted her to be truly assured I wasn't going to betray her trust.

"I think it would have to take someone pretty awful and cruel to tell your secret to the world," I said. "And I may be many things, but I'm not awful and cruel. I'm going back out there, and as far as everyone is concerned, everything is as it always was."

She nodded, looking like a lost little girl. I found I didn't like seeing her like that at all. "Okay," she repeated.

Satisfied she was as close to believing me as possible at this point, I slipped by Finn, squeezing his arm in support as I did, before leaving them alone in the pool house.

Once I stepped outside, I took in a deep, shaky breath.

"Holy crap," I muttered, staring up at the dark sky above.

Who would have thought I'd travel three thousand miles to a supposedly better life only to find two kids as messed up as me?

I didn't feel alone anymore at all.

And for their sake…I wish I goddamn did.

CHAPTER 14

Finn: Can we meet tomorrow? You can name the time and place...

India: Okay. 3p.m. Maggie's Diner. It's a little place in Waltham.

Finn: I'll be there.

I STARED AT the text from Finn for the millionth time. We'd swapped numbers at lunch one day when Gabe had insisted I get everyone's cell number. It was really just an excuse for Gabe to get my number so he could send me silly Snapchats throughout the day. Although, recently, I was happy to note that he wasn't sending me nearly so many, seeming focused on Charlotte these days.

This was my first text from Finn.

After I left him and Eloise, I had gone back into the party. Gabe had Charlotte cornered in the nook by the back stairwell, his hands braced on the wall above her head. They had seemed to be in deep discussion and not even aware of anyone else.

Bryce and Joshua had stopped me, though, asking curiously where Elle and Finn had gone. I made this "ugh" face and told them I'd accidentally walked in on them in the pool house together when I was looking for somewhere to get a breather.

Bryce had clapped her hands together like it was the juiciest thing she'd heard and I felt a moment of relief that Eloise's secret was safer than ever.

When Finn did appear again at the party it was alone, and he told everyone that he'd put Eloise to bed because she'd had too much to drink.

"Oh, sure," Bryce had teased, "after you two had fun in the pool house."

Finn had shot me a questioning look.

"What?" I'd shrugged with an air of casualness I didn't feel. "I just told them I found you two going at it out there. If you'd wanted it to be a secret I assume you wouldn't have chosen a semipublic place."

Grateful appreciation had lit his eyes and he'd smirked. "Not your business."

I'd rolled my eyes, keeping up the pretense. "Lock the door next time."

An hour or so later the party began to disperse. Finn left with the others before we could get a chance to grab a private moment together. When I finally dropped down on my bed, though, I found the text from him.

Now my alarm clock only read 5:43 a.m.

I hadn't been able to sleep a wink thinking about Eloise. Thinking about Finn. My head hurt from all the thoughts crashing into one another up there. My stomach felt that queasy, empty way it did when I'd had little sleep, and that feeling was only compounded by my nerves.

I wanted to see Finn. I wanted to know what this all meant.

But more than that I really wanted to talk to Eloise. This was too big to just leave it hanging. We may not be close but that didn't mean I wasn't worried about her. I needed to know for certain she trusted I'd keep her secret. I didn't want her agonizing over the concern that I might out her.

A sound in the distance drew me up from my pillow. It sounded like a door closing. Throwing myself out of bed I hurried over to my French doors and pulled the curtains aside.

My stomach fluttered with those aforementioned nerves at the sight of Eloise strolling by the pool. She had on jeans and a Tobias Rochester hoodie. A very casual look for her. I watched her as she disappeared into the tennis court.

I glanced back at the clock. Obviously she was finding it hard to sleep, too.

Well…if we were both up…

I dashed into my walk-in and grabbed the nearest pair of jeans and sweater I could find. After brushing my teeth, I threw on a pair of sneakers and hurried out of the house into the chill morning air.

I found Eloise sitting crossed-legged in the middle of the court. She startled at the sound of footsteps and her head whipped around.

Her pale skin looked stark in contrast to her deep auburn hair and she had dark circles under her eyes. It was the least put together I'd ever seen her and it was no wonder. I'd bet she was suffering a mad case of hangover blues.

Oh and of course there was the small matter that someone she barely knew had found out her deepest secret.

"What are you doing here?" she said wearily.

"I couldn't sleep." I sat down next to her, my legs stretched out, ankles crossed, my hands braced behind me. I hoped by appearing casual I could ease some of the tension between us. "Saw you come out here."

"I came out here to be alone."

"Okay. But I'm here now. You could talk to me."

Eloise scowled at me. "What do you want from me? To hold this over my head as blackmail?"

I flinched at the suggestion. "Maybe you've been living in your world for too long."

"Or maybe I just understand people and their motivations. I'm not stupid, India. I know all you want is to be popular and accepted. I know ambition when I see it, which is why you are the last person I'd ever want to find out about this." Her lower lip trembled and she bit it to stop it.

"You're right," I said. "I want to be popular and accepted. I was the most popular girl in junior year back in California. I liked it. Life was better when I was popular."

She narrowed her eyes on me. "Life was better? What does that mean? Has it got something to do with why you don't call Hayley 'Mom'?"

I let go of a long, shaky exhale. "You're not the only one with secrets. I went through something a few years ago. My dad…he wasn't a good man. Let's just leave it at that."

"Oh." Some of her defensiveness melted into uncertainty. "I'm sorry."

"It happens, right?" I shrugged it off with more nonchalance than I ever felt about it. "It made me stronger, though. It made me determined."

"To be popular?" Eloise studied me carefully. "Because you think no one can hurt you when you're at the top. You're in control there. You've got power. You have people to notice if something were to happen to you."

I flushed, embarrassed. Because she was partly right. "Yeah, that's why."

She kept staring at me, as if now that she'd uncovered some truth from me she was looking for more.

"I would never trample over someone else to be popular again. I am many things but malicious is not one of them," I said.

We were quiet awhile until I felt brave enough to ask, "Why are you afraid to tell people the truth?"

Her hazel eyes seared into mine at my question, and I was sure she wasn't going to answer. Instead she glanced around us and then stood up slowly. "Not here."

"Pool house?" Relief that she was willing to talk to me moved through me.

She nodded, and I stood up to follow her. The pool house was still unlocked, so we slipped inside. I turned on a few lights and wandered into the kitchen. "Tea? Coffee?"

"There should be some green tea in there."

I busied myself making us tea, glancing over my shoulder now and then to make sure she was still sitting on the couch. She sat staring at her hands.

"I wish I could say something that would reassure you that you can trust me." I handed her a tea and sat down on the chair across from her.

Her hands hugged the mug I'd given her.

I waited.

And waited.

Finally Eloise looked over at me, fresh tears in her eyes. "Sometimes I feel like I'm going crazy."

I hoped she read my compassion as that and not as pity.

She seemed to because she continued. "I didn't know what I was going to do today. Ignore you. Talk to you. Hate you." She offered an apologetic smile. "But I guess I'm just so tired of pretending."

"I know you probably don't believe me, but I understand that part more than you know."

"No, I believe you, India. I always saw something in you… I was just reading it wrong. Now I know." She shrugged. "You're damaged, too."

I winced. "That's not a great word."

"But it's true."

"Why are you damaged, Eloise? Why do you need to be? Why are you afraid to tell people the truth?"

"You know I was thirteen when I lost my mother?"

"Yeah."

"That damages you, India. Losing someone you love that much. Their loss leaves behind a wreckage. And my mom and I were close. I knew I was lucky. My parents really loved one another. I never thought Daddy would get over losing her." She relaxed back into her seat, staring off into space as she remembered. "For me it was different. I remember the pain of losing her and what it was like to suddenly realize that everything was temporary. The older I get, the more cheated I feel. Other kids my age…they didn't know what it was like to grieve. To feel pain like that. To look around at people your own age and not understand them because what they *think* is important seems so trivial and stupid in comparison to what I *know* is important.

"There was Finn, though. Finn got it. Daddy got it. He's my best friend, do you know that? My father is my best friend and my hero and my whole world." Her tears sprang free and she swiped at them hastily. "If I lost him, I don't know if I'd come back from that. And if I lost him because I'd rather fall in love with Angelina than Brad, I'd never forgive myself. Not for making that choice."

"Is it a choice, Eloise?" I leaned forward, wanting to understand. "You can't help who you're attracted to."

Her lips curled in bitterness. "No, you can't. Believe me, I wish I could. I wish I really wanted Finn."

I contemplated my mug, trying to gather the courage to ask. "How did...how did you know you were gay? When?"

"I was almost fifteen. I'd known something was different for a while. I never had crushes on boys and as we got older and my friends started dating I didn't want to. I tried to tell myself it was a maturity thing, that I just wasn't *there* yet. I kissed boys at parties but I didn't feel anything but uncomfortable, even repelled sometimes. One day Bryce was talking about a boy in our class. She was talking about how cute she thought he was and how she got butterflies every time he smiled at her.

"And that's when I realized I did feel that way—" more tears dripped down her cheeks "—but I felt that way about my French tutor."

"A girl," I whispered, my chest aching for her.

She nodded. "Audrey. She was French. Eighteen. A freshman at Boston University. And little fourteen-year-old me got butterflies when she smiled at me and my skin tingled whenever she touched me. I was aware of every little movement she made. I overanalyzed every little thing she said to me. And I cried the whole night when her boyfriend came to pick her up from tutoring me. I eventually told Daddy I didn't need her anymore so I didn't have to deal with my feelings. But it was like all my feelings were now unlocked. Soon after I developed a crush on Katherine Kelter."

My jaw dropped.

Eloise gave a huff of angry laughter. "I know. I'm full of surprises. But I've pretty much been mooning over her since ninth grade. And she'll never look at me twice. I'll never be able to go up to her and ask her out, or hold her hand or kiss her. How is that fair? Why do I have to hide who I want to be with?" Resentment flared in her eyes.

Until now Eloise had seemed so controlled—sad but controlled. But I saw more. I saw her fury at having to hide from the world. And now I also understood her reaction every time Bryce mentioned Katherine flirting with Finn. The jealousy in Eloise's eyes wasn't for Finn…it was for Katherine.

"You're not going to freak out, are you?" she snapped, her defenses up again. "Aren't you scared I'm attracted to you?"

I didn't know if she was testing me but I knew how I answered this was important in how we moved forward. So I raised an eyebrow and said, "I'm straight, does that mean I'm attracted to every guy in the world?"

"Of course not. But that doesn't answer my question. Are you freaking out that I might be attracted to you?"

"Are you attracted to me?" I said in a way that hopefully communicated I wasn't finding this conversation alarming.

She sniffed, wiping away the last of her tears. "You're gorgeous, but I put you in the 'familial' box before you even got here."

I thought about what Finn had said about Eloise's fears and how her mom had something to do with it. "So your mom never knew any of this? You realized after she'd passed away?"

Pain tightened Eloise's features. "Yes. But I know she wouldn't have accepted this about me."

Somehow I couldn't imagine anyone who loved their kid as much as I could guess Eloise's mom loved her wouldn't support her. "How can you possibly know that for sure? Because she was a conservative pro-traditional family person like your dad? That doesn't mean that she wouldn't come around if she'd known this about you, and loved and accepted you for who you are."

"Have you ever had memories from your childhood, stuff that confused you at the time, but when you remember them as you get older you start to realize a truth you were too young then to understand?"

"What do you mean?"

"When I about six, seven years old..." Eloise's gaze drifted over my shoulder as she seemed to search back into past memories. "My uncle Beau came over to the house while my dad was at work. There wasn't anything unusual in that. Beau was my mom's little brother. We weren't super close because he traveled a lot but he and my mom seemed close. But that day she didn't want him in the house. I didn't understand what they were yelling about or why they were both crying, and I didn't really understand why Beau left that day and I never saw him again.

"But during the weeks when I realized I had feelings for Audrey I started to remember that day. It was just weird. And I never got an explanation from either of my parents about it. However, I remembered something my mom said to him. She said that she could never support his lifestyle. I didn't understand what it meant then but that word, 'lifestyle'... I started to think maybe Beau was gay."

A heavy feeling settled in my gut for Eloise. "You don't know that for sure though, right?"

"No. But it would make sense, right? And if my mom could cut out her own brother for being gay then she might have felt that way about me, too. Ashamed."

"You're taking a guess here. You're afraid of something you don't even know is real. Not supporting Beau's lifestyle could mean anything. He might have been a criminal or a drug addict or something. It doesn't mean he was gay. And even it if did, their argument was a decade ago, and a lot can change a person's mind in a decade. Say you're right—and we don't know you are—and ten years ago your mom did stop talking to her brother because he was gay, that doesn't mean she wouldn't have eventually changed her mind, or that she would have reacted the same way to her own daughter. People can react differently to something when it affects someone they desperately want to protect. And I can only guess that your mom would have wanted to protect you from any kind of pain."

"We don't know that though," she argued. "And we'll never know because she's gone. I'm terrified of losing my father, too. I won't do anything that might cause me to lose him."

"And so no one else but Finn knows?"

"No one. And that's the way it stays."

"Elle, I've seen how your dad is with you. He would support you. You have to know that. He loves you."

"No." I saw the panic take over her anger. "You don't know him. He's backed a campaign against same-sex marriage. He's openly voiced his opinion on what he considers the traditional and 'right' American family, and that is a straight couple. I can't risk it. This would change the way he sees me."

"Or how everyone at school sees you?"

"Exactly. You have to get that, India. You need the popularity because it makes you feel safe—well, I feel the same way. I've never known anything but being Eloise Fairweather. I'm privileged and popular and people respect me. You know what kids are like when they come across someone who is seen as 'different.' Eloise Fairweather, blue blood, straight-A student and girlfriend to school legacy Finn Rochester...she's respected, envied and admired.

"Eloise Fairweather, gay girl...she'd be annihilated."

"No, you wouldn't. Back at my school in California I knew kids who were openly gay and no one tortured them for it. They just accepted them for who they are."

"This isn't California. This isn't even Boston. This is Tobias Rochester."

I still had a hard time believing she wouldn't be accepted at school. "There are openly gay kids at Tobias Rochester. The guy you're in *Our Town* with is gay. Gregg something..."

"Gregg Waters."

"So, I don't see kids following around Gregg, making his life hell because he's gay."

"Not Gregg, no. But last year a senior, Josie Farquhar, came out to her family and friends. Within hours it was all over social media. The next day at school it started—crass jokes, mean girls. They would scream if she passed them in the hall, lunging out of her way in fits of giggles, crying out how she'd tried to touch their boobs. They campaigned to the school to have her banned from the girls' locker room because they said they felt uncomfortable and sexualized by her. Every day they taunted her and they did their best to make her feel 'other.' She left. Her parents took her out of Tobias Rochester and out of the state to finish her senior year."

"That was one example and it was a bunch of mean girls who probably would have found something to bully the girl for, anyway. No one would do that to you. You're Eloise Fairweather."

"But I've lied. I've fooled them into believing I'm something I'm not. And they would come after me for that. Let's not pretend that there aren't people out there who enjoy watching someone's downfall. I can't go through that. I only have to look no further than my friends for a bad reaction—Bryce would not take the news well."

"Speaking of, why are you friends with her?" Bryce was... well, there was no nice way to put it: Bryce could be a bitch.

"Because we've been friends since we were little kids. Sometimes she can be sweet."

I made a face of disbelief.

Eloise laughed. "I promise. She hasn't been the sweetest to you but that's partly my fault."

"How so?"

"I made it clear before your arrival that I wasn't looking forward to having you here." She sat forward, placing her now empty mug on the coffee table. "You have to understand it wasn't personal. When I first met Hayley I was concerned, naturally, because my father, although he had dated, had never been serious about someone. I worried that she was a gold digger. But if she is one, then she's a very good actress."

"Hayley likes society life," I said. "I won't say that she doesn't. But she loves Theo. She's dated some idiots in the past but she was never serious about them. Theo makes her feel safe. You of all people should get that."

"I do. And that's the impression I got when I met her so I decided to give my support but continue to look out for my father's best interests. Keep my eye on things. You...you were a problem."

"How?"

"It's easy hiding a huge secret like this from my dad, because as close as we are, I'm a teenage girl and he gives me my privacy. But having another teenage girl in the house and hanging around my friends, I started to freak out that somehow you'd find out I was gay." She grunted. "Apparently not such an irrational fear, after all."

Suddenly everything started to make sense. "So that's why you were cold to me?"

"The only reason I even invited you to sit with my friends is because Daddy had Headmaster Vanderbilt spying on us, and he ratted me out." She narrowed her eyes on me. "I could tell you didn't trust any of us. Now I think it's got something to do with your dad."

"Yeah," I admitted.

"You should know my father is a really good man."

"Except for the whole intolerance to gay people."

She flinched. "It's not like he wants to burn gay people at the stake. He…just doesn't understand it. That means he's flawed, not that he's not a good guy. Okay. You *are* safe here."

I was grateful for her reassurances considering the emotional mess she currently was in over her own problems. "So are you. Listen to what you just said. You should consider telling your dad. It doesn't mean anyone else has to know."

"No." She stood up abruptly, anger filling her eyes. "And you have to promise you're not going to say anything to him."

"I promise." I held up my hands. After all, Eloise knew her father better than I did. "I promise. I will never speak of this to anyone. It's not my secret to tell."

Her shoulders relaxed, and she slowly lowered herself back onto the sofa.

We were silent for a while until she said, her voice so low I had to strain to hear her, "Have you ever been terrified of who you are?"

Fire burned in my chest as our eyes met across the room. I thought about how hard I found it to trust anyone, unable to let them truly in. "Yes. I'm scared who I am means I'm going to be alone for the rest of my life."

Her mouth trembled with emotion. "Me, too."

Something eased inside of me at having admitted that, and at having her understand. "Do you think it's supposed to be this complicated?"

"I don't know." Eloise sighed heavily. "Every day is hard and confusing and complex, and more times than I'd like I feel sad and furious at everything and everyone. But I do get up and I get through every day because I remind myself that I have things that other people don't, and I have love in my life, but most importantly I have hope, India. I have hope that someday, once I'm out of high school, things will change for me. That I'll be stronger and that this horrible fear I have of losing my dad over this will go away somehow, and I can be me. Really be me. *That's* what gets me through high school."

As her words percolated, I felt my admiration for her begin to grow. More than that, I felt like she was holding up a mirror in front of me, and I didn't like everything I saw reflected back at me. "You're stronger than you think. Jesus…"

"What?"

"I've spent the last five years holding people at a distance, especially my friends, because I thought I knew something they didn't. I was hurting so much that I couldn't see how anybody else could hurt more… I've been kind of a selfish, distant asshole."

"You're not alone in that."

"But that's the point. You and Finn…you have all this money and privilege and power…but it didn't save you from pain. I guess I thought you were narrow-minded overprivileged snobs who didn't know the first thing about life—turns out I'm the narrow-minded one."

"No, you're not," she assured me. "If you were narrow-minded, you would have failed to be kind to me today."

"There are different kinds of narrow-mindedness," I argued.

Laughing, she held up her hands in surrender. "Okay, you were narrow-minded about us. But now you know the truth. Life is what you make it, no matter where you come from."

"Life is what you make it," I murmured. "Yeah. That's kind of my motto."

"And you want to rule the school," she reminded me.

"I do." But I wasn't sure it was that important anymore. Still, it had been my focus for so long I was kind of scared to want anything else from life.

"I can help with that. You're now officially only the second person in the whole world that really knows me. And I'm not currently talking to the other person since he outed me. So you're it. That means we're stuck with each other, O sister-to-be, and I don't think that's a bad thing. You guard my secret, I'll take you to the top."

"I'll guard your secret without payment," I said, a little annoyed by the "bribe."

Eloise grinned. "And that, my friend, is why I'm *happy* to take you to the top."

Relief warmed me. "So we're definitely okay?"

"Yeah." She cocked her head to the side, contemplating me. "About Finn, though..."

My stomach flipped at the mention of him. "Yeah?"

"He and I made a pact, and I'm sorry but I have to hold him to it. It's just until college. However, Finn likes you, and as angry as I am at him right now...you've been cool so if you two want to see each other in secret then I guess I'm okay with that."

The thought of being able to touch and kiss Finn, to hang out and listen to him and to talk to him, and just *be* with him, was definitely exciting. I wanted to get to know him better. But I wasn't sure I could cope with a secret relationship, with being "the other woman." I wasn't sure how good a secret relationship would be for my self-esteem.

Eloise seemed to sense my reluctance. "I've never seen him so caught up in someone before. He really likes you," she insisted.

I exhaled, long and slow. "I don't know."

She held up her hands. "Hey, your choice. I'm just letting you know I'll be all right about it, as long as you both are supercareful about keeping it under wraps."

"We'll see. As for you and Finn…he loves you. I know you must feel betrayed by him telling me but I promise it just happened and he feels awful about it. Please forgive him."

Eloise lowered her gaze. "I know all that's true but it doesn't change what he did or how much it hurts. I just need time."

Those butterflies Eloise had mentioned raged to life as soon as I pulled into the parking lot at Maggie's. I parked Eloise's Jaguar next to Finn's Aston Martin and gave up any hope that the cars wouldn't draw attention to us. They were giant, expensive beacons. Alone they were bad enough. Together… well, I just knew as soon as I entered the diner the customers and staff were going to watch me with curiosity.

Hopefully we knew no one in Waltham.

I was right. I felt the burn of attention on me as I searched for Finn. I found him in a booth at the back. He must have requested it, because there were no other diners near it. He sat up a little straighter when he saw me.

Was his heart pounding as hard as mine?

To my surprise he got up before I could reach him and met me halfway.

He touched my waist and my whole body seemed to explode in tingles of awareness. "They stop looking after a while," he muttered, his eyes flicking around at the room.

"You sure?" I was uneasy about talking to Finn privately when there were so many eyes on us.

"Yeah. Let's sit."

I nodded, my heart pounding no less hard as Finn's hand moved from the curve of my waist to my lower back. He kept it there as he guided me toward the booth.

I was in my seat two seconds when a girl with dark blond hair dressed in the diner uniform appeared at the booth. "What can I get you?"

"I'll just have a Diet Coke and some fries," I said, not really caring what I ordered since it was doubtful I'd be able to eat anything.

"Same, but make mine a regular," Finn said.

Once she was gone I looked at Finn, our eyes connecting. Just that made my skin hot. Our silence began to stretch, however, and I knew one of us was going to have to speak before the tension proved too much.

"I hung out with Eloise this morning," I said.

His dark eyes lit up. "Yeah?"

"Yeah. Got her to trust me a little. Talk to me about it."

"She told me she needed space, so I've been worrying about her all day." He closed his eyes briefly. "It makes me selfish but I'm relieved—relieved that someone else knows. That *you* know. But I also feel like crap. Eloise has never been this mad at me before. Do you think she'll forgive me?"

"Yes," I said with certainty. "And forgive yourself, okay.

It must have been hard for you both that you were the only person who knew."

"Now you know, too," he said. "I'm sorry for making you a part of the secret."

"Don't be. It means she's got someone else looking out for her. She seems so scared."

"Wouldn't you be?"

"I don't know."

"This is Theodore Fairweather's daughter we're talking about, India. He's not exactly about acceptance when it comes to the gay community."

"That's what Elle said."

"Well, she's right. Which makes me blurting it out..."

"Hey." I touched his arm without even thinking about it. "Please stop beating yourself up about it. It's done. And, Finn, I know you blurted it out but do you really think that would have happened with just anyone? You trust me. Right?"

"I do." He stared at my hand on his arm before lifting his eyes to mine. Trust mixed with longing and affection and admiration and all these wonderful things were open in his expression for me to see.

I withdrew my hand, knowing I still wasn't sure what we were to each other.

He sighed at my withdrawal.

"You're worried about what Eloise will think, right? Once she, hopefully, stops being mad at me I'm going to talk to her."

"Actually, she talked to me about us. She said as angry as she is at you, she would be okay with us as long as you kept pretending to date her and we saw each other in secret."

Finn's whole face lit up in relief and then he immediately frowned at what he saw in my eyes.

"Two sodas and two fries." The waitress suddenly appeared and dropped our food on the table.

I waited until she'd left before answering Finn's silent question. "I don't know if I'm up for sneaking around behind everyone's back."

"Don't think about it like that. I owe Elle more than ever now. We'd just be protecting her secret."

"By making whatever is between us a secret."

"I made a promise." His tone was unapologetic, but his expression wasn't. His soulful dark eyes seemed to plead with me. "I can't back out of that promise."

"I understand." I stared at my fries, finding it difficult being around him without wanting to just throw up my hands and give in to the idea of us.

"What exactly about hiding us bothers you?"

"I don't know," I answered instantly. At his scowling silence, I insisted. "I don't. I'm trying to work that out myself. I just know it makes me uneasy. It doesn't feel right."

"It's not like I'd be cheating on Eloise." He reached for my hand and goose bumps rose up on my arms at the slide of his callused skin against my soft palm. Because of rowing, he was a rich boy with working man's hands.

I liked the contradiction of his hands. I liked the feel of them holding mine. I more than liked it.

"I know," I said. "I know that. I just..." Reluctantly I began to pull my hand away but Finn, even more reluctant to let go, held fast. I stopped moving and looked him straight in the eye. "I can't—"

"I can't stop thinking about our kiss," he cut me off.

My eyes grew round at the heat in his as he began to rub his thumb over the top of my hand. The heat he was feeling began to build in me.

"Finn," I whispered, pleading now.

"I'll tell you everything you want to know. About me and Elle. About other girls. Whatever you need. But you should know that our kiss blew my mind."

"Other girls?" I frowned and then bit my lip, annoyed that that was the thing that had caught my attention in all he'd said.

His smirk was a little smug and arrogant. I pulled at my hand but he held on even tighter. "Jealous?"

"Don't be a dipshit."

He laughed. Hard. And my God, it was such a good look on him. He needed to laugh and smile more. Definitely.

You could be the one to help him do that.

Ahh! I shoved that thought quickly out of my head.

"Okay." His chuckle trailed off. "I'll try not to be a dipshit. As for other girls—Florida. Every summer I stay at my mother's parents' house. They're not wealthy like my father but they retired there and have a good life. They're not close to my father. They had fights with him about getting to see more of me. He finally gave in and allowed me to have a month every summer with them. It's the best month of the year."

"I'll bet," I muttered. "Do they know the truth?"

"No. There would be no point. It would only upset them and there's nothing that people like them can do to win against a man like my father. According to him he has powerful men in his pocket. I'm not sure if it's friendship or blackmail, I just know my father is connected, ruthless, powerful and he never loses. So I'm stuck."

His dismal assessment of the situation only highlighted to me not only why Finn was so desperate to find small pieces of happiness, but also why he and I could never work in the long term. His father didn't like me, and when it came time for Finn and me to go public, his father wouldn't be happy. I didn't like to think what he might do in an attempt to put a stop to me and Finn as a couple.

Finn seemed to sense that was where my mind was going because he decided to change the subject. "There were girls in Florida," he admitted. "Nothing serious. Just girls to hang out with."

I read between the lines. "Have sex with, you mean?"

Finn wrapped his hand around my wrist and leaned across the table. Not for the first time I saw and felt the passion inside of him. "It was just sex. An escape. You're not that, India. You have to believe me. I would never have betrayed Elle for just some girl I wanted to sleep with."

His fervor was exciting, a little intoxicating. I was all logic and plans and keeping myself safe, whereas Finn was emotion and risk and right now all about diving off a very big waterfall with me.

"Does Eloise know about the other girls?"

"What would be the point? They were temporary in a temporary situation. And Elle and I are pretending, remember. All we've ever done is a quick kiss on the lips in public."

"Why are you telling me about the other girls?"

"I don't know." He sighed and glanced away for a moment, seeming to gather his thoughts. "I guess I want to tell you everything. I've spent the last few years of my life not telling people about my father or about Eloise. Over time I guess I just stopped telling them anything. It was hard, but it never bothered me until I met you. I want to tell you everything. I want *you* to tell *me* everything."

Oh my God, why did he have to be such a romantic pain in my ass?

"I'm getting to you, aren't I?" There was that smug smile again.

I rolled my eyes and managed to extricate my hand from his. I settled back in the booth, taking a little bit of distance from him. "You are so confusing."

He frowned. "How?"

"You can be so…"

"So what?"

"Arrogant. And then so…"

"So what?"

"Not arrogant."

His mouth twitched with laughter. "O-kay."

"Do you think I'm a foregone conclusion?"

All amusement fled his features. "No, India. I don't. I think you have more defenses than a citadel."

Now I struggled to contain my smile. "Yeah?"

"Yes. And it's annoying when I'm trying to get you to see how much I really want to try this with you. I want you any way I can get you."

"Oh, really?" I teased.

He laughed, rethinking his word choice. "I didn't mean it like that."

"So you don't want me?"

At the sudden burning in his eyes I wished I had stopped while I was ahead. "Oh, I want you."

I felt this strange but wonderful flutter low, low in my belly.

Oh boy.

"Say yes," he pressed. "I really do want to know everything about you. I can only do that if you say yes."

"Everything?" Fear mingled with excitement at the thought.

For so long it had just been me. That way I wasn't vulnerable to anyone hurting me. I'd wanted friendship with Finn knowing I'd be giving some of myself over to him.

But Finn was asking me for more than friendship. He was asking for secrets. Longings. Dreams. Fears. Kisses. Touch. Maybe even sex.

Everything.

Was I ready for that?

When I took too long to give him the answer he wanted, Finn pulled out his wallet and threw some money on the table. I watched apprehensively, wondering if I'd blown it and so goddamn confused at myself, as he stood up.

He held out his hand for me but I didn't know what that meant. It could have just been part of his breeding to not leave a girl sitting at a table alone even if she was driving him crazy.

I tentatively took his hand and he gently pulled me up.

He led me with long strides out of the diner and into the parking lot.

The blood was whooshing in my ears, my heart was pounding so hard.

As soon as we reached our cars Finn suddenly turned around and yanked me toward him. I slammed with a gasp up against his hard chest only to then find myself pressed up against my car.

His dark eyes were so hot they were almost black and his chest heaved hard against mine.

When I didn't say anything or protest at being sandwiched between him and the car, he slowly lowered his head.

My breath stuttered and my eyes fluttered closed in anticipation.

At the soft, feathery brush of his lips against mine I curled my fingers into his shirt and clung tight. It wasn't like the hard, desperate kiss of the night before but it was no less passionate. It was slow, tender and definitely meant to seduce me into Finn's way of thinking.

And it was more than working.

Finn broke the kiss, his hot breath tickling my mouth as he whispered, "Say yes."

I thought of Eloise today and how brave she had been to sit with me and let me in.

Be brave, India.

"Yes," I whispered.

The beautiful and entirely far too sexy grin he gave me was worth the courage. "I almost don't know what to do with you now."

I chuckled and bowed my head, resting my forehead on his strong chest. "I guess we'll just have to take it a day at a time."

"Yeah." His arms wrapped tighter around me and his chin came to a rest on my head.

We stood there just holding one another for a while and it was perfect.

Beautiful in a way I hadn't experienced.

"We should probably learn some ninja spy skills," he murmured.

Amusement made me shake against him. "Ninja spy skills?" I lifted my head to look up at him.

He was grinning at me like a little boy and it occurred to me that already I was getting to see a side of him I'd never seen before. "For all the sneaking around we'll be doing."

I cocked my head to the side. "And where would one learn said ninja spy skills?"

"From a ninja spy master, of course."

I giggled. "Of course. And where will we find him?"

"Or her."

"Or her." I liked that he'd thought of that.

"Car wash?"

"A car wash?"

"An antiques store? Library? Security room in a supermarket?"

Leaning into him I felt this giddiness burst through me, making me light and carefree in a way I couldn't remember feeling before. Finn Rochester had surprised me again.

And I loved it.

"He could be somewhere more obvious like a dojo."

"Do you really think a ninja spy master would be lurking somewhere so obvious?"

"Sometimes obvious is the least obvious."

He thought about that a second and then shook his head. "No. I'm definitely thinking antiques store."

"Okay, fine." I slid my hands down his chest to grip his waist and I noted how my touch made his eyelids lower in this really cute, sexy way. I decided touching him a lot would be on the agenda since I doubted physical affection was something he'd received a lot of in the last few years. "What kind of stuff will our ninja spy master teach us?"

He stepped closer, pressing deeper into my body in a way that made me lose my breath and the ability to tease. "All the ways in which I can get you alone without anyone knowing where to find us."

"Oh." I smiled slowly at the thought. "I think I'm going to enjoy the fruits of those lessons."

Finn grinned and held me tighter.

CHAPTER 15

"SO YOU AND Finn finally did it?"

Bryce skipped to a stop in front of Eloise. We were standing at Elle's locker Monday morning and Bryce had one perfectly waxed eyebrow raised in question.

Charlotte was behind her giving Elle an embarrassed, almost apologetic smile.

Eloise seemed to take a minute to register the question and then she looked back at me as if asking for guidance.

The truth was if she and Finn were to keep up their lie, then people had to think they did the things that high school couples in love did.

I gave her an imperceptible nod.

Still confused, she turned back to Bryce. "How did...?"

"India told us she accidentally walked in on you guys in the pool house Saturday night and then Finn returned alone with this lame excuse that you were so drunk he'd put you to bed. More like exhausted." Bryce nudged her and gave her a devious smirk. "Needed a little Dutch courage, did you? Well, who cares! The deed is finally done. Joshua and Gabe will finally get off Finn's back about it. I have to admit I was starting to feel sorry for the guy."

Elle glowered at her. "When have I ever discussed my love life with you?"

"Never. That's why I was so excited to hear you're actually human."

Ignoring that comment, Elle took a step toward Bryce and lowered her voice. "I am not a piece of juicy information on one of those low-grade gossip vlogs you watch. I keep my love life with Finn private because that's what it is. Private."

"Well, excuse me for showing interest in my best friend's life."

Not wanting Eloise's defensiveness to cause a fight that would only make her anxious, I hurried to intervene, verbal diarrhea launching out of me. "Well, I'm still a virgin."

Bryce's and Charlotte's mouths dropped open and they were successfully diverted. "You?" Bryce said in disbelief.

I decided to ignore the insult, already freaking out about the consequences of my confession.

"Really?" Charlotte pushed forward. "Because so am I. I have to admit, I was a little upset about being the last in the group but now I know you're one, too, I feel better."

"You're a virgin because you're a prude." Bryce waved her off and turned to me. "But why are you a virgin? I thought you had lots of boyfriends back in, ugh, California."

Charlotte flinched. I scowled at Bryce. "I never said I had lots. I said I'd dated quite a bit. Dated. Not hooked up."

"You don't present yourself as the shy, retiring wallflower type, so why haven't you done the deed? Is there something wrong with you?"

I shrugged. "I'll have sex when I want to have sex."

"I am not a prude," Charlotte muttered, her cheeks bright red with anger.

Bryce nudged her with her shoulder. "Oh, come on. You need to lighten up a little."

Eloise looked mad but she kept quiet, possibly afraid entering the conversation would lead Bryce back to questioning her about her and Finn's sex life.

I opened my mouth to suggest we walk to class but just then Finn appeared in the hall. He stopped between Bryce and Elle. "Hey. Why are you guys all huddled up? Something going on?"

"We're having an interesting conversation here, Rochester. Before I could get the juicy details on your deflowering of our queen, India announced that she's a virgin." Bryce grinned up at him.

My blood turned hot with mortification as Finn turned to me in surprise.

I wanted the ground to open up and swallow me whole.

"What is wrong with you?" Eloise stared at her friend in disbelief. "You know you've always been a bit of a bitch but lately you're taking it to new levels of mean."

Bryce flinched. "I'm just kidding around."

"Well, get a clue, Bryce, because no one is laughing." Eloise grabbed Finn's hand and gestured to me. "Let's get to class."

As we walked away, Bryce said, "So what? India is your new best friend and suddenly I'm roadkill? You ignored me on WhatsApp yesterday."

"Yes, I ignored the new, meaner you. Learn to apologize and maybe we can all return to normal. Are you coming, Charlotte?"

Relief flooded Charlotte's features that she wasn't in the doghouse with Elle, too, and she scurried over to us.

We walked into Microeconomics class, and I grabbed ahold of Eloise's arm and pulled her toward me before she hit her seat. "Do you think it's wise putting Bryce out in the cold?" I whispered.

I saw the worry on her face. "I'll talk to her," she whispered back. "Something's going on with her. She's not usually this cruel. I just couldn't take it this morning. And you said what you said to help me out. I didn't want her to be mean to you because of it. But I'll talk to her," she repeated.

Bryce appeared in the doorway with Joshua just as I was sitting down behind Finn.

As for Finn, he seemed to be avoiding my gaze.

Great.

Had the virgin thing flipped him out?

Bryce glowered at us but stubbornly refused to sit anywhere but her usual seat. Joshua seemed confused by the tense atmosphere as he sat down. "Does someone want to let me know what's happening here?"

"What's happening where?" Gabe appeared.

"Everyone is acting weird," Joshua said.

"Probably because everyone knows Finn and Elle had sex at her father's engagement party on Saturday." Gabe grinned.

I closed my eyes, feeling all eyes on us.

Because Gabe had said it loud.

Very loud.

Now everyone definitely knew the lie I'd spun.

I opened my eyes and peeked at Elle. She was blushing but didn't look too miserable about the whole thing.

I glanced back at Finn, who felt my stare and looked up at

me. His expression was embarrassed and apologetic, and I tried to communicate silently that he had nothing to apologize for.

"Thank you, Gabe, for that social news announcement," our teacher said. "Now if you're done embarrassing Miss Fairweather and Mr. Rochester, perhaps we can get on with class."

"Sadly that is all the juicy information I have to share today, so go ahead, sir." Gabe laughed, in no way apologetic.

Word spread quickly about Finn and Eloise, and while she was clearly embarrassed, her earlier defensiveness with Bryce was gone. Although Charlotte kept trying to reassure her friend, thinking Elle was miserable about the gossip, I knew Elle was now good with it. It was only authenticating her and Finn's relationship lie. She'd even mouthed, "Thank you," to me when we were leaving Microeconomics.

When I walked into Modern European History, however, Finn did not look happy. I sat down beside him and he immediately leaned over to whisper to me. "I'm sorry."

"Why?"

"I've got guys slapping me on the back and giving me their 'way to gos.' I don't want you to see that."

"Finn," I whispered back, "you have nothing to be sorry about. I'm the one that started the rumor. And I encouraged Elle to go with it."

"So you're okay?"

"I'm fine. I promise."

Franklin strolled into the class as Finn leaned back in his chair.

I tried to listen to Franklin, I really did. But it turned out that as much as I was aware of Finn before we confessed our feelings for one another, I was even more so now.

Last night I'd gotten home and after letting Elle know Finn

and I were going to try the whole secret relationship thing, I'd curled up on my bed with my ereader. The romance I was reading was suddenly more poignant, more engrossing, and the sex scenes woke up my body in a way they hadn't before.

I bit my lip, trying not to smile right there in class.

For a long while I'd thought there was something wrong with me because I didn't feel how my friends seemed to feel when a boy kissed them.

Now I knew it was because I hadn't met the right boy until now.

I snuck a look at Finn from the corner of my eye and felt my breath catch.

He was staring at me.

He caught me looking and quickly looked away.

I almost laughed.

Crap.

We weren't doing a very good job so far of keeping our feelings off the grid.

It looked like he and I needed to talk about what "covert" meant.

I was early, heading toward the media room for the *Chronicle* meeting. Eloise and I had just parted ways, as she headed toward the theater for rehearsals.

It had been a weird day.

The vibe I got from Finn and Eloise in the cafeteria was that they were happy. Everyone seemed to notice it and put it down to the fact that their relationship was now on the next level. Elle had obviously talked to Bryce because she sat at the table and seemed to be on good behavior. Well, good behavior for Bryce.

It all seemed hunky-dory in their world.

Our world, I should say.

Yet, as excited as I was about Finn and as relieved as I was for Elle, I felt uncomfortable with the lies. I'd spent a long time keeping my past a secret but I didn't think of that as lying so much as evading. Some might say there wasn't much of a difference but it felt like a difference to me. I never actually said anything that wasn't true. I just didn't say everything that could be said. In this case we were outright lying to everyone, and I suddenly realized what life for Finn and Elle was like all the time.

If I felt uncomfortable in my own skin, then surely they must feel a hundred times worse.

Today it wasn't showing on them, though.

My doubts about sneaking around with Finn were rearing their ugly heads again and, as if he knew that, Finn suddenly appeared by my side in the empty hallway.

He grabbed my hand, startling me, and I'd just said, "Finn?" when I found myself being jerked unceremoniously into the art room where Finn's darkroom was.

Butterflies raged to life in my belly as he marched me through the room, threw open the darkroom door, hauled me inside, slammed the door shut and pushed me up against it.

"Fi—" My question was cut off by his lips on mine. I sighed into his kiss, and as he pressed his body into me, his grip on my waist tightened.

Wrapping my arms around his neck, I held on for dear life as my doubts were obliterated by the excitement I felt in simply being with him.

When we finally came up for air, I gave a breathless little laugh and stared up into his shadowed face. "Well, that was some hello."

He kissed the tip of my nose, his hands sliding around my

back to pull me into him. "I've been dying to do that all day. I swear I thought I was just going to launch myself across the table at you at lunch today."

I chuckled. "As fun as that would have been it's probably good you didn't."

"Yeah. Things are a little crazy. But Eloise's happy. We talked today."

"You're good?"

"Yeah, she says she's still hurt, which kills, and I'm going to make sure I never hurt her again. Especially since she says she forgives me. Mostly because you're being so cool." He grinned now. "I think she really likes you."

"You sound surprised."

"I thought she'd see you as a threat. But you've won her over. You have a habit of doing that," he murmured, and brushed his mouth over mine.

My lips tingled. "I love how you kiss."

Finn looked pleased and a little smug. "Yeah?"

"Mmm." I decided to ignore his smugness. "I never liked kissing until now."

In answer he kissed me softly. "Never." Kiss. "Before." Kiss. "Now?"

"Nope."

"Is that why…?" He trailed off, suddenly looking unsure.

"Is that why, what?"

"I shouldn't ask."

"Well, you've started so you might as well finish," I teased.

His hold on me tightened, his expression sober. "Is that why you're a virgin? You didn't like this…stuff…?"

I answered thoughtlessly, so busy enjoying exploring him, feeling him close, I didn't think beyond my words. "I liked when the guys I dated touched me, just not the mouth-to-mouth part."

Finn tensed. "Touched you?"

"That—"

"Touched you how?"

It was my turn to tense. "You thought I wasn't a virgin, right?" I said softly, cajoling. "So why does this matter?"

"Touched you how?" he repeated.

"Finn." I hoped he heard the warning in my voice.

He did. "I just don't like the idea of you with anyone else."

I remembered how jealous I felt yesterday when he told me about the girls in Florida. "I get it. But it's the past, right? None of those guys made me feel the way you make me feel."

"Ditto on the girls." His voice was rough as he leaned his forehead against mine. "God, sometimes it feels like too much."

"Good," I breathed. "I'd rather you feel too much than too little."

In answer he kissed me again, this time harder, more desperate, until I felt his body pressing against me. Flushed, tingling all over, needy in a way I'd never felt before, I pulled away to catch my breath. "We need to stop. I need to get to the meeting, and I can't look like I've been making out with a hot guy in a darkroom."

He laughed, the sound low and delicious. "Yeah, I guess. When can I see you alone again, though?"

"Tomorrow? After school? We could pretend we need to study together."

"Eloise might cover for us—pretend I'm there to see her instead."

"Hmm, I don't know. I don't want to use her like that."

"Hey." He kissed my jaw, near my ear. "She's using me,

remember?" He bit my earlobe gently, making me shiver. He pulled back. "She's fine with this."

"But we should hang out with her, too. We're the only 'real' people she has in her life at the moment. We should be there for her."

Finn stared at me, his expression soft. "You're a good person, you know that?"

"No, I'm not," I said automatically. I was a selfish person. I'd had to be in order to survive the aftermath of my father.

"If you weren't a good person you'd be worrying more about where to find a place to be alone with your stepsister's boyfriend than whether or not your stepsister was lonely."

I almost laughed at the ridiculousness of his sentence. "I just… I feel like I get her in some ways. And I respect her."

"Okay. We'll hang out with her, too. I love Elle. I have no problem with spending time with her. But I do want to find time for just us."

"We will," I promised, sliding my hands down his back. "We need to."

He groaned and reluctantly stepped back. "You need to leave."

I gave him a quick kiss on his cheek, grinning mischievously as I did so. "Okay. See you tomorrow."

I left him, feeling light and happy. I'd forgotten about the lies and the discomfort and the doubt, and felt nothing but anticipation for the next time I could get Finn Rochester alone.

CHAPTER 16

"HEY, CAN I look at your notes for Microeconomics? I've been going over mine for the last few classes and they're useless," I said to Eloise over breakfast a few Saturdays later.

She swallowed a piece of croissant and nodded. "Would you like me to go over them with you?"

"Yeah, if you're offering."

"In exchange, maybe you can help me run some lines for the play? Bryce was doing it but she keeps making fun of the whole thing." She didn't have to say that Bryce was still acting like a hyperversion of her mean girl self over her father dating Charlotte's mother.

"Sure, no problem."

"I thought maybe we could talk Finn into hitting Charles Street before the movie today. I need new notebooks."

"Ooh, me, too," I said.

"Ah, two against one." Eloise smiled.

A throat cleared to our right, and we both turned our heads

that way. Hayley was sitting frozen with a piece of toast in her mouth, eyes wide, while Theo was staring at us in bemusement. He had been the throat clearer.

"You two are getting along," he said carefully.

For the past few weeks we'd hardly seen our parents. Hayley was always busy with wedding plans and Theo had a big case at work that was keeping him at the office late. They'd missed recent developments between me and Eloise.

"Yes, Daddy." Eloise shrugged and turned back to me. "Do you think it would be pushing our luck to get Finn to stop by Boylston Street, too? I have my eye on a Prada bag."

"Definitely pushing your luck."

She slumped with a sigh. "I thought so."

Eloise did manage to talk Finn into stopping by Prada but only in exchange for him getting to choose the movie.

That meant watching the latest bestselling thriller-novel-turned-movie, but Elle and I both enjoyed it so it wasn't such a bad deal.

We were sitting in Lulu's afterward, Elle and Finn sitting beside each other for the sake of keeping up appearances. I sat across from them sipping my latte and chuckling as Finn teased Elle about the girl at the popcorn counter of the movie theater.

"I'm telling you she was checking you out."

Elle blushed and gave me a pleading look. "Would you tell him to stop?"

I grinned but threw my napkin at Finn. "Stop it."

"Just sayin'," he murmured, still smiling to himself as he took a sip of coffee.

Elle rolled her eyes. "Can we talk about something that actually has a point? Like our Microeconomics assignment."

"It has a point?" Finn and I said in unison.

We grinned at each other.

That got us another eye roll from Eloise. "Fine. We won't talk about schoolwork. It's not like it's important or anything."

"We could think up a way of getting me out of going to Austria with my father at Christmas."

Elle and I shared a look. Although I was the only one who knew how bad things could get with Finn's father, Elle knew enough to wish things were better for Finn at home. "We could tell him I'm pregnant," Elle said deadpan. "You know, to lighten his mood when you explain you can't go to Austria."

I snorted.

Finn smirked at her. "I dare you to tell him you're pregnant."

"Are you kidding? I'm pretty sure that man can shrink someone with his steely stare alone. We'll think of something else."

"Hey, what are you guys doing here?"

We glanced up as Bryce and Joshua walked over to us, holding hands. Bryce had narrowed her eyes on me. "Third-wheeling their dates now, India?"

"Bryce," Joshua warned.

She shrugged and took a seat at our table. Joshua stayed standing. "Well?" she snapped up at him. "Coming or going?"

He scowled at her but took a seat at the table.

Bryce turned her attention to Elle and Finn. "We were passing and saw you guys in here. Thought we'd join. We haven't been on a double date in ages," she said.

Finn shot me an apologetic look while Elle shifted uncomfortably.

"You know what we were just talking about?" Bryce

grinned. "Do you remember two years ago at Honor Ruffalo's pool party—"

"The floater!" Elle laughed. "How did I forget about that?"

"What made you think of that?" Finn grinned at Joshua.

Joshua shrugged. "Bryce was talking about having an indoor pool party over winter break. I was reminding her of the downsides."

"He's being a downer." She threw him a dirty look. "But what's new?"

Before Joshua could react to her gibe, Elle tried to alleviate the tension between boyfriend and girlfriend.

"To be fair the floater culprit was never found." She shuddered in exaggeration.

"Oh, sweetie, are you thinking about how it nearly touched you?" Bryce reached over to squeeze her hand in sympathy. "Thank God Finn saw it and pulled you out of the way."

"My hero." She snorted and nudged him with her shoulder.

They all laughed, moving on from the story about the floater to another about a fifth grade party where a few kids got sick on punch and caused a vomiting domino effect.

I began to feel like the third wheel Bryce had accused me of being as it became more and more like a double date between the four of them. Finn and Elle naturally became more affectionate with each other as the trip down memory lane went on. They didn't cut me out deliberately. Bryce was leading this particular venture into nostalgia-land and I had no doubt she was doing it on purpose to make me feel left out.

But it wasn't really her I was upset with.

I hated that I couldn't sit beside Finn. I hated that his arm was around Elle and not me. I hated that no one knew he was my boyfriend, not hers.

None of that bothered me when it was just Finn, Elle and me in our little bubble together.

It bothered me in situations like this, and it bothered me that I had to pretend that it didn't bother me.

"I have this week's book to read and review for the *Chronicle*," I said, cutting off Bryce. "I'm going to head back."

"We'll come with you," Elle said.

"No, really, I have to work." I stood, grabbing my purse. "You guys stay."

Finn frowned up at me. "I'm your ride."

"I'll get a cab." I smiled, hoping it didn't seem false. "I'll see you guys later."

I avoided Bryce's smug smile as I left.

At the knock on my door two hours later, I rolled over on my bed. I sat up immediately at the sight of Finn in my doorway. "Hi."

"Hey." He stepped inside and closed the door. "Elle's downstairs. She said she'll keep a lookout for Hayley and Theo."

I didn't say anything, just watched as he made his way over to the bed and climbed on next to me. He stretched out beside me, his elbow bent, head resting in his hand, and he stared right into my eyes.

"Why did you leave Lulu's?"

"I had a paper to do," I said.

"Really?"

I actually did. "Do you want me to show it to you?"

"No." He reached out and curled a strand of my hair behind my ear. "I just want to make sure you're okay."

I gave him a reassuring smile. "I'm fine."

He shifted closer. "Promise?"

"Yes." I leaned in and pressed a soft kiss to his lips. When I pulled back he was frowning at me. "What is it?"

"Did you ever have a birthday party growing up?"

Surprised by the question, I shook my head.

"Not one?"

I moved to shake my head again and then I remembered... "No, I did. I sometimes forget stuff from then but before Hayley left...yeah... I had an eighth birthday party."

"Yeah? What was it like?"

"I don't know." I moved to sit up. "Do you want to listen to some music?"

"India." He rested a hand on my shoulder and gently pushed me back down. "You never talk about your life before your mom left."

"There's not a lot to say."

"What about your eighth birthday party?"

I remembered everything was purple and silver because I loved purple and silver. Purple and silver balloons and banners. A purple and silver cake. A purple dress, silver shoes. Even Hayley wore purple and silver. She made purple invitations and wrote them out in silver ink. She wrapped my presents in purple and silver, too.

It was the best birthday ever.

"I don't want to talk about this," I snapped, and twisted away from him, moving off the bed.

"Hey." Finn caught me around the waist and pulled me back against him. "I'm sorry," he said in my ear. "We don't have to talk about it."

After a moment I relaxed against him. "We can talk about anything else," I whispered, not wanting to disappoint him. "Just not her, okay?"

"Okay." He squeezed me.

A little while later we lay on the bed, his arms around me, my back to his chest, and there was no tension between us, just sweet contentment.

"So tell me about this floater?" I said.

Finn tensed at me ruining the moment and then he began to shake, the bed shaking with him, and his laughter filled my ears.

I relaxed, the crappy scene Bryce caused at Lulu's and the feelings it brought out in me disappearing at the sound of Finn's laughter.

When he sobered he held me that little bit tighter. "Instead of the floater, why don't I tell you about my mom?"

I had no objections to that at all. I wanted to know everything about Finn. "I'd like that."

"She liked a good birthday party," he said immediately. "I had one every year while she was alive. She liked themes. One year it was superheroes, another villains, another computer game characters, another Grimm fairy tales. I was Rumpelstiltskin that year. Very creepy."

I chuckled. "I'll bet."

"Just a little while before she got cancer, she had me help her throw a birthday party for this kid she was treating. This little girl had a problem with her heart and she was in the foster care system. While my mom treated her she was living in a girls' home so she had no one. My mom realized her birthday was coming up and we threw the little girl a party in the children's ward. Her name was Sophie. I made a banner for her. She looked so amazed. She cried and when I asked her why she was crying she said no one had ever thrown her a party before. I felt really bad. That year I'd complained because I didn't want a party.

"I wished I never complained. I wished I'd told my mom how awesome I thought she was."

At the sadness in his voice I turned around so I could see his face. "She knew, Finn. She knew."

I snuggled against him and he held me tight.

"She dressed me up as a sasquatch when I was five, though. I think I'm allowed to be mad at her for that."

I gave a bark of laughter, pulling back to gaze up into his eyes. "Is there photographic evidence?"

He grinned. "I'll never tell."

A few weeks later…

"You don't like Will Ferrell?" Finn said, his expression horrified. "No one dislikes Will Ferrell."

"Uh, correction, no one dislikes Steve Carell, but I didn't say I disliked Will Ferrell. I have no idea what he's like as a human being."

"I'm guessing awesome because he's awesome." Finn sat up on my bed. "Seriously? He creeps you out?"

I laughed. "You're really freaking out about this."

"What is it about him that creeps you out?"

"He has weird man-child eyes."

"Weird man-child eyes?"

"Yes. He has a man's face and body but the eyes of a child. They have this innocence that is completely incongruous to most of the stuff that comes out of his mouth. Why do you think he was so good in *Elf*? It was all in those man-child eyes. He has the eyes of a small boy who still believes in Christmas. It's creepy in the context of the rest of him."

Finn threw his head back in laughter, and I lay beside him, watching and enjoying every minute of it.

We'd now successfully been hiding our relationship from everyone for the last six weeks. During that time I'd seen Finn laugh a lot. It made me feel good that it was *me* who made him laugh so much.

The others had noticed the change in him, too. He was lighter, much less broody, and he cracked jokes and talked more. And of course he talked to me in public, which they all put down to his new good mood. And they all put his new good mood down to the fact that they thought Eloise was giving him some.

Honestly, I was a little disappointed that his friends thought Finn so shallow that his behavior could change so drastically over getting laid.

If they knew him, really knew him, they would know it would take more than that.

It would take someone to make him laugh, someone to listen to him, someone who was there for him in a way no one else had been before.

"What is so funny?" Eloise suddenly appeared in my doorway, grinning at us.

I patted the bed beside me. "Will Ferrell apparently."

"Nope," Finn corrected me. "India."

"Funny haha or funny strange," she said as she strode over and hopped up onto the bed beside us. "Because I'm voting funny strange."

"Har-de-har." I pushed her gently.

She grinned. "I didn't actually come in here to insult you. I heard a car on the drive. Hayley and Daddy are home."

I threw Finn a look. That could have been close. I turned back to Elle. "Thanks."

"No problem." She crawled over me and insinuated herself between us.

Our parents had still been caught up in work and wedding planning. The wedding was a few days before Christmas, only a few weeks away now. My life here was becoming more and more real, and I was daring to hope that it might be permanent, after all.

"I just got off the phone with Bryce." Eloise groaned and covered her eyes with her hand. "She and Joshua are still having problems."

"I wish he'd break up with her already." Finn sighed.

"Finn," I admonished.

"What?" He shrugged. "I've never been a big fan of Bryce. Josh is too good for her."

I didn't necessarily disagree. "She loves him."

"She should treat him better, then."

"She should treat everyone better, but I doubt that will happen."

"She *is* genuinely upset," Eloise muttered. "And my head is pounding from having to listen to her rant at me on the phone about how she suspects that he's cheating on her." Eloise peeked at me between her fingers. "Just a heads-up: you were a suspect, but I talked her out of that."

I made a face. "She has such a swell opinion of me."

Finn snorted.

Eloise giggled. "It's because you bond with him over music. I swear I've never met anyone as paranoid as that girl."

"I bond with Finn over music," I argued. It was true. Now that Finn and I were actually talking in public, it was mostly with Joshua about the bands we liked.

"Yes, but you *are* secretly hot for me." Finn winked at me. "So that's not the greatest argument in the world."

"Maybe I'm secretly hot for Joshua, too," I teased.

He gave me a look. "Don't make me hunt down and kill my best friend."

Eloise grunted. "Finn Rochester, caveman? Who knew?"

"Oh, that is tame for him," I told her. "Believe me."

"Huh." She grinned at him. "I'm seeing a new side to you these days, my friend."

I smiled because she looked genuinely happy for him.

Finn reached out and tapped the tip of her nose affectionately.

Her grin became a soft smile. "I started talking to this girl online."

His eyes grew round with curiosity while I nudged her. She looked at me, laughter in her eyes. "Tell us more," I urged.

"Her name is Sarah. She's seventeen. She's a senior at Cheltenham Girls' High School here in Boston. She's very witty and honest. I like talking to her. There's not much else to say."

"Is there flirting going on? Like hot flirting?" Finn grinned.

She smacked his arm. "I am not giving you material for lesbian fantasies."

I laughed. "I want to know if there is flirting going on, too."

Eloise rolled her eyes. She was grinning, though. "Lots of flirting."

Before I could dig for more information we heard footsteps outside my door.

We looked over and suddenly there was a knock.

Surprised, I called, "Come in."

We all sat up at the sight of Theo and Hayley standing in the doorway. They both wore huge grins on their faces as soon as they saw us together.

"We were going to order some takeout and wondered what you'd like," Theo said, his eyes moving from me to Eloise to Finn. "Finn, you're welcome to join us."

"Chinese?" Elle said.

"If you like."

"Chinese sounds good." I shrugged.

"Yeah," Finn agreed.

"I managed to talk Theo into cutting out of work early." Hayley was grinning at me, and I could sense she wanted to jump around all giddy at discovering me hanging out with Elle and Finn again. "Isn't this great? All of us together for dinner."

"We're having dinner together, Hayley," I teased, swinging my legs off the bed. "Not exactly enough to win us the Brady Bunch Family of the Year Award."

"You're such a smart-ass." Elle chuckled, moving off the bed after me.

"And good thing." I threw wide eyes at Finn, whose grin rivaled Hayley's. "Or what a dull life you all would still lead without me around to entertain you."

"Pfft, pretty full of yourself there, Maxwell," Elle retorted.

"I have reason to be." I winked at Theo as I slid past him and Hayley. "I am awesome."

Finn's bedroom was huge. It was also one of the few rooms in the big house that looked truly lived in. It was messy, with clothes strewn here and there, his schoolbooks piled on the floor, and books he was reading on his own time stacked on high bookshelves. The only not untidy thing in the room was the bed because of the staff. They tried to clean around his clutter. He had posters of bands on the walls, and nearly every inch was covered with photographs he had taken of the places he'd seen. His father wanted him to be well traveled and cultured, but unfortunately that meant Finn was forced to go with him somewhere new over Christmas every year.

Not so unfortunately that meant Finn had taken some beautiful shots of places he'd visited around the world.

The first time I'd seen his bedroom was only a week into our relationship. His father was away on business, and we'd gone to his room to hang out and get to know each other. Finn assured me the Rochester staff wouldn't say a word to his dad about me being there. He'd told them we were working on a school project together. If they didn't buy that story, I didn't know. They gave us total privacy.

"We were in Cabo." Finn had pointed to a beautiful shot of a huge rock formation that jutted out over the beach into the water. "That was the year I told my father that I didn't want to go to Harvard Business School. I told him I wanted to be a travel photographer. He broke my camera." He'd shot me a pained look. "It was the last time he hit me. I fought back. The staff at the resort must have known something was up. We were wandering around with bruised faces. It was so ugly." His voice had gotten hoarse. "Part of me felt good about standing up for myself but mostly I felt… I *knew* I was trapped. My father will do whatever it takes to get his own way. And my future is in his hands. I can't afford college without him. That means I have to do what he wants me to do."

I hadn't known what to say to him, to make him feel better, to assure him he wasn't trapped when the truth was I didn't know how to fight a man like his father any more than Finn did. Instead I'd wrapped my arms around his waist and leaned my head on his shoulder. "Did you buy the camera you have now?"

"No." He'd smiled down at me. "Eloise did. I didn't tell her about the beating I took but I told her about my dad getting pissed off about my photography and smashing my camera. I didn't know what she was up to but she made me open a late Christmas present in front of my father. It was a camera. An even better one than the last. And she gushed like an idiot about how she was so sad to hear I'd broken my camera and how I just had to have a new one." He'd given a huff of laughter. "She knew he couldn't say no to the camera when it was from her without embarrassing himself. He actually likes her."

I'd chuckled. "*I* like her. The more I know, the more I like. I'm glad you had her then. I wish she could have what we have. With this Sarah girl she's always talking online with or...any girl that she cares for. She deserves happiness."

"You are the sweetest person," he'd murmured, bending his head for a kiss.

"Stop saying that," I'd whispered against his lips, "it's not true."

He'd kissed me, long and tender. "You taste sweet," he'd murmured when we finally came up for air.

Now I was in his bedroom again for the fourth time. Mr. Rochester was away on business, this time for three nights, so Finn had the house to himself. He was always in a good mood when his dad was away.

I lay on Finn's big bed, staring at a picture on his bedside table.

It was a black-and-white photograph of his mother. It had been taken in the style of a nineteen-forties Hollywood starlet. She was so beautiful. Finn had her eyes.

We'd been lying in comfortable silence for a little while, lost in our individual thoughts, as Finn trailed the back of his knuckles over the top of my arm.

"I thought about being a doctor. A pediatric surgeon. Like her. Follow Elle to premed," Finn said.

I glanced at him, realizing he'd been watching me look at the picture. "Yeah?"

"If I couldn't be a photographer, maybe I could be the next best thing. Kind of a tribute to her."

"That's a good idea."

Darkness shadowed his face. "My father said no."

Your father is a monstrous bastard! I wanted to rage. But I kept it inside. Finn already knew his father was a bad guy. He didn't need the reminder.

He caught the heat in my eyes, anyway, and he leaned his head closer to mine. "Hey, it's okay."

"It's not." I looked back at the picture of his mother, wishing she were still here. Maybe she could have fought for him. Helped him. Because I was clueless, helpless and powerless, and I hated it.

In fact, I think I hated it more feeling that way for him than I ever did for myself.

That feeling seemed to expand inside my chest until I felt almost suffocated by the aching frustration.

"Hey, hey." Finn rested his forehead against mine. "It's okay. I'm okay."

I turned to look at him, forcing him to pull away from me. "Are you?" I practically begged.

He brushed his thumb over my bottom lip and leaned in to whisper, "I have you, don't I?"

"I'm not enough, Finn."

"God," he breathed against my mouth, "you have no idea how wrong you are."

"I want you to be happy," I said. "With more than just me."

"I am happy. I've never been happier. My dad can't touch me when I'm feeling like this. Believe me, he's tried."

"What has he done?" I frowned, jerking back. He hadn't mentioned his dad giving him shit.

"It doesn't matter."

"Finn." I sat up. "It does matter."

He sighed and sat up, too. "Look, he's just being his usual self."

"In what way his usual self? Is he hitting you?" I reached for him, turning his face to the light in case I'd missed a bruise or something.

Finn chuckled and grabbed my wrists. "No." He tugged me so I had no choice but to fall against him. "He…okay…he suspects I might be 'fooling around with you' in secret. His words not mine."

"And he's okay with that?"

"I'm still with Eloise so he's assuming I've taken his advice and that I'm using you."

"Arrgh," I growled. "I swear, Finn, that guy. Sometimes I think I have the better deal. My dad beat the shit out of me but even then I had the hope of a future away from him once I turned eighteen." If I'd made it to eighteen living with him, that is.

"Don't," he said through gritted teeth. "You weren't better off. This—" he pushed my shirt up, revealing my ribs "—is just a reminder." He bent his head and pressed a soft kiss to the only physical scar my dad left me. A burn from a cigarette he'd put out on me when he was wasted. The next morning when he found me crying in pain was the only time my father showed a measure of remorse. Carla had put some antiseptic on it so it wouldn't fester but because it hadn't been taken care of by a doctor it left a little circular scar. "Every time I think of what he did to you I want to hit something."

"Then don't think about it," I whispered as I ran my fingers through Finn's soft, thick hair. In answer he began to press kisses across my belly. This time a different heat flashed through me, and I sighed, falling back against his bed.

He looked up at me, his fingers trailing over the zipper on my jeans, questioning.

I nodded and squirmed in anticipation as he unbuttoned them and then pulled the zipper down. We hadn't had sex yet but we'd done nearly everything else.

It was exciting, exhilarating, and I was growing to crave him like I was addicted.

But sex—

As much as I wanted him something stopped me from going all the way with him.

I didn't know what it was and I didn't want to ponder it too much, so I just enjoyed what we did have.

I knew Finn enjoyed it, too, and he never pushed for more even though the question, along with a little frustration, was in his eyes. I had no answers, so all I could do was make up for it in giving everything over in my kiss.

CHAPTER 17

I WATCHED ELOISE disappear into the pool house still wearing the floor-length pale yellow Jenny Packham dress that had definitely made her the belle of the ball—or the Winter Formal, I should say. Most every other girl had turned up in silvers and pale blues, so Elle had really stood out. Me, not so much, as I was wearing a cobalt blue silk gown that swished around my ankles.

I'd been miserable the whole night as Elle and Finn held hands and danced when coerced to by Bryce and Joshua. Elle had insisted we do a group hang thing at the dance so I wouldn't feel left out, but it hadn't really worked out. Charlotte and Gabe barely looked at each other from the moment they got there, making me wonder what was going on with them. The tension between them was so thick Gabe got up and left the table. Five minutes later we saw him slow-dancing with a senior.

Poor Charlotte looked miserable and insisted on going

home early despite our protests. Elle and I tried to get her to talk to us but she wouldn't, and all we could do was put her in a cab and promise we'd call her the next morning.

Bryce and Joshua, who had gotten over their relationship problems, spent most of the night making out at our table, and that left the not-so-kinky threesome of me, Elle and Finn.

At home it never bothered me, but at the dance our threesome was awkward. I looked and felt pathetic hanging with them and was desperate to go home.

There had been times over the last few months that I'd found it hard to keep my relationship with Finn a secret. Those doubts I'd had way at the beginning would whisper to me sometimes. However, as quickly as they'd come to me, Finn would obliterate them with his kisses, his kindness and his devotion.

But he hadn't told me he loved me.

And watching him kiss Elle, even if it was all for show, was getting harder, not easier like I thought it would.

I was so lost in my own crappy thoughts that it had taken me until the three of us were back in the limo, heading to our house, to notice that Elle was also in a mood.

Theo and Hayley were staying in New York for the weekend so we had the house to ourselves. The intention was for Finn to hang out with me after formal to make up for the fact that we couldn't be together at the dance. But I wasn't sure I wanted to be alone with Finn.

And I still felt that way as he stood at my back. The limo had dropped us off at home and Elle had charged ahead of us, seeming lost in her own world. We'd followed her through the house and then watched her disappear out into the pool house.

"Something's wrong with you," he said quietly. "What is it?"

"There's something wrong with Elle," I evaded. "I should

go talk to her." I spun around. "You should go home, Finn. We'll talk later."

I hurried away from him and outside, ignoring the surprised look on his face. He looked as though I'd just slapped him.

The truth was it was easier to deal with whatever was going on in Elle's head than it was to deal with my own angst over Finn. I didn't want to argue with him or break up with him—not at all! However, I also didn't like how I was starting to feel.

Probably like how his father wanted me to feel.

Like a dirty little secret.

And as much as I knew that wasn't true, I couldn't stop the insidious thought from creeping in.

I shrugged it off and practically ran over to the pool house, lifting the hem of my dress out of my way to get there fast—it was cold!

I didn't bother to knock.

Eloise sat on the sofa in the pool house, looking so forlorn I felt an ache in my chest at the sight of her.

"Hey," I said, walking over to sit across from her, "what is going on?"

"Aren't you supposed to be with Finn?"

"I told him to go home. What's up with you?"

"You told him to go home?"

"Elle, what's up? You're acting weird."

"No weirder than you. You were upset tonight."

I frowned. "Is that what's wrong with you?"

She didn't answer but somehow I knew I was just an excuse for some bigger problem.

"Elle..."

"I just get mad, all right," she snapped. "These dances, they make me mad. I was with Finn the whole night and I felt all alone. These are the nights I just wish things were different, you know."

"Yes. I think I do."

"I'm sorry, India."

I thought about how truly lonely Eloise was and suddenly felt very petty for feeling resentful. "I'm sorry, too."

Her laughter was bitter. "What a pair, huh? You wishing you could hold your boyfriend's hand in public, and me wishing I had the guts to ask Sarah to this stupid dance."

"Have you ever kissed a girl?" I said.

My abrupt question caused her to expel a bark of laughter. "I hope you're not offering."

I rolled my eyes. "No. I just… I wondered… How do you really know you're gay if you've never kissed a girl?"

She stared at me for a moment before asking, "What age were you when you developed your first crush?"

"I was ten," I said, remembering it clearly. "His name was Logan and he punched my arm every time he passed me in the hall. If only I knew then what I know now." I grinned. "That boy liked me back."

"So you'd never kissed a boy but you knew you liked them?"

Her point hit home, direct and true. "Yes. I knew I liked boys before I kissed one."

"Same for me." She shrugged, giving me a sad smile. "Tonight I'd give anything to have a stupid crush on a stupid boy." Eloise lowered her eyes. "Do you know why I like being in the school plays?"

"Why?"

"Because I can be any kind of person at all without the fear of judgment." Her eyes glistened with tears. "Most days I try not to care. But today I care. Today is a day I wish I were the kind of girl who was so secure in her own skin she didn't care what anyone else thought of her. Today is the kind of day that makes me think of my mother, who loved formals, who could be kind and loving, but was my father's wife after all. And if it's true what they say, that somehow she really is looking down on me, then there is this huge possibility that she's disappointed in me...and no one can blame me for caring that my mother would have hated the person I truly am."

Chest hurting for her, I got up slowly and then sat down beside her. Without saying a word, because words would be superfluous at this point, I put my arm around her and drew her head down onto my shoulder. She slumped into me, and I felt her hot tears hit my bare skin.

My grip on her tightened, and I wished today had been a different kind of day for her, too.

A little while later I walked Elle to her room and headed back to my own feeling more confused than ever. I had to admit, if only to myself, that I'd started the night feeling resentful toward her. I didn't understand why Elle still needed Finn to help keep her secret.

They'd been in a relationship for two and a half years, and everyone thought they'd had sex. If they broke up, no one would automatically jump to the conclusion that Elle was gay. She no longer needed Finn to continue her lie. She could stay single for the rest of high school, going out on a date here and there to avoid suspicion, and no one would be the wiser.

It didn't mean Finn and I could get together right away but we could lead up to it in a way that people wouldn't jump all over us for it—especially with Elle supporting us.

But she couldn't seem to see past her irrational fear and I admit...it was beginning to bother me.

However, seeing her so sad and upset for the first time since she'd talked to me about being gay, I couldn't hold on to my resentment. What she was dealing with was bigger than my insecurities.

I strode into my room, ready to crash, only to come to an abrupt halt at the sight of Finn lying on my bed asleep.

Something huge swept through me, filling me up, as I stared at him sprawled out on my duvet.

And for the first time I let myself finally admit what all that hugeness was.

I was in love with Finn Rochester.

I love him.

Tears pricked my eyes, though I wasn't sure whether they were tears of happiness or confusion or fear or all three. I kicked off my shoes and climbed up onto the bed, trying not to wake him.

I gently laid my head on his chest and closed my eyes, listening to his heart thud in my ear.

No, I thought, I would put up with being his secret girl, because it was better than not having him at all. It was better than feeling lonely. And one thing was for sure: I never felt lonely when I was with him.

I was just drifting to sleep when I felt his arms close around me, and his lips brush my ear. "Don't leave me," he whispered. "Don't ever leave me."

I burrowed my head deeper into his chest and held on to him tight.

CHAPTER 18

"SO, JUST US, HUH?" I stared across the cafeteria table at Gabe.

For the first time ever I found myself alone at lunch with him. Finn had booked the darkroom out to finish a project he was working on; Joshua and Bryce were extra-loved-up these days and were off doing…well…probably each other, somewhere. And Eloise was in dress rehearsal for the play that was opening that night.

Charlotte was mysteriously absent.

Gabe grinned at me. "Your wish finally came true, Maxwell. So what will you do with me now that you have me alone?"

I smiled with faux sweetness. "Ask you what is going on with you and Charlotte?"

The cocky look on his face was quickly replaced by discomfort. He shifted uneasily in his seat and looked at his plate. "I don't know what you're talking about."

Oh, yeah, sure.

"I'm talking about the fact that you and Charlotte looked mighty cozy at the engagement party and then suddenly you could barely look at each other at Winter Formal. What's up with that?"

Gabe glanced around, as if he was checking to make sure no one was listening. He leaned across the table and said quietly, "Charlotte hasn't said anything?"

My curiosity peaked to new heights. "Not a word. Why? What happened?"

He frowned down at his plate. "I'm not sure I should say anything, then."

"You can't not say anything now," I argued.

"If I do tell you… I mean…shit." He rubbed a hand over his head.

"Gabe."

"Can I trust you, Maxwell?"

"Of course."

In answer to that, he got up out of his seat and came down to sit in the seat next to mine. I turned to him, eager to find out what was going on between them.

"I haven't told anyone else this…"

When he didn't say anything else I punched his shoulder. "The suspense is killing me here."

"Fine." He glanced around us again and then looked me directly in the eye before he muttered something.

"What was that?"

He muttered it again.

"Gabe, just spit it out."

"Charlotte and I hooked up," he hissed.

I think my jaw might have hit the floor. "No."

"Yes." He looked pained, not happy, and I suddenly started to understand what was going on here.

"You dumped her, didn't you?" I glared at him, thinking how devastated Charlotte must be after giving up her virginity to him, only for him to reject her.

"We weren't going out. It just happened. And now shit is weird between us."

"Weird how?"

"Charlotte wants to date." He said the word *date* like it was dirty.

My irritation at him was growing steadily worse. "And what is wrong with that?"

"Come on, India, you know I don't date. After I've been with a girl I get bored."

I thought of how badly Charlotte must be hurting right then and I wanted to punch him. Gabe must have seen my thoughts in my expression because he held up his hands in defense. "Look, I'm not a total asshole, okay. It just...she was coming on to me at the engagement party and I got carried away a little. The next day she came over to my house to study and she practically jumped me."

"You could have said no if you aren't into her." I really, *really* wanted to smack him.

He glared back at me. "I didn't *want* to say no."

Interesting.

"So...you like her?"

"It's Charlotte. Of course I like her. She's one of my closest friends. And that's the problem. If we dated and we broke up, I lose my friend."

Slowly the anger seeped out of me. "Can I ask a question?"

He nodded.

"You said that you get bored with a girl after you sleep with her. Does that mean you wouldn't want to sleep with Charlotte again?"

Gabe's lips tightened. It was the most serious I'd ever seen him in my life.

"Gabe."

He shot me a tortured look. "I can't stop thinking about her."

Hope began to blossom in my chest for my friends. "Then what's the problem? Give it a shot."

"No." He shook his head adamantly. "I don't date. I'm not good at it. And I would end up hurting her. So no."

I wasn't exactly following his logic but I'd never seen such a mulish expression on his face so I knew he meant it. "So you'll be cool with her dating other guys, then?"

"How? Is she dating someone? What do you know?"

What a dipshit. I made a face at his obvious jealousy. "You are so screwed."

His eyes grew round with alarm. "How?"

"Because you've slept with her now. Things will never be the same between you and she's just going to resent you for hurting her, anyway. If you date, she'll be even more hurt. If she dates, it's going to drive you crazy. So it's up to you…do you give dating her a chance with the risk that it might not work out? A risk, I might add, that we all take when we date someone. Or do you be the guy that slept with his best friend who's crazy about him, and then reject her. There is really only one scenario there that *guarantees* you lose her friendship."

Gabe scowled at me. "Nah-uh. I'm very charming if you hadn't noticed. I can win Charlotte's friendship back."

"It's good that you're optimistic. That's nice." I bit into a fry. "Delusional. But nice."

His chair scraped across the floor as he pushed back from the table. "That's what I get for seeking advice from a girl."

"I know," I called out as he was walking away. "The truth hurts."

He flipped me the bird without turning back and I ignored the curious looks around us. I couldn't care less. Gabe needed to hear the truth, so he could pull his head out of his ass and ask Charlotte out.

As for me, I needed to find her and make sure she was okay.

The school felt flooded with people, an expectant and electric atmosphere in the air. It was a mix of excitement over the upcoming Christmas break and anticipation for the first performance of the school play that evening.

After having a heart-to-heart with poor Charlotte, who was so hurt and rejected by Gabe that she hadn't wanted to tell any of us about it, I'd stayed behind after school with Elle for the last-minute rehearsals. Since she and Elle were so close, I made Charlotte promise to tell Elle about Gabe. It would make her feel better to talk to her friend, confide in her. She agreed, as long as we didn't tell Bryce, who was still extra mean around Charlotte these days because of their whole parents dating situation.

For now I kept Charlotte's secret, knowing Elle needed to stay focused on the play. Being sound assistant hadn't involved much so over the last few months I'd become a general assistant, running around after crew and actors and getting them what they needed.

Walking through the halls that night with a cooler filled with bottled water, I passed students and their parents as they milled around before curtain-up, smiling at those I recognized.

"India!"

I whipped around and found Patrick striding toward me.

"Hey."

"Let me help you." He took the heavy cooler out of my hands before I could protest. "Where are we taking it?"

"Backstage."

"Ah, behind the scenes." He grinned. "Lead the way."

"Thank you."

"You're welcome."

I began leading him toward the backstage door. It was awkward between us because I'd been deliberately keeping my distance from him. He seemed more than a little confused considering I'd flirted with him at Hayley and Theo's engagement party.

I led him inside and we headed to the large dressing room. "We come bearing water!" I called out cheerily, and we hadn't even breached the doorway when we were bombarded by actors.

When the crowd dispersed I found Eloise.

And she wasn't alone.

Finn stood next to her…and he did not look happy to see Patrick next to me.

Ignoring his narrowed eyes, I strode over to Elle, sensing Patrick fall into step behind me. "Here," I said, handing her a bottle. "Hydrate."

She smiled wanly. "Thanks. I hate that I get so nervous."

"It goes away, right?" I said.

"Yes. As soon as I hit the stage…" She trailed off, turning pale. "Excuse me." She pushed past us, possibly heading somewhere to upchuck.

"Will she be okay?" Patrick said.

Finn didn't do a very good job of not scowling at him. "She's always sick before a performance. She'll be fine." He looked at me. *What is he doing with you?* his look said.

I shrugged.

"Should you go after her?" Patrick said.

Finn looked insulted by the implication that he wasn't fulfilling his boyfriend duties. He was. Just...to me. I was getting the possessive boyfriend treatment.

"I will." I brushed between them, wondering if Finn ever gave a thought to how it made me feel when he and Elle got affectionate in public. At first it seemed to bother him, but now he didn't give me silent "sorrys" with his eyes. It was like he thought I was used to it or something.

But God forbid I should walk by another boy's side.

I thought of Gabe and how much of an idiot he was acting about Charlotte.

Finn wasn't looking any smarter than his friend.

Guys were such dumbasses.

As it turned out, Elle did get over her nerves as soon as she set foot onstage. The audience was, like me, mesmerized by her. In the last act, when I watched the scene again when the boy playing Emily's husband, George, throws himself on his wife's grave as she looks on, and she turns to her mother-in-law and says, "They don't understand, do they?" I knew now why I got those goose bumps every time Elle delivered Emily's line. The real emotion she put in it didn't just come from losing her mom; it came from having her secret. It came from knowing and feeling things her classmates just couldn't understand yet, and maybe never would.

And while last time I watched Elle on that stage I'd been in awe, now I knew her, now I cared about her and now I was proud of her.

When the play was over, after her roaring standing ovation, I left Elle to get dressed and take off her stage makeup and I headed out front to see our parents.

Hayley's cheeks were flushed, and her eyes were bright as I approached.

"Wasn't she wonderful," she gushed. "I just… Theo, you never said how talented she was."

Theo frowned. "I think I did, you know."

"You did," I agreed. "So did I. But I guess you have to see it for yourself."

"Why isn't Eloise pursuing acting?"

"Eloise is going to do something useful with her life and become a doctor. Don't fill her head with nonsense about acting."

Hayley raised an eyebrow at Theo's tone. "It's not nonsense."

"Hayley," he warned, and I stepped back, not really wanting to be there for a public spat.

"Don't Hayley me," she said, glancing around to make sure no one was listening. "Eloise can be a doctor, a pilot or an actor for all I care…as long as *she's* happy."

They had a stare-down but Hayley refused to *back* down. I was kind of impressed.

Theo finally sighed. "I see Donald Keating." He disappeared, and Hayley glowered after him.

"Was that your first disagreement?" I teased, trying to lighten the mood.

Hayley shot me a look. "No. It's not."

I frowned. "Trouble in paradise?"

"No." She hurried to my side, threading her arm through mine. "Our different backgrounds make for different attitudes. Theo has expectations for Eloise and now for you. I just don't want either of you to feel pressured by them."

"I don't feel pressured," I assured her.

Hayley brushed my hair from my face, her expression turning tender. "Have I told you lately how proud I am of you?"

I tensed, still not so evolved that I could easily accept praise from her.

"I am," she insisted, her grip on me tightening ever so slightly. "You came into this strange Boston world, not happy to be here, and yet you grabbed it with both hands and made it your own. And you've charmed everyone, including Eloise." She smiled. "That kid was so lonely before you got here. You know, I think you might be her best friend."

The truth was Hayley wasn't wrong. And she'd shocked the heck out of me with her perceptiveness. "Elle wants to be a doctor," I said. "Just to reassure you. It is what *she* wants."

"Good to know." Hayley grinned. "Guess I should go find my fiancé and smooth his ruffled feathers."

"Ugh, Hayley, no dirty talk, please."

She guffawed and lightly pushed me. "You're so bad."

And just like that she reminded me of a teenager again. But instead of it annoying me, it made me laugh as I watched her float through the crowds, oblivious to other men looking at her, when her entire focus was Theo.

"What are you laughing at?"

I glanced up at Finn, sobering. "Hayley."

He nodded absentmindedly. "Can I have a word?"

I nodded and followed Finn as he led me through the crowded hallways and into a part of the school that was empty. The lights were low here and it felt eerie and quiet.

"Finn," I whispered.

But he ignored me until he found a classroom door that would open. He gestured me inside and then closed the door behind us, pulling the blind down over the small window at the top.

"What's going on?"

He leaned against the door and crossed his arms over his chest. "Why is it Patrick Donaghue can't seem to stay away from you?"

I rolled my eyes at the exaggeration. "Oh, come on. I've spoken to him twice in the last few weeks."

"I heard he's going to ask you out."

"Finn, I'm not doing this." I was tired and hungry and so not in the mood for Finn in jealous boyfriend mode.

"Do you like him?" He narrowed his eyes on me.

Apparently when hungry and tired it didn't take much to blow my fuse. "Are you kidding me?" I snapped.

"Well?"

"Are you listening to yourself? You can't get mad at me for talking to a boy, Finn! I spend nearly every day having to watch you hold hands with Elle, give her kisses and hugs. You don't seem to care how that makes me feel. You do not get to be pissed at me for talking to another boy—another boy who would have no problem holding my hand in public!"

Finn's head jerked back, like I'd hit him.

My words seem to echo all around us as we stood staring at one another in silence.

"It's..." Finn looked flabbergasted. "It's just Elle. You know it's... How can you be jealous?"

It wasn't about Eloise. I knew rationally there was nothing going on between them.

Honestly, I didn't know for sure what exactly it was that was driving me so crazy about the situation. "Forget I said anything," I said. "I'm tired, that's all."

The apprehension didn't leave his eyes but, as if he, too,

was scared to take this conversation any further in case it led somewhere we couldn't turn back from, he strode carefully toward me, cupped my face in his hands and pressed the sweetest kiss to my lips. "Let's get you home," he murmured.

Two days before Hayley and Theo's wedding, I couldn't believe we were finally becoming a family.

I stood in my walk-in staring at the bridesmaid gown I'd be wearing. Finn was in my bedroom, lying on my bed with the freedom of knowing that Hayley and Theo were out.

"Fast-forward ten years," I called into the other room. "If you could have it exactly as you want it, what would your future look like?"

"I travel the world taking photographs for a living," he answered immediately. "When I come home it's to Boston, to an apartment in Back Bay where I live with you. You have a rock on your left finger that I put there, and we're arguing about what we should name our first kid. My dad is not a part of our lives. At all."

I smiled at the thought of that future, taken aback Finn was even thinking of "us" that far in the future, never mind the marriage and babies bit. I didn't know a lot of guys our age that wouldn't run screaming in the other direction just thinking about it. But Finn wasn't like other guys our age. He got what was important. Like me. "Eloise lives a few blocks from us with her girlfriend, who happens to be very understanding about Elle's crappy hours as an intern." I strode out into the bedroom, and my smile died.

Finn wasn't laughing. He looked completely serious. "Do you know why Patrick's interest in you drives me crazy?"

I shook my head, surprised he'd mention it after we'd done

such a good job these last few days pretending there wasn't this horrible friction between us.

"Because you're right. If you were with him he would have no problem telling the whole world you were his girlfriend. I can't do that and I hate it."

I stared at him, blown away by his honesty, and not quite sure how to reciprocate without giving away too much of myself.

Finn's smile was tired. "So it's hard for me, too. Just so you know."

I leaned against my bedpost. "Okay."

He nodded and shifted on the bed. He frowned as his hand moved under my pillow, and when he pulled his arm out, he was holding my ereader.

My heart lurched as he moved to switch it on. "Hey." I jumped on the bed. "Private." I waved my hand at him, gesturing for him to give it to me.

A slow smile lit up his face as he handed it over. "You can chill. I know you read romance novels."

Heat flooded my cheeks. "Wha—how—what?" I sputtered.

He laughed and sat up, grabbing hold of my wrist so he could haul me none-too-gently against him. I collapsed onto him as he fell back against my pillows. He cupped my too-hot face in his hands, looking deep into my eyes. "I've known about your secret for a while," he whispered. "Don't worry, I won't tell anyone."

"I—" I realized I didn't know how to explain why I liked romance novels so much, or why I was so embarrassed by my addiction.

"It's okay. You want the happy ending. There's no shame in that, India. No shame in that at all."

It was the way he said it. Just something in his voice.

It was like it flipped a switch inside of me.

I started to cry.

I pressed my face into his neck and bawled like a baby while he held me tight in his arms.

Sometime later, once I had calmed down, I settled my cheek on his chest and took a deep breath. "I'm sorry."

"Never be sorry," he said.

"I want to feel happy for her without resenting her, without resenting myself," I blurted. "Before I got here, met you, Eloise, I was this awful person who didn't want Hayley to have happiness. I didn't think she deserved it. Now… I want her to be happy but I'm not even sure if it's because her being happy means my life here is permanent or if I just want her to be happy. And if I do just want her to be happy, then I feel angry at myself for giving her that. It's so messed up."

Finn stroked my back. "Hayley left you. She walked out on you for years and left you to a man who abused you. And the only reason she's back in your life is because he almost killed you. I'm the last person to give you perspective on this because I'm angry at her, too."

"Hayley did what?"

We bolted upright at the furious tone, my heart dropping to my stomach at the sight of Elle standing in my doorway. She was pale, with two red spots flushing high on her cheeks. Disbelief, horror, blazed in her eyes.

"Eloise." I scrambled off the bed. "Elle, please."

"No!" She held up a hand to ward me off. "You tell me everything, right now."

Stomach sick, I could only stare at her, because I knew the moment I opened my mouth there was a possibility everything Hayley and I had built here would just go up in a puff of smoke.

"If you don't tell her, she's just going to make it up in her head for herself out of what she heard," Finn said.

"I know you want to protect your dad," I started, "but it's not—"

"My dad," Elle cut me off. "Yes, I do. But it's not just about that… Jesus, India, is what Finn said true? Did that happen to you?"

Eventually I sat with my back resting against Finn's chest, him supporting me physically and emotionally, as I told Eloise my story. Every little piece.

"That night with the food," she murmured, looking a little lost. "That was because of your dad?"

I nodded.

"Oh God, I told Bryce of all people." She squeezed her eyes shut. "I'm so sorry."

"It's okay."

"It's not okay!" Her eyes flew open and her anger blazed out. "Hayley left you to a monster! She just left you!" She stood up, hands shaking. "Does Daddy know?"

Fear choked me and I shook my head.

"About any of it?"

I swallowed past that fear and it was painful. "He knows my father wasn't a good man. I don't think he knows Hayley wasn't there for all the times he wasn't a good man."

"Or that Hayley is the reason he wasn't a good man," Elle snapped.

"Elle, please. Please don't tell Theo."

Her eyes grew round with shock. "You want me to let him marry her not knowing who she really is?"

"She's not a bad person," I found myself arguing. "She made a mistake."

"That mistake almost cost you your life. Do you forgive her for that?"

"I don't know," I whispered. "I don't know. But I don't think I could forgive myself if I destroyed what she has with Theo. She loves him, Eloise. We can't take that away from her."

"But what about my father?" she cried. "He doesn't know what the woman he's marrying is capable of."

"Yes, he does, because I told him."

I immediately jumped away from Finn as Hayley pushed her way inside my room.

"People really need to stop eavesdropping around here," I heard Finn mutter, and a little hysterical giggle escaped from my lips.

Hayley drank us all in, her features tight with pain, especially when she saw my reddened eyes. Finally she focused on Eloise. "I told Theo last week, a few days before your play. Things have been a little tense between us, but he's come to forgive me. You can ask him yourself when he gets home."

Eloise glowered at her. "He may have forgiven you, but that does not mean I have."

"I don't expect you to."

"Why did you leave her? My mother was dying and all she cared about, all she kept apologizing for, was leaving me." Tears glimmered in Elle's eyes. "How could you willingly leave her?"

I tensed at Elle's question and the way Hayley struggled to control her emotions. For some reason it was the question I'd never had the guts to ask Hayley, and she'd frustrated me over the years for never having the balls to bring up the answer herself.

Now she turned to look at me. "May I speak to India alone, please?"

Finn touched my arm, and I looked over my shoulder at him. Although my heart was pounding in my chest and I thought I might be sick, I nodded.

He slowly got up and walked, stone-faced, by Hayley before taking hold of Eloise's hand. She stiffened and shot me a look.

I nodded at her, too, and she reluctantly let Finn lead her out of the room.

The door clicked softly shut but the noise might as well have been as excruciating as nails down a chalkboard for the way it made both of us flinch.

Hayley shook out her hands and lowered herself onto the stool by my vanity table. I sat on my bed and let the silence thicken. My stomach churned.

"Over the years, I've wanted to try to explain…but how do you explain the unexplainable?" She shrugged helplessly.

"You try."

She winced at my cold tone. "It's easier said than done."

"Try," I reiterated. "I know this is probably the last thing you want to be discussing before the big wedding but if you do anything for me, just for me, then please do this."

Her eyes shone with emotion. "I guess I should start at the beginning, then. The truth is I had a shitty upbringing. We've never really talked about your grandparents because you've never really asked me anything, but you should know they weren't loving parents. My dad slapped us around, and my mom would use me as a shield. Better me than her, she used to say."

I stared at her, appalled, shocked and begrudgingly sympathetic. It was jarring to realize that all this time I'd had someone in my life who actually got what I'd gone through. Never could I have believed Hayley and I would have something like that in common.

"I never had grand dreams as a kid. I didn't want to be a lawyer or a doctor. I just wanted to be out of that house, that's all I wanted. And I don't want sympathy, India, I don't, not from you. I don't deserve it. I just need you to know why I ran into your father's arms at eighteen. At the time he was this escape and he loved me. No one had ever just loved me. I hadn't ever heard someone say those words to me until your father did."

I remembered how much he loved her. His love for her made me feel resentful because every punch, every kick, every time he starved me or punished me, was a reminder of his love for her and how that love had turned to the darkest kind of hurt.

Hayley flinched at whatever she saw on my face and looked down at her feet. "By the time I realized I didn't love him back, I'd already had you. I stuck it out with him because I didn't want you to have a broken family." She laughed bitterly at the irony. "Oh God, kid, I messed up so bad. I stayed instead of taking you and getting out of there. I thought it was better to be loved by him than to be scared on my own. But over the years I started to think about all those things that everyone dreams about when they're kids. I thought about what I wanted from my life, just for me, and I knew your dad would never let me have them because he loved me too much—if it meant splitting my focus from him, he'd never let me have it."

She was telling the truth because I also remembered that. I hadn't seen his behavior as possessive or controlling when

I was a kid, but looking back he was that way with her. I remembered one night she came home from her part-time job at a supermarket. It was only months before she left. She'd brought leaflets home with her and had sat down with him to show them. She'd wanted to go to community college. My dad had gotten frustrated. I remember him shouting at her that they'd already talked about it and they couldn't afford it. Hayley had argued with him until he screamed in her face and slammed out of the house. She'd cried in her room all night.

I'd been so scared they'd split up and I was angry at her for making him mad.

I was such a stupid kid.

Hayley's expression was a mix of pleading and apologetic. "I'm ashamed to admit this, more than you'll ever know, but I started to resent you. I looked at my beautiful kid and I resented you because I was stuck in another shitty situation but this time for you. I'd stayed with him for you. And I hated myself for blaming you. I hated myself so bad and I was scared that I would turn into my father and that I would hurt you.

"So I left."

I stared at her, barely able to make her out for the tears clouding my vision. "And he hurt me instead."

She nodded, her own tears finally breaking free. "When they came to tell me what had happened to you… I wanted to die, India. I wanted to die. I thought I'd left you for the better. I knew he was controlling but I never knew what he was capable of. You have to believe me. I left to protect you… If I had known what he would do…"

"Why?" My voice broke. "Why didn't you tell me this long ago and save us from all this crap between us. I would have understood. Or I would have tried to understand."

"You wouldn't talk to me…" She shrugged helplessly. "You

scared me because you were just so angry all the time. And honestly, I didn't think you'd trust a word I said."

The anger, the pain and the words I needed to express all that had lodged in a tight ball in my throat and I couldn't get them out. I'd stopped counting how many times that ball had burned there, preventing me from letting the words go.

But I needed to let them go.

I finally needed to.

I forced the words out with everything I had.

"Do you know why I was so angry, Hayley?" I said, my voice hoarse. "Because I want to hate you. I want to hate you but I can't. I love you. I love you more than I love anybody, and you hurt me more than anybody else. Even more than my father, because you left me. *You* left me."

Hayley stared at me, pale, eyes wide at my confession.

And then her face crumpled under the weight of my words and a sob burst out of her. Hayley rushed at me, and I was in her arms before I could stop her.

I stood frozen. Uncertain. Afraid.

And then my fingers bit into her arms and it took me a moment to realize I was holding on instead of pushing her away.

CHAPTER 19

"I'M NOT GOING to start calling you 'Mom,'" I said quietly.

Hayley sighed with her whole body, her shoulders brushing mine as they lifted. We sat next to each other on my bed and had been quiet for the past five minutes after our tearful confessions.

I felt strange. I felt vulnerable in a way I didn't think a kid should feel with their parent. But I also felt something else. Something hopeful.

I was reminded of Eloise's words to me not too long ago in the pool house.

"But most importantly I have hope, India. I have hope that someday, once I'm out of high school, things will change for me..."

Somehow along the way I'd stopped hoping for a lot of things. One of those was the reconciliation of my relationship with Hayley. It was too painful to hope for it, and honestly, I just couldn't see it ever happening when it hurt too much.

Hearing her side of the story finally, however, helped. I

guess my fear all along had been that she didn't love me and that's why she left, and that she'd been forced out of guilt to bring me back into her life. It was still bullshit that she left me, but maybe over time I could try to see it from her side.

Most importantly, though, I had hope that over time I would start to believe that she loved me.

Still, baby steps.

"I guess that's fair," she said. "I'm not expecting things to change miraculously overnight."

I looked at her and she turned to me with a love I wanted to believe in in her eyes. "Things will change, though," I said. "How could they not?"

Her lips trembled with renewed emotion. "Yeah?"

"One day at a time."

"Thank you," she whispered.

"Thanks for telling Theo the truth."

"He deserved to know. For him and for you." Now I swore I saw wonder on her face. "He needs to know who he's marrying, and I wanted him to know just how amazing you are."

I thought about who I'd been only months ago while I was living in California. The truth was I wasn't sure I was that girl anymore or if I'd ever be her again. It seemed true for Hayley, too. "He's not marrying the woman that left me," I said. "You've changed since you got here."

"Maybe." She nudged me. "For the better, right?"

"Well, except for the shopping, yeah."

Hayley laughed and gripped my hand. "I'm going to get some sleep. You should, too."

I nodded and followed her to my door. We were both surprised to find Finn and Elle down the hall, leaning against the wall waiting on us. We'd been in my room for at least an hour.

Hayley rolled her eyes. "Okay, guys, India is fine, but she

needs some sleep. Finn, it's time you got home, and, Eloise, Theo will be home soon. I'm sure you want to talk to him."

Elle nodded and then looked at me.

"I'm fine." Finn was staring at me like he wanted to steamroll Hayley to get to me. "Really."

They left quietly, both shooting worried looks over their shoulders at me, and I disappeared back into my room because the truth was I *was* exhausted.

I thought I knew who I was but every little revelation, every little significant encounter…it seemed to change me infinitesimally. And if that were really true that meant that I'd never stop changing, and if that were true, then there was no guarantee of anything.

There was no safety in that, no power, no control—all the things I needed. And they would always be out of reach.

It was a terrifying realization.

My phone suddenly buzzed on my nightstand, and I rolled over to check who was calling. At the sight of Finn's name I pushed through my exhaustion and fears to pick up.

"Hey."

"Are you okay?"

"I… I guess so. I'm tired."

"I'm sorry."

"For what?"

"Tonight you needed me. I should have been able to hug you, comfort you, and I couldn't because Hayley was there."

"It's okay."

"It's not okay. You're right. This is hard."

"Yeah." I didn't know what else to say. There seemed to be no solution so I was stuffing the concern down deep inside in order to deal with all the other issues in my life.

Finn was quiet, and I wondered if he had guessed what was

going on in my head regarding our relationship. If he did, he chose to ignore it. "I'm really proud of you. The way you handled tonight. It was a lot and you…well, you're amazing."

"Thank you. I don't feel amazing."

"How *do* you feel?"

"Are you driving?"

"Hands free. Now, how *do* you feel?"

I breathed deep, the sound causing static to crackle between us. "I'm scared, Finn."

"What are you scared of?" came his gentle reply.

"Change."

"Everything changes, India."

"I know that. But there were things about me that I thought were fixed, you know. Now I don't know who I am."

"Yeah, you do. Things change us, things will always change us, but *who* you are, that thing inside you that determines your choices, controls your actions, your reactions, it's still yours. If something bad happens it's up to you how you let it change you—you either become more compassionate or you let it make you bitter. I already know how you've let the mess your parents made change you. I see it in the way you are with Elle, I see it at school in how you refuse to bully or be bullied, and I saw it in your bravery when you told me about your dad so I didn't feel alone anymore. You're strong. Stronger than you realize. *That's* your safe place, India."

Part of me was glad he wasn't in the room to see the fresh tears scalding my cheeks as I heard the words—the only words—I needed to hear.

A bigger part of me hated that the most important conversation I'd ever had in my life was happening on the phone.

He understood me. He got me.

And I was beginning to think that there was no safer place than that.

I love you.

I closed my eyes, more tears squeezing out. “Thank you,” I whispered.

“No. Thank *you*.” He released a long sigh. “I wish I was there right now.”

“Me, too.”

After a few seconds of silence he sighed again. “I’ll let you go. Get some sleep.”

But I didn’t want to lose him so soon. Not after everything he’d just said. “Stay. Until you get home, stay.”

“I can do that.”

“Finn…” I felt the words bubbling up inside of me, desperate to say them now when I felt it more than ever, but I didn’t want to say it for the first time over the phone.

As I trailed off I heard him take a shuddering breath. “I know,” he whispered. “Me, too.”

CHAPTER 20

THE WEDDING AND its reception took place at a fancy country club just outside Cambridge. Hayley wore the dress that made her look like a starlet and Theo couldn't take his eyes off her all day.

Many of the male guests were openly envious of their friend.

Many of the female guests were openly envious of the bride. I had to wonder how many of them actually saw her as a usurper and how many were genuinely willing to admit her into their fold. I knew Hayley had already made some friends but I guess I was worried for her and I could admit that now when I couldn't before.

Right then it was better to worry about Hayley than to worry about Finn and me.

"This is supposed to be a happy day," Eloise teased as she took in my dour expression.

"Are you happy?"

"My father is happy." She shrugged. "And if he can forgive Hayley and, God, if you can forgive Hayley, then who am I not to?"

The last twenty-four hours had been emotionally draining, to say the least. Eloise did confront her father, and Hayley had not been lying—she had told him the truth. After he had a heart-to-heart with his daughter, Theo came to find me.

"I understand now," he'd told me, his eyes filled with a compassion I was actually starting to believe in. "Hayley made a huge mistake, and I'm not ever going to tell you that you *have* to mend fences with her. What I can tell you is that I truly believe in her deep regrets, and I truly believe she loves you."

"I'll try…to mend fences. But I can't promise anything."

"India, it's just amazing that you'll try." He had shifted closer to me. "I want to tell you something Hayley confessed to me even though she knew it could cost her…well, me."

My heart thudded in my chest, but I nodded for him to go ahead.

"Your mother loves me, I know that, but she also chose me because she was…*is*…attempting to make amends with you."

"I don't understand."

"I can offer you opportunities you didn't have before."

Suddenly I'd remembered Hayley's words to me when we first arrived in Weston.

"This is the best thing that will ever happen to us. I know you don't believe me but Theo is a good man, and he can take care of us. No one can hurt us here."

Understanding had dawned. "Your money."

He'd looked uncomfortable but nodded. "That, among other things."

"And you're okay with that?"

"I'm a father," he'd said. "I would do anything to protect my daughter."

"Is that what she's doing...marrying you to protect me?"

"No and yes. It isn't one or the other. It's complicated."

I'd frowned because as wonderful as it was to think my mother would make such a huge decision with my best interests in mind, I didn't want to be the cause of someone else's hurt. "I don't want her using you for me."

Theo had grinned. "I'm going to take that to mean that you're warming up to me. However, you know your mother isn't using me. She's doing this for all of us. She loves me. I love her. She loves you."

And so Elle and I had watched them get married in front of a bunch of people I didn't know very well and two people I thought I knew better than anyone else in the room knew them.

Those two people were at the wedding as boyfriend and girlfriend, and I didn't know if it was the giddiness of the happy couple but Finn and Elle were playing their own version of happy couple better than they ever had before.

As a groomsman, Finn had walked Eloise down the aisle, while some distant cousin of Elle's walked me down the aisle. For the last few hours I'd watched my two best friends laugh and touch, and even kiss when prompted to for photos, while I felt further away than ever from them.

It was jarring considering how close I'd felt to Finn just a day before.

The truth was it wasn't their fault. It was the situation. People who'd known them for years (and the damn photographer) forced them to play boyfriend and girlfriend. The fact that they were best friends just made it easy for them.

They were coupled up, and there was no time for us to be our usual threesome.

I was out in the cold.

The toasts were over, dinner had been served and now people were either sitting around their tables chatting, mingling on the perimeter of the dance floor or actually dancing.

I was seated with my friends at our dinner table. The only one missing was Charlotte because Elle's cousin had asked her to dance.

Since Gabe had done not one thing to fix things between him and Charlotte, the tension was still palpable between them. As she swayed in the college guy's arms, Gabe glared so hard at them it was a wonder he didn't set them on fire with the heat in his eyes.

"Okay, I've had enough," he finally snapped, pushing his chair back and slapping his napkin against his plate.

We all stared up at him in confusion as he stared out at the dance floor with determination. It looked like he was just about to make a move when the music ended and Charlotte separated from her dance partner.

"Oh, screw it." Gabe strode around the table toward her, her pretty eyes growing large as she stuttered to a stop at her chair.

"What the—"

"Char." Gabe gripped her petite shoulders in his big hands and bent his head to hers. "Let's cut the crap, okay."

She wrinkled her nose. "Cut the crap?"

"Yes. Cut the crap. I miss you. Okay. I miss you…like…a lot. And not just my friend. I miss the other stuff." He grinned at her boyishly. "A lot."

She stared up at him, a small smile beginning to play on her lips. "What are you saying?"

"I want to be with you." He glanced toward us, realizing we were all watching intently. As were the table next to us. Gabe straightened, and slid his arm around Charlotte's shoulders, drawing her into his side. "That's right," he told us, puffing his chest up with pride. "Charlotte and I are together." He looked down at her. "You still want us to be together, right?"

She giggled. "Yes."

His answering grin was huge. And then he kissed her. A deep, embarrassingly long kiss that made Joshua wolf-whistle, and a guy at the next table shout, "Get a room!"

I was happy for my friends.

I was. Truly.

But Gabe's public declaration of his feelings for Charlotte only made my already raw feelings over my secret relationship with Finn worse.

Elle and I shared a smile, and I tried my best to hide my pain, and probably failed. Luckily Elle didn't have time to question my sad smile because Bryce was kicking off.

"What the hell have I missed?" She glared at us all. "And why are none of you surprised by this *development*?" She threw a hand out at Gabe and Charlotte.

Charlotte and Eloise started to mollify Bryce but I wasn't paying attention anymore.

Maybe it was the heaviness of the last few days, maybe I'd been ripped open and that gaping wound would take time to heal and in the meantime was causing me no small amount of sensitivity, but those doubts I'd had about keeping me and Finn a secret came rushing over me in powerful waves.

"Open your eyes, Trash."

I squeezed my eyes closed against the memories and when I opened them again I homed in on Finn's father across the room.

"My son does not date trash."

I felt an uncomfortable buzzing in my ears as my heart began to pound. I dragged my eyes from Mr. Rochester and they landed on Jasper Oliphant, who had been invited with his parents.

"Do you think I really need to force myself on a piece of trash like her?"

I pushed away from the table in an effort to push out their words.

"India?" Elle looked at me in concern.

"You okay?" Finn said quietly.

"I'm fine. I just need to use the restroom." I hurried out of the ballroom, but instead of going into the busy restroom I wandered the country club until I found a large empty conservatory on the other side of the building. Inside it was filled with patio tables and chairs piled on top of one another—their summer garden furniture taken inside during the winter months. I pulled a chair down carefully and sat in it with relief. It was so quiet here. I could hear myself think.

And what I thought was that I was jealous today.

Hurt and jealous.

I knew Finn cared about me, I knew I was his girlfriend, but there was something to be said for a guy being proud to share who his girlfriend really was.

I knew if Finn could he would—at least, I hoped he would. The truth was I didn't know. His father would give him so much shit over it that I had to wonder: if Eloise wasn't standing between us…would he tell the world I was his girl?

I'd worried over that from the start but I'd buried the fear because I knew how it would make me feel.

Like I wasn't good enough.

Like I was trash.

And Finn was right, I guess. I was strong. Strong enough

to realize that I couldn't cope with that kind of poison in my head, not after I'd fought so hard to suck out the toxic crap my dad had tried to seep into my blood with his abuse. I had worked my ass off. That's why I cared so damn much about being popular, because I felt worth something—my classmates, my teachers, they made me feel worth something. Not one of them ever made me feel like trash.

And I couldn't have that in my head again...and if I couldn't...

I choked on the thought, my hands curling into fists.

"There you are."

I stiffened at Finn's voice and turned to watch as he strolled into the room. He squeezed past a pile of furniture and lowered himself to his haunches before me. "Hey." His eyes roamed my face. "What's going on?"

"You're strong. Stronger than you realize. That's your safe place, India."

This boy had been kind to me, loving, devoted. I needed his brand of kind like I needed food. To have him care about me, to kiss me, to touch me, felt just as important as not feeling like I wasn't good enough.

So how did I decide what was better for me?

Apparently, Finn knew I'd already decided before I did.

He put a knee to the ground, his whole body slumping forward as his eyes grew wet. "No. You're not doing this."

I blinked and tears I hadn't even realized were there fell hotly down my cheeks.

"Why?" he said, the word cracked and broken.

I forced myself to look at him even though it killed me. "Because it hurts too much. Watching you with Elle and everyone thinking she's yours, that you're proud that she's yours. And then Gabe... He finally got his head out of his ass about

Charlotte and he wanted the whole world to know how he feels about her. It hurts that we can't do that."

"Then I'll try harder." He grabbed my hands. "We can make it work."

"No, we can't. Not in secret. I can't feel that way about myself."

"What way?"

"Like I'm not good enough. I thought I could put it aside but I can't. It's too big. It's too dangerous for me. I can't go back to feeling the way *he* made me feel."

He dropped my hand, shock and hurt slackening his features. "You're comparing me to him?"

"No," I hurried to assure him. "Not like that. It's not your fault. But hiding us makes me feel like I'm a dirty secret, like I'm trash you're not proud to be in public with."

"I can't be in public with you because of Eloise." He told me what I already knew, sounding exasperated and panicked. "You know that. If we could be together in public I'd be bragging about it like a smug ass, like Gabe. You know that. I told you how it makes me feel that I can't tell everyone we're together."

"Is it true, though?" I dared to whisper. "Could you really? Say Elle wasn't in the picture…could you cope with the pressure from your dad?"

And there it was.

Finn's whole body seemed to deflate in defeat. He didn't want me to do this, but he wasn't sure of the truth himself.

I swiped angrily at my tears, not wanting to blame him, attempting to understand because I knew I should. I stood, and he looked up at me like I was taking away his whole world.

There was sharpness in my chest, lodged deep, painful and unmoving. "Thank you, Finn," I whispered, and then I laughed sadly. "It's funny...no one has ever made me feel so good about myself, not like you have, and yet it's ending because of how bad our relationship makes me feel. Go figure."

"India." He stood suddenly, towering over me. He ran a hand through his hair, his fingers curling tightly into the strands. "What can I say? Tell me what to say."

I brushed another tear aside. "How about... I hope you have a great life and that you get everything you want."

His mouth trembled.

"Finn," I whispered, unable to speak louder because of the tears in my throat, "I hope you have a great life and that you get everything you want."

At that, Finn, a boy who could hide pain so easily before, began to cry, and before I changed my mind and threw my arms around him, I did the hardest thing I'd ever done so far in my short, chaotic existence.

I walked away from him.

I don't remember the rest of the wedding reception. All I remember was that I didn't see Finn again that whole night.

The next morning I knew I didn't have to be up for breakfast because Hayley and Theo were staying at a hotel in Boston. They weren't going on their honeymoon until the day after Christmas. I'd have to put my game face on for a few more days.

But for now, in their absence, I could wallow.

I hadn't slept a wink. Nor had I cried.

I think I was somehow trying to numb myself to the pain.

I was *that* girl. The one who gets her heart broken by a boy and doesn't know how she's supposed to put one foot in front of the other without him. I didn't want to be that girl.

How did I become her?

I groaned and pulled my duvet up over my head.

"Hiding won't help."

Yanking the duvet back down, I narrowed my crusty eyes on Eloise. She stood in her pajamas by my doorway, her features strained. "He told you," I surmised.

She strode inside and hovered over me. "Do you blame me?"

I frowned. "Is Finn blaming you?"

"He's..." Pain darkened her expression. "He says no, but he's mad at me. I can tell."

"Misplacement," I promised her. "Even if you hadn't asked him to maintain the pretense of being your boyfriend, we'd still be in this mess. I won't pretend anymore, and he probably would have asked me to so he didn't have to deal with the fallout from his father, who thinks I'm trash."

"I don't believe Finn would have asked that of you," she said, hopping up onto my bed. "He can deal with his dad."

Elle didn't know what his father was fully capable of. I looked away. "Doesn't matter now, anyway."

"Why does this have to be so melodramatic? Couldn't you just put up with this for another couple of years? A few years in the grand scheme of things is nothing. Please, India." She grabbed my hand to draw my focus back to her face. "You broke Finn's heart last night."

I flinched and pulled my hand away. "You don't get it."

"Then make me get it, because I'm the one stuck in the middle."

Suddenly I was flooded with anger. "Trash!" I yelled, pushing up into a sitting position. "Trash, trash, trash!"

Eloise winced. "Wha—"

"My dad called me that all the time. Among other gems like 'nothing,' 'worthless,' 'useless.' And since I got here Finn's father called me trash, your friends have called me trash and Jasper called me trash. I worked my butt off back in Cali to not let that piece of crap that shared my DNA win the battle of destroying my self-worth. I will not think of myself as trash. And being Finn's dirty little secret because his father thinks that's what I am would eat at me and eat at me, and in the end I'd hate myself for ever letting them win."

My stepsister stared at me wide-eyed.

"You've got nothing to say?"

"Not anymore." She got off the bed. "Just that in light of that…I think you did the right thing. Pancakes?"

"What?"

"Do you want pancakes? I think this situation warrants pancakes, because as badass as you just sounded I know you're in love with Finn and I know your heart is breaking. You might think that makes you weak but I don't, so we're having pancakes and a whole day of ice cream since I've been led to believe ice cream is a balm for a broken heart."

I sighed and pushed the duvet back, rolling out of my bed. "I really didn't want to like you, you know that. You're a pain in my ass, Fairweather."

"Right back at ya, Ma—" Elle stopped and turned to me. "Are you keeping the name Maxwell?"

"I hadn't really thought about it." I shrugged and moved past her out the door. Now that she'd mentioned pancakes I wanted to see if there was enough maple syrup to drown my emotions.

"You should really consider Fairweather. That's a name that will open doors in this town."

"I'll think on it, then."

"Plus, India Fairweather sounds like a very important person, don't you think?"

I snorted, shocked she'd managed to amuse me when I felt like my insides had been put through a meat grinder. "I said I'll think on it. India Fairweather does have a nice ring to it."

It would mean another change, but a better change than the last one in my life.

Christmas came and went quickly, and it turned out, unsurprisingly, that Christmas at the Fairweathers' meant getting spoiled by gifts and way too much food. Eloise bought me a diamond tennis bracelet and Hayley and Theo bought me my very own Jaguar.

My very own *Jaguar.*

Expensive jewelry and cars for Christmas. This was my life now.

The amazing gifts, however, couldn't fill the emptiness I felt in my life. If Hayley and Theo wondered what was up with me they didn't ask. Whether to give me privacy or to preserve holiday cheer, I didn't know. All I knew was that if I hadn't missed Finn with every fiber of my being, it might have been the best Christmas I ever had.

Worse, I hated knowing Finn was in Austria with his father, suffering in the presence of that awful man, and he didn't have me to turn to.

"How is Finn?" I'd found the courage to ask Elle, hoping that at least she was there for him.

She'd given me this sad look. "He's not answering my texts."

Great.

I had well and truly annihilated our threesome.

Hayley and Theo took off for their month-long honeymoon trip to Europe, and Elle and I had little else to do but hang out with each other. When she wasn't talking online with

Sarah, Elle shared FaceTime chats with me and Anna (who thought Eloise was awesome) and hung around the house with me and then with our friends when they got home from their own Christmas breaks.

It was through Joshua that we finally heard word of Finn.

"I can't believe Finn is skiing in Austria while we're stuck here," Bryce complained as we sat around the roaring fire in her father's mansion.

"Oh, yeah, because we have it so bad," Eloise snarked.

"Hey, I'd rather be here than in Finn's shoes." Joshua sighed. "His dad is such a dick."

"How so?" I said, attempting not to sound too interested.

"Well, I'm sure Elle already told you, but Finn's dad is trying to get him to sign an *actual contract* stating that he intends to attend Harvard Business School if he gets in."

Elle hid her surprise by ducking her head but I'm pretty sure my eyes were popping out of mine. "What?"

Joshua looked grim. "He takes the overbearing successful parent cliché to a new level."

"He can't make Finn sign that," I said vehemently. "That's not even legal, right?"

I felt Eloise's touch on my leg and flushed, realizing my reaction might seem like an overreaction.

"Sorry." I shrugged. "I just… I hate bullies, you know."

"Yeah." Gabe scowled. "I really don't like that guy."

"None of us do," Bryce said. "He's not exactly full of warmth, and that's coming from me."

I smirked at her rare moment of self-deprecation.

"I wonder how Finn turned out so well," Charlotte said a little dreamily.

Gabe shoved her gently. "Hey. I'm sitting right here."

She blushed and mouthed her apology.

"His mother," Eloise said quietly. "Finn is like his mother. She was kind. Warm."

"You remember her?" I said.

"Yes. Her mother and mine were best friends. She worked a lot but when she was around it was kind of magical." She smiled, remembering. "She had this ability to make you feel like you were the most special person in the whole world and she had nowhere else she'd rather be. I bet that made her a great doctor."

"I'm sorry." I realized that she'd lost Finn's mom, too. That was a lot of loss before she'd even hit fourteen.

Her grateful smile was sad. "Thanks."

"Well, it just got depressing in here." Bryce jumped to her feet. "I say we break into my dad's liquor cabinet."

CHAPTER 21

THE REST OF vacation flew by. I'd stayed at home while Eloise attended Gabe's parents' New Year's Eve party and I had to admit it was the loneliest New Year's I'd had in a while. Even with a strained relationship with Hayley, my New Year's had always been nice. When it wasn't spent with her, it was at parties my friends threw. This was the first one I'd spent alone. As if Elle had some kind of spider sense, she'd come home five minutes before midnight, and we sat in the back living room with a mug of cocoa saying everything we felt without saying anything at all.

Before I knew it, the days were racing toward the new semester, and somehow I found myself standing by Eloise's locker on the first day back at school, feeling like I was going to upchuck.

"Stop it," Elle admonished.

"Stop what? I'm not doing anything."

"You're emitting extremely high levels of nervous energy, and it's making me nervous."

"You should be nervous. Finn hasn't spoken to you since the wedding. Doesn't that upset you?"

"Of course it upsets me." She slammed her locker closed. "But Finn and I have been friends for years, and I have no doubt that we'll work things out."

"Unlike him and me," I muttered.

She didn't need to say anything. It was true, after all.

"Shh." Eloise turned to me. "Bryce and Charlotte."

I glanced beyond her shoulder and saw our friends strolling toward us, as always looking like something out of the pages of a high-fashion spread.

Bryce frowned at me as they drew to a stop. "You look terrible. Are you bulimic again?"

"I never was bulimic."

"You know if you don't deal with your denial you'll never get better."

I looked at Eloise. "I'm going to punch her in the face."

Elle's mouth twitched and she shot Bryce a look. "Stop it."

Bryce shrugged, amusement dancing in her eyes. "What?"

"Maybe we can get through this semester without you trying to rile someone?"

"And where is the fun in that?" Bryce grinned just as the first bell rang.

The butterflies in my stomach suddenly went on a rampage.

I drew in a shuddering breath and followed the girls to Microeconomics.

Tentatively I stepped inside the classroom and I felt like I'd swallowed a gust of wind when I saw Finn sitting in his usual seat. He glanced up at us, before focusing solely on Elle.

He didn't even look at me.

Rubbing my sweaty palms on my outer thighs I made my way over to my chair, watching as Elle stopped to talk to Finn.

Their words were too quiet to hear but I guessed all was forgiven when Finn took hold of her hand. They stared meaningfully into each other's eyes and relief lit up Elle's face. She kissed him on the cheek and took her seat beside him.

I waited for him to look up at me, but instead he stared at his desk.

Rejected, guilty, angry, hurt, I practically fell onto my seat with the weight of my emotions and stared straight ahead.

I didn't feel his burning eyes on me the entire time.

It was like I was invisible to him now.

That stung.

When the bell rang I was already packed up. I hurried from the classroom before anyone could say anything, desperate to get away from Finn.

In Fiction Writing Charlotte attempted to ask me if anything was wrong but I shut her out, hurting her, and adding more guilt to the smorgasbord of feelings I was currently experiencing.

Knowing Modern European History was coming up, I contemplated cutting class. I even contemplated cutting school for the rest of the day, but in the end I knew it would just be delaying the inevitable. I couldn't exactly cut class for the rest of my life, now could I?

If only there was a way to do that and still become an attorney.

I got to history class before Finn did, and it made things a tiny bit easier because I could keep my head down, focus on my desk and pretend that Finn wasn't ignoring me.

When he came into the room, I felt it. I was aware of every move he made as he slid into the seat next to mine. It was almost like how things were between us when we couldn't admit to ourselves that we liked each other.

But it was worse. Much worse.

In the last romance novel I read, the heroine had said to the hero after he broke up with her that it had been better not knowing what she was missing, and she wished she'd never met him. I was kind of pissed at her at the time because secretly I liked to think Tennyson had it right—*it was better to have loved and lost than never to have loved at all.*

Now I got where the heroine was coming from. Right now it didn't feel better to have loved and lost. Right now I wished to God that Finn and I were strangers, because I felt ready to burst into tears every five seconds, and crying in public, in *high school*, was in the top five most mortifying things that could happen to a teenager.

By the time class ended I had a bunch of notes I'd written that I would really need to take a look at later because I had no memory of writing them. I'd been on autopilot, Franklin's words a blur.

This time I waited for Finn to pack up his stuff and leave the class first. When he leaned down for his book bag, I got a whiff of his cologne and the pleasant flip that I got in my belly now radiated up into my chest and seemed to pulse against the sharpness that was lodged in there.

It hurt like a mother-effer.

"Paper tonight," Franklin reminded me as I was leaving.

"Sure thing." I smiled wanly, ignoring his answering frown of concern.

If class had been bad, nothing could prepare me for the excruciating hour at lunch. I'd thought for sure Finn would go off with his senior buds to Lulu's, but it seemed he was a masochist (or worse, no longer cared), because there he was, sitting next to Joshua and talking to Elle.

Elle looked over at me as I waited in line for food. I gave

her a shrug. Thirty seconds later my phone buzzed in my pocket.

Eloise had sent a text.

Eloise: If you want I could make up a terrible excuse to get out of here…

I smiled in gratitude at the message and quickly texted back.

India: Thanks for the offer but let's just act like there's nothing up.

With that in mind I strode over to our table with my shoulders back and took my seat, wearing what I hoped was a perfectly bland expression.

Since Finn and I had become friends over the last few months I knew they'd find it weird if I didn't acknowledge his presence. Again.

"Hey, Finn," I said quietly, not looking at him as I opened up my sandwich. "How was Austria?"

And for the first time in what felt like forever I felt the comforting heat of his eyes on my face. "Cold," he said.

I almost closed my eyes at the sound of his voice.

Jesus, I was such a goner.

"Shocker." I threw him a quick smile and looked back down at my food.

"You're certainly Mr. Monosyllabic today," Bryce said to him. "Was Rochester an extra pain in the ass on the skiing trip?"

This time I couldn't help but look at Finn. I wanted to know the answer to that.

He frowned at Bryce. "Yeah. It was a nice break from your brand of pain in the ass, though."

Gabe choked on his burger while the rest of us tried to contain our reactions to the uncharacteristic dig.

Bryce handled the gibe with the aplomb of a seasoned mean girl. She quirked one finely waxed eyebrow at him. "Well, look who decided to get a personality in Austria. I have to say I'm impressed."

Finn snorted. "Of course *you'd* be impressed by someone being a shit to you."

"Ooh, stop, Finn, or I might just have to dump Joshua for you," she said.

Joshua made a WTF face. "By all means."

"And get my dick frozen off by the ice queen?" Finn curled his lip. "I'll pass."

"Hey, man," Joshua warned.

"Oh, sweetie, I appreciate it but I don't need your help." Bryce turned from Joshua to sneer at Finn. "Whatever has crawled up your butt, Rochester, don't take it out on me. There's friendly hissing, like what India and I share—" she gestured to me casually "—and then there's drawing blood with a few well-placed scratches. That's called crossing the line."

They were locked in a staring match for a few seconds.

Was Finn's attitude because of me? Was he ignoring me as a way to deal with the breakup?

And maybe talking to him was so not a good idea.

Suddenly Finn shook his head. "You're right. I'm sorry." He looked down at the table.

Bryce sniffed and shrugged back her shoulders. "You're forgiven, since I know your father is an asshole."

I couldn't help my smile at her retort and watched as Joshua grinned and leaned over to press a kiss at the corner of her mouth. For a moment her expression softened on him and for the first time since meeting her I saw what Joshua saw in her. There was possibility for Bryce. There was kindness and even understanding in her. It was too damn bad they lost out to her bitchiness so much.

The rest of lunch was excruciating for me, and I was guessing for Finn, too. He didn't say another word for the rest of the period and no one expected him to. I could only imagine our friends blamed it on whatever had occurred between him and his father.

As for me, I tried to say a few words here and there so that they wouldn't connect our bad moods to each other. It was difficult, and I thanked God for Elle, who was a lot more talkative than usual in an attempt to make up for us.

It had been a while since I'd been so thankful for a lunch period to be over.

"Are you going in or are you just going to stare at the door?"

I blinked at the voice, pulled from my thoughts of turning tail and heading home. I wasn't sure if Finn would be present at the *Chronicle* meeting, and despite my brave words to Eloise earlier, I wasn't really keen on repeating our lunch period.

I glanced up and found Patrick smiling quizzically down at me.

"Patrick?"

"India." He grinned. "You have a *Chronicle* meeting, right?"

"Right. How…?"

He shrugged. "Katherine told me the paper schedule."

"Oh. So what are you doing here?"

"I stayed late. Studying. I saw you standing here and couldn't leave without saying hi." He gave me this soft, flirty look. "How was your break?"

I shrugged. "It was fine."

"Are your parents back from their honeymoon?"

"Another ten days."

"Are you sure you're okay?"

I shook my head. "Stressed already."

He stepped closer, ducking his head to look deep into my eyes. "I guess this would be a bad time to ask you out, then, huh?"

I stared back, speechless with surprise.

Someone cleared their throat. Loudly.

Patrick and I jerked away from one another and turned toward the intruder.

My heart immediately started acting like that damn metal detector again.

Beep. Beep. BEEP. BEEP. BEEP BEEP BEEP BEEP!

Finn stared stonily at us. "Can I get by, please?" he bit out, gesturing toward the door we were blocking.

"Finn," Patrick said, "how are you?"

I stepped aside so Finn could pass and as he did he put his back to me, giving his entire focus to Patrick. "I've been better."

Patrick raised his eyebrows, watching Finn as he pushed into the classroom. "Sorry to hear that," he called after him.

Finn's acknowledgment consisted of him slamming the door shut behind him.

Bemused, Patrick looked at me. "Something I said?"

"No," I assured him. "I better go in."

"And the answer to my question?" He gave me another charming grin meant to entice me.

Months ago I might have considered it a good idea, a distraction, but now the thought of dating anyone else made me cold inside and out. "I'm sorry. I'm concentrating on school right now."

He looked genuinely disappointed but also something else. Something I recognized well.

He looked determined.

And I wasn't wrong.

"I'm not giving up," he said as he backed away.

"Patrick, I—"

"Nope." He waved me off as he kept walking backward. "Nothing you say will change my mind. I like you, Maxwell, and when I want something I don't throw in the towel the first time I strike out."

"Patri—"

He cupped his ear. "What's that? I can't hear no or any word filled with the intonation of a no."

I laughed despite myself. "You're nuts."

He grinned. "I'm patient." He winked and turned away, striding off with the confidence of a good-looking guy from a good family who apparently didn't care if their son dated someone like me.

Sighing, I pushed inside the media room, my eyes automatically searching out Finn. He was talking to Franklin and he glanced up at my appearance only to glower at me for a split second before going back to ignoring me.

Great.

Now I was not only the girl who broke his heart, I was the girl who broke his heart and was flirting with his teammate.

Good job, Maxwell, good job.

I heard Eloise yelling as soon as I walked in the door. Gil had just dropped me off after the *Chronicle* meeting, and I had fully intended to go to my room and wallow for the rest of the evening. I couldn't really talk to Eloise about Finn because she got this look on her face, like she felt guilty but was also pissed off for feeling guilty. And I couldn't talk to Anna about it because she didn't know I was seeing Finn.

There had been more than one time over the past few months that I wanted to tell Anna everything. I needed someone, a friend, outside of the situation to talk to. But my promise to Eloise had kept me quiet. It was easy enough to hide the truth from Anna when all we did was FaceTime. But I knew, with how emotional I was feeling, that if I took up Theo's offer to go visit her I'd take one look at my friend, break down and tell her everything, and that's why I hadn't yet.

So wallowing alone it was, then.

That is, until I heard Elle's yelling.

Elle wasn't generally a yeller.

I followed her voice to the dining room where she was pacing beside the table with her phone to her ear. A plate with a half-eaten sandwich was laid there with a can of diet soda. She'd obviously been interrupted midsnack, but by who?

She saw me and her eyes flashed angrily.

Uh-oh.

"You know what, Finn," she suddenly snapped. "Go screw yourself!" She hung up, breathing heavily, and I braced myself. "You!" she yelled, pointing at me. "You! He's yelling at me when he should be yelling at you!"

"Elle—"

"No, what did you do? Because he and I were fine at school today. We were back on track. So what the hell happened?"

"He caught Patrick flirting with me."

"Oh, of course, and so the first chance he gets he calls me up to yell at me for being a bad friend and not wanting him to be happy."

I moved toward her as soon as I saw the tears hit her eyes.

She held up a hand. "Don't."

"Look, Elle, he knows it's not your fault. I broke up with him because I know that even if you hadn't asked him to pretend for you, that *he'd* ask me to pretend for him. He's just… lashing out."

"At me." She pounded her chest. "*I'm* his best friend."

No, *I* was his best friend.

"You two should never have started this. It ruined everything." She pushed past me, and I sighed heavily.

I slumped down onto her vacated seat and picked up her sandwich. I bit into it and chewed sullenly.

Right then and there I made a promise to myself: if I could get through the next couple of weeks I would avoid drama like the plague.

Confusion was my first emotion when I heard Eloise singing in the informal dining room. I stepped inside, curious to see if it really was her singing and stopped short, watching her cheerily put pastries on a small plate.

As she was pouring orange juice into a glass she finally became aware of me.

I'd barely slept a wink worrying about Elle and Finn.

In light of last night something was definitely wrong with the picture in front of me.

Eloise grinned at me, seeming to read my thoughts. "Finn called to apologize."

"Last night?" I moved into the room, sadly eager to hear any news about my ex-boyfriend.

"Yup. He said he was out of line and that he didn't want anything to come between us. He sounded better. A lot better."

I was weirdly both relieved and disappointed to hear that.

What did it mean exactly? Had he just decided "Heck, she's not worth it, I'm going to get over her now"?

"Huh."

She rolled her eyes. "I thought you would be happy to hear he sounded better."

"I am." I turned away to pour out some cereal, hiding the lie in my eyes.

"But you're not better, so the idea that he might be hurts you," she said gently.

"Yeah, I'm a selfish bitch that way," I singsonged dryly. I shot her a look over my shoulder. "I'm glad you two are friends again, though."

Elle's expression softened with sympathy. "This will get easier."

"Can we fast-forward to that part?"

"If I find a genie to grant me three wishes the first one will be a remote control for life, just for you, I promise."

I chuckled. "Thanks."

"Hayley and Daddy are back soon. That's something to look forward to, right? I mean, things were nice between you and Hayley before they left. Don't you want to explore that?"

I took a huge spoonful of cereal, leaning against the sideboard as I stared at my stepsister. I chewed and swallowed and said, "Do you know what I want? I want to go back to the days of worrying about history papers. I don't want to worry about finding my way on new ground with Hayley and Finn."

"Well, tough," Elle said. "This is your life. Deal with it."

I snorted. "You really need to work on your bedside manner."

She smirked. "I'm trying to help. If you overthink everything that's happened in the last few months, you might stop functioning. And I need you to function." She suddenly seemed shy as she looked anywhere but at me. "I'm not sure I can do this…you know…*life*…without you. It felt like it was running away from me before you found out the truth. It wasn't a nice feeling."

Her confession settled over me. Turned out being needed was kind of nice. But I couldn't just turn off all the crap going on in my head even if I wanted to. "I know. I feel like my life is racing away from me right now."

"Well." She shrugged, seeming even more uncomfortable. "Just remember you have me when you start to feel that way."

Pleased, I grinned at her. "Are we having a moment?"

"Not one I will ever admit to." She smiled sweetly before tearing a big chunk of a croissant with her teeth.

And just like that, life slowed down again, and I decided to enjoy the feeling while it lasted.

Has there ever been a moment in your life where you thought, *Wow, that would have looked cool in a movie*?

Me, neither.

Until that morning.

Like every other day before it, Gil took Elle and me to school (I had my Jaguar but no parking permit for school) and we made our way to my locker before heading to hers. We stood beside it until Bryce and Charlotte showed and then the bell rang and we headed to our classes.

First period went like it always went—slowly.

During second period a freshman delivered a note to the teacher. Apparently they wanted to talk to me in the admin office. Confused, I'd gathered my stuff and left class. I'd been heading toward the admin office when someone grabbed my wrist and I was hauled to the left.

A door slammed and I blinked, disoriented.

Finn stood inches from me. We were in an empty chemistry lab.

"Finn—"

My words were cut off by his mouth. On mine.

Just like that I forgot all the reasons why his lips shouldn't be touching my lips.

I kissed him back because it felt right, and when I did he crushed me closer and kissed me deeper.

When we came up for air, reality came with it. "No." I pushed away from him. "What are you doing?"

"I'm not hiding anymore," he said, looking determined. "Not from Elle or our friends. Not from my father. I'm done pretending you don't matter to me. You matter, India."

For a moment I wanted to kiss him again, relief flooding me. But that moment only lasted a second or two before the thought of Eloise drowned the relief with concern. "We can't. We can't do that to Elle. It would hurt her."

"But we're hurting, and I know Elle. If we could just talk to her, make her see sense, we can all get what we want. I'm talking to her tonight. I just couldn't let another day of school pass without you knowing that I'm ending the fake relationship."

"People will talk," I said, feeling uneasy just thinking about it. "They'll think the worst. Elle shouldn't have to go through that."

Finn strode over to me, his eyes pleading. "Talk to Elle with me. Let us all work something out. Please."

I nodded reluctantly because I wanted that. I wanted it to work out for all of us.

"I don't understand," Elle said.

Finn and I stood in Eloise's bedroom. She was sitting at her desk looking up at us as if we'd just crushed her whole world.

Guilt immediately made me want to take back our words.

"Please try and see this our way." Finn lowered himself down beside her, his hand on her knee. "No one is trying to hurt you, Elle. I know you're scared about people finding out, but I wouldn't do this if I thought they would. As far as everyone else is concerned we're just an ordinary high school couple who decided to break up."

"But if you start dating India right away everyone will think it's weird if I'm okay with it," Elle protested.

"What if we didn't start dating right away," I said, and then hurried on at Finn's horrified expression. "I mean, in public. We'll keep dating in secret for a few months until enough time has passed for it to seem okay."

"It'll never seem okay that my stepsister is dating my ex-boyfriend."

"I agree, it'll definitely give the gossips something to talk about, but we're all friends. After three months everyone will see that you're over Finn, and then you can tell Bryce and everyone else that Finn and I want to go on a date and you don't see a problem with that. We'll just play the relationship out slow. We won't act like we've been dating for months. And you could even go out on a date with a guy before Finn and I go public so it looks like you're moving on first."

Elle considered this. "I could do that," she said carefully, "but I thought the whole point of this was that you didn't want to date Finn in secret?"

"I don't. But three months isn't two years. I can handle three months." It wouldn't feel great, but I could handle it better if he and Elle weren't pretending to be a couple.

"Please, Elle," Finn said.

Her gaze moved from him to me and back to him again. She looked worried. "I'm still scared."

"No one will ever know your secret," he reiterated. "Not unless you want them to."

Elle heaved a shaky sigh. "All right. If you guys are sure this will work."

"We're sure." Finn grinned with relief.

I could barely contain my own relief. I'd been miserable for the past few weeks. I was kind of done with that.

His lips trailed down my neck and tingles shot through my body.

I gasped lightly at the touch of his fingertips trailing the curve of my breasts through my shirt.

He pulled back and stared into my face as I sat straddling him in the driver's seat of his Aston Martin. The look in his eyes brought tears to mine and I cupped his face, bringing my lips to his.

"Thank you," I whispered against them. "For choosing me."

CHAPTER 22

I STUCK TO Elle's side like glue the next afternoon as we walked toward the cafeteria. Everyone was looking at her and whispering. Already rumors were flying.

Once Elle had decided to go along with breaking the ruse between her and Finn, she wanted it done right away. She'd called Bryce and told her that they'd broken up because they were too young to be getting so serious, knowing Bryce would spread the news faster than anyone. The story was that the decision had been mutual.

However, Bryce kept wanting to force sympathy on Elle like she was the wounded party and it was catching. Everyone was treating Elle like a victim, and Elle was pissed and upset.

I felt guilty as hell.

"The best thing to do is sit with Finn at the lunch table. Once they see you two are trying to be friends, they'll get bored. Rumors don't follow a friendly breakup. People want scandal."

"Right," she said, but she didn't sound like she was totally convinced.

I was glad to see Finn sitting at the lunch table and proud of Elle when she walked up to him and placed a hand on his shoulder, knowing everyone was watching her every move. "Are you okay?" she asked, her voice just loud enough to attract attention.

Finn gave her a small smile. "I'm good, Elle. You?"

"Yeah." She smiled back and took the seat across from him.

"You two are really okay?" Gabe asked, bemused.

"Yes," Finn said. "We both decided we're better as friends."

"Just out of the blue?" Bryce looked suspicious.

"No," Elle corrected. "Not out of the blue. We've felt this way for a while, but were both just too afraid to bring it up to one another. We finally did and I think it's safe to say we both feel better than we have in a really long time."

"But we don't want any weirdness between any of us," Finn added. "We're really okay. Elle's always been one of my best friends. Nothing will change that."

Joshua clamped a hand on Finn's shoulder and grinned cheekily. "Well, I'm proud of you. It's all very mature."

We laughed, easing some of the awkward tension at the table.

"Seriously," Charlotte said, "you two really do seem good. So I'm happy if you two are happy."

"Hey." Gabe slid his arm around Charlotte's shoulders and drew her against him. "Don't go getting any ideas. *We're* not breaking up. You're stuck with me."

She giggled. "Oh, no. How horrible." Her giggles were swallowed in his kiss.

Elle cleared her throat loudly and the couple broke apart. She smiled at Charlotte. "Thank you. We *are* happy."

Bryce almost looked disappointed there wasn't going to be a scandal, after all.

★ ★ ★

It took two days for our friends to relax and realize that Finn and Elle were being honest when they promised there would be no awkwardness between them.

It took the rest of our classmates another two days to come to that realization.

Unfortunately (and it was *unfortunately*), I didn't have to keep our secret for three months.

"I love that it's set in Boston," Alana said at the *Chronicle* meeting a week later. She was holding the paperback of the latest bestseller I was reviewing for the paper. "Are you enjoying it?"

"Yeah. It's got plenty of suspense."

"You know what would be great?" She had that focused, intense look she got in her eyes any time an idea struck her. "If instead of a large picture of the cover we put a thumbnail. The larger area for an image could be an original photograph of somewhere iconic in Boston. Somewhere mentioned in the book. Finn could give it a daguerreotype finish so it's moody and dark to fit the book."

"That's a cool idea."

"Great. Is he here?"

"I think he's working in the darkroom."

"Okay, go tell him he has another assignment." She handed the book back to me and turned to Honor. "Now please tell me you have a better idea for an article than plagiarizing the plot to a Kate Hudson movie?"

I snorted and got out of there before I got dragged into the argument like I knew everyone else would.

Excitement unfurled in my belly as I hurried down the hall toward Finn's darkroom. We hadn't actually had the chance to spend much time together alone because our friends had kind of closed ranks in an effort to protect Finn and Eloise from any more gossip. We spent most nights all hanging out together.

I rushed into the art room and up to the darkroom door. Alone time with Finn.

Yes, please!

"Come in," he called at my knock.

I pushed inside, my belly doing that little flip thing at the sight of him hanging a photo up to develop. He grinned when he saw me. "Hey, you."

"Hey." I grinned back. "I'm here to tell you that Alana would like a moody photo of somewhere in Boston to go along with my book review."

Finn turned his whole body to face me. "So you're just here on official business?"

I dropped my book bag. "Nope."

He met me halfway, cupping my face in his hands as we hurried for a kiss. It had felt like forever since our last kiss.

Finn groaned against my mouth, and I found myself being lifted up onto a countertop. He pressed between my legs and my hands gripped his T-shirt as our make-out session went from hot to scorching in zero point five seconds.

Longing and frustration fueled us as our hands roamed over each other. One of Finn's hands slipped under my skirt as his lips trailed down my throat. I closed my eyes, soaking in the heat, the excitement, the rightness of being with him.

"Well, well, well."

We froze at the familiar voice.

I didn't want to open my eyes. I was scared that voice was real.

Finn pulled away from me and I had to open my eyes,

catching a glimpse of Jasper in the doorway of the darkroom before Finn blocked me from his view.

I peered over Finn's shoulder.

Jasper grinned at us. "So this is why you really broke up with Eloise."

"Get out," Finn demanded, his whole body tensed for a fight.

"Oh, I'm going. Alana just wanted me to tell you the Friday meeting is canceled because she has an appointment and she's a control freak who can't allow us to meet without her. I added that last bit."

"You told us. Now get out."

"Sure." He grinned, wickedness in it. "I think I'll go find Eloise." He was gone before we could protest.

"Finn—"

"Shit." Finn dug into his pocket and pulled out his phone. Two seconds later I listened, feeling shaky and sick with worry, as Finn told Eloise what had happened. He put his phone on speaker.

"He won't know that you already know about us," he said. "What are you going to do?"

"How could you two be so careless!" she snapped.

"We're sorry," I said quietly. "But it's done. What should we do?"

She was silent awhile and finally she said, anger and disappointment dripping from her words, "I'll deal with it." She hung up.

"I have a bad feeling about this."

Finn didn't reassure me with words. I think he had a bad feeling, too. Instead he pulled me into his arms and hugged me.

Until I got scared we'd get caught again and hauled my ass out of there.

* * *

The whispers and gossip followed me into class the next day, disrupting lessons and annoying the teachers as well as making me supremely uncomfortable.

The night before I'd gotten home to find Elle shaken up.

Jasper had called her. She'd pretended to be shocked by what he had to say because she didn't know how else to react without causing suspicion.

By morning everyone knew and Elle refused to talk to me the whole way to school after she'd gotten off the phone with an enraged Bryce.

Our classmates sneered at me in accusation as I walked through the halls, but worse, they gave sympathetic looks to Elle, casting her in the role she'd feared—humiliated, dumped girlfriend and betrayed stepsister.

"All because you two couldn't keep your hands off each other at school," was the last thing Eloise snapped at me before we left for school that morning. "And after all your promises that I could trust you."

Things only got worse that night when Finn dropped me off at the house just after dinnertime. I saw the suitcases in the hall and to my surprise found I was actually happy to see them there. That feeling didn't last long.

My footsteps a little quicker, I moved through the house, following the sound of voices. I found Theo and Hayley in the back sitting room sipping a glass of wine.

I felt the strained atmosphere as soon as I walked into the room and if I hadn't felt it I would have known something was up by the stony look Theo gave me.

On faltered footsteps I drew only a little closer, coming to a complete halt when Hayley and Theo rose to their feet.

Where Theo looked mad, Hayley looked confused.

"What's going on?" I said, even though I already knew.

"Really?" Theo said. "You're going to pretend innocence?"

My stomach fluttered unpleasantly. "How did you find out?"

"Well, I received a phone call from Bryce while we were at the airport today asking if I knew my daughter had been betrayed and humiliated by her boyfriend and new stepsister. Coming home to find my daughter crying into her pillow was confirmation." Theo's face got redder the more he said. "How could you?"

I flinched at the pained reproach. "Theo, I—"

"She befriended you!" he snapped. "She went out of her way to make you feel welcome and at home."

"Theo." Hayley stepped toward him but he shrugged her off, refusing to tear his accusatory eyes from me.

"I thought you were made of finer stuff than this," he said, voice hoarse with disappointment. "I cannot believe I've returned from my honeymoon to this—to a brokenhearted daughter and a stepdaughter I can barely look at."

And on that cutting note, he strode out of the room.

I felt a stinging in my chest. Funny, but until his disappointment in me, I hadn't realized how much Theo's opinion of me mattered.

I was almost afraid to look at Hayley but somehow I forced myself to. "Do you hate me, too?"

She took a step toward me, cocking her head in curiosity, which was a weird reaction. "He doesn't hate you. He's angry. And he's wrong."

My head jerked back with surprise. "What?"

"I know my kid." Hayley gave me a wry smile. "I know you think I don't, but I know you. You would never betray family because you know how that feels."

I could only guess I must have looked like a gaping fish right then.

"You're a good girl, India. The three of you are good kids. Something here is…off. The three of you are hiding something." She brushed my hair behind my ear. "Tell me."

With the gentleness of her touch, gratitude, fierce and winding, barreled into me at her words. It took me a minute to swallow past the emotion. "It's not my secret to tell," I choked out.

Hayley heaved a sigh. "Okay." She drew herself up and threw back the last of her wine. "I better go see to Theo. I'll talk to him."

I nodded and turned to watch her stride from the room. "Hayley," I called just as she reached the doorway.

She glanced back at me.

I gave her a little smile. "Thanks… Mom."

Her whole face lit up. "Sweetie…"

"Okay, enjoy the moment because it felt really weird, and I might never say it again."

Hayley burst out laughing, and she shook her head at me. "There is no one quite like you in the world, India Maxwell."

"Fairweather," I corrected. "Once Theo stops hating me I think I'll change my name to Fairweather."

She gestured to me with her empty wineglass. "Contrary to current evidence, this is a damn good day."

I laughed as she walked out of the room with a happy sway to her hips, but as her footsteps faded my smile did, too.

Theo's expression, his words, came back to wind me. It was only the beginning. The kids at school had been mostly too shocked to say anything mean but I knew by tomorrow it would have sunk in and things were going to turn bad for Finn and me.

Patience was the key, because one day this would all blow over and I could just enjoy being Finn Rochester's girlfriend.

I nearly guffawed out loud at that, but the truth was if ever there was a time for wishful thinking to get me through, it was right now.

CHAPTER 23

EVERYONE WAS LAUGHING. I looked up through my hair and watched them, disgusted.

They were like a pack of hyenas.

And this…

This was my worst nightmare.

Bottom of the rung on the high school social ladder.

Literally—I was currently flat out on my face on the floor of the hallway since someone had stuck a foot out when I was passing.

Day Four in Finn and India's Now Open to the Public Love Story.

We even had our own hashtag on social media.

#Finndia.

You might have guessed that #Finndia wasn't going too well for me.

The sick thing was Finn wasn't getting any crap from anyone.

No. Apparently he was a victim just like Eloise.

I was the cheap hussy who had stolen the prince from the princess.

As I pushed up on my elbows Elle came into sight. She was standing in the middle of the hall staring at me in horror.

Embarrassed, I lowered my eyes and got to my feet. Attempting to ignore everyone, I grabbed my fallen books and walked in the opposite direction of my stepsister.

My knee throbbed like a mother.

For the last three days, Finn and I had eaten lunch at a table by ourselves. We got stared at and sneered at but when we were together the abuse wasn't so bad. It was when I was alone that the name-calling and spit balling happened. I could now add physical assault to the list.

Home wasn't any better than school.

Theo acted like I didn't exist and his attitude pissed off Hayley so much they got into a huge argument, so the newlyweds were no longer talking.

Eloise kept avoiding me so I had no idea what was going on in her head. All I knew was that our friends had turned against me, my stepfather had turned against me, Patrick turned in the opposite direction when he saw me, my entire class hated me and even some of my teachers looked at me with derision.

And Eloise had the power to stop the character assassination.

I needed my friend back.

Finn was silent the whole time he drove me to his place after school. He was mad.

Not at me.

At everyone else.

Word had gotten back to him about my little "stumble" in the hallway.

I'd tried to tell him I was all right but I don't think it helped.

"I used to think the brain was the most important organ," I quipped. "But then I thought, look what's telling me that."

A reluctant smile pulled at Finn's mouth. "What?"

"It's a joke."

"It's a bad joke." He pulled into his driveway. Rochester was away on business again so we had the house to ourselves.

The tug at Finn's lips was gone, and he was back to Mr. Brooding as he came around to the passenger's side, opened the door and helped me out. He held my hand as he led me into the house.

I searched my brain for more material to lighten his mood. "Where do animals go when their tails fall off?"

Finn glanced back at me with a cool eyebrow raise.

"The retail store."

"You tell really bad jokes."

"So bad they're funny, right?"

He didn't answer as we walked upstairs to his room.

I decided to persevere. "What kind of shoes do ninjas wear?"

"I don't know." Finn sighed as he tugged me into his bedroom and closed the door behind us. "What kind of shoes do ninjas wear?"

"Sneakers."

He pressed his lips together.

"Aha!" I pointed at him, grinning. "You want to laugh, I can tell."

"I don't. I want to cry they're so bad."

"How do you make a Kleenex dance?"

"I'm afraid to ask."

"Put a little boogie in it."

Finn threw back his head and scrubbed his face with his hands. "Oh, man," he groaned, but I could hear the laughter in his voice.

I giggled. "What time is it when you have to go to the dentist?"

He dropped his hands from his face and crossed the small distance between us to pull me against him.

"Tooth-hurtie," I said.

Finn shook his head, staring down at me with so much tenderness my smile fell under its beautiful weight. "I love you," he whispered. "So much."

My breath caught, wonder flowing through me in tingling warmth. "Really?"

"Truly."

I slid my arms up and around his shoulders and pressed deeper into him. I prepared myself to say something I hadn't said to anyone since I was eight years old.

"India?"

"I love you, too, Finn."

He kissed me, sweet and tender, seeming to savor every little taste of me.

I pulled back, a little out of breath. My skin was hot, my belly in flutters and my heart was racing so hard. There was no guarantee that I would ever again feel the way I did right then as I stood in Finn's arms. I didn't want to waste that feeling.

"I'm ready," I told him, gazing meaningfully into his eyes.

His grip on me tightened. "Are you sure? This isn't just because you want to take your mind off all the crap that's going on at school?"

Butterflies raged to life among the flutters in my stomach.

But they were the good kind. The great kind. I kissed him lightly, breathing him in. "It's got nothing to do with that." I told the absolute truth. "I want this. With you."

And that's how on a day that could have been one of the worst in my teenage life, one of the best and most significant things happened.

I led Finn Rochester to his bed, we undressed each other and I lost my virginity.

I had always found that phrase strange—"losing your virginity." How could you lose something that you willingly gave up, right?

It was like by using the word *loss* it was really about the idea of losing your innocence.

I'd lost my innocence a long time ago.

I didn't see the loss of my virginity in that light.

It was more that I lost every part of me in Finn, and he in me.

I never knew being lost could be so beautiful.

CHAPTER 24

ALL MY HAPPY disappeared as soon as I stepped inside the house.

Theo was passing through the hall with a newspaper in his hand. He looked up from it to stare at me.

I was frozen by the weariness I found in his eyes.

He sighed, dropped his gaze and walked away from me.

Even though I understood he was hurting because he believed his daughter was hurting, I was wounded by his refusal to believe in me.

With that feeling digging deep in my chest, the last person I wanted to see waiting for me in my room was Eloise.

My afterglow sex buzz died completely. "What are you doing here?"

"I've been avoiding you."

"Really? I hadn't noticed."

She ignored my sarcasm. "I've been avoiding you because I knew this would happen. I knew they'd murder you for this, and it's not exactly easy for me to watch. You are the last person in the world I want to hurt," she said, her eyes wet. "Please, India. Please. If I could tell them the truth to save you from all of this I would. I'm just so scared. I don't want to be. I want to be stronger, but wanting it doesn't make it true. I'm sorry." She gave me a sad, lonely smile. "I miss my friends."

I took in the way her hand shook as she raised it to her forehead. She pressed it there as if somehow it would stem the flow of tears but it didn't.

The last time I'd watched Elle cry was when she told me the truth about her sexuality.

With the memories of that night and the night Finn had told me, when she threw up from too much champagne and too much fear, the hurt I'd felt at her anger began to drain out of me.

"Eloise…argh." I threw my hands up in exhaustion and aggravation. "I know. Okay. I can deal with the kids at school and with Theo's dirty looks. I can deal with it. Bigger picture, right?" I gave her a reassuring smile. "But I miss my friend, too."

"You were angry at me. I saw it today in the hall."

"I needed you," I said. "Now you're here."

Three seconds later I was rocked back on my heels by the impact of her body hitting mine. Surprised, it took me a moment to return her hug.

I put my arms around her, feeling her tremble against me and wishing I could do something, anything, to make everything okay for her, for us all.

Just as quickly as she'd embraced me, she jerked away from me, straightened her clothes with her usual primness, nodded at me like we'd just finished discussing a bake sale and strolled out of my room.

I shook my head, laughing to myself. I wouldn't change her for the world.

India: You should call Elle. She misses us.

Finn: I will. But we have bigger problems than Elle right now.

India: What's going on?

Finn: My father knows about us.

"Well, if it isn't the traitorous whore."

I rolled my eyes at Bryce's greeting as she sidled up to me in the hall the next day at school.

"How can you even show your face around here?"

"Simple, really—it is attached to my head and my head is attached to my body and my body makes these actions called movements and these movements take me places like school."

Unamused by my sarcasm, Bryce got in my face. "Just because Eloise has stupidly proclaimed you off-limits does not mean you are safe. I will find a way to destroy you, with or without her permission."

"And why do you care?"

"She's my best friend. Loyalty actually means something to me."

I grunted. "I'll believe that when I see it."

"Back off, Bryce," Finn said as he approached. My eyes immediately narrowed on his cut lip.

"If it isn't the man-whore." Bryce zeroed in on his lip. "I see someone finally taught you a well-deserved lesson."

I didn't even notice her walk away. My blood was too busy boiling as I stared at Finn's mouth.

He grabbed my hand. "You okay?"

"Am *I* okay?" I snapped, leaning into him. "He hit you?"

Finn glanced around us quickly. "Not here."

"Fine. Let's get out of here."

"We can't cut class."

"Right now, I couldn't care less about class."

He grinned and then winced, touching his thumb to the cut.

I seethed. "I'm going to kill him."

"He's not worth it."

"What the hell happened?"

"I'll tell you at lunch. We'll go somewhere. Meet me out front."

"I got a text from Elle," Finn said as soon as we got into his car. "She wants to know who hit me."

"What did you tell her?"

"Nothing yet."

"Finn, what is going on?"

"Once we park."

We drove in a thick silence, a silence that only allowed my growing anger to build. I'd been agitated all morning, thinking about Finn's lip and the son of a bitch that had punched him.

Thirty minutes later we were parked in an isolated spot near a wooded park where people took their dogs for walks. It was dead at night—I knew because Finn had taken me there over the last few months to have some alone time. Now, during lunch hour, there were a few cars parked but we still had privacy.

"Start from the beginning," I said as soon as he switched the engine off.

He exhaled heavily. "When I got home from dropping you off last night, my dad was home and he was waiting for me. His company attorney knows Theo and somehow he found out about everything and mentioned it to my father yesterday at work. Obviously my dad was surprised to hear I'm now dating you."

"I can see he didn't take the news too well."

Finn smirked bitterly. "It seems he didn't like me walking away from him while he was talking."

"Did you…" I was almost afraid to ask. "Hit him back?"

"And become like him?" he said gruffly. "No. Like I said, he isn't worth it."

"What did he say to you?"

His grip on my hand tightened until it was almost painful. "He's going to ruin my future if I don't break up with you."

I wrenched my hand away from him. "What does that mean? And why does he still care? Technically I'm a Fairweather now."

"Because he's messed up in the head, India. It's got nothing to do with you. It's about him and me, and him controlling my life, it having to be the perfect image he has in his head. He respects Theo and he wants me to be with his daughter. Not his stepdaughter. He basically wants to live my life for me. You aren't *his* choice. That's all that matters to him. This is about him proving he has control over me.

"So if I don't break up with you, he's going to make sure I don't get into college. Not even Harvard. Without his money I couldn't afford to go, anyway."

"He'll cut you off?" I cried. "That piece of—that son of—that hateful piece of shit!"

"India." He reached for me. "It doesn't matter. None of that matters. I have you. That matters."

"No." I shook my head adamantly. "Your future matters, Finn. He's not taking that away from you and you're not going to let him because of me. He can't stop you from getting into college!"

"He might not be able to pull the strings he says he can… but, India, I can't afford to go if he cuts me off."

"Scholarships," I reminded him.

He shook his head. "I will never get financial aid. My father makes too much money. And art schools tend not to have crew teams."

"Your grandparents, then."

"They're retired. They live comfortably, but they would stop living comfortably if they had to pay college tuition. But I could move out, get a job…"

"No." I scowled at him. "That is not how this ends. You will go home and tell your dad you broke up with me."

Hurt flared in his eyes. "Are you kidding me?"

"We're not breaking up," I promised. "But right now he needs to think we are until we can figure something else out."

"Like what?"

"I don't know. Let me think."

"And while you're thinking you'll start to feel terrible again about being my—what was it you called it? My dirty little secret."

I saw his deep-seated worry about that. "No. This is temporary, *very* temporary."

Finn contemplated me a second, seemed to believe I meant what I said and then reached for me. He gently hauled me over the center console until I was sitting in his lap. I touched his lower lip, my thumb just a breath from the cut. Gently, so gently, I pressed a kiss to his mouth. "I love you," I murmured.

"I love you, too," he breathed. "India, I swear…that's all that matters to me."

And as much as I believed him, as much as it lit me up inside, I knew better. Love, our love, was great and all, but there was something else just as important, and I wouldn't stop until I found a way to get it for this boy.

Theo sat in his office chair staring out of the window with this unfocused look in his eyes. I wondered what he was thinking about. It certainly didn't look like work.

Okay, here goes nothing.

"May I come in?"

He startled out of his daze, his lids lowering over his eyes when he saw it was me that had interrupted his daydreaming. "I'm a little busy."

"Make time." I stepped inside and closed the door behind me.

Theo sighed and gestured to the seat in front of his desk.

Once I was sitting I searched his face, seeing more than an angry, hurt father figure. I saw confusion in his eyes, too, and wondered if Hayley's avowals of my innocence were starting to get to him. "I realized something last night."

"And what was that?" His tone wasn't warm with tell-me-mores but he wasn't throwing me out, either.

"When Hayley told me she'd met you and that we were moving here, I started having nightmares."

He frowned. "About what?"

"They were memories, really. Of the things my dad did to me."

Concern flashed in his eyes and right then I knew I was doing the right thing.

"I'm sure Hayley has told you that he would punish me by starving me…among other things."

"Yes," he whispered, clearly horrified by the thought.

"I started dreaming about those days again and I hadn't in years. All because Hayley was dragging me across the country to live with a man I didn't know. I didn't know what kind of man you were, or if she was dragging me into another nightmare."

"India." He scrubbed his hands over his face. "I didn't know that."

"I know. But that's why I wasn't very warm with you, because…I don't trust easily. For God's sake, I'm just learning to trust Hayley. For the first few months here I had those nightmares, those memories, every now and then. And last night I realized that they'd stopped a while ago. They stopped, and I didn't even notice."

He looked torn for some reason, but I understood when he said, "Are you going to tell me they stopped because you met Finn?"

"No," I said, nervous now. "They stopped because I started to believe in *you*."

Surprised, Theo slowly sat back in his chair.

I smiled shyly. "I didn't know that, though. But I was thinking about a problem and the only solution that felt okay was to come to you with it, and I was surprised by that. And that's when I thought about the dreams and how they had disappeared." I looked at my hands. "I know I've disappointed you." I gave him an apologetic smile. "But you have to believe me that I'm not the person you think I am right now."

"India, I'd like to understand what's going on. Eloise says she doesn't hate you and she doesn't want me to be upset with you. She's being awfully understanding for a girl who just got her heart broken."

"There's a bigger problem than me and Elle right now."

He scowled. "How so?"

"I found out something about Finn that no one else knew and that's where our friendship sprang from. I'm going to tell you what that thing is because he needs your help."

"Okay." He leaned forward. "I'm listening."

Cheeks pale, Theo stared at me for what felt like forever once I'd finished telling him about Finn's father—his abuse over the years and his subsequent threats. I also explained that Eloise had been pretending to be his girlfriend to keep his father off his back.

"Does Eloise know? Has she known this whole time?" Theo bristled.

"No," I rushed to assure him. "Finn kept the abuse to himself. She just knows that his dad is hard on him emotionally."

"I will deal with Eloise pretending to be his girlfriend later. Right now what's important is finding evidence to back up your claims."

Anger rushed through me. "They're not claims. His lip is split right now from his father's right hook."

"India, I believe you, but legally I can't do anything without evidence."

"Theo…think about who we're talking about here. You've known this guy longer than I have. I'm not asking you to do anything legally. That's not what Finn would want. I'd hate for him to be dragged through a court trial. I'm asking you to think of some way to convince him to let Finn go."

He was quiet so long I was afraid I'd made a huge mistake.

"I need to talk to Finn," Theo said. "Get him here."

"He's a little reluctant to do anything that might mean leaving me behind, so involving him might not be a good idea."

"India, I'm not going to do something that will change Finn's home situation without talking to him first. Get him here."

I swallowed, my heart pounding at the idea of convincing Finn to get on board with my plans. "Yes, sir."

Finn stared at Theo in shock before turning his accusing eyes to me. "How could you tell him?"

"We can't fight your dad alone."

"And you think he can?" Finn gestured angrily to Theo.

"Finn," Theo said firmly, drawing my boyfriend's attention back to him. His eyes narrowed on Finn's lip. "How long has Gregory been beating you?"

It was the first time I'd ever heard Finn's father's first name. It made me flinch because it made him more human somehow, which in turn made the fact that there was a monster in him more horrifying.

"This is the first in a while." Finn touched his lip.

"But before then?"

"A few months after my mother died. He used to hit her before she got cancer. But in places people wouldn't see."

Any color Theo had left in his face just drained right out of him, and he sank back in his chair looking suddenly much older and more tired. "Jesus Christ," he breathed. "Why didn't she come to me?"

"My father can be a pretty scary guy."

My stepfather's face hardened. "The Rochester and Fairweather friendship goes back a few generations, but your father and I were never that close. He has always been a controlling, ruthless bastard. Still…if I had known…" He shook his head and stood up. I watched him pace behind his desk, suddenly restless, it seemed. "Why didn't you tell me?"

Finn ducked his head. "I was ashamed."

"All this time," Theo muttered. "God, I sent my daughter over to that house."

"He never touched her," Finn assured him. "She doesn't know a thing."

"Just enough to pretend to be your girlfriend to get him off your back."

My boyfriend shot me a quizzical look. I shot him a "just go with it, and no, I didn't tell him his daughter is gay" look.

"I'm going to call your grandparents," Theo said, turning to him resolutely.

"What? Why?" Finn looked suddenly afraid.

"Because...you're going to go live with them."

His head immediately whipped to me. "This is you, isn't it? This is your plan."

"Actually, that wasn't India's original plan." Theo drew our gazes back to him. "She wanted you to stay in our pool house. Considering the situation, however, I think it would be highly inappropriate for my stepdaughter's boyfriend to live with us." He gave Finn a look of apology. "I'm sorry, Finn. If things were different, perhaps...but even then... I considered your friends' parents. Joshua or Gabe—"

"Yeah, Josh's parents would let me stay with them. It wouldn't be a problem."

"I imagine not," Theo said, his expression grave. "But maybe what you need is to be with your grandparents. Maybe what you need is to be reminded that you have family that wants the best for you—"

"But—"

"More than that, I think what you need is distance from

your father. If you stay, there will be questions that neither of you want to answer. Situations that may throw you together at school. You know him better than anyone. Can you honestly tell me he won't try to interfere with your life as long as you're here?"

Finn was silent.

Because he knew—we both knew—Theo was right.

"You don't need that worry, Finn. You need a chance to be a kid. For once. Go to Florida. Be with your family. And be a kid."

I was heartbroken when Theo turned down my suggestion that Finn stay with us. It was agony to know that my decision to bring Theo into the situation meant sending Finn far away from me. The pain in my chest was unbearable, and a huge part of me wanted to scream and shout and say I'd changed my mind about this whole thing. But I couldn't be selfish. I had to put Finn first. That's what you were supposed to do when you loved someone, right? Even if it was tearing you up inside. And the truth was that Theo was right. "Finn, it's the best thing for you."

He pushed up out of his chair. "Forget the fact that my dad will never allow it... I told you I don't want to leave you!"

"I will persuade your father to let you go and to give you the money you need for college tuition," Theo said.

I gave Theo a sad, tremulous smile, relief shuddering through me that I actually *had* made the right call in coming to him.

"How?" Finn demanded. "How can you do that?"

Suddenly a hard, determined anger filled my stepfather's expression. "Leave it to me."

"But—"

"You don't need to know how. You just need to know that I can fix this."

"No." He crossed his arms belligerently over his chest. "I'm not leaving." He glared at me. "I'm not leaving you. I love you."

"Finn, just because you'll be in Florida doesn't mean you'll stop loving me. I get that."

"No, you don't." He sat back down, pulling his chair toward me so our knees touched. "If I leave we don't know what will happen. There's a chance that this—" Finn gestured between us "—won't work out. And that scares me more than the future my father has planned for me."

"I'm scared about that, too. But I know something you don't… There was this moment back when I woke up in the hospital all those years ago. A moment that I totally forgot about until recently. I was so busy being mad at everyone that the memory just…disappeared. But I remember it now.

"Hayley came to my hospital room and it was the first time in five years that I'd seen her. She was a mess, she couldn't stop crying." I heaved a shaky sigh, the image of her so clear it could have happened yesterday. "She came to tell me what the authorities hadn't yet. That my dad was so drunk the night he attacked me that he ran his car off a bridge. He died. He was gone. She told me she was taking me home with her to California. That it was over.

"I can't describe the relief I felt. This sheer relief that he was out of my life for good. In that moment I didn't care about Hayley's betrayal or how shitty life had been so far. All I cared about was that I was free.

"I love you, Finn—you have changed my life for the better—but that freedom I felt… I am telling you that freedom is bigger than us, and the best thing I can give you right now is the promise that being free of your dad is worth risking us."

He drank in my words like they were sweet wine laced with razor blades, the pain so clearly etched in his face. After what felt like forever he grabbed my hand in both of his, bowed his head and pressed his lips to it.

With my free hand I reached up to stroke his hair in comfort, fighting back tears when I felt the wetness of his on my skin.

CHAPTER 25

THERE WERE MANY things in life that I was unsure about, but the one thing I was sure of was that Theo Fairweather would never tell me what he'd said (or threatened, I guess) to Gregory Rochester to convince him to let Finn go live with his grandparents.

What I did know was that Finn's dad let him go but refused to back down on the money situation.

"Then what will he do?" I'd said as we piled Finn's suitcases into the pool house where he'd stay for a few days before he got on a flight to Florida.

"I don't want you to worry about college," Theo had said to him. "You're covered. I've already spoken to your grandparents."

"How?" Finn said. He looked so exhausted and all I wanted to do was wrap my arms around him.

Theo gave him this no-nonsense, don't-even-think-about-arguing-with-me look. "I will pay your tuition."

"No!" Finn shot to his feet. "No way, I'm not a charity case."

"Of course not," Theo said. "You're Kelsey Monaghan's son. I held you when you were a baby and I've watched you grow up into a smart, talented young man. You're like a son to me, Finn, and I will not see your future ruined because of your father."

Finn blinked in surprise and I watched as that surprise turned to emotion. The muscles in his jaw flexed as he tried to fight it. "Sir, I don't know…"

"Just say thank you." Theo held out his hand to him with a smile.

They shook hands, and Theo clapped him on the shoulder, and all the while I watched a silent conversation pass between them. Watching them together I realized if Theo had known about Finn's situation long ago he would have saved him, just like he was saving him now. But what really made the breath catch in my throat was that I believed, really believed, that if Theo had been around when I lived with my dad, he was the kind of person who would have stepped in to save me, too.

Once Theo had left us alone in the pool house we stared at each other.

Suddenly it came crashing down on me that we only had a few days left together. Finn's grandparents were devastated to hear the truth and quite rightly desperate to have Finn come stay with them where he'd be safe. He'd been withdrawn from Tobias Rochester, and they'd enrolled him in a good (but tuition free) school a five-minute walk from their beach house.

I felt a little breathless at the idea of not seeing him every day.

"You want a soda?" I said, desperate to find a distraction, any distraction.

He looked a little confused by the question in light of the heavy atmosphere, but nodded. "Sure."

I hurried toward the door.

"Aren't there any in the kitchen here?" Finn called after me.

"We're out." I didn't know if we were out of soda in the pool house. I just needed a momentary breather from the tension between us. I knew I had done the right thing for Finn and I knew one day he, too, would fully come to understand that.

It didn't mean the sacrifice didn't hurt like hell.

I strolled into the house, coming to a stop when I saw Hayley watching television in the family room.

"Hey, sweetie." She looked up at me. "Finn getting settled in okay?"

"Yeah. I'm just getting him a soda."

"Gretchen made some brownies. Take him a few."

"Okay." I moved to leave and then thought better of it. "Hayley."

"Yeah?" She glanced back up from what looked like a soap opera. My silence drew her focus completely away from the screen, and once I knew I had her full attention I said something I never thought I'd hear myself say.

"He's kind of awesome."

It took her a moment and then a slow smile lit up her face as she worked out which *he* I was talking about. "Yeah," she whispered. "He kind of is."

Theo wasn't perfect. Of course he wasn't. Elle wouldn't be so scared to be herself with her dad if he was. The test would be when Eloise's truth was revealed. Would he be a hero to his daughter the way he had been to Finn and me?

I believed, deep down, he was the kind of man who would get over himself for Eloise.

"I'm happy for you," I told Hayley.

And you know what the great thing was?

I finally meant it.

★★★

"You need to talk to Finn."

I looked up from my ereader and the romance novel that I was attempting to read. I'd been reading the same page for the last ten minutes.

Eloise stood in my doorway, her arms crossed over her chest. "He's down there in the pool house, confused, relieved, probably scared, but mostly brokenhearted because the girl he's in love with organized his departure from the state and now refuses to be alone with him."

I dropped my ereader to scowl at her. "Do you think this is easy for me?"

"No. I think it's incredibly hard and I think what you did for him makes you the strongest person I know." She gave me a sad, guilty look. "I can't believe I didn't know what was going on with him. But you did. You caught it. He told me all about it. And, India…that's just one more thing in my life I have you to be thankful for."

"You don't need to thank me, Elle."

"But I do. Because you saved him. And he's my best friend." Her mouth trembled with emotion, and she shook herself as if to shake it off. "I have cried buckets recently and I refuse to do any more crying. You need to go down there. I know it's hard. But keep being strong. You're the girl who somehow managed to fix *everything* without anyone ever finding out that I'm gay. I think you can handle going down to the pool house to make out with your boyfriend."

I snorted. "When you put it like that…I guess so."

Finn was lying on the sofa bed, his hands behind his head, staring at the ceiling light, when I stepped inside. He looked at me. "She appears," he murmured.

I hurried over to him and got onto the bed beside him. He immediately moved one of his arms to put it around me, and I snuggled into his chest. "I'm sorry," I said.

"It's okay."

"It's not… I just…do you feel like I railroaded you into this?"

His silence began to make me panic, but just as I was about to freak out, he spoke. "No. If I really didn't want to I wouldn't be going to Florida. I heard what you said, India, and you were right. I'm worried about leaving Boston, my friends, my life… I'm terrified to leave you and have things not work out between us…but the biggest thing I feel right now is relief."

I relaxed deeper into him. "I'm glad."

"He's out of my life. I feel like there is this weight off me I didn't even realize I was carrying. I almost don't know what to do with myself—I feel so much lighter, like I might just take off and start floating around. I guess I just need to find myself on new ground."

"Exactly. And it's scary in itself but, Finn, it'll be so worth the fear."

"Yeah."

I heard the anxiety in that one word. "It doesn't mean you won't miss it here. I know that." I kissed his chest. "What will you miss the most?"

"You."

I smiled. "I know that, too. Other than me?"

"Elle, Josh and Gabe. My crew. Although they're pretty pissed I'm leaving so I don't know how much they'll miss me. And I'll miss all the main stuff—Fenway, the burgers at the Bristol Lounge, Cafe 939, Mike's Pastries, Maggie's Diner." He stroked my arm lightly. "You," he repeated.

"You and I will be okay. And I'll send you boxes of goodies from Mike's Pastries."

"What makes you so strong, India?"

I thought about it, how not too long ago I'd thought I was strong but the truth was I hadn't been…not until recently. What I'd told Finn was true. When I realized my father would never be able to hurt me again I'd felt the relief of being free. But somehow over the years I'd built a new prison out of my fears of being hurt. I'd taken my own freedom away. Until Massachusetts. "You. Elle. Anna. Maybe even Hayley and Theo. We'll see about those two," I joked.

We were silent awhile as we lay together, just enjoying each other's warmth.

Finn's voice broke the quiet but barely, it was so low. "Whatever happens, I'll never forget what you've done for me."

My eyes stung, and I pressed my cheek into his chest. "Back at you, Finn."

I thought the worst thing that could happen the next day when I woke up was to remember that Finn was leaving the next morning.

Unfortunately, it wasn't.

I was shaken awake by a hysterical Eloise.

"What, what, what is it?" I swatted at her drowsily.

"India, wake up now," she said, her voice frantic.

I pried my eyes open. "What?" A horrible thought hit me and I sat up, almost slamming my face into hers. "Did Finn leave already?"

"No." She pushed her hair off her face and I saw her cheeks were wet, her eyes red, and there was nothing short of horror in them.

"Elle." I felt my heart slam against my ribs at the sight of her. "What's going on?"

She shoved her phone at me.

I took it, blinking until my vision cleared, and what I saw made my blood turn cold.

Eloise's Twitter stream was full of tweets about her from our classmates.

Tweets about her being gay.

I looked up at her. "How?"

More tears slipped down her cheeks as she took the phone back, pressed some buttons and then handed it back to me.

Bryce: I thought we were friends.

Eloise: We are friends. Are you drunk?

Bryce: I came over last night to see what was going on with Finn. I overheard you telling HER that you were gay. HER. Really? You tell HER your biggest secret. Well, guess what...secret's out.

Eloise: Oh God, what did you do?

I'd suspected all along that Bryce was jealous of my friendship with Eloise, but despite how mean I knew that girl could be, I didn't think she'd take her envy and use it as a weapon, let alone that the blood she'd spill would be Elle's.

"What am I going to do?" she whispered.

I looked up from the phone and told her something I knew was the last thing she wanted to hear. "You need to tell your dad the truth before he finds out from someone else."

Her chest began to rise and fall in a fast, sharp rhythm.

"It's okay." I pushed my duvet off me. "I'll come with you. If you want?"

Elle nodded before expelling a long, shaky breath. "How do I do this? I've thought about telling him a million times but right now my mind is just blank."

"Let's just sit him down, and we'll see how it goes from there."

I pulled on a robe and directed a reluctant Eloise out of my room and down the hallway. We walked past her room, following the wide corridor around the house until we got to the other side where Theo and Hayley's huge bedroom suite was.

Just as I raised my hand to knock on the door, Elle grabbed my wrist.

I looked at her and read the fear in her eyes.

Whatever happens, I'm not going anywhere.

Her grip relaxed and she let me go. She nodded even though she looked ten seconds away from upchucking.

I rattled my knuckles against our parents' door.

At the silence beyond it, I rapped harder. "Theo! Hayley!"

That seemed to do the trick as we heard soft sounds beyond the doors. A few seconds later one of the double doors swung open, and Theo stood in silk pajamas, squinting at us, his face creased with sleep. "Girls, what is it?" He yawned. "Everything all right?"

"No. Um… Eloise needs to talk to you. Downstairs. Back sitting room. Now."

Suddenly more alert, Theo's attention moved to his daughter. He immediately paled at her complexion. "Please tell me you're not pregnant."

"I'm not pregnant, Daddy. I'm gay."

I was physically jolted by her abrupt announcement and I swung my eyes from her to her father.

He stared at her, confused. "What?"

Elle's lips started to tremble. "I'm gay."

Hayley appeared beside Theo, her eyes on Eloise, her own face pale. She'd obviously heard. "Uh…sweetheart, why don't we take this downstairs…"

"I don't understand," Theo huffed. "Is this a joke?"

"No." She shook her head frantically. "I wasn't just covering for Finn by dating him. He was covering for me. I've been too afraid to tell you and everyone else the truth. I'm gay. I'm gay, Daddy. I'm gay."

"Stop saying that!" he yelled, throwing his hands up in disbelief.

"Why?" Elle began to cry. "Because you think it's a dirty word?"

"How…what… I don't know what's going on?" He looked to me as if for answers.

Eloise's "throw him into the deep end" strategy hadn't worked. Perhaps I should have coached her before we did this. "Bryce found out last night. She overheard Elle and me talking. She's told everyone. It's all over social media. Eloise wanted you to find out from her, not from someone else."

Theo looked horrified, which was probably the reaction Elle had been fearing since she was thirteen. He stared at her, wide-eyed, like he'd never seen her before.

And then that's when Elle started to tell him her story—everything that she'd told me, about her tutor, about her fears about her mom and her uncle, how she thought it would have made her mom feel about her, how much that hurt and scared her… "So Finn and I thought we could help each other out," she said, her voice shaking so much I wanted to grab her hand. "We agreed to pretend to be in a relationship to keep his dad off his back and to protect me from anyone finding out that I was gay. To protect me from *you* finding out I was gay.

"I love you more than anyone in this world and I know how you are. I'm terrified—" she began to visibly tremble now "—terrified of losing you over this. But I'm still me, Daddy. I'm still Eloise. *Please.*"

I'd never been as proud of anyone in my life as I was right then. Hayley was crying quietly beside Theo. Her tears had started as soon as Elle mentioned how she wanted to die when she first realized the truth about herself. She'd never told me that before. I wanted to cry, too, hearing it.

There was nothing but kindness and compassion in Hayley's expression and I could only hope that her feelings would help Theo come to accept the truth about his daughter.

My hope was shattered into smithereens when he shook his head and dropped his eyes. "I can't," he said hoarsely. "I can't even…" He sucked in a huge breath of air and then turned around, pulling away from Hayley's touch as she reached for him.

"Theo!" she called as he stormed into their room and disappeared into their bathroom. The door slammed shut in his wake.

Eloise stared into the room.

If someone wanted to paint heartbreak, they need look no further than my stepsister's face.

"Oh, sweetie," Hayley breathed, and she reached for her, pulling her into a tight embrace.

Elle's arms dangled at her sides as she continued to stare after her father like the whole world had just come crashing down.

CHAPTER 26

OUR HOUSE WAS a big house. For four people it was a big house.

A lot of rooms.

A lot of empty space.

And yet somehow Eloise and her father's grief seemed to fill every inch, every corner, until it felt like you couldn't move without wading through thick cloying mud while the rain soaked you through.

Eloise and I spent most of the day with Finn in the pool house. The three of us lay on the sofa bed together and in a strange way the distraction of looking after Elle was a good thing for Finn and me. It reminded us of who we were, and a big part of who we were was being friends to Elle. Our concern for her seemed so much stronger than the fear of what our future together held.

"Theo is a good guy." Finn finally brought up the subject as the light outside began to wither. "He'll come around."

"This is my worst fear realized, Finn," she said. "What do I do if I've lost him?"

"You haven't lost him," he promised.

"I'm going to kill Bryce," Elle seethed. "I mean, I am going to annihilate her."

"You're not going to war with Bryce," he said. "She's not worth it."

"The scandal she created..." She shook her head in disbelief. "I can't go into school tomorrow. Not alone."

I was going with Theo and Finn to the airport in the morning and had decided that I'd probably be too much of a mess to go to school at all. "Then don't."

"I can't come to the airport, either." She shot Finn an apologetic look. "Not with Daddy there."

"It's okay." He slid his arm around her shoulders and pulled her against him. "We'll say our see-you-laters here tomorrow."

"See-you-laters?"

I smirked. "Finn is refusing to call it goodbye."

"Because it isn't," he insisted. "I'll visit when I can, and you guys can come to Florida whenever you want. Plus... Harvard is Theo's alma mater. There is a ninety-nine percent chance both of you will apply and get in there. Am I right?"

I nodded because it would be a dream for me to be prelaw at Harvard and I'd seen Elle's Harvard sweater and T-shirts. Theo had pretty much brainwashed her into going there.

She nodded, the pain in her eyes making me believe she was thinking about that, too.

"I love Boston. I won't lose this city or you guys because of my father. I'm going to apply to the Massachusetts College of Art and Design. They have a great fine arts program where I can study photography." He grinned at us. "I'll be back, ladies."

Elle hugged him hard. "You'll call all the time and email and text and communicate in any way you possibly can," she ordered.

Finn laughed. "Yes, ma'am."

The forced levity between us soon became too hard to maintain and the weight of our reality settled over us as we lay together. Somehow over the last few months we'd become this family unit, and it almost felt like we were going through some weird divorce.

Finn leaving would change everything.

Despite that, I knew I would have to get up every morning and let each day take me on whatever journey life had in store for me next. But that didn't mean that I couldn't let myself be sad. Being sad didn't mean I was giving up on the idea of Finn and me having a future; it just meant that I was sad our present had to turn out the way that it did.

Theo hugged Finn hard, clapping him on the back before stepping out of the embrace.

With his hand cupped behind Finn's head, Theo ducked his own so he had Finn's full attention. Staring deep into his eyes, Theo said, "You call me if you need anything."

"Yes, sir." Finn nodded. "Thank you for everything."

Theo squeezed his nape and reluctantly let him go. He gave me a bolstering smile. "I'll let you two say goodbye. I'll wait out in the car for you."

I watched as Theo strode away, my stomach churning for many reasons. Theo still hadn't spoken to Eloise. I didn't know when he'd gotten home yesterday but Elle was in bed. This morning she'd said goodbye to Finn and then hid in her room, refusing to go to school. Theo wouldn't talk to her, despite Hayley's increasing frustration. I think he was glad for the excuse of taking Finn to the airport.

At least he had to take me back to the house, and hopefully he'd talk to Elle when we returned.

It was difficult for Finn and me not to be openly angry with Theo. We both were so mad at him for his reaction to Elle. But Finn was also grateful to Theo for all his help, and so was I. The situation was so messed up. It felt impossible to know how we should act.

Finn had decided to be respectful. His leaving was already hard enough without causing a scene with Theo.

"Hey." Finn took hold of my wrist, pulling me out of my musings and toward him.

And this was the other reason my stomach was churning.

I was dreading this moment.

"They'll work it out. Theo is conservative, but I can't believe that he'd disown Elle. He loves her." He rested his forehead against mine. "I can't believe I'm leaving when she needs me the most."

"I'm here for her." I slid my hands up his back, curling my fingers tight into his shirt. "I promise to look out for her for you."

"That's the only reason I'm getting on this flight. I know she's in good hands."

I smiled and tipped my head back so I could touch my lips to his. As soon as our mouths met, the emotion just exploded out of me, and I sobbed against him.

He slid one arm around my waist, and his other hand cupped my head to press my face gently against his neck. Embarrassed but unable to control myself, I let it all out, my tears soaking his skin, and my body shuddering against his.

"India," he breathed into my ear. "I love you. I'll never stop loving you."

"I—I..." I pulled back, and he let me go but only to cup my face. He wiped away my tears with his thumbs. "I don't—I—I don't want you to ever think that I wanted this. If we could have had it all I would have found a way."

"I know." He kissed me, fiercely, so hard it was almost painful. "I would have, too."

"We just have to remember this is a good thing."

"Right. It is. Doesn't mean I'm not going to miss the hell out of you."

I reached up for another kiss and when I pulled back I whispered against his lips, "You're my safe place. Florida, Boston, Timbuktu...it doesn't matter where you are."

He squeezed his eyes closed, his tears falling silently. I studied his face, every piece of it, memorizing it even though I knew I'd see it soon when he called.

Finally he got himself together and he opened his eyes to study me, too. "I'll call you when I get there," he said.

I nodded, speechless against the sobs that were trying to escape out of my throat.

He kissed me hard, quick, like one more taste was exquisite torture and then he turned and strode away into Security without looking back.

For a brief moment I wanted to scream. I wanted to give in to the idea that life was cruel and unfair to me, that I'd had too much taken away too young.

Instead I began to concentrate on just breathing, the simple act calming me down until I could see sense again.

The truth was I didn't know whether or not Finn and I would make it. Would we end up together? Have a happily-ever-after?

Did it even matter?

We'd changed the course of our futures.

We'd saved each other.

I could live with whatever came next because now I had something I hadn't had a year ago. I now knew there were people like Finn in the world. That was something he gave me, and with that gift he gave me more.

He gave me faith.

Hope.

He gave me the things that would last long after everything else faded to an end.

CHAPTER 27

ELOISE AND I sat on the stairs, listening to our parents' voices rise upward in anger. I imagined we looked like two scared little girls huddled together.

I felt torn.

Theo was capable of a lot of kindness, and I would never be able to thank him enough for whatever it was he did to get Finn out of his father's clutches.

But his refusal to talk to Eloise was making it hard not to be openly pissed off at him.

Apparently Hayley was done with his attitude, too.

After another night of not talking to Elle, Hayley had cornered him the next morning when he'd been trying to escape to work.

"I can't believe you're not even willing to talk to her!" she yelled.

"How I conduct myself with my daughter is none of your business."

"Oh, you made it my business when you married me. And I will not stand by while you make that child feel unloved for just being who she is!"

"Stop it! Just shut up!"

"No, I will not shut up. I am telling you right now, I will not stand by and let another man destroy a little girl. If you don't do the right thing I swear to God I will pack up my stuff and their stuff and take both of those kids away from you so that Eloise never has to deal with your judgment again!"

"Don't you threaten me with my daughter!" Theo roared. "No one is taking my daughter away from me! No one!"

Eloise tensed beside me, and I gripped her hand harder.

There was an unearthly silence below and finally as we strained to listen we heard Hayley say, "Do you hear yourself? She's your daughter. You don't want to lose her. You still want to protect her and love her and that is all that matters here, Theo."

"I just..." His voice had gone so quiet I nearly toppled down the stairs I was leaning forward so far. "Losing her mother...her life has been so hard already. I can't bear the idea of anything making her life harder. This...she's not ready for how people will treat her."

"Maybe not. But I think you have a pretty strong kid. All she needs is for you to love her and support her, no matter who *she* loves. She'll be all right, Theo. But she won't be if she thinks for one second that this changes how much you love her."

We heard a choked sound and then Hayley's soothing mutters of comfort. I glanced at Eloise and watched the tears score silently down her cheeks as she listened to her father cry.

"Go to him," I whispered.

There was still fear in her eyes.

"Go."

On trembling legs my stepsister stood up and very tentatively made her way downstairs.

I watched her disappear out of sight, wishing Finn were here with us. I knew that it was only the first of many Finn wishes to come.

Hayley appeared at the bottom of the stairs. She gave me a shaky smile and climbed up to sit down beside me. "They're hugging," she whispered.

"Will they be okay?"

"It won't be easy, but I read somewhere that nothing worth fighting for is ever easy."

"Was that in one of your romance novels?" I teased, needing to lighten the atmosphere.

She shot me a look. "I knew you found my stash."

"If it makes you feel any better, I haven't borrowed from your stash in a while."

"Well, it's a little late now. I'm sure you now know every euphemism for the word *penis*."

I snorted. "And my vocabulary just keeps expanding. I bought an ereader. It's like romance novel heaven on there."

"Yeah? Should I get one?"

"Oh, yeah."

"Reading anything good right now?"

"I'm venturing into the world of historical romance at the moment." I paused. "Finn said I read romance because I need the happy ending." I looked at her, wondering if she thought that were true.

She bumped me with her shoulder. "That's why I read them."

We were quiet a moment and we could hear the gentle murmurings of Eloise and Theo downstairs.

Relief started to untie the knot in my stomach.

"I'm thinking about branching into other genres," I said.

"Why?"

I shrugged. "I guess I don't need the happy ending anymore. Maybe it's okay to just have the *right* ending."

Hayley smiled thoughtfully. "Even if it doesn't look like it from the outside, I think if you look closely enough you'll see the right ending *is* the happy ending."

I contemplated that and then shot her a surprised smile. "That's kind of deep."

"What can I say? I'm an unexpected sage."

Maybe it was how intense the atmosphere was in the house, maybe we were growing hysterical with it, or maybe we just needed some light relief and the idea of Hayley being a sage was funny. Whatever it was, when our eyes met, giggles bubbled unexpectedly out of us, and we had to muffle our laughter with our hands.

The grandfather clock in the dining room was really annoying. I'd never noticed how freaking loud that thing ticked.

A fork hit a plate and the ting of it made me flinch.

Maybe the grandfather clock wasn't the problem.

Even the sound of Theo crunching on garlic bread sounded incredibly loud.

Nope.

Not the clock.

It was the silence.

The silence was unbearably noisy.

Sitting at the dining table, I glanced over at Elle. She was concentrating on her dinner. *Really, really* concentrating hard on that plate of food.

I looked at Theo.

He was staring at his garlic bread like he was in conversation with it.

My eyes locked with Hayley's. She looked as concerned as I felt.

After their talk, Theo had gone to the office and Elle had wanted to be alone in her room. Theo promised to come home for dinner and he stuck to that promise.

But it seemed like things weren't just going to magically be okay between Eloise and her father. I wished I knew how to speed up the process.

My phone buzzed in my pocket and since no one was looking I snuck it out.

Finn: How's dinner going?

India: It's as silent as the grave :/

Finn: Tell one of your bad jokes. That should crack the mood.

I glanced back up at my silent family. What the hell. It couldn't hurt. "I went to the zoo the other day," I said, and they all looked at me. "It was empty except for a single dog." I paused briefly. "It was shih tzu."

Hayley snorted into her wineglass.

Elle and Theo both raised their eyebrows at me and then returned to staring at their food.

I took my phone back out of my pocket.

India: Apparently bad jokes only work on you.

India: And Hayley.

Finn: Just give them time. Call me later, okay. I love you.

India: I love you, too.

Now I stared dazedly at my food. Finn had been gone a day and I already missed the heck out of him.

"Have you talked to Finn?" Hayley broke the silence, as if reading my mind.

I nodded glumly. "He called earlier. He arrived safe and sound. His grandparents are really happy he's there."

"That's good," Theo said. "They're good people."

"I know. It's just going to be hard. I miss him already. So does Elle," I said pointedly.

Eloise's head came up at the mention of her name and Theo finally looked at her. He gave her a sad, strained smile. "He can visit anytime he wants. And you can go there."

A grateful smile lit up Elle's face. "Thanks, Daddy."

Something wistful entered his expression, and I would have given anything to know what he was thinking. I just wanted everything to get back to normal between them. But Finn was right. It would take time.

"You're welcome, sweetheart," he said softly, and looked back at his plate.

I smiled at the hope on Elle's face at his endearment.

Baby steps.

"The awkward strain between you two will eventually go away," I assured Elle.

She lay on my bed, hugging my pillow. Theo had gone into his office after dinner and Elle had been about to hide herself in her room when I practically dragged her into mine to make sure she was okay. "Yeah," she said despondently. "Maybe. Until the first time I bring a girlfriend home."

A knock at my bedroom door stalled me from having to come up with a reassuring answer to that. Hayley popped her head around the door when I called, "Come in."

"Gabe and Charlotte are here to see Eloise."

Elle paled.

"Let them in," I said.

"No," Elle whispered. "I'm not ready to face their judgment or their anger."

"Do you really think they'd come to the house if they were mad at you?"

She glowered at me but I ignored it and nodded at Hayley to let them in.

Gabe and Charlotte walked tentatively into my bedroom not even a minute later and stood awkwardly staring at Elle.

Elle stared back at them, hiding her fear with a defiant tilt of her chin.

And then Charlotte flew across the room at her and hug-jumped her.

"Oof!" Eloise was flattened against the headboard as Charlotte landed on her and locked her arms tight around her.

"Are you okay? I've been so worried!"

Elle's whole body seemed to deflate with relief and she smiled at Gabe over Charlotte's shoulder as she hugged her back. "I've been better."

Gabe leaned against a post of my bed, throwing me a sad smile. "I'm sorry about Finn."

"I'm sorry, too."

"It sucks he's gone."

Charlotte pulled back from hugging Elle. "The whole

school is buzzing. No one can believe Finn is gone. No one can believe you're—" She stopped, looking mortified.

"Gay," Eloise supplied dryly. "You can say it. It's not a dirty word."

"I know. I just… I don't want to say the wrong thing."

"You won't. I'm sorry I hid it from you."

"Don't worry about it," Gabe said. "We get it."

"We so get it." Charlotte squeezed her arm. "Remember Josie Farquhar."

Elle winced.

Charlotte blanched. "See! I'm saying the wrong things."

"Josie Farquhar?" The name sounded familiar but I didn't know why.

"The girl I told you about," Elle said. "She came out last year."

Oh, yes. I did remember. She was the girl that got ostracized at school until her parents yanked her out of Tobias Rochester.

"That won't happen to you," I promised hotly.

"Nah, it won't," Gabe said. "You've got us."

Eloise shot him a grateful smile. It withered quickly, though. "What about Bryce and Joshua?"

"Bryce is on the warpath against you," Gabe informed us. "She's pissed you confided in India and not in her. And I get the feeling she's a little weirded out that you like girls. You know Bryce when she doesn't know how to deal with something—she just takes that shit out on someone else. Joshua isn't sure what to do. He's taken Finn leaving pretty hard. He lost his best friend. He doesn't really want to lose his girlfriend and Bryce says she feels lied to, betrayed. He told me to tell you that he is on your side, that he gets it, he accepts you…but he has to lay low with you for now for Bryce's sake."

"But we won't," Charlotte said, a fierce expression on her face the likes of which I'd never seen on her before. "We're here for you. Always."

Eloise nodded and leaned back against the headboard, looking bone tired. "Thank you. I'm going to need you."

EPILOGUE

LIKE EVERY SCHOOL day since I'd arrived in Massachusetts, Gil dropped Eloise and me off at school.

But unlike those other days, today we were late.

Theo still seemed stiff and unsure when he said goodbye to us that morning, but that didn't mean anything bad. He and Elle would find their way back to an easy relationship again. He loved her too much. He had said we could cut school again today because of how emotional the past few days had been but I talked Elle into going.

Over the last forty-eight hours she had gone through a lot of emotions. The positive obviously being that her dad was willing to get over his own prejudice for the love of his kid. Also, Elle had told Sarah about everything that had happened and they finally talked on the phone and were going to meet up that weekend for their very first date. Elle had confessed to having butterflies about the date but the giddy, excited kind.

The last few days had been intense for her and on top of it she missed Finn, too.

It was a lot for one person.

And although we had Charlotte and Gabe on our side, Bryce was a force to be reckoned with. There was no doubt in my mind things at school were about to get hard for Eloise.

But I had more faith in our class than Eloise did. I believed that they would accept her for who she was. It wasn't them or their acceptance I was worried about. It was Bryce and how far she was going to take this war against Eloise.

But there was no point in delaying facing Bryce and the rest of our classmates.

Eloise looked up at the school gates and then turned to me. "If you walk in there with me, you lose everything you ever wanted when you first got here."

"I know. That doesn't mean I'm not walking in there with you."

Her expression softened. "Do you remember the first day we met? We were by the pool and I had Bryce and everyone at my back in support against you."

I thought of the irony of it all. "I do."

"Life is so strange."

Life was definitely strange, but standing outside those gates, no longer afraid to be just another person in the hallways, no longer fearing the lack of safety in the basement of the social hierarchy, I had to think that there was beauty in strange.

I had everything I thought I never wanted.

I had never felt more lost.

Or more found.

Or more safe.

Or more scared.

I had never felt more *free.*

★ ★ ★ ★ ★

ACKNOWLEDGMENTS

THIS BOOK HAS undergone an evolution unlike anything else I've written. India, Finn and Eloise's story was quite different when I started it and I'm proud of the journey it took to its completion. For that reason, my biggest thank-you is to my tremendous agent, Lauren Abramo.

Thank you, Lauren, for all your wisdom and brainstorming; for our phone calls in which you were so insightful I'd immediately get off the phone to get back to this manuscript, totally inspired. And thank you for helping me shape the friendship of these characters into something beautiful. India, Finn and Eloise would not be the same without you.

I relied on the honest opinions of a few essential beta readers to help keep me on the correct path in my endeavor to write the best possible version of this story. Thank you, Rebecca Pappas and Claribel Ortega, for taking time out of your very busy lives to read *The Impossible Vastness of Us.* Your kind words, perspective and insight helped to make sure all aspects of the story were given the care and authenticity they deserved.

I also want to thank my always extremely honest and loving mum, and my good friend Tammy Blackwell, whose wisdom also found its way into this book.

Of course India, Finn and Eloise's journey still had some evolving to do when it made it into the hands of my wonderful editor at Harlequin Teen, Margo Lipschultz. First I want to thank you, Margo, for believing so passionately in me as a writer and in this manuscript. There are no words to describe how much that means to me. Second I want to thank you for taking this book to the next level; I had so much fun editing this with you. And third, I think gratitude should be expressed for you creating the hashtag #Finndia.

Furthermore a big thank you to the art team at Harlequin Teen for creating cover art that made me do an actual happy dance in my kitchen when I first saw it! Thank you to the entire team at Harlequin Teen for your hard work on *The Impossible Vastness of Us.*

And finally, as always, to you my reader:
the biggest thank you of all.